Pelican Books

'Just Like a Girl'

How Girls Learn to be W

Sue Sharpe was born in London in 1945 and
educated at Heriots Wood School in Harrow
Weald. After working in a medical research
laboratory for a year she went to Leicester
University to study psychology, sociology and
philosophy for a Combined Studies degree. She
returned to London in 1968 to take an M.Sc.
course in Social Psychology at the London
School of Economics and stayed on there to
work in research and to begin a Ph.D.

Since then she has worked in research and
teaching and has taught courses for the
Workers' Educational Association, and in
polytechnics and adult institutes. She is a
member of the Women's Liberation Workshop,
and contributed to *The Body Politic* – an
anthology of Women's Liberation writings,
edited by Micheline Wandor.

Sue Sharpe

'Just Like A Girl'

How Girls Learn
to be Women

Penguin Books

Penguin Books Ltd,
Harmondsworth, Middlesex, England
Penguin Books,
625 Madison Avenue, New York, New York 10022, U.S.A.
Penguin Books Australia Ltd,
Ringwood, Victoria, Australia
Penguin Books Canada Ltd,
41 Steelcase Road West, Markham, Ontario, Canada
Penguin Books (N.Z.) Ltd,
182–190 Wairau Road, Auckland 10, New Zealand

Published by Penguin Books 1976

Made and printed in Great Britain by
Hazell Watson & Viney Ltd, Aylesbury, Bucks
Set in Monotype Times

Contents

Preface and Acknowledgements

The girls who form the central part of this book were originally the focus of research for a thesis in Social Psychology. My interest in feminine ideas and attitudes at this time (1972) was intensified by my growing involvement in the Women's Movement and I had decided to explore the present situation of girls at school and their future ideas about work and marriage. I ambitiously planned not only to look at girls from English families and backgrounds but also to make a comparative study of English, West Indian and Asian girls. (When I refer to 'English girls' and 'Ealing girls' in chapters 4, 5, 6, 7, this denotes those who are white and whose families are long-established in Britain. For simplicity I have referred to the black girls as 'West Indian' and 'Asian' regardless of whether or not they were born in Britain, (most of them were not), or whether or not they classify as British citizens. This may be technically incorrect but it seemed the clearest way of distinguishing between them and implies no denial of status. They appear separately in chapter 8.) Subsequently, 249 girls from the fourth forms of four schools in the London borough of Ealing gave me information about themselves by filling up a questionnaire, and some were interviewed in depth. Three of the schools were comprehensive, one was secondary modern, and all were mixed. One hundred and forty-nine girls came from English families, fifty-one were of West Indian origin and forty-nine were of Asian origin. Most of them were working class.

By the time I had completed the research and was getting into complex data analysis I had become increasingly alienated from the work. The warm and living nature of the feelings, ideas and hopes of the girls who had participated had been frozen somehow and lost within long computer sheets covered with endless statistics and calculations. Useful as this type of analysis can be in other contexts, I put it to one side in favour of writing about the girls in a more comprehensive way. I tried to locate their own personal statements within the general situation of girls and women in a way that would be more meaningful. They would then be contributing, not as statistics or as typical examples, but as separate individuals who share patterns of personality and experience through growing up in similar environments and having similar social positions and prospects.

Consequently, this book does not set out to be a definitive sociological or psychological study, nor does it present or test any grand theories. It is intended as a descriptive and analytical account of the situation of young girls in Britain today, set in a historical and social context and illustrated by girls themselves. (Although the characteristics of their situation and the problems they face will be found in many countries outside Britain as well.) It does however, contain two biases: the first is that I am more interested in the situation of working class girls, because their social and economic position provides fewer alternatives than their middle class and better-off sisters. The reality of their lives is often denied by the freewheeling assumptions of sexual equality and opportunity put over in popular ideology, and neglected in the evaluation of women's progress towards 'emancipation'. The second bias is that my account is intentionally feminist and as such is of course no less valid, and may help to counter the opposite bias contained implicitly in so much that has been written about girls and women in the past.

The girls quoted in this book come predominantly from one area of London, and their position should be distinguished from that of girls living in other parts of the country: in industrial cities, provincial towns and rural villages. As the capital and central city of England, London differs in its range and number of opportunities; and in ideology too, it is easier in London to express and distribute new or radical ideas such as those about women and equality. In other areas, limited opportunities and the trenchant hold of traditional views about women leave many girls with little to look forward to outside marriage and mother-hood. And in regions such as Lancashire, women's work in the textile industries has always been an economic necessity both for the women themselves and for the continuation of the industry. Women there have no illusions about liberation through working as the sort of work available is usually tiring and badly paid. Girls growing up around these areas are well aware of this and look with relief towards marriage, unless they have the education, initiative or other means necessary to change their situation.

Nevertheless, girls from different regions share many things in common as a consequence of their sex. Their upbringing in the family prepares them for 'femininity', their education reinforces the sex divisions through school organization, and the curriculum teaches them 'skills' suitable for 'women's work' in which they encounter some measure of discrimination throughout all parts of the occupational structure. Popular ideas and beliefs still see all but the most talented (and usually middle class) women as primarily wives and mothers, while at the same time acknowledging that today a large proportion of women are regularly employed. Changes in the nature of women's role are being recognized, discussed and acted upon to varying degrees all over the country. For some women greater economic independence has led to social and personal changes in their lives and a readjustment of their domestic role. For others more economically dependent the construction of new towns and tower blocks has increased isolation, and the incidence of mental illness in housebound mothers has risen drastically. In this context the desirability of work, marriage and motherhood perceived by girls everywhere takes on new significance. The sorts of ideas expressed by the Ealing girls about their present and future lives will also be echoed by others, and while their own statements are personal and individual the subjects of which they speak are those faced by all girls.

The girls contributing to this book have had their ideas and hopes caught and held like stills from a film. They are suspended in time while real life moves on relentlessly, each day bringing more knowledge and experience to change or define their lives. They will all have left school by now; a few will have gone on to college or university, but most into a job. Some will probably be getting engaged or married and a few may already contemplate motherhood. Whatever they are doing I would like to think that if they read this book they would be pleased to recognize themselves in it. I would like to thank them for contributing so much. I am also grateful for the cooperation of the teachers in the schools involved. Many other people have given me help and support, in particular David Phillips, who gave me the confidence to write a book about the girls themselves when I was in despair at losing them in statistics, and then had to live with the consequences. Thanks also go to Sheila Rowbotham for reading it and making helpful comments and giving constant support, likewise Hermione Harris, Liz Waugh, Joanna Bock and all the members of Arsenal Women's Liberation Group.

CHAPTER I
A Century of Changes

The situation of girls growing up today can be understood better when it is seen as part of a wider historical process. The popular view of a linear progression towards greater freedom for women is in fact an over-simplification. In Britain the story has been one of constant adaptation to changing circumstances. The education available to girls has, for instance, depended on social class and the demand for labour, and on the role of the state, as well as on the prevailing notions of feminine roles. The Industrial Revolution transformed women's working lives by changing their role in the labour force. It institutionalized the division of labour between the sexes by creating a formal division between work inside and work outside the home.

For working class women, the growth of factories gave them a place of work outside the household, while the production of goods that had previously been made at home reduced the labour of the middle class woman. The Victorian middle class ideal of the wife and mother concealed the real helplessness of the married middle class woman and was irrelevant to the harsh conditions of most working class women. The middle class feminist movement which emerged in the 1860s put forward a cautious alternative to this ideal of genteel leisure. But the main concerns of most feminists in the nineteenth century were the education and employment of middle class women; the narrow futures of working class women were not fundamentally questioned.

Working class girls' education was to be affected not by the efforts of middle class women, but by the intervention of the state and by the growth of new types of work within capitalism. In the mid nineteenth century the job opportunities for the genteel and unsupported were limited in the extreme. But by the end of the century, young women from middle class families and from the respectable upper working class were entering jobs as typists – called 'typewriters' – or becoming teachers, telegraphists and telephonists. Mass education played an important part in this.

I am therefore concerned to look first at a brief history of the nature and provision of girls' education up to the present day, and to women's changing position in the labour force in order to shed light on the situation today.

EDUCATION

The 1870 Education Act made schooling available for all children up to ten years of age, and this became compulsory in 1880. Before this, education had been left on a voluntary basis, which meant that while middle class boys were sent to school, middle class girls were given sparse and irrelevant teaching at a few boarding schools, or at the hands of poorly taught governesses. Poor children if they went to school at all, went to a dame school, or one founded by a charity or religious society, or perhaps a 'ragged school', a part-time factory school, or just Sunday school. Proposals for a system of state education had been unsuccessfully introduced in parliament in the early part of the nineteenth century, but it was not until 1870 that the effects of a combination of motives and forces brought it into being. As capitalism and industry had developed, so its technology and administration had become more complex, and it became increasingly important to have a working class with some minimum education and literacy. Even semi-skilled workers needed to read, write and obey written instructions. Social control was another requirement for an efficient mass labour force, which caused the ruling classes anxiety throughout the nineteenth century. It was thought that mass education would help socialize the working class by imbuing them with new attitudes to work, teaching them deference to the middle class, and raising the standard of living in their homes, and would thus allay the threat of their discontent. It was also seen as contributing to national power as strength in mind would make up for lack of strength in numbers.

The Newcastle Commission, inquiring into popular education in 1858, discovered that relatively few children went to school, few could do sums, read or write, and girls knew little of needlework or cookery. It pointed to the inadequacy of the voluntary system of education. If the standard of living of the working class was to be raised, then the education of girls in the area of domestic economy was essential. Emphasis had been paid on the 'three Rs' and since the children's results in these determined the financial position of many schools, domestic education for girls had been neglected and was taught much less than in the charity schools of the previous century. Lord Shaftesbury said in 1859, 'I would like to see every woman of the working classes have some knowledge of cookery, for . . . I am certain that they are ten times more improvident and wasteful than the wealthiest in the land.' There was therefore a need to educate boys and girls of all classes. On this educational platform, campaigners with very different motives stood together. Socialists, trade unionists and radicals saw it as a way to raise working class consciousness, while feminists saw it as a way of helping women. The success of their campaign lay in its agreement with the state's need for a more literate, educated and disciplined work-force which would work skilfully and efficiently and thus result in increased production and profit. By making school compulsory for those between the ages of five to ten years, the state made its influence felt on the working class family, steering it towards the small unit of today. Children were taken out of the home, where they had previously contributed to family survival, and made dependent. Capitalism was helping in education as an investment in a more 'rational' exploitation of future workers.

The 1870 Act was really only a compromise, to fill the gaps where voluntary schools were inadequate to non-existent. In such places, school boards were elected, to set up elementary board schools at public expense. These were attended by children of the very poor and working classes. Middle class girls made other private arrangements, or attended endowed secondary schools or public day schools. (Secondary education was assumed to be the prerogative of a minority, and for girls it was usually arranged privately.) But while the Act applied equally to girls and boys, in practice their attendance at school was not at all equal.[1] The working class family had been very dependent on the work and wages of its children, and schooling conflicted with this role. The consequent clash of demands caused frequent non-attendance at school, when children were required to earn essential money or look after younger brothers and sisters. Few schools provided crèches for infants, and since working class wives worked on and off for most of their lives, the only alternative was a paid child-minder or nurse. Therefore girls were used for this instead because they did not need paying. The school board, through experience, turned a blind eye to these activities by girls – their being 'needed at home' was reasonable since schools could provide no alternative. The school board attitude to boys was different, and therefore a double standard came into being. Their non-attendance, for whatever reason, was viewed as truancy and was strictly followed up and dealt with.

In the previous collective working class family, there had been a tendency for boys to earn money or do work in kind, while girls were more involved in service roles, especially child-care. 'One effect of compulsory schooling was to emphasize this difference, bringing wage-earning under an increasing sustained attack, while extending a certain tolerance to unpaid domestic labour, especially child-care. Another effect was probably to strengthen the tendency for child-care and other domestic work to be seen as the province of girls.'[2] By the end of the nineteenth century, differences in boys' and girls' attendance had narrowed, but there were still more girls missing from school.

Teaching methods were mechanical, often just rote learning, and the books used were both sexist and moralistic. Discipline was strict and 'drills' were frequent. For girls, there was an emphasis on appearance: neatness and cleanliness were exaggerated as part of the concerted effort to raise working class standards of home life. A lesson in 'getting on in life' told girls, 'If you are a housemaid, it is "getting on" if your rooms look cleaner and fresher, your fire-irons brighter, your steps whiter, your whole house neater than other people's . . .'[3] Families were made to feel ashamed if they did not reach these standards, but many were too poor to fulfil any such demands.*

Needlework was considered a subject of central importance for girls, and they spent about a fifth of their time on this while boys did other things – usually more technical, scientific and arithmetical. It became compulsory to teach needlework to get a government grant, and in 1882 cookery also became grant-earning. Spending so much time on this made girls get behind in other subjects, but it was considered that they were being fitted for their present and future roles in life. The stipulations regarding girls' subjects severely limited any other opportunities, as for instance in the 1876 Code, when every girl presented for examination in the higher standards of elementary school had to take domestic economy as one of her subjects. Since most schools only entered children for one subject, there was little choice for girls. They were completely excluded from science work when it was introduced, and few girls' schools took it when it was established. Where it was taught, scientific principles were often only applied to illustrate domestic contexts, like ventilation, and evaporation for use in drying and airing clothes.

Education for working class girls therefore concentrated on the domestic skills, a content that was determined by ruling class and educationalists' assumptions about limited ability and future role. For instance the stringent needlework requirements would qualify any competent girl as a very skilled needlewoman. However, their training was less geared to either working, or making things for themselves, than towards family responsibilities, and being useful and thrifty wives. Similarly, cookery was seen as being of major importance, and investment in education in this and in needlework and domestic economy was an investment

---

*The increasing awareness of 'respectability' among sections of the working class had other effects, one of which was to restrict girls' freedom as family status improved. It became necessary to show visible concern about girls' welfare and activities. In 'respectable families' mothers would ideally not have to work and could then more efficiently prevent daughters from roaming the streets. Girls with working mothers were able to snatch a little more autonomy.

in social welfare for the people. 'In the rhetoric of the time, the family was in decay, and the state therefore threatened, but if women could be taught to be good cooks and housewives, all might yet be well: their men would be tempted home by the prospect of a tasty meal (concocted thriftily out of next to nothing) pleasingly served in a bright clean room, so they wouldn't retreat to the pub; family life would be saved, and the good of the country therefore secured.[4]

In the eyes of the upper class, the education of working class girls was domestic in order to prepare them for every eventuality: either becoming wives and mothers, or taking the 'appropriate' job of domestic servant. Therefore, in the period up to the beginning of the twentieth century, when compulsory state education was founded, the roles of working class girls and women were already circumscribed. They entered the new century with inferior schooling due to absenteeism; and the low standards of teaching and limited content in girls' schools ensured that there was little opportunity for them to become proficient in any area other than housewifery and domestic service.

By this time it had been acknowledged that the education system was in a chaotic and inadequate condition. Elementary and secondary education had operated on parallel lines instead of providing continuity of schooling. Working class children who made up the bulk of pupils at elementary schools still had little chance of going further and class differentials were therefore being preserved and reinforced. The Education Act of 1902 was intended to remedy this situation by putting responsibility for all levels of education – elementary, secondary and technical – into the hands of local education authorities, who could then organize some continuity and attempt to increase opportunity. But secondary schooling was not free and this severely limited working class entry, although a small gesture was made in 1907 by the introduction of a certain number of free places – a so-called 'ladder of opportunity'. The class duality of this system was also perpetuated in other ways. For instance secondary education became academic-oriented while elementary and technical had a more practical emphasis. This division has remained pervasive up to the present.

Following on the 1902 Act and the supposedly increased access to secondary education, the Elementary School Code of 1904 laid down that the curriculum should be widened to include (as well as the 'three Rs'), instruction in English language and literature, history, geography, music, physical training and hygiene, etc., and for girls cookery, laundrywork and housewifery. Critics of this expansion complained that girls' education should be linked more thoroughly with the 'chief business of their lives'. However, the curriculum in elementary girls' schools continued to be very concerned with domestic activities, while in high schools for middle or upper class girls, these were rarely emphasized and were even looked down on as something done by less intelligent girls – an attitude that is still found today. The curriculum for boys expanded to include science and mathematics at the end of the nineteenth century, but these subjects were minimized in the education of middle and upper class girls. Elementary school girls probably learnt most of their mathematics in lessons for increasing thrift in the home. 'Mathematics should be kept at a minimum for girls, it does not underlie their industries as it does so many of the activities of men,' said Sara A. Burstall, a distinguished high school headmistress in 1907.[5] It is easy to see how a basis was laid for girls to consider mathematics and science as beyond their capabilities. This attitude was reinforced by the poorly qualified science teachers that were the inevitable result of this circular process of education.

At this time, adolescent girls were very susceptible to 'over-pressure' of work. This condition of physical and mental strain was induced by the time spent on housewifery and other domestic activities at school, while the widened curriculum also demanded that they do more languages, music and art. This, on top of the duties they had to carry out at home, put tremendous stress on many girls. By 1913, 'over-pressure' in L.E.A.-maintained schools was giving cause for concern and appropriate recommendations were made to ease the situation, although these were largely ignored. In 1923, it was reconsidered in a report on the 'Differentiation of Curricula between Sexes in Secondary Schools'. It was noted that similar stress and strain was seen in women teachers, which was affecting the quality of their teaching.

Many sensible recommendations were again made but they inevitably had little effect.

The aims of education were made public in the official reports of this time. In 1906, the 'Report on Higher Elementary Schools' put great stress on character and subservience, noting the characteristics that employers said they would like to see in the 'products' of these schools. Over-all the emphasis was on children being educated as efficient members of the class to which they belonged. Boys and girls should be fitted for their appropriate stations in life, which were determined by class and sex.[6] Feminists at this time were working ardently for the vote. Their ideas for obtaining increased educational opportunities for middle class girls were clear but they made no adequate analysis of the situation of working class girls, whose opportunities were limited to a few low level jobs and scarcely any apprenticeships. Some feminists thought that they were best taught to survive poverty as thrifty wives and conscientious mothers. They did not consider the situation in the light of changing the class inequalities. Meanwhile, more jobs were opening up for middle class women: in the Post Office or as typists and secretaries, as well as in the liberal professions like nursing and teaching. Middle class girls' education was now beginning to be recognized as having a possible occupational outcome, although this was seen as being of minimal importance in schools, and work was assumed to end with marriage.

After the First World War, the 1918 Education Act raised the school-leaving age and made recommendations for day-continuation schools in an attempt to check impending juvenile unemployment and as a compensatory gesture to counter the post-war inadequacies of the 'land fit for heroes'. Then came the economic slump and depression of the twenties and thirties. In 1926, the Hadow Report on 'The Education of the Adolescent' considered post-primary education in the light of the unemployment situation, and concentrated again on emphasizing women's place in the home. Once again the focus was on the teaching of housecraft to working class girls in order to help the national situation:

They should also be shown that on efficient care and management of the home depend the health, happiness and prosperity of the nation.

Distaste for the work of the home has arisen, in great measure from the fact that housecraft has not been generally regarded as a skilled occupation for which definite training is essential, and it has too often been practised by those who, through lack of training or underdeveloped intelligence, have been incapable of performing it efficiently and of commanding the respect of their fellows . . . Greater efficiency in the housewife would go far to raise her status in the estimation of the community.

Class equality of education took yet another step backwards in the thirties when the cutback in education abolished the system of free places to secondary schools and for the first time the 'means test' was introduced into secondary education. Another significant development was the rise in educational psychology which began officially with the appointment of Cyril Burt on the London County Council. Intelligence tests were introduced and Cyril Burt and others claimed that it was possible to predict accurately at an early age the ultimate level of a child's intellectual powers. This was used to justify streaming, the eleven plus, and the consequent segregation into different types of school according to ability, which laid the basis for the tripartite system of education brought in by the 1944 Education Act. This changed the elementary and secondary system into one of primary schooling to the age of eleven years and subsequent allocation to either grammar or secondary modern school on the basis of the eleven plus examination. Technical colleges were also provided to supply specific technical knowledge and skills. This system made no progress towards equalizing educational opportunity for the working class, who tended to fail the examination for reasons that had more to do with social and economic deprivation than innate lack of intelligence. Once allocated, they absorbed the inbuilt status and assumptions of the school and it became very hard to break out of this channelling process. It is only relatively recently that this system has been largely replaced by comprehensive schooling.

At every stage in the development of state education, the question of the domestic training of girls has been considered. The importance attached to teaching girls, especially working class girls, to become efficient housewives and mothers appears ironic when it is compared with attitudes expressed outside the education system which define housewives as inferior and non-productive. While middle class girls' education is today officially aimed towards some skill or profession in the labour market, working class girls, with their long history of necessary and exploited labour, are still viewed in the context of domestic life; either in order to improve working class home life, or because the girls are implicitly considered to be less able, and early leavers, who will not benefit from other kinds of education. Only seventeen years ago, the Crowther Report looked at education for fifteen- to eighteen-year-olds and recommended that for 'less able' girls, for whom marriage loomed nearer and nearer, the prospect of courtship and marriage should influence the course of their education, and the curriculum should be framed to respect the different roles of the sexes. 'It is plain, that if it is sound educational policy to take account of natural interests . . . [the direct interest of a girl] in dress, personal appearance and in problems of human relations, [these] should be given a central part in her education.' This report set alight many arguments in newspapers on the issue of similar education for girls and boys. Four years later, in 1963, the Newsom Report ('Half Our Future') on thirteen- to sixteen-year-old children 'of average or less than average ability', expressed similar suggestions for girls' education, suggesting that girls unenthusiastic about housework 'may need all the more the education a good school course can give in the wider aspects of home-making, and in the skills that will reduce the element of domestic drudgery'.

Higher education has had a relatively recent expansion for girls. Although campaigners like Emily Davies were trying to get girls admitted on an equal basis to Oxford and Cambridge as far back as the 1860s, this did not happen until well into this century (1948 for Cambridge University). Provincial universities were allowing women in before the end of the last century, but it was not until after the Second World War that the growth of universities and some decline in sex discrimination combined to give many more girls the opportunity for higher education. This progress was interlinked with changes and demands in the economy and in ideology. Developments in capitalism again needed more educated workers, and could not officially deny 'equal opportunity' for girls. The 'Robbins Report on Higher Education', 1961–3, emphasized the need for professional women to return to work, especially in teaching, where there was a great shortage at that time. It noted that a new career pattern had emerged which consisted of a short period of work before marriage, and a second period starting about fifteen years later and continuing for twenty years or more. Details were given of the unequal ratio of women to men entering university (one woman to every four men over-all in 1963) and the opposite trend in training college (two women to every man), as girls channelled off into the lower levels of higher education. Robbins was very keen on higher education for girls, and suggested that more girls would probably stay on at school in the future, this being welcome 'if only from the national point of view of making better use of what must be the greatest source of unused talent at a time when there is an immediate shortage of teachers and many other types of qualified person.'

The Robbins Report also exposed the large class bias in higher education, showing for instance that only 25 per cent of under-graduates in 1961 came from families in which the father had a manual occupation. Educational sociologists in the fifties, had already attacked this waste of ability, and had pointed out the low proportion of working class children who went to grammar schools. They suggested that it would be useful to look more closely at the relationship between home background and school. This was subsequently demonstrated by researchers such as J. W. B. Douglas[7] who found that the social conditions under which most working class children lived contributed greatly to class inequalities at primary school. These included the facilities at home and relative lack of parental interest and encourage-ment, which were themselves rooted in the conditions of the working class in society. It was these aspects rather than ability that were non-conducive to educational performance and there-fore the talents of huge numbers of working class children were being wasted. Similarly, he found that amongst secondary school children matched for academic ability, those from middle class backgrounds were twice as likely to stay on at school as working class children.[8] This confirmed the decision to raise the school leaving age to sixteen years implemented in 1972.

This century has undoubtedly produced a great increase in girls' secondary and higher education, but this has still largely benefited the middle class, whose access to better education, and aspirant backgrounds have led them more easily into relatively higher status jobs and into the professions. Working class girls have been viewed, and tend to view themselves, in a different educational perspective. Historically, the concern given to domestic subjects has reinforced their traditional role, and up to the present day the official reports on their schooling concentrate on this aspect. By being defined as 'less able' they are excluded from any of society's so-called more 'useful' occupations.*

The publicly professed principle of equality of opportunity, and the switch from streamed to comprehensive schooling has unsurprisingly made little impression on class or sex inequalities. It has a wider foundation since we live in a society whose efficient running is dependent on maintaining class and sex divisions. However, in such situations there are inevitably contradictions, and some of these have been felt strongly by many middle class girls, who have absorbed both the high aspirations of their class and the ideology of equality. They are finding that despite higher education and raised expectations, their real position and opportunities are by no means equal. Although there is equal pay in more occupations at the top end of the job scale, they are expected to preserve most of the other aspects of their role and status which define their positions as lower than those of men. Women are excluded from the top positions and when they have children they are expected to step down and slip quietly away to their domestic place at home. Women teachers have particularly been conscious of this, and have become aware of their own roles in transmitting the basis of these inequalities in school. It is partly out of such conflict that feminist consciousness has been raised, and the Women's Liberation Movement contains many women in these situations.

Working class girls experience the most inequalities, both in

---

*As expressed for example in the Crowther and Newsom Reports discussed above.

education and later at work, but experience potentially less role-contradiction because their expectations are less often expressed through success in education. Historically, these expectations have been denied or channelled off into domestic subjects and concern with the primary role of wife and mother. The opportunities for unqualified girls are usually in semi-skilled and unskilled work, and in low level clerical work which may seem exciting at first; but all these are jobs characterized by unequal pay and a low level of organization (although this is slowly beginning to change). These conditions have been accepted as a result of women's need to work and their belief that their major role is in the home. Lack of knowledge about alternatives and ignorance about status, wages and position relative to other sorts of workers contributes to their acceptance of circumstances. School attempts to groom girls for its main goal of academic success but neglects those for whom this has been made to appear meaningless or plainly out of reach.

The present education system can be viewed through its historical growth from the 1880s. But rather than being a straightforward and positive progression, the nature of girls' education at any particular time reflects the outcome of a number of inter-related factors. These include the stated (official) aim of education, the prevailing idea of 'femininity', the sexual division of labour, and the demand for certain types of labour and levels of skill.

WORK

Middle and upper class girls in the last century looked forward to a womanhood of leisure and home management, and participated little in any outside work. Working class families, however, could ill-afford any idleness and both girls and women laboured in industry and domestic service. In 1861, about 2·7 million women over fifteen years old were gainfully employed – 26 per cent of the total female population (this proportion remained stable in later decades). Very nearly 2 million were in domestic service, while the rest were mainly in textile factories, millinery, 'sweated' and 'outwork' trades. Very few had any kind of skilled work. In the textile industry children were often taken on as 'pieceners', dealing with broken threads on spinning machines. One young girl of fourteen years, for example, worked on this from 6 a.m. to 5.30 p.m. with one and a half hours break. She only moved on if someone left or died. She was earning two shillings and sixpence per week at fourteen, and by twenty-one years, when she left, she was getting nine shillings per week.[9] Women usually stopped this sort of work on getting married, and took on some work at home instead.

Many women worked in the sweated trades and did 'home-work' – trying to fit family needs around getting the essential few pence to survive. They worked as milliners and seamstresses, washerwomen, framework knitters, straw-plaiters, nail and chain makers, box-makers – and at many other exploited home-based occupations. There were apprenticeships for girls which were low-paid or unpaid. A stonemason's daughter in 1891, who had been apprenticed to a dressmaker in Dalston, was lucky enough to earn a small wage – but never more than ten shillings a week – and she eventually left to go into domestic service.[10] For some sorts of home-work, the children would be drawn in to help. For instance, the stages of matchbox making would be divided up amongst everyone. At the beginning of the twentieth century, a number of inquiries had exposed the sweated trades and the situation of outworkers, and the government tried to regulate wages (through the Wage Boards Act, 1909). By 1915 the wages of about half these workers were regulated, though still relatively very low, and sweated exploitation on a major scale showed a decline. For many, however, their dependence on this sort of work guaranteed their continued exploitation.

Domestic service was the largest single employment for English women, and the second largest employment for all people in the nineteenth century up until the First World War. There was little else for an unskilled girl to do if she had to work, and living within another household also provided a relief for her own family, as it meant one less mouth to feed. Domestic service paralleled the growth of its employers, the middle classes, and reflected the development of their Victorian family pattern. It was a very acceptable occupation at first, because girls of twelve or thirteen with no experience or training would be taken on, but it suffered a decline in the 1870s, as it got more unpopular. It began to be avoided by young girls, partly due to developments in education, but partly also due to new employment opportunities. For those with some education, teaching, nursing and clerical work were becoming more acceptable and available, while for most working class girls, shop and factory work offered higher wages than domestic service, shorter and more regular hours, freedom from constant attendance and duty, and also provided more independence and sense of identity. The *camaraderie* found on the factory floor was far more enjoyable than the subordinate atmosphere of servant life.

By 1901 domestic service still accounted for 40 per cent of employed women, but its decline continued and was greatly accelerated by the 1914–18 war, when masses of kitchen maids, parlour maids and cooks moved into munitions factories, public services and subsidiary armed forces (400,000 of the girls and women in domestic service left it at this time). It had become regarded as low status by society in general, but out of all its disadvantages, like the long hours and the symbolic servility of their uniform – it was the social one, that of isolation and lack of freedom, that contributed the most to its downfall.

The First World War

In 1914 the outbreak of war greatly changed the position of women in the labour force. At first the general dislocation of industry caused unemployment, which affected women more severely than men. But soon an increasing number of women were entering the new openings in munitions factories and other industries that were being created as men went off to fight. In March 1915 there was still a surplus of unemployed women, and the government launched a scheme of national registration inviting women willing to do work of any kind to enter themselves on a Register of Women for War Service. This was aimed at finding out what sort of reserve women's labour force they had, and within two weeks, 33,000 women had enrolled, and a total of 87,000 registered in all.*

At first there was a transference from slack to busy trades, like women moving from dressmaking to grocery shops. Middle-aged professional women who could not do 'ordinary' occupations often took positions in banks, insurance and other forms of business, which were opened to women for the first time. Married women returned to work in industry, and soldiers' wives entered munitions in large numbers, probably motivated by rising prices and the inadequacy of their 'separation allowances'. As the war continued, there was a transference from 'women's occupations', to the more highly paid jobs like munitions. For instance, as skilled women left laundry work, their places would be filled by charwomen or girls fresh from school. Often skilled women moved into almost unskilled work in the munitions factories.

The proportion of previously unoccupied upper and middle class women going into war work was small. It was confined to some young girls who would not normally have worked, some older women who entered clerical work, and some educated women who were taken on as a weekend force for munitions – known as the Weekend Munitions Relief Workers (W.M.R.W.). They were quite enthusiastic, although their husbands often were not so keen, being worried about the class of girl with whom they would mix.

Therefore the new needs of industry were mainly filled by working women or wives of working class men. Former factory hands, charwomen and domestic servants were found on heavier work, while shopgirls, dressmakers and milliners undertook the lighter work. The increase in women workers can then be accounted for without saying that a great number of women new to work were employed, since lots of home-workers, half-employed charwomen, small shopkeepers etc. suddenly became regular workers.

* Many workers' and women's organizations were very worried about the government's plans for introducing women workers without making certain guarantees both for women and for the men displaced. Resolutions and demands connected with this were made by, for example, the National Workers' Committee, the Women's Freedom League, and Sylvia Pankhurst.

Women entered all kinds of work, previously the protected provinces of men. Although it was not possible to replace men in very heavy work processes, there was success in fairly heavy work, like rubber manufacture, paper mills, shipyards, iron and tube works, chemical and gasworks, stacking coal, brickmaking, flourmilling and other trades. But this level of work was not really so new, as Miss Anderson, the Principal Lady Inspector of Factories pointed out: 'It is permissible to wonder whether some of the surprise and admiration freely expressed in many quarters over new proofs of women's physical capacity and endurance is not in part attributable to lack of knowledge and appreciation of the very heavy and strenuous nature of much of normal pre-war work for women, domestic and industrial.'

Women were moving into lots of other areas. The pre-war expansion of clerical work opportunities for girls was speeded up by the war, and in shops the demand for assistants, doorkeepers and lift-attendants was great. Waitresses were replacing male workers in hotels and restaurants, and the Waiters' Union, in contrast to the attitudes of most other male unions, was actually training them for the work. Munitions work was very popular, and large numbers of girls were transported away from home to work in the big new factories. This work included some very dangerous processes, as the shells had to be filled with T.N.T. Many girls suffered from T.N.T. poisoning which caused very unpleasant skin eruptions.

In the transport industry, women were taken on as carriage cleaners and ticket collectors. In the then new Maida Vale underground station, the staff were almost all women, but they were getting lower wages than men would receive for the same work. This often happened in other areas of work, and was usually further complicated by the male unions' reluctance to allow women to join. Many women who had previously been domestic servants became tram conductors. Entry into this work was successfully resisted by the unions at first, who said that it was 'most uncongenial and ill-fitted for women', but by 1917, there were 2,500 women tram conductors.

In 1916 and 1917 the Women's National Land Service Corps, and the Women's Land Army, sent women to help on farms.

These women did a lot of tough outdoor work for relatively little pay, and usually proved to be excellent workers. Another profession that was opened up for women by the war was the police. The women's police force was first formed on a full or part-time volunteer basis. Its main purpose was to protect women and girls who were living in hostels as a result of being brought together to work in munitions, or who lived in towns near large military-encampments. At the end of the war 100 policewomen were taken on into the Metropolitan Police Force, full-time and paid.

Lots of inquiries and committees looked into the effects of war work on women. In terms of health, conclusions were mixed, because many married women with children were unsurprisingly exhausted by working all day (or night) and dealing with the home as well. But on the other hand, many girls had benefited greatly from outdoor work, and from improved diets. Rationing, introduced in 1917, actually improved the standard of living for many working class families as their meat rations were more than they could ever have afforded before the war. In the munitions factories, girls also got regular meals. Reports by some women Labour leaders on home life deplored the disintegration that resulted from long hours, hard work and bad accommodation, but they did not think of questioning either the social conditions or the organization of domestic work.

Other reports noted the change in personality and attitude of the women factory workers, and one writer in the *New Statesman* (23 June, 1917) declared that they had developed a new independence: 'They appear more alert, more critical of the conditions under which they work, more ready to make a stand against injustice than their pre-war selves or their prototypes.'[11] Dr Marion Phillips held that the roots of change lay in the absence of millions of men from home, and in the fact that for the first time the demand for women workers exceeded the supply. Away from the influence of men, women had been able to form independent opinions, and had gained 'a new grasp of experience, a widened outlook and greater confidence in their own judgements'.[12]

When the war ended, unemployment hit women first, because so many had been involved in war industries. The popular press exhorted women to go home after their war effort. Women were dismissed in thousands, often with little or no notice. Twenty thousand women who had been made redundant by Woolwich Arsenal marched to Whitehall, and this demonstration effectively convinced Lloyd George of the need for some unemployment allowance. At this time however, a system of 'out of work donations' was introduced instead of unemployment insurance benefit, and in New Year 1919, 225,000 women were receiving this compared with 101,000 men. This reached a peak in March when 494,000 women and 234,000 men were receiving 'donations'. After thirteen weeks, donations were reduced, and they were finally discontinued in November 1919. The system was particularly unsatisfactory for women, because they were refusing to take the alternative employment offered to them, which was generally in sweated industries, or in places either too skilled, or underpaid and unattractive. Eighty-one per cent of women were being refused donations because they would not accept 'suitable employment'.

The Ministry of Labour admitted that an unsatisfied demand existed for women in domestic service, laundries, needlework trades and textile industries, at the same time as half a million women were unemployed. But women did not want these jobs. At one point the Association of Laundrymen even appealed to the government to put pressure on women, but fortunately no action was taken. Women themselves said, very reasonably, that since the government had raised the rate of unemployment donations from twenty shillings to twenty-five shillings per week on the grounds that it was not possible for a single women to live on less, they could not be expected to enter laundries at eighteen shillings per week. There was a general unwillingness of women to move to work with lower wages, and also to places lacking the many conveniences of the new munitions factories. After much criticism of the donation system, a committee examined it, but they concluded that applicants should not expect the same sort of work or wages they had had during the war, and donations should be stopped if 'similar' work was refused.

Women were however staying on in certain jobs, such as at the lowest level of bank clerks and other clerical positions; also in shops, hotels and restaurants, in transport, and in some light unskilled work in the engineering industries. But it was clear that many processes, like flourmilling and sugar-refining, and other trades where women had worked satisfactorily in the war, were now closed to them. The protective legislation for women, which had been waived for the period of the war, now forbade them to work nights or on Sundays. The attitude towards women industrial workers as weaker and 'not quite adult', was reinforced by such legislation whose purpose was to protect jobs for men rather than to protect women. It was significant, as Winifred Holtby[13] noted, that this protection only applied to occupations that were quite well-paid and where women entered into competition with men. Others – like charwomen, domestic servants, nurses etc., had no such prohibitions on nightwork, or Sunday working, and infringed the Factory Act conditions relating to lifting heavy weights and having statutory mealtimes. Similarly ironic was the difference between the capacity for work of the undernourished girl working in sweated trades, compared with that of a similar girl who had been well-fed in munitions in the war.

The middle classes were very concerned by the post-war unavailability of domestic servants, and set up committees to inquire into the problem. It seemed that nothing would tempt them back, and such committees were aware of the low status and contempt that being 'only a servant' had acquired, and were concerned to change this. For instance, amongst the training courses for unemployed women set up after the war, there was a special one in housekeeping. The Ministry of Labour Committee investigating the problem again in 1923 suggested that training in domestic service should form part of the education of all elementary school girls between ages of twelve to fourteen years. As we have seen, this emphasis on domestic work was again expressed in the 1926 Hadow Report on elementary education.

The war had changed women's assumptions about work – upper and middle class women started assuming they had the right to work, and working class women who had done a man's job began to question their subordination. The number of women in Trade Unions rose at this time, and women contributed to the general labour unrest. They were especially concerned with issues of equal pay, together with various feminist and other women's organizations who were very anxious not to return to a pre-war situation. Women of different classes had also mixed and worked together during the war, and some of the rigidity of the class barriers had been broken down. In 1919, various working women's organizations arranged a meeting in the Albert Hall attended by women representing nearly every trade, at which speakers dwelt on the folly of unemployment at a time when the country was in need of all sorts of manufactured articles. Resolutions were passed giving three points of a 'Women's Charter:' the right to work, the right to live, and the right to have leisure.

Post-War and the Depression

There was a short boom in industry after the war, and more jobs were opened for girls. Clerical work saw a great expansion – demanding typists, secretaries, telephonists and post office clerks. Office-work was considered a respectable job for a middle class girl, who moved into the secretary position, while the lower level work was taken by a new sector that was emerging – the lower middle class. The office girl had now really arrived, clutching on to her newly acquired but limited sexual and economic independence. There was a surplus of women over men, and many young single girls were willing and wanting to work. But unemployment was increasing all the time, and the economic slump followed a number of strikes which reflected the militancy and discontent of the working class. After the defeat of the General Strike in 1926, both men and women were demoralized, and the gains previously made began to slip away.

There was antagonism between men and women workers, as men were afraid for their jobs, and accused women of causing unemployment. The majority of women were non-unionized (it was estimated that only one-sixth of working women were in unions in 1926), and men made little effort to change this situation, preferring to ignore it and concentrate on men at the expense of women. Women who needed work were getting desperate. They took work at appallingly low pay, and between

1921 and 1931 200,000 re-entered domestic service. In the 1930s typists sat with blank paper in their machines, trying to look busy. Office workers were rarely allowed to stay on after marriage, so they had the choice between spinsterhood or losing essential money. Some compromised by either not admitting their marriage, or settling for a 'common-law' arrangement. On 14 November 1933, Central Hall Westminster was packed by a mass meeting of women's organizations which proclaimed the right of married women to paid employment; and in March 1934, a similar rally was held over 'equal pay for equal work'.

At this time women often obtained jobs more easily than men since they were cheaper to employ, less well organized, and their numbers in industry and the professions were constantly being diminished by the drain of marriage and family obligations. Children were also more easily employed than men, as, like women, they were cheaper. As a result a new social phenomenon emerged: the earning woman supporting the unemployed man. Men found this very hard to come to terms with as it represented a denial of their masculinity: 'There are men who will not even kiss a girl in a taxi for which they have not paid'.[14] But taxis were not in the experience of most of the working class, and working class women employed in industry did not get much money. During the worst years of the Depression they were often lucky if they got a full week's work.

Unemployment hit its peak in 1933. Means-testing was introduced, and a man often lost his unemployment benefit on the basis of the whole family's income. The early 1930s saw a general narrowing of ambition, ideas and opportunities, and a lapse into defeated resignation. Feminism was still voicing demands and mounting campaigns, but these were more in the context of seeking reforms from the state in the way of welfare* and family allowances, than demanding radical change in structure or

* Some welfare reforms had been introduced around 1910–11, prompted by the concern expressed over the health of the working class, and over the declining birth rate and high infant mortality. Free milk, school meals, health visitors and midwives set off a glorification of motherhood which for the first time placed before the working class the opportunity of adopting some of the family patterns of the middle class, hitherto out of reach.

organization, and woman's role was universally accepted as being in the family and domestic scene. The consequence for most working class women was that they had two heavy roles, at work and at home, and most were worn out by the time they were thirty.

The generation of girls growing up in the twenties and thirties had little of the feminist consciousness that had been so high before and during the war. Above the life-draining struggle of working class girls and women to keep their families going, the dizzy frivolity of the 'flappers' provided a public and superficial shield. The atmosphere of liberty, emancipation and sexual freedom* that had been around after the war was confined mainly to the middle class young. It was also reflected in women's fashions which showed a rejection of strait-laced Victoriana, and expressed itself in short skirts, cropped hair, flattened busts and no waists. The leisure industry was expanding to lap up the new earning power of the young working girl, and providing the beginnings of the mass market in clothes and cosmetics.

Towards the end of the twenties a wave of cultural anti-feminism began. New images of femininity were projected on a mass scale, both through fashions, which showed a swift and dramatic change in the thirties to deliberately ladylike styles – busts came out, waists went in, hair was long and hemlines dropped – and through the expanding entertainment industry, which produced a spate of romantic films in which mean men heroically dominated soft helpless starlets, and popular songs echoed the joys of love and marriage. Women's status was seen as being at its highest in their 'natural' role and was supported by a false comparison with emancipation. This was paralleled by fascist ideas and activities that were developing at this time. Reports of the position of women in Nazi Germany had filtered through, where the govern-

---

*The idea of sex for solely reproductive purposes was being eroded by such people as Marie Stopes, whose writings about the importance of sexual compatibility and pleasure were put into practice with her birth control clinics. The campaigns for contraception and abortion that were ultimately to have a great effect on women's lives, were fought at many informal and formal levels. The association of birth control with obscenity which made it a publishing risk, weakened in the twenties with the growing support of the labour movement. It remained a controversial subject, however, for many years.

ment had manipulated women using both psychological and direct measures to get them out of any employment and into the home.* In Britain, it was implicit in middle class ideology that it was preferable for a wife not to work, and that any aspiring husband should be able to earn enough to keep his wife at home. This was the situation when the Second World War broke out in 1939.

The Second World War

Despite 10 per cent unemployment at the start of the war, mass mobilization soon absorbed this and by 1940 it was clear that the need for men in the services and the expanding war industries necessitated again calling on women to provide the extra workers. At first, this was dependent on women's voluntary entrance into such employment, but in March 1941, it became necessary to register women of twenty and twenty-one years. By July, the situation was again desperate, as women had proved very reluctant to volunteer, especially for the services,† which had gained some reputation for impropriety. There was obviously a need for draconian measures and it was announced that all people, from eighteen-year-old girls to men and women of sixty, would be obliged to take some kind of war work. But the most striking development was that for the first time women were to be conscripted. No other country involved in the war went as far as this, and the War Cabinet were rather unhappy about it at first. It became law on 18 December 1941, but only applied to unmarried women between the ages of twenty and thirty (extended to nineteen-year-olds in 1942). They all had the choice between the auxiliary services and important jobs in industry. Entering the services meant the A.T.S., the W.R.N.S., or the W.A.A.F. where they were mainly employed doing the inevitable clerical or

* In his statement on fascist policy (*The Greater Britain*, 1932), Sir Oswald Mosley declared the need for 'men who are men and women who are women'.

† Women's auxiliary services consisted of the W.R.N.S. (Women's Royal Naval Service), the W.A.A.F. (Women's Auxiliary Air Force), the A.T.S. (Auxiliary Territorial Service) and various nursing services.

domestic work (canteens etc.). They would take no part in combat unless they expressly volunteered.

The reluctance of many women to volunteer for war work was in direct contrast to the First World War, when girls and women in jobs like domestic service and the sweated industries had eagerly exchanged these for the prospects offered by munitions and other essential war industries. In spite of active campaigns over the country, this time the response was very poor. Surveys conducted at the time[15] put forward several explanations for this reluctance. Women did not want to move, girls had been put off by stories from the First World War about the poisonous processes in munitions work, they were afraid of what industry was like, and seemed generally unaware of the urgency of the situation. Between the wars many other openings had expanded for working women (clerical, commerce, shops, etc.) and factory work had lost its advantages. A survey in Worcester gave the main objections to munitions work as follows: domestic problems (children, shopping, etc.), long hours, dirtiness of the work, monotony, impossibility of getting out of such work, and degradation of doing factory work. For married women with families, or young typists and shop assistants, the work had little appeal. Those who had already volunteered had done so through either patriotism or economic necessity, and in certain areas of depressed employment (like South Wales and the North-east) women were very glad of the opportunity for work.

Although the public attitude to conscription of women was favourable, and the result of one survey found that 97 per cent of women agreed 'emphatically' that women should undertake war work, many were in a state of confusion and consternation about the prospect. One typist wrote, 'I can lay my hand on my heart and say truthfully that I have not yet met a woman in the twenties who is not in an awful state about conscription.'[16] By 1943, it was almost impossible for women under forty to avoid war work unless they had heavy family responsibilities or they billeted war workers. In July of the same year, it was announced that all women up to fifty years of age had to register for employment, in an effort to release younger women for work in aircraft factories. There was an outcry against the 'direction of grandmothers' but it was passed. Most of the regulations, however, fell on the young unmarried women. Women were classified as 'mobile' or 'immobile', and girls could be 'exported' from their homes to work in war factories, a situation that was especially resented in Scotland when it was discovered that girls were to be sent south of the border.

The number of women new to work in this war did not show a vast increase, but again more an acceleration of peace-time trends. In 1943, the proportion of women aged from fifteen to sixty in the forces, munitions, and essential industries was about double what it had been in 1918.[17] Nearly 3 million married women and widows were employed compared with 1·25 million before the war. Of women aged from eighteen to forty, 90 per cent of single and 80 per cent of married women were in the forces or industries. The rest were looking after children or doing part-time or home jobs. It was estimated that without a war, there would have been about 6·75 million women working in 1943, and in fact there were about 7·5 million – representing an increase of only about 0·75 million. Women had worked in industries like the aircraft industry before the war, and within the engineering and metal industries; a quarter of working women had some pre-war experience, half came from different jobs, and the rest from school or from looking after the home.

As in the previous war, women entered many male-defined jobs, and usually proved to be as good as men. Their enthusiastic efficiency was again viewed with great suspicion by male workers. Although they did not go into mining, there were not many jobs below that requirement of physical ability in which some women could not be found. They worked on the railways as porters, in shipyards as welders, in the aircraft and other essential war industries. They produced work previously done by skilled men. Relations were not always easy between women and the men who trained them and with whom they worked. Men saw the threat contained in the 'dilution' of their jobs by women, and were often reluctant to give away all their knowledge. At the same time, many managements were loath to train women whom they considered to be a temporary labour force. Surprise was expressed at the ease with which the girls picked up skills – an ease which quickly reinforced male fears. When girls were first introduced into male-dominated factories, men often looked at them as if they were some new species. One girl, who proved to be a very competent worker, was described thus by her male workmates in an aircraft factory. 'We looked at her, nine of us, for days as though we had never seen a woman before. We watched the dainty way she picked up a file, with red-enamelled fingertip extended as though she were holding a cup of tea . . . her concern for the cleanliness of her hands, her delicate unhandy way with the hammer.'[18] In a northern foundry an ex-waitress became the best machine operator in the shop, but an observer noted: 'This girl has so taken to machinery that she would like to become an apprentice and go right through the works. This, of course is not possible on account of Union agreements. There is a feeling among men that at the moment women must be in the factory solely because of the war, but really women's place is in the home.'[19]

Women's real place at home was endorsed also at governmental level, and concern with the welfare of family life, particularly that of the working class, caused Beveridge to produce the basis of the Welfare State in his report in 1942. He made these views very explicit, and they provide a complete contrast to the national situation of the time, in which women were being exhorted to leave their young children in nurseries and go to work, young girls were being conscripted, and other women being directed from less to more important occupations. It is obvious that in looking forward to the end of the war, the state is stepping in to ensure the maintenance of Britain as a nation. The position of women working was officially classified.

The attitude of the housewife to gainful employment outside the home is not and should not be the same as the single woman. She has other duties . . . Taken as a whole, the plan for Social Security puts a premium on marriage in place of penalizing it . . . In the next thirty years housewives as mothers have vital work to do in ensuring the adequate continuance of the British race and of British ideals in the world.[20]

The 'temporary' nature of women's work was reflected in the

attitudes of men, management, and many women themselves. Trying to assess the potential state of women's demobilization, a special survey[21] found that most women were looking forward to going home when the war was over. It was the young unmarried women who were the most worried about their position and who welcomed the idea of staying on at work. This was also felt by elderly women who had been working for some time and were very financially dependent on their work. Married women, it was suggested, and those expecting to be married, saw their future goal as settling down to domestic life. This was unsurprising since much of the full-time factory work was very tiring and women with families became exhausted by their double job-load. For part-time workers however, the situation was different. The war had made many employers offer part-time work to women for the first time, and those taking it on were often women of about forty or fifty years of age from quite comfortable backgrounds. They were delighted with the outside interest and freedom that this gave them, and were very keen to continue.

A different attitude was expressed by many girls, generally young and from families of high income levels, who had gone into the services. They were reluctant at the thought of settling down, and expressed a longing for travel and adventure. 'The wanderlust is very widespread in the women's services.'[22] They were anxious about their post-war destinies, especially as war had reduced the prospect of marriage, and yet their training in the anti-aircraft service had not trained them for any peace-time job. The survey suggested that these girls were having to think for themselves for the first time, and were beginning to exchange frank and political ideas. 'Women in uniform have become far more independent-minded, first because there is no male member of the family available from whom to take a ready-made opinion, and secondly because in this new communal life, private hopes and fears are being brought into the daylight and related to wider plans for reconstruction on a national and international scale.'[23] They were in favour of equal competition with men, while those working in industry were content to accept continuing inequalities.

Female inequality at work carried on in its historical tradition.

Women in government training centres received just over half the pay of men, and sometimes this was even further reduced when they started full-time work! This happened particularly in the engineering industry. It was significant that although resistance to women working was not great, it was concentrated in the key places, and the A.E.U. for example, excluded women right up to 1943. The belief that things were going to be really tough for the working class after the war reinforced men's inclination to cling on to their present advantages. Very few women were to be found in the higher grades of industry, or on the Joint Production Committees formed during the war. Unequal pay was fairly universal, and when the railway companies were challenged to pay women clerks the same rates as men, they replied that 'Since the managers had been unable to find any industry where the principle of equal pay for equal work was applied, they did not see why they should apply it on the railways.' Despite agreements in the engineering industry to give women the full male rate after thirty-two weeks, this was easily and usually evaded. The unions did in fact recruit a lot of women – more in the general unions (T.G.W.U. and G.M.W.U.), although 140,000 women joined the A.E.U. when it finally opened its doors to them. The number of women in all trade unions had nearly doubled by the end of the war, but inequality was taken for granted. Even a demand for equal pay for teachers, at first passed, was revoked by the House of Commons in 1944.

Women of different class backgrounds worked and mixed in the same jobs, although sometimes their status was reflected in the positions they took – for instance women who had been teachers or had held other supervisory positions were often made supervisors in the factories, which was not always a successful arrangement. The influx of women into industry stimulated attention to working conditions, personal relationships, and welfare as related to industrial efficiency, and there was a significant increase in welfare provision and training of personnel managers.

The entry of girls from non-working class backgrounds shamed many firms into reconsidering the conditions under which women had to work. They were faced with the choice of either giving these girls clerical positions where conditions were better, or improving their facilities by providing better canteens and sanitary arrangements than those that 'the local factory-class girls had got used to'.

Married women had many problems with both shopping and child-care, as few firms gave regular time off for this purpose. The consequent absenteeism and bad time-keeping of many women reinforced management's already prejudiced views that married women were unsuitable employees. At first mothers had to leave children with relatives or neighbours, but the obvious unsuitability of many arrangements emphasized the need and demand for state-sponsored nurseries. This, in combination with Britain's overwhelming need to free women for essential work in industry gave the final impetus to the delayed question of day nursery provision, which began a great expansion from mid-1941. Many mothers were reluctant to use these facilities at first, but attitudes did change.

Young working class girls leaving elementary school in the war years usually made their choice from factory, shop, domestic or office work. Office work was more often the preserve of girls with secondary school education and the 'snob' division between clerical and manual workers in the same factory was quite high. The most important aspect was the money, which made a much needed contribution to family income, as well as providing the important (though meagre) pocket money. Girls took on a multitude of different unskilled jobs both before and during the war. This often happened in very quick succession, and they slipped from one to the next with an easy and indifferent attitude reflecting the labour shortage. Here for instance is the career of a girl of sixteen and a half in 1942 who left school at fourteen and has never been without a job for more than two days, except during evacuation.[24]

Job 1. 2 months: Calendars. 'You shove a piece of paper over a machine that is printing calendars. It got on my nerves.'
Job 2. 2 months: Pipes. 'You just polish them.'
Job 3. 1 week: Playing cards. 'You make up the pack.'

Job 4. 3 months: Darts and Fishing Rods. 'You fit the flight into the base with two pairs of pincers. That was a nice job. Interesting.'

Job 5. 3 days: Electric Irons. 'You had to fit wire into an adaptor.'

Job 6. 1 month: Batteries.

Job 7. 1 year 8 months (present job): Petrol Tubes. 'You stick a little rod into the solution and seal the top of the tube. I might "stick up" or go on to the filling machine or do other jobs as I fancy. We can swap jobs amongst ourselves. It's alright.'

The same situation was found in clerical jobs, although this is more typical of London than the north, and one girl was known to have had twenty-four jobs by the time she was twenty-two. Such young girls were used as a very cheap source of labour, and were employed on the most tedious and insignificant of tasks.

Money and leisure became important to them, and they had more of both than their mothers had had in their youth. Much of their leisure time was spent at the pictures or dancing, and some enthusiasts saw films three to five times a week. It was often a relief to get out of the house, where lack of space gave little privacy. After the age of about seventeen most girls' dominant interest was marriage, and this crucial part of their future was discussed frequently with friends and mothers. The war speeded up the tendency towards early marriage, and the idea of women's domestic careers became strongly established.

Practically every girl says that she will want to give up her job when she gets married, and expects her career to continue for another five years at most. Even when the girl, like one very capable clerk who had risen from twenty-five shillings at fifteen to fifty shillings at eighteen, says that she herself would probably like to go on with her job after marriage if her husband were away, her boy does not favour the idea, nor do the older people at her home.[25]

Those who considered continuing to go out to work did so only in the case of financial necessity. 'They see marriage as a full-time career, and want literally to make a job of it. It is a matter of principle ... that a woman's first duty is to look after her own home ... Their boys take the same attitude ... and what "my boy" says carries much weight.'[25]

After the war, women were called upon to go home again, and although many did, it was not without a change in attitude that would bring them back to work later on. The post-war withdrawal of nursery facilities made it harder for women who did want to carry on, but the relative independence that many women had experienced left them discontented with work solely at home. Some part-time workers were allowed to stay on, as employers had found them useful and another way of extorting cheap labour. It was however not totally an employer's market in labour terms. Unlike the First World War, there was very little unemployment after this war – in fact there was a labour shortage in many areas. This meant for instance that part-timers who would have otherwise been forced to either leave work or continue full-time, were allowed to stay on. In some cases special shift systems were even worked out to best suit these women.[26] It is not absolutely clear how far women did follow the order to return home, or whether they were displaced out of men's jobs into perhaps more suitable 'women's work'. This is what appears to have occurred in America. Working class girls and women carried on working as they had always done, combining the belief that women's primary place is in the home with its economic contradiction. It was middle class women once more who saw the most change, clinging on to their part-time jobs, although certainly not denying their primary duties to the home.

Up to the Present

The period after the war and in the fifties saw a general cultural reaction against the independent woman who had demonstrated her capabilities briefly in war-time. Fashion and the female image became restrictively feminine, and marriage was held out as the most normal and desirable state for women to be in. The implications of John Bowlby's* studies exaggerated the need for mothers always to be with their young children. The terrors of 'maternal-deprivation' laid the responsibility for children's future development at the mother's door. It served as a dis-

---

* On the effects of 'maternal deprivation' on young children, and the importance of the mother–child tie, 1946. See also chapter 5.

couragement to would-be working mothers and placed most of the guilt on the working class since they were assumed to be the main perpetrators of this psychological offence. In spite of this, women (particularly married women) were still going out to work. Thus they contributed to expanding industries and provided extra income for the family, giving everyone the illusion of being better off. The Tory government patted itself on the back for the affluence of the 1950s and said 'You've never had it so good.' But the credit was as much due to these women's labours as to government policy. It was the simultaneous expansion in the 'women's work' areas – the administrative, educational, welfare and service sectors, that created a demand for women and made it inevitable that they should be increasingly drawn into the labour force.

The 1950s saw more and more married women going out to work. Many factors had contributed to this situation: an earlier marriage age, falling birth-rates and shrinking families, reduction in time necessary for housework as a result of household gadgets and ready-to-cook foods, increasing demands for female labour, and the changing ideology of the modern world in which women were theoretically free to compete with men. Development of birth control, and changed attitudes to family size which emphasized the advantages of smaller families, meant that a smaller proportion of a woman's life-time needed to be devoted to motherhood.

In the period from 1881–1951, there was little significant change in the proportion of gainfully occupied women in the total female population: 25·5 per cent in 1881 and 27·4 per cent in 1951; although this obviously conceals the great changes in regions and types of occupation. But in the period 1951–61, this went up to 37·2 per cent, and this increase was almost totally through the employment of married women.[27] The public acceptance of the notion of women as an integral part of the labour force was hastened by the post-war situation of full employment, which meant that employers had to look to women as the only available source of reserve labour. The resulting opportunities for part-time work opened the door for many more married women. In the estimates made of women workers between 1951–61 through census figures, and by such studies as Dr Viola Klein's,[28] it appeared that over 80 per cent of part-time workers were married women. In 1957, almost half the population of married women were working, and half of these had children under fifteen years. The range of work, particularly for part-timers, was very limited, and reflected a high proportion of working class employment. In Klein's study, 45 per cent of working women were domestic workers, cleaners, canteen helpers and the like; then came clerical workers (15 per cent) and shop assistants (12 per cent). Altogether 67 per cent of part-time married women were in unskilled or semi-skilled work,* endorsing the continuing predominance of working class women's employment.

These trends continued into the 1960s, when the expansion of higher education for girls reinforced the idea that women could make a meaningful contribution to the work force, while also endorsing the class divisions in education and employment. Girls taking O- and A-levels in grammar schools were being groomed for work in the higher status jobs and professions (teaching and nursing being two areas currently having labour shortages), while in the lower forms of these schools and in the secondary moderns, girls left early for lower-level jobs needing the minimum qualifications. The reasoning then seemed to be that if you had a good job, especially a higher status one with training, like teaching or medicine, it was a pity and a waste to give it up. It became acceptable for a girl in such work to carry on with it after both marriage and children. On the other hand, unless women were short of money there was little recognized reason for them to return to low status jobs like routine clerical and unskilled work. Even financial need was often lost in the myth that women only worked for 'pin money'. It was thought to be unacceptable for women to work because they wanted to get out of the home.

But as the sixties wore on, cultural changes occurred which questioned the strict gender definitions separating masculine and feminine. The expanding youth movement rejected the tradition of their elders. They were helped in self-definition by the need for new markets within capitalism, which exploited their earning

* These figures approximate to the distribution of employment for the mothers of the girls in my research.

power and manipulated their tastes. Teddyboys, beatniks and hippies demonstrated their ideas of alternative cultures. Boys and girls grew long hair and wore unisex clothes. The militancy that had started in the days of C.N.D. exploded on student campuses in the late sixties and challenged the system that had put them there. Women's Liberation emerged as a movement partly out of this new radicalism and in 1970 the first organized conference was held in Oxford.

Working class girls who have been picking their way through school and adolescence in the 1970s are relatively untouched by this upsurge of feminism although some may encounter teachers in the women's movement. But their position has been changed and complicated by developments in women's role and attitudes. Like all girls, they confront a situation that is the product of historical change – embracing economic, technological and ideological developments. For instance middle class girls have come to accept and expect their right to work. They take their choice from a better selection of jobs than working class girls, but are still barred from easy entry to men's jobs or high positions.

This may provide conflict for some girls, but other contradictions particularly affect working class girls. The idea of job involvement for example, which is so implicit in school careers teaching, clashes with the routine and monotony of most jobs open to them. It clashes too with the deep investment that many of their own mothers have made in family life. The resolution and outcome of contradictions like these in girls' lives will depend not only on changes in the economic and labour position in the immediate future but also on the active response of the girls themselves.

WOMEN AND THE FAMILY UNDER CAPITALISM

Women's role in the home is of fundamental importance to the working of our society, in all its social, political and economic spheres. I have looked at how the role and expectations of girls and women have been transformed and developed through time, and it is now necessary to examine their present situation more deeply. Through such an analysis, it becomes clear that the attitudes and ideas of girls are not only formed through tradition, teaching and their own interpretation of the world, but can and should be understood by examining the social conditions of their lives under capitalism. They have an integral part to play in the organization of work and of the economy, and therefore the way these operate will affect their position. At the same time if women's actions and demands are strong enough they can exert their own influence on the course of capitalism.

A family without a woman is not a proper family. She is seen as the necessary element, although apparently insufficient if the official views on unsupported mothers are to be taken seriously. Subject to influences from outside the family, her role within it changes with any alterations in its form and functions. Conversely, as women have made modifications and extensions to their role, the family has had to adapt itself or be propped up with state aid.

There have been several important changes in the family which have affected women's situation. When most people lived on the land, the peasant family made up a production unit and the whole family was involved in working. Similarly in domestic industry men, women and children worked together. These economic functions of the family have been gradually whittled away since the growth of the factory system. The movement towards towns and work in mass production, and the emphasis on accumulating capital contributed towards reducing the extended agricultural family to the small nuclear unit recognized today, and reflected the effects of demands for different sorts of workers within capitalism. State intervention through education and social welfare has taken over and made public some of the private informal education which existed in the family, thus also altering women's role in the family. Every generation of girls grows up in a family situation which is trying to adapt and survive within present economic and social conditions, and eventually plays its own adult part in continuing this process.

The division of labour in society thus puts production into the hands of men, leaving reproduction and child-care to women. Production is thus separated from both reproduction and consumption. From the time of the Industrial Revolution class divisions rigidified between the ruling class, who owned the factories and most of the other means of production, and the working class, who made up the mass labour working for them. The middle classes emerged in between, striving and aspiring towards the upper echelons of power and wealth.

Instead of working in family workshops and on smallholdings, men increasingly went *out* to work, and a consistent wage became the criterion for survival. A man's capacity for work, his labour, was exchanged or 'sold' in return for money with which he could then purchase back, at a higher price, the finished products of his or others' labour in order to maintain him and his family. Since the main emphasis is on accumulation of capital, making profits is essential to success within capitalism. Therefore a worker never receives back the real value of his or her labour. It is implicit that the relations of production – the relationship between worker and employer – capitalist – should be exploitative. The worker performs surplus labour producing surplus value which ends up as accumulated capital (profits). The aim of any capitalist is to compete successfully in the market place of commodities. The greater his profits the more capital he can accumulate, and the more he can expand his enterprise and keep up with competition. Within this process, workers have the dubious 'freedom' of selling their labour. They are 'free' to work their lives away and yet always remain powerless and subordinate to those who own capital and the means of production.

The relationship between men and capitalism, as described above, is direct and exploitative. That between women and capitalism has been kept deceptively separate. Contributing to this has been the dominant set of beliefs and values of society, which stressed women's place within the home. As a result there was no official recognition of women as part of production despite centuries of their essential labour. This separation of work from home and family also led to neglect of any proper analysis of women's contribution through their husbands and children. In order to begin to rectify this, it is necessary to examine more closely the role of the family and the parts women play inside and outside the home.

The shrinking of family structure was accompanied by a corresponding erosion of functions. Children were taken out of the home for compulsory schooling; and other home duties, such as nursing, were eased by the provision of hospitals. The creation of the welfare state in this century made a great impact, giving aid to the sick, unemployed, elderly, pregnant and poverty-stricken. The changing image of women's role is intimately connected with these state interventions, which in turn were determined by the need for a more efficient society, a more rational capitalism.

To illustrate this point, we can look at the pattern of goods that were produced in the last seventy years. At the beginning of the century, Britain was an important exporter of goods, but with increasing competition from abroad, was forced back on to the previously protected home market. The Depression in the thirties led to severe crises in some of Britain's older industries, such as steel, shipbuilding and textiles, which in turn led to mass unemployment. Simultaneously, newer home-based industries concerned with the manufacture of consumer durables were growing rapidly and helping to maintain a crippled economy. These products brought technology to the household and consisted of articles like washing machines and vacuum cleaners, which would eventually reduce the amount of labour necessary in the home. These domestic aids started being used in middle class homes, also helping to compensate for the declining number of domestic servants. This growth continued and was joined after the Second World War by the self-service catering development and the expansion of ready-prepared foods. Therefore, during this period an increasing proportion of capital was indirectly being made by easing women's domestic work in the home. Combined with other factors: such as the tendency towards smaller families, the development and use of contraception, and increases in allowances and welfare, this facilitated the conditions for women to work outside the home. Thus the changing pattern of economic production had its ultimate effects in the organization of domestic work.

Women's position at home and at work is also bound up with the demands of capitalism for different sorts of labour. In many areas of work, women need not be drawn into the labour force while there is a surplus of men, except into specifically female employment. But when this surplus decreases, or new sorts of employment open up, capital has to look towards other sources of labour power. This has happened particularly with the increasing demand for white-collar office-workers and secretarial staff, and the recent growth in computer work. In the last twenty years capital has drawn on immigrant labour (predominantly for manual work) and female labour to fill the demand. The wars accelerated this process for women, when they discovered for themselves that there was a far greater range of jobs within their capabilities than had previously been provided by domestic service. This has increased to such an extent that the rate of acceleration in the growth in female labour is probably about four times that of the rate of increase in the population.

Although recently there have been severe economic crises and large-scale unemployment, which are still continuing features, so far there has been no obvious redeployment of women back to the home. This is because they are now an accepted and integral part of the labour force (although in some manufacturing areas they are still very much a source of cheap surplus labour and the first to be paid off in the event of cutbacks). But women are also becoming unionized and more militant about their rights, especially over the crucial issue of equal pay It is harder to disperse and crush them. Also, the demand for women has continued in the administrative, clerical and secretarial fields, in which there is no competition with men. Therefore it is no longer so easy to manipulate a female labour force, and in fact it is not rational to lay women off in the present economic situation, since their contribution to the family income is becoming increasingly important. In all families, middle class as well as working class, women's wages ease the situation within capitalism.

Under capitalism, the family therefore lost a lot of its earlier functions in production, education and welfare, and women have experienced corresponding effects. The modern family now has two major purposes in which women still play the principal part.

The first is in producing and maintaining the present and future elements of the essential work force. This means a woman looks after her husband, bears his children and brings them up to the best of her ability. In this she is supplemented by, and herself contributes to, the welfare state, which gives token assistance to her work in the home, like providing the meagre child allowances. Within this function lie several other useful areas of indirect control: the family unit provides the most socially recognized and approved place for sex and reproduction; the cheapest place for the early care and socialization of children; and a private sanctuary to accommodate the passions and emotions so inappropriate and disruptive if they occur in the outside world of business and production.

The second major function of the family is avidly to buy and consume the products, useful and useless, that capitalism continuously makes available. To provide the maximum market for these, the 'privatization' of the family is essential – an infinite duplication of needs. Every family buys individual foods, cooks on individual cookers, in individual pans. Each buys the products and gadgets that are supposed to make work and leisure more enjoyable. Each is encouraged to compare itself with others to assess relative affluence and status. A family may be judged by what it consumes. An immense consumer market is being built up in which expensive luxury goods – cars, televisions, stereos, washing machines etc. take their place beside the basic needs for survival. Advertising has helped both to produce and maintain the demand, dwelling on a man's wish to compete and prove himself by encouraging him to buy certain large commodities, and on a woman's anxieties about being a 'good' wife and mother for which she has to buy the 'right' things.

The economy rests on such individual consumption – collectivization would be disastrous for capitalist profits, although beneficial for people. But the system is based on the needs of capital rather than those of people, and any slump, for whatever reason, is bounced back on to wages, which are then cut or frozen to preserve profits. Workers, like capitalists, are taught to believe in the importance of the 'national economy', and assume that its healthy growth is also theirs. To some extent this seems to be true, because in a prosperous economy, the capitalist class can afford to make more concessions to the demands of the working class, but these are fragments compared with the corresponding profits.

To carry out these two important functions, it is therefore necessary to preserve the small autonomous family. But instead of helping in this, capitalism shows one of many inherent irrationalities: for while expressing deep anxiety about any possible break-up or disruptions of family life, like the hypocritical Victorians, industry today consistently introduces schemes of shift-work and night-work, or demands mobilization, all of which take their inevitable toll on family life.

The Parts Women Play

Women today have two recognized roles: one at home, and the other increasingly in the work force. But rather than these being alternatives, the domestic role is assumed to be natural part of being a woman. Any other activities like having a job are then performed as additional work. In the isolation of every home, women perform never-ending tasks of cleaning, cooking, washing-up, washing clothes, and all the repetitive services that maintain the home. Mothers have the more exhausting demands of child-care. This work seems very far away from the grind of production. It is not counted as 'real work' because it is unpaid and done in the privacy of home. Here, women are given the illusory freedom to organize these tasks. It is an implicit part of being wife and mother, although the same things done for other people are counted as employment. The work itself is not light, and mothers may often work eighty or ninety hours a week in their homes. Housework has become easier and less time-consuming through domestic technology, but there are no consumer products to make children less demanding.

This unrecognized work is in effect the service and maintenance of the workers of today and tomorrow. It *is* related to the external world of production, but indirectly. A man is forced to rely on his wife's labour at home in order to be fit and able to earn a wage. With his wage he is expected to provide for a wife and family. Their survival on this money is dependent on a wife's economical shopping, and the provision of her free services. Every day she reproduces labour power, her man's capacity for another working day. Her work produces things, not for exchange, but for immediate consumption. Meals are eaten, floors and clothes are made dirty over and over again. It is because she does not produce for exchange that a woman's labour is deceptively unconnected with the 'real' economic markets. Therefore it is seen as 'unreal', or 'invisible labour', but it is certainly real enough to greatly reduce the cost of maintaining and reproducing workers (and to be, at least at present, cheaper than any other method), and therefore makes an important contribution to the total profits received by capital. Women have accepted this definition of themselves enough to say, 'I don't work. I'm only a housewife.' Their sons and daughters also absorb this perception of women's role and develop their appropriate relationships to production.

Home-making and child-care are obviously real work in every physical sense, but as women's work and as so-called 'unproductive' work they are different because they operate on a social and personal level.[29] The power of labour lies usually in its capacity to be sold and withdrawn at will. If housework is 'real' work, then a woman should be able to withdraw her services. But the crucial difference here is that it is not alienated labour but 'love-labour'. The relationship between man and wife is not that between worker and employer. The emotional ties and responsibilities run very deep: 'love-labour' is capable of sustained production out of all proportion to that of wage-labour. It appears disguised as something that has escaped reduction to sordid economic terms, and yet without it the cost of reproducing and looking after the workers would have to be borne by capitalism itself.

From childhood, women have learned to give themselves freely as a natural extension of character and role. The reward is love and security, which is highly valued by women in a society where love is a human feeling out of place and often distorted in the productive world, and where the development of capitalism has forced women to become dependent on finding a husband for their support. In such a society, what you are worth is more important than what you are, and it is no wonder that women stand aloof from this and express views like that of the fourteen-year-old girl who said: '. . . when you have a career you just work, and you might have a lot of money but you never have love'.

But what are the consequences for a woman whose whole life is measured in terms of the love she gives and receives from her husband and children? Often her identity gets lost, submerged within her caring. Her success is the reflection of their success, their problems are treated as her problems, their happiness becomes her happiness. At first, her own self may hang suspended, sometimes returning for moments of expression, but when the children come, and life gets filled with immediate demands, this becomes a luxury, drawing further and further back and finally forgotten. Her world is encapsulated within home and family.

A man's relationship to the home is very different. He has an independent role at work where he becomes someone in his own right, whatever his job and however well he does it. For him home is a place to return to, to relax in and be recharged for the next day's work. It is the place where he is by tradition the head, however token this has become. Here he can dominate and satisfy expectations of masculinity denied to most workers in their subordinate position within capitalism. The masculine ideal demands assertiveness, aggression, competitiveness and initiative, and such attributes are valued as necessary for success within capitalism.

But men also need to express emotions and have personal intimacies, and these have been partitioned off and channelled into the narrow confines of home. Women in roles of idealized femininity are supposed to soothe away the stress and tension of the male working day. The stereotyped characteristics of femininity make women seem totally unsuitable as successful capitalists, but are designed to equip them perfectly as receptacles for a man's bursting emotions and passion and as a sop to his frustrations at work. In our society, it is sad that the family is the only place where people are allowed to be themselves, safely prevented from disrupting the organized alienation that exists outside.

Women at home have adopted many strategies to cope with their situation, to refract its real causes and transfer them into some other form. They often develop minor illnesses and nervous complaints. They may become neurotic and obsessional over trivial things, over-reacting to small crises. To ease these symptoms, doctors prescribe tranquillizers or sleeping pills, which dull the senses enough to enable them to do the family duties. But the main criterion of women at home's 'normality' is how far they stay within the domestic role. If they reject this in an exaggerated way, doubts may even be cast on their sanity.* In traditional social work, a woman may be judged according to her 'femininity' and domesticity, and increased neatness and cleanliness is seen as 'improvement' in her condition. But on the other hand, intense concern with domestic tasks is rational if there seems to be no alternative, and many women draw much of their self esteem from their indispensability to the family. To deny this seems to remove the whole purpose of their existence.

Very few women today spend all their lives at home, and girls growing up now have lots of ideas about vocations. But this has not necessarily changed women's dependence on home and family as much as may be expected, as the ideology defining their role as wife and mother has lagged behind. Women's primary place is still at home with work running a closer second place than before, but still only acceptable with convincing reasons and adequate provision at home. This has masked the fact that many women, especially working class women, have been doing two jobs for many years, accepting their 'love-labour' and blaming themselves if they could not cope with the double work load. These beliefs work within the interests of capitalism now, but we have seen how the state can acknowledge and intervene in women's situation at times of critical labour need, as it did in the Second World War.

The same ideas that support the oppression and exploitation of women at home also form the basis of their conditions in work outside. The view that this is secondary is still held by both

---

* Phyllis Chesler[30] notes that it is often when women stop performing domestic tasks as part of their 'illness', that their husbands tend to have them (re-)admitted to mental hospital.

women and employers to justify low-level jobs at low wages. This is reinforced by regarding them as a temporary, transient and unreliable work force. They have been little helped in the past by male trade unions, who have neglected them for similar reasons, even seeing them as a threat to their stability. Women themselves have been slow and difficult to unionize and organize, partly because they have accepted their priorities at home. Many factors have combined to give women little protection against exploitation, but within the recent upsurge of industrial militancy, some male unions and workers have begun to realize the need to support women's demands as strongly as their own.

Women's work has mainly consisted of a large-scale continuation of the tasks that are involved in work at home. This includes work in textiles and tailoring, food and catering, nursing and teaching, secretarial and other clerical work. In the work of nurses, social workers and teachers there are elements of 'love-labour', since they are concerned with caring and being responsible for people. This has the effect of weakening the power of their labour. Withdrawal of labour means that a lot of people will suffer in some way. In the present economic crisis, these obstacles to action have been declining, as teachers and nurses have become militant and held demonstrations and short-term strikes. Through miserable wages and conditions, they have started to organize and to realize that their own self-sacrifice, cushioned within an ideology of dedication, is conditioned by capitalist demand for cheap services and as such has to be attacked.

Beliefs, Attitudes and Values

For a social system to work people must believe in it, and for its survival it must have a convincing way of putting over its ideas. Political power is not only a matter of economic dominance, it requires an ideological hold over how the world is presented. It would be too simple to regard this as a plot or conspiracy. The existing values of dominant groups are reproduced through the structure of institutions like the family, schools and the media, and women play a crucial role in this process.

From all these sources, people pick up an apparent consensus of what has been, what is and what ought to be. This is the way little girls learn to be 'proper' little girls, and then big girls, housewives, mothers, underpaid workers, and old-age pensioners. Boys similarly learn their appropriate gender roles, and grow to accept the class structure and their particular place in it. They all absorb an ideology which has its own self-perpetuating and circular justification. It is put over as natural, and because it seems to fit in with the way things are organized and most efficiently run, it is not challenged as a total system. There may be complaints about some of its workings, but it is hard to stand outside it and confront the whole immorality of its organization. It is easier to fiddle around with a few parts here and there.

Much of morality itself is confined within the context of capitalism, which defines what is good and bad for society. In this way, strikes and demonstrations are portrayed as socially disruptive and threatening to social order, while the exploitation that is at the heart of capitalism passes largely unquestioned. Similarly, changing the 'feminine' role is portrayed as trying to disturb something natural, pure and good, while women's subordination and oppression is overlooked. The professed principle of equality suggests that everyone can compete and succeed: you can make it if you try, providing of course that you are not working class, female or black.

Children spend their first few years helpless and dependent within the family. As they grow up, they learn the rules for living, the difference between right and wrong and who to obey. They are socialized into the customs and values accepted as 'normal', and taught to accept exploitation and inequality as part of the way of the world: for each according to his or her position in life. There are differences according to class, as the middle class are encouraged to achieve more, while the working class are exhorted to be thankful for what they have. Girls grow towards their future as wives and mothers and the increasing expectation that they should incline towards a career presents implicit contradictions to many of them. It is seen as particularly important that girls develop and believe in the female role and in preserving the established order, because they are the major agents in transmitting this ideology to their own children. It is significant that while the state has taken over so many other functions of the family, it has left parents responsible for the behaviour of their children. Therefore they have to control their sons and daughters, making sure they keep within the rules and expectations of society. Any misdemeanours are first reflected back on the family, before other social conditions are considered.

Although the whole family takes part in this process, and even children can be seen teaching younger ones what they should and should not do, women take another part as the gentle defusers of rebellion. They are a constant reminder of male responsibilities towards them and the children, and they discourage husbands from becoming militant at work. They are often more concerned to cope with their own struggle in the home, which is made even worse if their husbands become redundant. If they are unable to work themselves, they are dependent on the man's continuing wage. The different relationships that men and women have with production has shaped their consciousness, and for women the family usually comes first. They rarely identify with a class struggle that seems to have little direct connection with their lives, although they are generally the first to feel its effects.

This framework of ideas, beliefs and values helps to validate the divisive social and economic conditions under which people live, and gains expression through the ideas and attitudes of girls like those described in this book. Their class, sex and ethnic backgrounds have already moulded their interpretation of life. They have a long-held understanding of the differences between themselves and boys, and the different work roles laid out before them. The ideology of marriage, husband, home and children as the most integral parts of the future has been passed on, usually through their own mothers. It is on this acceptance that the economic system of capital accumulation has been able to reproduce the conditions for its perpetuation. And it is through attacking ideology as well as the material basis for class and sex exploitation that people can learn and understand their own roles in the process, and themselves take part in their own liberation from it.

There are many contradictions and irrationalities in women's situation under capitalism. For example, the family itself presents a problem. While on one hand it carries out economic and ideological functions necessary to capitalism in its present form, its existence as a retreat from the harsh productive world represents a place that is comparatively archaic and inefficient. In order to maximize the amount of labour that could be extracted from everyone, it would be rational to socialize most of the work done in the home, freeing women for labour.* But this would result in a disastrous collapse of much of the vast consumer market, and enormous capital investment would be needed in large-scale and cheap services to replace women's free labour in the home. Justification for this would also have to be introduced, since belief in the traditional domestic role of women has been very deeply instilled. Taking women out of the home would be interpreted as leading to the breakdown of the family, a possibility which has caused great concern in the past as it was seen as a symptom of impending chaos and as a threat to the social order.

As many girls have realized, the present situation demands their work both inside and outside the home. Consideration of jobs and careers forms an important part of girls' latter school years. Yet they are still individually responsible for looking after homes and children when they are married, and little nursery provision is made to help them. Those who plan to place their future young children in nurseries and return to their jobs will find this difficult to do. At first it will seem less of a struggle to conform to the role that capitalism makes most acceptable and whose basic principles have been made explicit throughout childhood and indeed history.

* This assumes an expanding economy. In a depressed economic situation the removal of women from the labour force would help to ease official unemployment figures.

Notes

Chapter 1

1. Much of the information about working class girls given here is taken from work done by Anna Davin into children's conditions at the end of the nineteenth century; to be published in the History Workshop Series, *Childhood*, vol. 2.
2. Anna Davin, op. cit.
3. ibid.
4. ibid.
5. Josephine Kamm, *Hope Deferred*, Methuen, 1965.
6. These class-biased assumptions are expressed in education reports such as the board of education 'Regulations for Secondary Schools' (1904) and 'Report upon Questions affecting Higher Elementary Schools' (1906).
7. J. W. B. Douglas, *The Home and the School*, Panther, 1967.
8. J. W. B. Douglas, *All Our Future*, Panther, 1968.
9. Quoted in J. Burnett, *Useful Toil*, Allen Lane, 1974.
10. J. Burnett, op. cit.
11. Quoted in Irene Osgood Andrews and Margaret A. Hobbs, *Economic Effects of the World War upon Women and Children in Great Britain*, Carnegie Endowment for International Peace, Preliminary Economic Studies of the War, no 4, New York, 1921.
12. Reviewing the effects of war on women at a conference of working class organizations in Bradford in March 1917. Also quoted in Irene Osgood Andrews, op. cit.
13. Winifred Holtby, *Women and a Changing Civilization*, John Lane, 1934.
14. Winifred Holtby, op. cit.
15. Mass Observation, 'People and Production', in *Change*, no. 3, 1942.
16. Mass Observation, op. cit.
17. Figures quoted in Angus Calder, *The People's War*, Panther, 1971.
18. M. Benney, *Over to Bombers*, quoted in Angus Calder, op. cit.

19.   Mass Observation, op. cit.

20.   Beveridge Report, 1942.

21.   Mass Observation, 'The Journey Home', *Change*, no. 5, 1944.

22.   Mass Observation, op. cit.

23   ibid.

24.   Quoted in Pearl Jephcott, *Girls Growing Up*, Faber & Faber, 1942.

25.   Pearl Jephcott, *Rising Twenty*, Faber & Faber, 1945.

26.   This happened at the Peak Frean factory in Bermondsey which was the subject of an investigation by Pearl Jephcott *et al*, *Married Women Working*, Allen & Unwin, 1962.

27.   Table given in Edward James, 'Women at Work in Twentieth Century Britain', *The Manchester School*, vol. 30, no. 3, quoted in S. Yudkin and A. Holme, *Working Mothers and their Children*, Sphere, 1969.

28.   Viola Klein, 'Working Wives', *Occasional Papers* no. 15, Institute of Personnel Management, 1960.

29.   Within the Women's Liberation Movement, Marxist feminists are attempting to analyse this sort of work, see for instance: Mariarosa Dalla Costa and Selma James, *The Power of Women and the Subversion of the Community*, Falling Wall Press, 1972; Isabel Larguia and John Dumoulin, 'Towards a Science of Women's Liberation', *Red Rag Pamphlet* no. 1; Jean Gardiner's reply to Wally Secombe ('The Housewife and her Labour under Capitalism', *New Left Review*, no. 83, January–February 1973) in *New Left Review*, no. 89, January–February, 1975; also *Women and Socialism Conference Papers* 3, 1974.

30.   Phyllis Chesler, *Women and Madness*, Allen Lane, 1974.

CHAPTER II

The Social Construction of Sex Differences

'Bet she's sugar and spice
And everything nice,
A pink and petite little treasure
Your new little "she"
Who's certain to be
A wonderful bundle of pleasure!'

'A SON IS FUN!
He'll keep you busy
With blankets and pins
And charm your hearts
With his boyish grins!
What's more he'll make you
Proud and glad
Congratulations mother and dad!'

Birth congratulation messages.

An understanding of how the position of girls and women is crucially affected by economic factors overlaid with ideology helps us to make sense of the nature, origins and perpetuation of existing sex roles. So far, I have examined these from a historical perspective and through the demands of the present economic and social structure. Another dimension can be added by looking more closely at the ideas, beliefs and values about men and women which are embedded within biology and psychology, and the ways that these are passed on.

The economic requirements which demanded certain sorts of labour and technology and which developed efficient contraception, have combined with women's own demands and attitudes to transform the position of women throughout this century. It has been accompanied by an ideology of sexual equality, thought to be fitting in a modern civilized society. Officially, this gives the same opportunities to both sexes, and has meant that formal sanctions previously preventing women from straying too far from conventional sex roles have been lifted. Nowadays women are apparently 'free' to enter any area of education and occupation, and are allowed to go into politics and other male-dominated spheres. The emphasis on people's rights and participation in a 'democratic' society makes it impossible formally to deny opportunity, although discrimination is still required by our social organization and division of labour.

To compensate for this, more pressure has been laid on 'informal' beliefs and sanctions in order to preserve these divisions. These are based on the biological and psychological differences thought to determine masculine and feminine personality, which are often used to justify role and job segregation. Consequently, the 'socialization' of boys and girls into contrasting personalities and roles has now a more significant part to play in the perpetuation of the social structure. In a society in which obvious discrimination is condemned, 'natural' sex differences help to preserve the separation of roles and thus the inequalities upon which the economic system still depends.[1]

It is therefore not surprising that theories and empirical evidence that question the whole basis of innate and psychological sex differences have made little impact. For instance, the cross-cultural studies carried out by anthropologists such as Margaret Mead[2] have shown that there is no universal 'masculine' or 'feminine' personality. The tribes she describes either show characteristics that are undifferentiated by sex or they reverse the sex stereotypes found in modern industrialized society. The Arapesh for example are a passive, gentle and non-aggressive people, all of whom take responsibility for looking after the children. In contrast to this 'femininity', both sexes of the Mundagumor tribe demonstrate the characteristics that we understand as 'masculine', while the Tchambuli reverse many of our accepted differences. Other examples can be found in anthropology[3] to show further constellations of characteristics and behaviour.

The existence of so many differing types of masculinity and femininity contributes towards undermining the system of sex stereotypes. However, it is important to remember that sex differentiation and its surrounding values and attitudes does not develop in an arbitrary way. It is vitally influenced by the nature of the economic structure of a society and the division of labour that has been developed around it. Some cross-cultural studies have tried to show how a particular economy affects sex roles and the socialization of boys and girls and thus their resulting personality formation.[4] For instance, in examining the training of boys and girls in reports of 110 cultures, Barry, Bacon and Child found that 'pressure towards nurturance, obedience and responsibility is most often stronger for girls whereas pressure towards achievement and self-reliance is most often stronger for boys',[5] as in Western society. But they also notice that where the economy depended on constant care of animals or regular tending of crops it was necessary that both sexes be similarly taught to be compliant, obedient and responsible (traditionally 'feminine'), because the economy needed these qualities. In cultures where the economy centred around hunting and fishing however, children were encouraged in assertiveness, achievement and self-reliance (traditionally 'masculine'), although boys were still rather more assertive than girls. For both kinds of subsistence economies there was greater variation in the work of men and boys than there was in that of girls and women, whose reproductive role defined certain regularities and meant that they had to stay fairly near home.[6]

Barry, Bacon and Child also concluded that the largest sexual differentiation and male superiority occur together in 'an economy that places a high premium on the superior strength and superior development of motor skills requiring strength, which characterize the male',[7] such as in a society where hunting, herding or warfare are important. This superiority has entered the value structure of most societies, related to other factors such as access to defined sources of power, and has pervaded many areas other than the original one based on primitive survival. Superior male status has been preserved while the situation it accompanies has changed many times. Applied to our society, it is clear that the division of labour and the separation of work from home and child-care is linked to personality, and that this is assumed to derive from innate male and female characteristics.

Anthropological evidence must not be used uncritically however, as small societies are subject to many influences, such as the effects of colonization and the impact of Western culture. When these are taken into account, the dynamics of change become clearer, but it is still hard to dismiss the example of 'primitive' tribes as merely deviant and irrelevant. The argument put forward that every powerful culture such as our own has similar sex differences and that therefore it may be the fact of not having these that contributes to the continuing insignificance of small societies, can be countered by understanding the demands of a specific economic system; we have seen how this evolved in our society by tracing the effects of industrialization and the development of capitalism on the roles of men and women.[8]

Another kind of evidence has questioned innate and predetermined explanations by focusing on the social influence of assigning a masculine or feminine personality to people at birth. This has developed out of research carried out mainly in America on patients with various kinds of endocrine disorders which cause them to develop ambiguous sexual characteristics. The researchers, John Money and John and Joan Hampson,[9] distinguish between 'sex', meaning the physical characteristics such as genitals, hormones, gonads, internal reproductive organs and chromosomes, and 'gender', meaning the amount of 'masculinity' or 'femininity' shown and felt by a person. In most people, agreement exists between their sex, 'gender role', and 'gender identity', but there are some who are born with a discrepancy within their physical sexual characteristics. Such people are termed hermaphrodites or inter-sexuals. The contradiction usually occurs between the external genitalia and some internal feature, but this may not be discovered at birth. A baby with apparently normal male or female genitals will be seen, named and brought up in the appropriate way, and it may not be until the onset of puberty and physical maturity that an incongruity is revealed. By this time, the individual's assigned gender identity is so well established that it is very difficult for them to adjust to the idea that some of their internal characteristics such as chromosomes or reproductive organs define them as being of the opposite sex.

Therefore the sex label assigned at birth determines the way the baby is brought up and the appropriate gender role and identity development. The social factors of rearing over-ride the biological structures. For instance nineteen patients who had been brought up in a way that contradicted the sex of their chromatin pattern had all developed a satisfactory gender identity. Another thirty-one patients had gender identities in contrast to the sex of their hormones and also to their secondary sexual body development. It is found that the upbringing of a child as male or female can only be successfully changed before the age of eighteen months to two years. This coincides with the learning and growth of language which greatly expands the child's scope of social learning and cognitive understanding.

John Money and the Hampsons feel that the influence of upbringing is so strong as to suggest that

... an individual's gender role and orientation as boy or girl, man or woman, does not have an innate preformed instinctive basis as some theorists have maintained. Instead the evidence supports the view that psychologic sex is undifferentiated at birth – a sexual neutrality one might say – and that the individual becomes psychologically differentiated as masculine or feminine in the course of the many experiences of growing up.[10]

This sort of evidence has however been used to support both sides of the argument and other researchers have used it to draw the opposite conclusions.[11] For instance they point out those individuals who go for medical advice because they are unhappy about some aspect of their own masculinity or femininity and are then discovered to have been 'wrongly assigned'. However, this does not negate the weight of evidence that shows gender to be no simple biological heritage. Genetics and biology do have a part to play in the process and should not be ignored for the sake of the argument. It is not necessary or reasonable to attempt to prove that men and women are exactly the same, but rather to show that the ways they do differ are not important and do not warrant their exaggerated consequences in the separation of sex roles and personality. It seems more likely that the biological factors provide the individual variable basis on which is built the appropriate 'masculine' or 'feminine' personality and behaviour for a particular society. These factors in themselves do not appear to have a powerful predetermining role.

A basic biological difference does however lie in women's

capacity to bear children and this has had crucial implications for their consequent role in production. Many of the stereotyped female characteristics are appropriately linked with the caring role of motherhood. But the reproductive role alone does not necessitate the assumptions of women's incapacity in other spheres of work, which can also be questioned through cross-cultural and psychological evidence.

Anthropology and psychology therefore both provide reasonable grounds for rejecting the 'natural' masculine and feminine roles that have grown into stereotypes. But no matter how many individuals are personally convinced, the many features of social and economic organization and functioning that use and exploit sex differences will not radically change unless capitalism either no longer needs these divisions or is itself replaced.

IDEAL IMAGES AND UNEQUAL VALUES

The wedge between male and female has been driven deeper by the stereotyping which pretends to represent the typical or ideal characteristics of men and women. It becomes a prescriptive process in which concepts of 'normal' behaviour are contained. 'Feminine' becomes the opposite of 'masculine'. Through books and other literature, and the great expansion of mass media, ideal images are created and reflected which force comparisons on their recipients. The extent to which these have effects must depend ultimately on the individual, but the barrage of images most people are subjected to, and especially children growing up, must carve out unconscious impressions about the nature of their world.

It is in the media* that the most conventional and exaggerated stereotypes are found, parodying the ways in which people are supposed to live. Although it is to be expected that the 'heroes' and 'heroines' of any situation would possess many of the socially desirable attributes of a particular place and time, much of what

---

* The nature and effects of certain aspects of the media on young children are examined separately in chapter 3.

is portrayed about women seems to have its roots in an older tradition. This is an expression of the 'informal' ideology reinforcing the continuing sex differences and male superiority. The gentle, demure, sensitive, submissive, non-competitive, sweet-natured and dependent dream-girl is not going to get very far with the 'equality' that modern civilized society is supposed to be offering her. Her mid-Victorian virtues, although loosened here and there, are still more appropriate for the care of husband, home and children.

The class basis of these ideals should not be forgotten, for inasmuch as it is the ruling class that defines these and other aspects of morality, so they also have the greater means to achieve them. For instance, the value of beauty for a woman is still very high and is seriously pursued. But housework, child-bearing and general worry soon take their toll on this. ('You're not the woman I married!') With money, however, the means of preserving looks and a good shape can be bought. On another level, and resulting from women's increased opportunities, the 'ideal woman' is now expected to be able to hold an intelligent conversation, and have an interesting job. Even Miss World must now express something of more social importance than a passion for horse-riding. But working class girls have less access to the education that secures the interesting jobs, and should they wish to continue work while they have very young children they are hindered by the lack of free nurseries. It is the middle class and above who have the independent means to hire nannies and *au pairs* and to pay for private nurseries. The adoption of these ideas in practice is clearly limited, and despite the long working history of working class women, they are naturally less motivated towards continuous pursuit of the variety of boring and monotonous jobs that are the only choices for many of them.

The stereotypes presented to boys and men are very different from those of 'femininity', although these too vary according to social class. On the active side, opposing the alleged passivity of women, men are supposed to be physically strong, aggressive, assertive and to take the initiative. They are supposed to be independent, competitive and ambitious. Their ideal masculine characteristics coincide by no accident with those necessary for success within a competitive economic system. In comparison, feminine ideals serve mainly to exclude women from this.

The success of working class men has traditionally been more confined to practical and technical skills. These are seen as essentially masculine pursuits, while paradoxically the academic studies that take men to the top are perceived as more passive and 'feminine'. A 'swot' runs the risk of being labelled as a 'sissy'. Upper class boys at public schools are trained for leadership, business and the professions. At the other end of the scale, working class boys are schooled for a mass labour force which constrains many of the 'ideal' characteristics such as aggression and dominance, which in their work situation are potentially disruptive. These are then transferred out on to leisure activities like sport, and particularly into their relationships with girls and women.

The implications of both male and female ideals and stereotypes are not beneficial to those striving to follow them. For women, following the sterotype can lead to self-sacrifice and an implicit acceptance of inferiority. For men, the active pursuit of ambition can consume their lives and destroy intimate relationships with other people, especially women and children. The changes that women wish to make in their role in this society should never be equated with the self-destructive position of men.

The active and passive dimensions of traditional male and female roles can be seen clearly in the way that a man's major activities are outward-directed and a woman's are inner-directed. He goes out to confront and capture the outside world while she constructs a cosy inside shelter for them both. The masculine role involves action and external achievement. It has no continuity and has to be 're-earned' every day. His success at any time can instantly be obliterated by failure. Man is judged by his success and his position in the social structure. Women on the other hand can be excused such failure because this is not their natural sphere. Their role is given them by default, without any activity being necessary. Their position in the social structure is defined by that of father or husband. Theirs is a role of 'being' while men are always in the process of 'doing'. The only thing that a girl has traditionally had to 'do' is find a husband to look after her.

The movement of women out to work has slightly altered this situation but boys still face an open and outward-looking future compared with the foreshortened perspectives that so many girls have on their lives. Their mental independence is blocked by a preoccupation with men and marriage. But for both sexes, the 'freedom' to explore life is limited, and usually confined to the rich and privileged. Most would have to work very hard to afford brief glimpses of other possibilities, and later, with a family of their own, the economic struggle for survival transforms these into fantasies, or obliterates them. A man's need always to be proving himself and his masculinity becomes more a reaction to insecurity than an independent creative activity, and a woman's acceptance of her position at home becomes more a resigned acceptance of inevitability than a positive choice from alternatives.

Although the official view may try to persuade us that women are equal but different, this is contradicted by the value-laden characteristics that are used to differentiate men and women. All the most socially desirable traits are ascribed to men, while to women are attributed those of a lower or negative value. In this way, the inferiority of women is directed away from its redundant basis in an out-moded way of life and traced to aspects of 'feminine nature'. If in becoming 'equal' they have to change some of these characteristics, women will also have to lose some of the ingredients of so-called 'normal' femininity.

The operation of this double standard is well-illustrated in the results of a study in America showing the way in which clinical psychiatric judgements are made about the mental health of male and female patients.[12] A group of clinicians and students were given a scale of sex-role characteristics such as 'aggressive' versus 'non-aggressive', from which they had to describe in turn a (mentally) healthy male, a healthy female, and a healthy adult (of no specified sex). The resulting picture of a male coincided with that of an adult, but the description of a healthy female was significantly different. This difference was not neutral however, for the qualities judged to be healthy in men and general adults were positively related to the social desirability of these traits. Therefore the concept of a 'mentally healthy' woman requires that she maintain qualities that society looks down on. The researchers themselves comment,

... clinicians are more likely to suggest that healthy women differ from healthy men by being more submissive, less independent, less adventurous, more easily influenced, less aggressive, less competitive, more excitable in minor crises, having their feelings more easily hurt, being more emotional, more conceited about their appearance, less objective, and disliking maths and science. This constellation seems a very unusual way of describing any mature, healthy individual.

In America, where people are more aware of their mental 'health' and more likely to seek help for psychological problems, the treatment of women would therefore involve a return to conforming to a 'healthy' state however inferior and unenvied it may appear. In Britain, there is as yet less selfconsciousness about mental health and people are less likely or able to seek professional help for minor psychological crises. However, the study, in terms of the ways in which men and women are implicitly viewed, is valid for this society too, and the double standard works at many other levels.

Talking about ideals and stereotypes is neither easy nor satisfactory because they represent intangible and abstract ideas that can be felt but do not stand up to examination because so many of them are denied by the great variation between people. Nevertheless, opinions and behaviour based on their implicit assumption can be seen everywhere.

THE VARIED 'NATURE' OF GIRLS

The sweeping generalizations embodied in these stereotypes obviously conceal the broad boundaries and overlap of characteristics between and within each sex. Amongst girls for instance there is a wide range of attitudes and behaviour that have very diverse expression. In general, and particularly within the social sciences, it is tempting to over-simplify and use classifications that are often superficial and misleading. Sex differences have frequently been studied as a major distinction, and social class differences have also been assumed on many levels, but many of the simple dichotomies that are drawn between both of these are not real.

For example, this is illustrated in the 'unfeminine' nature of aggression and forcefulness which can be seen both in the sporty toughness found in girls' boarding schools where it is popular and acceptable, and also in the activities of gangs of young working class girls which have developed in other schools. In one such school in London, it is quite common for girls to fight each other until they are fourteen or fifteen. At the same time, they are very concerned about keeping up with female fashions and boyfriends, and cannot simply be classified as tomboys. Some of the same girls were shocked at seeing a film about a female 'Hell's Angel'.

On the surface working class girls seem to be more verbally aggressive. They are often very noisy and swear a lot. But again it is important to consider the form of expression, and middle class girls, whose upbringing has often been more constrained, are still capable of delivering equivalent verbal attacks. Out in the country, a different standard of behaviour is expected and girls automatically help with the rough and dirty work of the farm. Over-all it is perhaps the lower middle class and upper working class girls living in towns who feel the most pressure to conform to demure femininity as their opportunities for doing anything else are fairly narrowly confined.

There are also interesting differences between girls of similar class backgrounds who have moved towards different kinds of education and training. For instance, in a college of Further Education in London, a teacher noted that the girls who were taking hairdressing, commercial and typing courses, which lead them into very sex-defined jobs, 'dress according to *Girl, Petticoat*, and "Brook Street Bureau" ads. They are totally immersed in self-image: nails, eyelashes, platforms and accoutrements.' The girls taking O-levels however, studied subjects which were far less sex-typed, and which might eventually lead them to Teacher's Training College, Art College or University. 'Often their whole attitude is different – they are more mature, more likely to be interested in general topics. And this is reflected in their dress which is correspondingly more relaxed: jeans, T-shirts and not so much make-up.* Other teachers in Further Education colleges have noticed the same differences.

In some ways working class girls are likely to become more immediately aware of the different expectations and roles of men and women. Their parents are often working in sex-defined jobs and they see girl friends and relatives leaving school, marrying and having children at an early age. The differences in the educational and vocational opportunities for them compared to middle class children help to ensure this. Often bored and indifferent about school, the most obvious course is to concentrate on going to work – thus entering lower level (and more sex-typed) jobs, and having a good social life which ultimately provides a husband. Conformity to more 'traditional feminine' dress, behaviour and attitudes are then more appropriate.

Family attitudes and values have an enormous influence even if there is conflict between the generations at other levels. For instance, teachers have noticed that working class girls from families who are politically active, either in the Labour Party or within a union, are often much more receptive and aware of class and sex inequalities. A mother's attitude to her role will also have some influence on her daughter, and on the sort of person that she encourages her to be. This again cannot simply be divided according to class. A socially aspiring middle class mother may just as easily encourage her daughter to do well through marriage as to succeed academically and independently. Working class mothers are not necessarily all so accepting of the feminine role that they have been often prematurely thrust into. Differences in status and standard of living are deeply rooted in the social structure and the lack of alternative ways of living, but these cannot just be polarized by class.

There are, however, many more fundamental ways in which the family plays the earliest part in training children to be 'acceptable' people. Its influence on sex role stereotyping at this time occurs regardless of class, and some parents who are beginning to

---

* Personal communication with Liz Waugh.

make conscious efforts to counter this are finding it far from easy.*

INFLUENCES OF FAMILY LIFE

A child's early experiences are almost all contained within the family, and it is here that the direction of personality development is set. It is parents, and more specifically mothers, who have the closest interaction and relationship with children in our society. Their deliberate and incidental influence teaches children the intricacies of acceptable and appropriate behaviour. They accept the existence and validity of sex differences and pass them on intact.

Social conditioning is both handed out and received in conscious and unconscious ways. In the light of the cross-cultural research and social-psychological studies examined above, its supposed influence in producing sex differences becomes exaggerated as theories based primarily around biological determinism become untenable. The child's social learning, which occurs initially in the family and is gradually extended outside, is then seen as being responsible for his or her behaviour and personality. But is this enough to account for the content and depth of emotion that is involved in being male or female? Can it explain the ways in which the differences are individually felt and enthusiastically defended, and the apparent need to pre-define sex roles and expectations in order to form and maintain self-identity? The mechanics of learning processes seem rather unsatisfactory and lacking as a total explanation.

One approach which has attempted to fill this gap has examined the central importance of family structure and the nature of early child-care.[13] This explanation, by Nancy Chodorow has a psycho-

* It is interesting that in recording interviews with working class women, most of whom had been fairly active politically through trade unions, or had been brought up in socialist families, Sheila Rowbotham and Jean McCrindle found that many of them had had an upbringing in which their parents, particularly their fathers, had tried to break down sex roles and bring their sons and daughters up in the same way. But each woman independently thought that they were alone and unusual in this experience of childhood.

analytic orientation, and traces the development of masculine and feminine personality and the relative status of the sexes back to the universal mothering role of women. It focuses on the conscious and unconscious effects on boys and girls of their early involvement with women. Each sex experiences this differently, and it is such aspects of growing up that contribute intitially to sex differences in personality. As a girl begins to form ideas about herself there is (universal) internalization of certain features of the mother–daughter relationship. Through this process the individual characteristics of society are reproduced, and this explains why although cultural differences in 'femininity' can and do exist, the majority of societies show similar female personalities and roles.

According to psychoanalytic theory personality develops, not as a result of conscious or deliberate efforts by parents or other adults, but out of a child's earliest social relationships, the nature and quality of which are appropriated, assimilated and organized by the child to form her or his individual personality. These aspects become internalized, and although they arise out of an ongoing relationship, they continue to exist independently and are organized to constitute a permanent personality. The unconscious operation of this process has a crucial influence on consequent behaviour, whether it be the 'normal' behaviour expected by society or that which is unique to the individual. The more conscious areas, like the way people see themselves (their self-concept), and the nature and extent of their feelings of femininity or masculinity (their gender identity), are thus dependent on the stability and consistency of the unconscious organization of personality. Therefore the different experiences of girls and boys in their early relationships make an important contribution to their consequent development.

Children are normally very closely attached to a woman in their earliest years, usually their mother. During this time, they become involved in the issues of separation and individuation (developing some independent 'sense of self'). This involves weakening the primary identification* with their mother and becoming less

---

*'Identification' usually refers to the incorporation into oneself of a 'model' person with whom there is a strong emotional tie. As children grow older it refers to the tendency for them (or a person of any age) to take on

orally dependent on her. Nancy Chodorow suggests that it is the experience of this process that differs importantly for girls and boys. For girls, early experience involves a 'double identification' in which not only do they (like boys at this age) identify with their mothers, but mothers themselves, as former daughters, identify strongly with their own daughters. This identification involves feelings of empathy towards the daughter's present and future, physical and emotional predicaments. A particular sense of attachment can develop from this which makes separation more difficult.

For boys, however, it is more usual for mothers to encourage a relationship that emphasizes their opposition and one which reinforces their son's self-awareness of the male role. Therefore, during the time covered by Freud's 'pre-Oedipal period',* the quality of relationship between mothers and their sons and mothers and their daughters is not the same.

After a child has reached about three years of age, (the beginning of the 'Oedipal period')† the different development of boys and girls is commonly acknowledged. During this period, a more specifically masculine identification must replace a boy's early identification with his mother and this coincides with the time when fathers appear more frequently in the child's world. However it is harder for this to happen under the conditions of modern industrialized society. Here, men's work takes them away from home most of the time and therefore a boy's identification often has to be reinforced by his fantasies of the male role instead of through a consistent relationship. He may consequently resort to a more negative way of asserting his masculinity: by identifying with what is *not* feminine. This involves repression of things in himself that are seen as potentially feminine (thus rejecting and

and reproduce the attitudes, behaviour and aspects of personality and emotional response exhibited by real life or symbolic models (for example characters in books, films etc.).

*Freud sees the pre-Oedipal period as a time in which there is no differentiation between the sexes, both identifying equally with their mother.

†This period is interpreted by Freud in sexual terms: a boy represses his sexual attraction for his mother because of the (fantasized) power of his father as potential rival, to kill or castrate him. He therefore replaces mother-attachment by identifying with his father.

denying his attachment to his mother), and devaluation of whatever he sees to be feminine in the world outside the home. Thus the superiority of maleness is asserted against the inferiority of femaleness. Boys are the best and girls are sissies, and this is reinforced through independent experiences outside the family.

For girls, the development of a feminine gender identity is more continuous. They do not have to reject early identification and attachment with mother since their final identification is with women, who are also the central characters of early dependence. Femininity and the female role are easily seen first-hand in daily life. There is no great need to reject mother-dependence, nor will a mother be very likely to encourage this, as she may still be identifying strongly with her daughter. Therefore a girl's identification with her mother is not the rather distanced position of a boy trying to identify with a male role and its concomitant behaviours, which he has to 'take on', but is more a close personal identification with a mother's characteristic traits and values.*

Therefore boys' and girls' experiences of the inter-personal world in which they grow up may affect the different development of their 'masculinity' and 'femininity'. Thus Chodorow suggests that 'certain features of social structure, supported by cultural beliefs, values and perceptions, are internalized through the family and the child's early social object-relationships. This largely unconscious organization is the context in which role training and purposive socialization take place.'[14]

Girls' training in the 'traditional' aspects of female role can be viewed as fairly easy and continuous and involve many diffuse and affective relationships between women. They are drawn into helping their mothers, and practising this role as part of growing up. Pressure is put on them to become involved with others, and

* According to Freud's theory the 'discontinuity' for a girl comes when it is necessary to transfer the sex-object choice from mother to father and men, and the discovery that she has not got a penis, the shock of which results in her blaming and rejecting her mother, and turning to her father. Freud suggested that girls' development of femininity via the 'Oedipal phase' is more difficult than that for boys because of this, but it seems more reasonable to view boys' development as more discontinuous and problematic.

to be concerned with nurturance and responsibility. It is later that they find that the outside world, unlike the early home world of women, is dominated by men.

Boys do not practice their adult role in this way – this has to wait until they reach adulthood. Meanwhile they are encouraged towards achievement and self-reliance, and away from dependent and close relationships. They tend to go off on their own or with a group of boys of a similar age. Girls participate more in the home, and are involved in an inter-generational world of women. They are not encouraged to go off and to develop individually and independently. They concentrate on 'relational' activities, and in our society they are even defined in these terms, as someone's wife, mother or daughter, which reinforces their dependence on these relationships. This means that unless she consciously counters this, a woman's individual sense of herself remains embedded within her relationships to others. She cannot clearly differentiate herself from the rest of her world, and this hinders the development of self-esteem* and self-confidence which would help her to change her position and status.

This unconscious process of internalization can reasonably explain how male and female personalities in different cultures occur and are reproduced through time. The material and economic basis of a society will be important in determining which characteristics are exaggerated, and which differentiate the sexes according to their roles in production. The fact that many societies are in approximate agreement about feminine personality and tend to see women as inferior can be traced back to their common practice of holding women responsible for early child-care and socialization. This has important implications for sexual equality. Both boys and girls would benefit from having close relationships and identification with more than one adult of both sexes, from men's increased involvement in child-care, and from

*However, after comparing different societies, Chodorow suggests that although men usually maintain their socio-cultural superiority over women, they always remain psychologically defensive and insecure, while women in certain circumstances can, in spite of their lesser status, feel a sense of security and self-worth.

seeing women in a recognized and valued role and area of control inside and outside the home.

The earlier unconscious process of differentiation is later overlaid with more explicit practices. In one study[15] of children between one and five years of age, four such processes were observed in the family situation, and it is reasonable to assume that they occur to some extent in most families. There was firstly an observed tendency for mothers to make more fuss over the appearance of their daughter. This involved fiddling with her hair, dressing her up, and frequently commenting on her looks. The emphasis on external features will consequently be absorbed and later reinforced by society's views on the importance of a woman's beauty.

Secondly, parents inadvertently focus their children's attention on certain more 'appropriate' objects and activities. The most obvious example of this is with toys and games. Toy-makers, sellers and buyers are all agreed in their assumptions of what is more suitable and enjoyable for boys or girls, and this reflects children's supposed interests, skills and future roles. Boys' toys are more active and technical, and include cars, trains, planes, spacemen and cricket bats, chemistry sets and miniature microscopes. Girls have a selection of far less active or exciting toys which stimulate a rehearsal of women's traditional role. They have dolls,* teddybears and other animals, doll's houses and prams, tea-sets, miniature ovens, pots and pans. There is usually some overlap, especially through sharing toys with brothers, but children soon become able to distinguish girls' toys from those of boys.

It is significant that many toys for boys are not only more technical and scientific but also involve the formation of plans, plots and strategies. Forts and toy soldiers provide plenty of scope for this. The analytic abilities that appear to differentiate boys from girls later in life may be reinforced by these sorts of

---

*We tend to assume that girls 'naturally' play with dolls but this is denied by some societies which do not have dolls. When for instance Margaret Mead presented dolls to Manu children, the boys ran off and played with them. This reflected the men's responsibility for children which was a characteristic of this tribe.

activities.* Piaget's work has shown that becoming familiar with an object can induce positive reactions towards this and similar objects or activities.[16] Therefore it is easy to see how a boy's apparently 'natural' leanings towards science can be elicited. His lack of mystification about these types of subjects compared to that of girls can be similarly accounted for, and is reinforced by the assumption that boys are better at them. Girls are often given toys which help them to practise playing 'mother', or they have dolls and animals with which playing takes the form of developing relationships: this includes feeding, dressing and talking to them.

The content and style of language provides another process of differentiation. Parents and other adults distinguish between the words and phrases they use to praise or criticise children, and whether they do it intentionally or not, it helps to build up the child's self-concept. The answer given by a fourteen-year-old girl in a Social Studies lesson about sex roles gives a good example of this:

In most families the girl learns from a very young age that she must behave in a very different manner from her brother, from the day she is given her first doll and is told she cannot go outside and play because it is raining and yet her brother can. Children learn how they are different from one another by the way the parents and their friends talk about them. Example – 'Oh what a sweet little girl you have and so pretty, does she help you around the house?' 'What a rascal of a son you have, always getting into mischief. Oh well I'd worry and think there was something wrong with him if he didn't.'

The fourth process† is really an extension of the second, in which the sorts of activities that children are exposed to, and required to do at home, rehearse children for their future roles. Girls are expected to help with household domestic work, and look after younger children. Boys are shown how to do repairs and to construct things. They may give token help with domestic

* The development of analytic ability is more crucially related to independence and mastery-training, and this is discussed together with intelligence and school achievement in chapter 4.

† Ruth Hartley labels these processes 'manipulation', 'canalization', 'verbal appellation', and 'activity exposure', respectively.

chores but it is not seen as a skill that they should acquire. One girl protested to me that whenever her brother did any housework he was paid for it as it was not 'boys' work', whereas when she or her sister did it, payment was out of the question!

Parents are usually quite unaware of a lot of their own efforts in the manipulation and production of sex differences. They believe themselves to be responding to innate differences that they presume to be present, and interpret similar behaviour differently for each sex. For instance, the way in which parents discipline their children may differ in that boys have more physical punishment and girls more often suffer the withdrawal of parental love and affection. Discipline may also be allocated more to fathers for boys, and to mothers for girls. The psychological effects of withdrawal of love are deep and long lasting (except where there has previously been little affection and therefore there is not much to lose). It is reasonable to assume that if girls do tend to be disciplined more like this, then this would increase the need for affectionate relationships, and dependency. It has been found that children disciplined in this way tend to be less aggressive than those who are punished physically. However, the process of individual development is complex and interactive and much use of the other physical forms of discipline can be destructive and equally constraining.

Girls generally receive more affection, more protectiveness, more controls and greater restrictions. They are not encouraged to be dependent but the relative lack of encouragement or opportunity for independence and autonomy has equivalent effects. In one long-term study[17] girls with very protective mothers were found to develop more feminine interests during childhood and adulthood. 'Overprotection' has also been found to have a 'feminizing' influence on boys' personalities. It has been suggested that fathers distinguish more in their treatment of children, emphasizing the 'masculine' elements of achievement in boys while giving nurturance and protection to their daughters.[18] Whatever intricate operations are involved in the relationship between parent and child, there is much evidence that boys and girls are taught differently with different roles and goals in mind and that this has moulded the consequences. Dependency, social pressure and expectations combine to tell their own tale.

Aggression is sometimes seen as a characteristic which distinguishes the sexes more than almost any other. In tracing its biological origins to the endocrine system people who hold this view often reinforce their argument that it is 'natural' for men to be more aggressive than women. However in any situation an interaction occurs between a person's hormonal activity and their own interpretation and assessment of that situation. Individuals have a choice of action, which may or may not be aggressive, and this makes it untenable to suggest an explanation solely in terms of hormone levels. People are not at the mercy of their endocrine systems.

Therefore although hormonal action can play some part in producing characteristics such as aggression this will vary between individuals of either sex. Their expression of aggressiveness is influenced by past social experience and knowledge in which being male or female has played a major part. Differences in aggression between boys and girls appear substantial and are assumed to be 'natural' but these have been exaggerated out of all proportion by the process of social learning and identification. Physical aggression is more appropriately displayed by boys who more often (but not always) have a greater capacity to use it successfully and so to gain prestige and status. Aggression in girls is disapproved of and they often re-channel it into more acceptable forms.[19] It is significant that it has been found possible to predict degrees of adult aggression from that displayed by boys, but not from that displayed by girls.[20] For women, something has happened along the way that has led to their more 'passive nature'.

But I wonder whether there is much to be gained by showing that girls have equivalent aggressiveness which is either displaced into another form or extinguished altogether. It seems more realistic to view most aggressive behaviour as misplaced in everyday life and to see boys and men as demonstrating an exaggerated form of competitive behaviour that is in fact self-destructive and damaging to their relationships compared with the more 'civilized' ways of girls and women. Girls may use verbal forms of aggression and hostility, but men are also no strangers to these, and need continually to score points off one another in order to maintain their place in the masculinity competition. Personal relationships are not facilitated or enhanced by the need for either exaggerated or repressed aggression, and its overt expression has to be suppressed at work. Therefore although the capacity for aggressive behaviour may be distributed within both sexes it is no longer very useful unless displaced into some form like ambition. Nevertheless it continues to hang on grimly to the myth of its status, supporting and supported by the sex divisions in the economic and social structure.

Tomboys and Sissies

One feature that characterizes much of childhood is the mix-up of traits and behaviour which is allowed to occur. This is usually tolerated differently for each sex. Boys are monitored more closely than girls from about the age of four years for the development of appropriate personalities and interests. As children begin to take on their more recognizable individual characters, parents and other adults, and children themselves, start to judge them according to the stereotypes for either sex.

. . . my brother . . . he gets treated like a little boy. My mother doesn't seem to realize that he's nearly thirteen, he gets treated as if he was ten . . . He's more babyish – I used to say he was sissyish when he was little, I used to take him around with me . . . I used to look after him a very great deal, even to parties for little girls, and he's a very feminine boy. He's gentle and good with children, and has ideas that are almost fatherly, he's not boisterously masculine or anything like that. He likes dressing nice and things you would associate with girls. And then there's my sister, who although she's a girl, she hates nice clothes, hates looking nice, can't stand her hair – she's got long beautiful hair. She's like a boy – it's got mixed up. I'm not sure how they'll land up. Now my little brother, he's a typical boy, he's only five and yet the other day he punched me and it nearly killed me.

Fourteen-year-old Ealing schoolgirl.

The presence of 'sissie' characteristics in a boy is viewed much more seriously than the 'tomboy' activities of girls, and this is reflected in the difference in value of these labels. Being called a 'sissie', with its feminine connotations, has a negative value. It is an insult, laced with contempt and derision. Being a 'tomboy' is much more positive, and is a label that can be taken with pride. These differences mirror the wider values of society which devalue feminine against masculine activities. In their efforts to structure their world, boys are quick to grasp and exaggerate the perceived inferior quality and status of girls and women. This is reinforced by the action and excitement that seems to be embodied in the activities and toys deemed more suitable for boys. Girls carry on playing with a wide range of toys while boys soon leave more 'girlish' toys behind them. Boys express a far higher preference for 'masculine' activities than girls of the same age do for 'feminine' activities. Many girls also choose to take specifically boyish roles and interests as there is certainly no difference in their capacity to enjoy action and adventure.

Boys are constrained far more within the boundaries of accepted behaviour than girls, who are allowed access to many expressions that are not strictly 'feminine'. Some tomboy girls go as far as taking over the attitudes of boys towards girls, and reject other girls as being boring and 'soppy'. Parents are not very concerned about their tomboy daughters who are after all indulging in the more prestigious activities of boys. They are considered to be going through a transient phase which will pass, to be replaced by one characterized by a heightened interest in clothes and boyfriends. By mid-adolescence, exuberance is expected to be toned down in favour of a more demure self-consciousness.

The exaggerated disapproval and parental anxiety attached to 'sissie' characteristics in boys should be considered more closely. I have already pointed out that many aspects of 'masculinity' are synonymous with the personal elements necessary to succeed within capitalism. If a boy is therefore lacking in these, or seems to move into areas of 'femininity', his future success is potentially jeopardized. So also is society, for the present system of production depends on the reproduction of appropriate characteristics in men and women.

Parents are unconsciously endorsing this when they become

anxious for their sons to be accepted and successful. Fathers more than mothers are concerned that their sons grow up in a suitably 'masculine' way. They perhaps wish to identify with their son's emerging interests and activities and would have difficulty in relating to a 'feminine' boy who exhibited traits that they had been taught to despise in men. They want boys to avoid most of the lesser-valued characteristics assigned to women. They often reinforce their son's and society's devaluation of women by trying to steer his behaviour towards acceptable 'masculinity' using jeers and threats: 'Surely you don't want to grow up a sissie boy?' It is symptomatic of this that a guide has been developed in America 'to provide parents with a monitoring system for their child's sexual development'.[21] The guide gives a list of games and activities classified as 'masculine' or 'feminine', and a boy's participation in these is checked off. If he has the misfortune to emerge from this as 'effeminate', his parents are recommended to encourage him to take up 'masculine' pursuits to put him back on the road to manhood. The enthusiastic authors even hope to restrain the relatively free tomboy in a similar way. 'At present the guide only helps to distinguish effeminate boys, but the doctors, John Bates and P. M. Bentler from Los Angeles, are also working on a modified version to identify extremely masculine girls.'

For a tomboy girl, it is of less consequence either to her future or to society that she is acting in an 'unfeminine' way as the lagging 'informal' ideology still sees her adult role as 'unproductive'. Providing she does not completely reject her reproductive and domestic role, she is allowed some eccentricity. Again the 'doing' and 'being' aspects are relevant, because it is far easier for a girl to give up tomboy behaviour and settle down than it is for a 'feminine' boy to suddenly take on the active components of the male role. The resultant insecurity involved with perpetually proving 'masculinity' is expressed in childhood through the often cruel treatment of boys by other boys who have labelled them as 'sissie' and use them as scapegoats.

An underlying fear of homosexuality should not be overlooked. Sex has had a long history of repression and 'normal' sexual behaviour has been narrowly and rigidly defined. It is only relatively recently that sex without reproduction has been officially accepted. Through repression and ignorance, people have developed an irrational horror or contempt for homosexuality. Parents see the development of this in their children as a stigma that reflects back to them. Much of society still views it as illness or perversion. Homosexuality questions the divisions between men and women that are believed to be 'natural' and right. It implicitly suggests a form of relationship which runs counter to male supremacy, the family, and the fundamental values of capitalism.[22] The fact that male homosexuality is more likely to be feared as a consequence of effeminacy in boys than lesbianism is for a tomboyish adolescent girl again reflects the values placed on traditional characteristics of the masculine role in this society.* It is also supported by a belief that women cannot have a sexuality independent from men.

The basic distinctions between male and female are therefore laid down within the family, and children learn these in a number of ways. The initial unconscious process of identification and assimilation is built on by the operation of social learning or conditioning, in which the 'right' behaviour is reinforced through a system of rewards and punishments and becomes 'generalized' out on to many other situations. This may be done consciously or unconsciously by parents and other adults and children. Once children are old enough to recognize themselves as boys or girls, they take a more active part in the process, seeking to discover what boys and girls do, and what they are like. Out of this, they observe, imitate and identify with people, often parents, and usually those of the same sex as themselves.[23]

Identification is not a straightforward process, it occurs in a variety of ways.† Children may identify with one or both parents, and sometimes with adults outside the family. It seems to depend on a number of factors which interact and combine within any specific (family) situation. The person chosen by the child as her or his 'model' appears to be selected on the basis of their per-

---

*It is not only our society that has seen homosexuality as a threat to social order. A lot of pre-capitalist societies do not tolerate it.

† Freud for instance sees the identification of boy with father and girl with mother as a result of successful resolution of the Oedipal complex.

ceived power (usually in terms of control of economic resources), the type and extent of discipline they use, and the closeness and affectionate quality of their relationship with the child. On this basis, boys and girls may identify with their father on account of his economic power and status and this for girls will combine with their greater freedom in taking on aspects of 'masculine' tomboyish behaviour. On the other hand, the warmest and closest relationship may be with the mother. However, models for behaviour are also chosen on the commonsense grounds of their similarity to the child, and therefore a girl will identify with her mother in recognition of her own future female role and will take on relevant behaviour. Identification is greatest when the adult–child relationship is very warm and close, when the child wishes to be like a particular person, and adopts their values, attitudes and personality traits and judges herself or himself through their eyes. But a girl for instance whose relationship with her mother is not close will still identify with aspects of feminine role in her that are common to women as a whole and which exist independently in the culture outside the family, exemplified in other adults and passed on by other children and through the media.

In this context it is interesting to see whether today's working mothers who are earning money and thus changing the balance of economic power have any effects on the characteristics of their children. Some American studies of this have found that daughters of working mothers are more independent and aggressive, while their sons are more conforming and dependent. However, I would still question the simplicity of these implications as working mothers change not only their economic status, but many other things: such as their relationship with their children, their conception of themselves, and how far the father takes over or helps with the domestic work. Whether they work from necessity or choice may also affect these issues. Identification is thus very important where taking on the features of feminine or masculine role is concerned, although those features that are 'inappropriate' become subject to increasing social pressures, as 'sissie' boys and tomboy girls discover. When women's position at work, their economic independence and their consciousness of themselves begins to rise, and child-rearing and other roles are equally and cooperatively shared, girls and boys will be a step closer to growing up with a choice of positive characteristics from either sex.

Although the foundations of 'feminine' and 'masculine' development as we understand them are built early in life they are not predetermined and unchangeable. Anthropological and social psychological evidence has at least told us that. At present, however, their validity is protected through the needs of industry and capital which fosters and reinforces an unofficial ideology of assumed sex differences. Changing the economic base can therefore open the door to changing sex roles and their accompanying attitudes and beliefs more effectively than the other way round. But even in the event of replacing capitalism, change in sex roles and personal relationships must be consciously sought by both sexes. It is not an automatic process.

Already many of the characteristics that are used to stereotype and polarize the sexes have become redundant in real life while their image and implications persist. I have already suggested aggression as one example of this, for while continuing as a distinguishing masculine trait, it is too disruptive to be useful to a society organized around maintaining a conforming labour force and is constantly being defused and diverted. Many jobs in which men succeed through ambition and assertiveness rather than aggression are seen by women as requiring them to become 'aggressive' and 'unfeminine' and are avoided for this and other reasons.

There are as many variations within sexes as between them. I am not suggesting that women should be like men, or vice versa, or that we should all be exactly the same. What we should do is to understand how and where artificial differences have been created, exaggerated and exploited, and to change this process in its totality. Men and women are undeniably different in their physical sexual characteristics and for women this has had far-reaching effects on their role and status and possibly (as Chodorow suggests) can explain the development of the 'feminine' personality. It is bad enough that girls and boys are socialized into different and often exclusive roles and personalities which deny many opportunities to both of them, but that those of girls should be deemed and treated as inferior is a criminal anachronism.

The real life situation has changed for women, particularly since the last war, and the formulation of legal bills of equality and shouts for liberation have somewhat confused the old ideological tortoise that lags behind and still clings to the stereotypes. In their 'pure' form however, these stereotypes mainly exist in the media. Here they exert an insidious influence, mixing fantasy and reality in such a way as to complicate the nature of their indirect effects. It is the representation of these images in the lives of young girls that we must examine next.

Notes

Chapter 2

1. See H. Holter, 'Sex Roles and Social Change', *Acta Sociologica*, 1971, 14, reprinted in H. P. Dreitzel, 'Family, Marriage and the Struggle of the Sexes', *Recent Sociology* no. 4, Macmillan & Co., New York, 1972.
2. M. Mead, *Sex and Temperament in Three Primitive Societies*, William Morrow, 1935; and M. Mead, *Male and Female*, Penguin, 1950.
3. See Ann Oakley, *Sex, Gender and Society*, Temple Smith, 1973, chapter 5.
4. See B. B. Whiting (Ed.), *Six Cultures: Studies of Childrearing*, John Wiley, 1963. Also H. Barry, M. K. Bacon and I. L. Child, 'Relation of Child Training to Subsistence Economy', *American Anthropologist*, 61, 1959.
5. H. Barry, M. K. Bacon and I. L. Child, 'A Cross-Cultural Survey of Some Sex Differences in Socialisation', *Journal of Abnormal and Social Psychology*, no. 55, 1957, p. 330.
6. For more discussion of the relationship of child-rearing to the economy of different sorts of society, see N. Chodorow, 'Being and Doing', in V. Gornick and B. Moran, *Woman in Sexist Society*, Signet New American Library, New York, 1971.
7. H. Barry, M. K. Bacon and I. L. Child, op. cit.
8. Discussed in the previous chapter and also in greater detail in Sheila Rowbotham, *Woman's Consciousness, Man's World*, part 2, Penguin, 1973.
9. See J. and J. Hampson, 'Determinants of Psychosexual Orientation' in F. Beach (Ed.), *Sex and Behaviour*, John Wiley, 1965; and J. Money, *Sex Research: New Developments*, Holt, Rinehart & Winston, 1965.
10. J. and J. Hampson, op. cit.
11. See for instance M. Diamond, 'A Critical Evaluation of the Ontogeny of Human Sexual Behaviour', *Quarterly Review of Biology*, 40, 1965, pp. 147–75; and C. Hutt, *Males and Females*, Penguin, 1972.
12. I. K. Broverman *et al.*, 'Sex Role Stereotypes and Clinical Judge-

ments of Mental Health', *Journal of Consulting and Clinical Psychology*, no. 34, 1970.

13.   Nancy Chodorow, 'Family Structure and Feminine Personality', in M. Z. Rosaldo and L. Lamphere, *Women, Culture and Society*, Stanford University Press, 1974. Her theory of the early unconscious socialization of boys and girls was stimulated by being a member of a women's group consisting of mothers and daughters who were consciously analysing their early inter-relationships.

14.   Nancy Chodorow, op. cit.

15.   R. Hartley, 'A Developmental View of Female Sex-Role Identification', in J. Biddle and E. J. Thomas (Eds), *Role Theory*, John Wiley, 1966.

16.   J. Piaget, *The Construction of Reality in the Child*, Basic Books, 1954.

17.   J. Kagan and H. A. Moss, *Birth to Maturity: A Study in Psychological Development*, John Wiley, 1962.

18.   U. Brofenbrenner, 'Some Familial Antecedents of Responsibility and Leadership in Adolescents', in L. Petrullo and B. M. Bass (Eds), *Leadership and Interpersonal Behavior*, Holt, Rinehart & Winston, New York, 1961.

19.   For more discussion about aggression and sex differences see Ann Oakley, 'Sex, Gender and Society', and R. Sears, 'Development of Gender Role', in F. A. Beach (Ed.), *Sex and Behavior*, John Wiley, 1965.

20.   J. Kagan and H. A. Moss, op. cit.

21.   Featured in an article in the *Sunday Times* by Peter Watson, 1973.

22.   See the more detailed account in Don Milligan, *The Politics of Homosexuality*, Pluto Press, 1973.

23.   For more lengthy discussion on these methods of developing sex differences, see articles by W. Mischel and L. Kohlberg in E. Maccoby (Ed.), *The Development of Sex Differences*, Tavistock, 1966.

CHAPTER III

Reflections from the Media

Grasping the ever-expanding contents of the less immediate world is a fascinating process. Children stare in wonder at the horizons that roll back before their eyes. The blur that surrounds the distinguishing reassurance of their mother's face begins to clear and is filled with shapes, colours and movement that can be focused, followed and felt. Consciousness opens and spreads, and becomes ready to receive and absorb all the experience it can. But it is not only to be filled with real people, toys, games, visits and outings; there is an increasing variety of other worlds, beckoning with their images of fantasy and adventure. The television is a window of excitement and surprises, the radio a hidden source of singers and storytellers. Picturebooks create characters and tales with every turning page, first stared at with absorbed yet illiterate comprehension, then gradually with words taking form and sense, completing, and in some ways restricting the stories. Young imaginations start devouring comics, and magazines, and books.

Capturing the attention of children, all these worlds present image after image, story after story, adding layer upon layer to the process of assimilating knowledge. Presented alongside reality, fantasy is a wonderful escape into danger and unpredictability, into envied skills and success. Children are astute enough seldom to confuse these two worlds while they innocently absorb the impressions given about ways of life, boys and girls, men and women. In discovering how girls arrive at their views of themselves, and their relationships with the world, it would be wrong to dismiss the effect of books, comics and other sorts of media.

READING PRIMERS

A host of ideas spring out of the drawings of a picture book, but it is with the studied concentration of learning to read that the images are caught and anchored in the verbal world. In the readers, which are usually meant to represent some sort of reality for children, the writers have portrayed their own ideas of a real or ideal world, showing implicit discrimination by sex, and often by race and class as well. In so doing, they provide simple and effective reinforcement of traditional divisions in society and of its prejudices. A child struggles slowly towards literacy, staring at pictures, repeating words and sentences over and over, vocalizing and unconsciously absorbing any sexism or racism contained in them.

Reading primers usually focus on a family, especially the children and their activities. They are meant to seem 'normal', and because of this, they present people who are exaggerated and even caricatured: for instance mothers who seldom go outside the home and never have any sort of job, and working class women with hair tied up in Mrs-Mop-style scarves. Since life appears largely like this anyway, sexism is not always obvious and has to be blatant before many people notice it and complain. An apparently neutral world is presented, filled with those traditional roles and stereotypes which confirm a child in what she or he, to a lesser extent, sees happening within her or his limited experience. There have been some slightly less biased books produced, but the majority of children are still learning from the well-thumbed pages of readers like *The Ladybird Keyword Reading Scheme*, *Janet and John*, and the *Beacon Readers*.

The heroes and heroines of these books are found living happily and peacefully in sunny suburbia, and in the Ladybird books it always seems to be summer or Christmas. They occupy a large roomy house with a big beautiful garden full of birds and flowers, in which they can play monotonous games. Their toys are large and expensive. Jane, the little girl from the Ladybird books, seems to be a very well-brought-up middle class girl. She always smiles sweetly, dresses nicely, never quarrels or gets angry and jealous, and is never aggressive or self-assertive. Her brother Peter, however, is just the opposite. He is a very active and assertive little rascal, with lots of energy, and is often to be found making things and controlling situations, with Jane as patient onlooker. In this unreal world neither of them appear to encounter the day-to-day problems of living and there is no conflict. They have parents with the temperaments of saints whose patience and understanding is limitless. It is hardly a reflection of average family life. Any child reading these words and seeing these pictures is being shown the idealized and serenely repressed world of the middle class adult.

Looking more closely at the parts played by girls and women, it becomes clear that they are cast as the passive supporting characters for their vigorous male counterparts. 'Mummy' seems to have a particularly dull time – all her life revolves around servicing 'daddy' and the children by preparing food and making beds, by cleaning, washing and ironing, with sewing and knitting as her leisure activities. When she ventures outside the home, it is only to shop. 'Daddy' is the pampered breadwinner. He is the person who goes off into the unseen outside world, and who eventually also returns from it. He will never be seen washing or making beds. He is the one who drives the car, paints the house and plays with the children, especially with Peter. In his leisure time he also reads the newspaper, a pastime in which 'mummy' shows little apparent interest.

The different characteristics for boys and girls are implicitly endorsed. Little girls are good, sweet, quiet and thoroughly angelic, and they like helping mother in the home. Boys are not expected to behave like this and are seldom involved with anything very domestic. It is their prerogative to be naughty, which is assumed to come naturally with being a boy. When brother and sister are portrayed doing things together, the boy is clearly the active, commanding and dominating figure, while the girl is a pliant and passive observer. For example, Jane has to watch Peter make a sandcastle, a go-cart, a doll's house. At his command she watches him: 'Look at me Jane, look at me in the boat.' If Jane asks to join in when Peter is playing with his toy train and station, then she must obey his orders: '"Yes," says Peter, "I have the train. You play with the station."' And Jane always obeys. When they are seen with their parents, they imitate appropriately. 'Peter helps daddy with the car and Jane helps mummy with the tea.' 'Jane wants to make cakes like mummy.' '"I will be the man in the shop," says Peter. "Then let me be mummy," says Jane.' Girls only seem to show any active spirit when they are given the opportunity to help mummy with the dusting, sweeping and polishing, or pretending to prepare tea.

It is often the pictures as much as the written sentences that impress readily absorbable images on minds and imaginations. It is the illustrations too that tend to go even further than the words. The method of teaching that uses a technique of 'Look and Say' is frequently used, and relies heavily on pictured interpretations. A short and simple sentence is illustrated by a colourful and detailed drawing showing the words in action. For instance, a sentence such as 'Here we are dressing up' would be accompanied by an illustration in which girls and boys are seen donning the garb of traditional feminine and masculine characters, or possible future roles. Boys put on costumes of cowboys, policemen, firemen, while girls are dressing as princesses, nurses and brides. Toys that are pictured also follow the traditional roles. Girls have the inevitable doll, while boys play with cars, boats, planes and trains. The innocence of a sentence 'Peter has a toy and Jane has a toy' is soon lost in its interpretation.

These transparent messages, completed with brightly coloured illustrations, clearly lay out children's separate roles. They put girls squarely in the conforming passive role, quiet shadows beside lively brothers. Both girls and their mothers rarely go outside the domestic sphere, and mother invariably wears her apron. Boys' activities manage to transport them outside, following more active and interesting pursuits, usually with their father. Thus the sex roles are divided very effectively in these and similar primers. They discriminate between the sexes and present a basic grounding in those attitudes and that behaviour from which women are now struggling to escape.

It is not only this portrayal which is wrong, but also the way that the conditions and standard of living are represented. Most children are nowhere near the upper middle-class world in which Peter and Jane live. Some primers have started to try to correct this fault,* by recognizing the modern world of tower blocks and supermarkets, and in doing so, come to life with lots of bright images. Some are also recognizing that many children come from other countries. However, the basic parts played by girls and women are little altered by their change in surroundings. Their place is still a domestic one. This is well illustrated in a number rhyme about 'Ten Busy Housewives'.[1] These industrious ladies gradually increase from one to ten, each involved in tasks of dusting, washing, cleaning etc., until eventually they have 'nothing left to do'. But of course, what else could housewives possibly do?

When children have mastered the basic skills of literacy, the door opens on to a vast spread of books that promise action and excitement. The story is the most important thing and children judge how interesting and exciting this is, and whether it has enough to stir their imagination. Once again the position of women and girls in these books shows little improvement on the passive and restrictive roles already crudely portrayed in reading primers. It is still clearly boys and men who are given the most active adventures and take the most initiative, and women play all the traditional parts they are meant to take in 'real' life. There are a few books in which girls do come through very positively, but these are a tiny minority. The same situations are found in the fiction for older children, and the 'career novels' in which John is always the doctor and Anne the nurse. In America much has been and is being done to combat sexism in children's literature, and things are beginning to move in Britain too. Several groups have been set up to work specifically on this question. They are demonstrating publicly just how stereotyped the present books are, recommending those which are not sexist, and are trying to change the policies of publishing houses.†

*For instance, Nippers, a series of children's readers written by Leila Berg.
† These groups include C.I.S.S.Y. (Campaign to Impede Sex Stereotyping the Young), a women's group who are trying to influence publishers etc. and who produced the children's books issue of *SHREW* cited earlier. There are also the Leeds Women's Liberation Literature Collective, who

COMIC REALITY

One of the nicest things I remember doing as a child, especially on rainy days, or during long school holidays, was lying on the floor reading comics. They seemed very innocent then, but looking back, and reviewing them today, it is clear that they too endorse the same roles and images as children's books and readers. From the simple picture strip papers, to pop and love stories and the glossy magazines, the portrayal of girls and their concerns and interests is narrow and circumscribed. Reality is supposed to be reflected while it is all the time directed.

For very young children who are just beginning to read, there are girls' comics like *Twinkle* ('The Picture Paper especially for Little Girls.') and others for both sexes like *Jack and Jill*, *Playhour* and *Robin*. In *Twinkle*, little girls are shown doing various activities, but many of the stories have a similar theme, involving the familiar stereotypes. One recurring theme is that of helping people and doing good turns. 'Babs the Brownie' learns 'Kim's Game' (remembering lots of items that have been shown for a minute or so) – which turns out to be extremely useful when her mother forgets her shopping list the next day. Goldilocks gets her three bears to perform for the little girl in hospital who could not go to the circus. Patty Pickle wants to help her mother with the housework, but she is so clumsy and inefficient that she is set to clean her doll's house instead. I'm sure it wouldn't happen to Peter Pickle! Familiar roles are seen in 'Nancy the Little Nurse', who mends the broken dollies in the Dollies' Hospital with her grandad, who is the dolly doctor. Apart from mummy, who is either doing housework, or taking her daughter walking and to the shops, adults rarely enter the scene. The comics for both girls and boys are marginally better, if only because they often feature animals instead of children, like 'Harold the Hare' and

have been issuing newsletters reviewing non-sexist children's books, the Children's Books Study Group, and the Children's Rights Workshop Book Project, and several others at the time of writing.

'Fliptail the Otter' who engage in slightly more activities that are neutral and less sex-biased, although the animals are still given a gender and often act accordingly. When children do enter however, the same themes occur – like 'Nurse Susan and Doctor David', a 'Let's Pretend Story'.

For children of seven or eight, up to about thirteen years of age, comics are divided sharply into those for boys and those for girls. Girls read *Bunty*, *Judy*, *June*, and *Mandy*, among others, all titles taking the form of a girl's name. Boys read comics with names like *Victor*, *Valiant*, *Hotspur*, *Lion*, *Thunder* and *Hornet* – names which embody virile masculine associations. The differences in the style of the titles implies and reflects the orientations of the contents. The majority of boys' stories are action-packed adventures, taking place in wild and remote lands, on spaceships or other planets, or on football pitches and racetracks. Physical feats are performed against inestimable odds; contests and conflicts, battles, tests of skill and ingenuity pour continuously out of every page. Stories are loud and noisy – 'VROOSH! SKREECH! CRUUUSH! BAAANG! VROOM! AAAARGH!' ricochet round the pages.

Girls' comics conspicuously lack this sort of action. Stories tend to involve coping with unexpected situations, or taking part in individual competitions, trying to prove the innocence of someone wrongly accused, or helping people to rediscover their lost families. Almost every story seems to contain some personal or emotional element. Heroines have to be able to inspire sympathy in the reader for what they are fighting for, or against, in order to be recognized in all their true worthiness. Personalities are laid out in much more detail than in stories for boys. Much more care is taken to show either the sincerity or the wickedness of the characters. Because the hopes and beliefs of the heroine are so fully set out, it is much easier to identify with her, in her vulnerable and exposed moments. In all these stories the message comes across that it is girls alone who are sensitive enough both to have feelings themselves and to be able to detect them in others.

Backgrounds to girls' comic stories are much narrower in range than those for boys. Male action can take place in any part of this or, indeed, any other world. But for girls, most stories are based in the home, the family or the school, which also therefore provide the main restricting authorities. The action, potentially defined by the background, is restricted from the start. It has been claimed that girls' comic stories benefit from having more 'realistic' elements in them[2] and that this is better than the extreme fantasy found in boys' comics. However, all imaginations, regardless of sex, need to be, and enjoy being, kindled, and fantastic action is probably more creative and exciting than the slower more 'inward-directed' stories that are presented to girls.

Since background confines characters, it is significant that most of the boys' heroes are adult men – soldiers, spacemen, cowboys, footballers and scientists. They don't have restricting families. They can go where they like and do what they want. None of them are married. By comparison, the chief characters produced for girls are usually in their teens. Their families have to be accounted for somehow and often large parts of a story are devoted to the problem of coping with a family or with trying to survive without one. In stories where parents play a major role, they are usually in some difficulty and the daughter comes to the rescue. But for a heroine to have any sort of adventure she needs autonomy, for romance she needs tragedy, so writers of comics dispose of parents with few qualms. It is amazing in comics to see how frequently and tragically orphans are made or children separated from their parents. Here are three examples:

Helen May was alone in the world until she traced her twin sister Linda to a home for bad girls and took her home to live with her.

Jennie Smith and Rose Brown were two thirteen-year-old orphans. One day Mr Carter came to Sunnydale Orphanage looking for his daughter. He had been stranded on a desert island for eleven years and when he was finally rescued he discovered his wife had been killed in a train crash ten years previously. His baby daughter survived and he managed to trace her to Sunnydale Orphanage.

When Agnes Hobbes' father was put in prison, she went to live with her selfish aunt.

In talking about their choice of books, some children have said that they prefer it this way: 'We like stories about children on their own, children who don't like their parents, orphans, animals who go out to seek their fortune.'[3] In real life, parents are the ones who, by the exercise of their powers of veto and punishment, most limit the freedom of their children. Fantasy can allow children to experience some freedom and for boys this means identifying with their autonomous heroes. But for girls, who are even more circumscribed than boys, this escape is diminished. They are fed on a diet of stories in which, even if the parents have been safely explained away, the heroine is tied by other factors, often by small brothers or sisters, or by close friends or relatives.

The odds with which girl heroines have to battle are not the easily identifiable monsters, spacemen, crooks etc. that the boys' heroes conquer, but rather their own isolated existences. They spend their time finding lost relatives, winning the final gymnastics competition, detecting and combating people with jealous and evil motives. They are shown to be adept at fighting emotional rather than physical battles and their 'villains' tend to be adults – relatives, teachers, occasionally crooks or kidnappers of heiresses – or other girls. There is little solidarity between girls in these stories and collective action is rare. The world of these stories is full of nasty and jealous people, often apparent friends, who cannot be trusted and who will stoop to anything to prevent the heroine from winning. Thus Glynis locks Smash-hit Cindy in the storage shed to stop her entering the tennis tournament; Olive gives Gymnast Sylvie the wrong message to put her off her performance; Sadie gives another girl sleeping pills to prevent her singing in a show.

The opposite sex are featured in differing degrees. Men and boys feature quite prominently in girls' comics, often as close relatives, figures of authority, or as unscrupulous villains, but seldom as simple friends. In boys' comics, however, women and girls are almost completely excluded. Occasionally a sister or a niece may appear, or a girlfriend is mentioned (never for the hero!), but in general boys' stories show a totally male world. One story in which women did appear concerned a cricket match between the young heroes ('the strongest boys in the world'), and a ladies' team called significantly 'The Ashford Amazons'. These large, hefty, unattractive girls were finally defeated by the ingenuity of the heroes who let mice run all over the pitch. Then what weak and silly creatures the Amazons were made to look. Just like girls! Another story for boys had a girl heroine ('Tomboy Jo Tallon') hired as trainer to a speedway team, an ace rider who neatly demolished sneering Duke Kilroy. There are few stories like this in girls' comics, and although defeating male opposition is an inadequate alternative, it is better than the equivalent girls' stories which often end with a moral like: 'We don't have to compete with boys – that's where Pauline was so wrong. They're better at some things, we're better at others – like tending people when they're hurt. We've learnt our lesson.'

A few comics, *Diana* and *Tina* for example, published for younger girls, incorporate stories and features about the pop world. These often include the boy-meets-girl theme and are merely a younger version of the love-story comics. The readership for which the publishers of these papers are aiming is indicated by the advertisements they carry for dolls. They have turned away from the simple comic-strip style of *Bunty*, *Judy* etc., and point their readers towards a world of pop-idols, teenage infatuations, fashion and beauty tips, horoscopes, letters and advice. They are a child-like warm-up to the magazines devoted entirely to the pursuit of romance. In these comics girls are also seen rehearsing for their future roles in the family. In the absence of parents, heroines struggle at home to carry on looking after their brothers and sisters. In those stories where girls have got careers they are usually either glamorous, like modelling, singing, theatre management or road managing for a pop-group, or they are traditional like nursing. Occasionally there is an original tale like that of the cockney girl mechanic, but she shows that she is a proper girl after all by secretly becoming a beauty queen. Characteristically, these comics never reveal what becomes of their bright, ingenious and persevering heroines when they get older. If these publications, unlike comic fantasy for boys, are trying to be realistic, then perhaps they are right. There are very few successful women in our society and it is difficult to write drama and adventure stories about housewives and mothers. But whatever the reasons, the future for these heroines is always left blank.

FALLING IN LOVE WITH LOVE

After reading ordinary comics until the age of about twelve, girls move on to the romantic papers like *Jackie, Melanie, Valentine, Mirabelle* or *Popswap* (for junior pop music fans). These comics are saturated with romantic love. Finding the right man is the only road to true happiness. Stories begin with the inevitable encounter between boy and girl, who then meander their way over various obstacles ultimately to find true love together in each others' arms. 'It's so easy to fall in love . . .' runs the blurb, and so it seems. Inexpensive too, at 4p, and if the best-seller *Jackie* has a circulation of almost a million copies a week, the actual readership is probably more than double this.

The plots (if they can be called that) unfailingly contain some perspective on love. Whatever contrivances are made to draw out a story, the final picture is inevitably a familiar locked embrace, a thought bubble encapsulating the satisfaction of this position. 'But I always knew it would come to this in the end . . . Mm . . . Me too . . .' Tragedies are again very popular, and the death of a lover is possibly more romantic than his survival. 'Oh Dave, why did your van have to crash that night, you died homeward bound – you were coming home to me. But wherever you are now I'll always wait for you.' But there are also morals to be learnt about love, for you cannot just fall in love with anybody, like falling for your teacher, or for a married man. This is deceitful and perilous. 'Oh she mustn't let that faithless fella soft-talk her into breaking up a marriage – happy or otherwise.' The idealization of romance is completed visually with over-glamourized illustrations (apparently drawn by members of the cheaper artistic labour market in Spain),[4] in which men and women have regular film-star features, flowing or curly hair, model complexions and figures.

These stories, which show girls as having an overwhelming need to find a man, obviously run counter to all the notions of Women's Liberation. They obliterate any idea of girls as independent individuals having interests of their own. Now that women's liberation is publicized and talked about, comic writers too have absorbed these ideas, which are thrown back, caricatured and defeated. Young girls who read *Bunty* in August 1974 were vaguely introduced to the idea in the form of a female magician called 'Libby Wimmin' who claimed that lady magicians were as good as men but who was persuaded to change her mind by Merlin's daughter. Love comics often become even more explicit when they defend love against liberating ideas. An American girl for example, who is shown independently travelling around England with her guitar, is revealed as doing this to forget her unhappy love affair. She reflects bitterly at the end, 'All the hardness, the being like a boy, it's just a front. And I thought for once I'd found somebody who'd seen through it, so that I could stop the search and relax.'

Another heroine, back in Victorian days, declares, 'There's got to be somewhere I can go. Something I can do. Cos if one more person tells me a woman's place is in the home, I'll hit them! I'm not ready for domestic bliss and pots of aspidistras! I want more than that from life!' She manages to get transported to the present day, but cannot cope with girls' relative independence of dress and work, and returns to her own century leaving readers with the moral of her tale, : 'I'll give you one word of warning – don't complain too loudly about your lot in life cos it'll take a Prosper (the man who transported her) to show you how lucky you really are.' Women's Liberation itself is revealed, in a story about two Martians on Earth here to study human behaviour. They witness a tiff between Sue and Ben. Following Sue home, they hear her say 'Men. I'm finished with them, I'm through with being a slave.' Then she goes off on a Women's Liberation demonstration, carrying a placard saying 'Down with Slavery'. The Martians construe this as a slave revolt – the long-haired ones are slaves, and the short-haired ones are their masters. In the middle of this, Ben arrives, snatching Sue's placard and saying that she is making a fool of herself. They begin another quarrel until suddenly 'Oh no, the demo's gone on without me, I suppose you'll be satisfied now.' 'Course,' says Ben, 'You were only doing it to make me mad anyway.' And he throws her placard away. They move off, still arguing. But by now the Martians' 'shield of invisibility' is wearing thin and Sue catches a glimpse of them. She gets faint, and, trembling with shock, gives Ben the opportunity to take her in his arms and embrace her – 'I won't let anything hurt you.' The picture brims over with hearts and all ideas of liberation are extinguished and forgotten. The writers of the comic strips absorb and reflect topical aspects of everyday life but nothing must upset the theme of true love. Nor would the clamouring readers seem to want this for as well as being tantalized by the implications of sex, they have learnt that finding the right man is the fulfilment of every young girl's dream.

Features appear in these comics, showing the lives of the latest pop stars, with meticulously posed photographs to cut out and keep. Articles give advice on make-up and fashion, and simple cookery. These are similar to those found in the bigger glossy magazines and women's papers, but there is nothing yet about babies. Nothing about how to get them, or how not to get them, or how to look after them. After all, first get your man. Babies are a bit too domestic at this stage, and are catered for by the straight women's papers where pop stars fade into insignificance. The agony column is another popular feature in every such comic paper or magazine, with correspondents ranging from very young girls (and some boys) who are struggling to experience friends of the opposite sex, to those who have found a mate and are trying to untangle the resulting complications. In the romantic comics, these often tortuous letters illustrate the multitude of problems that gaining or keeping a boyfriend seems to involve. They appear in marked contrast to the picture stories accompanying them, in which couples walk into the sunset of eternal happiness.

PAST AND PRESENT

Comics and love story papers are not new, they have been read by girls (and boys) for years. I have discussed some of those read by contemporary teenage girls, with their imaginary worlds filled with deceitful rivals and lost relatives or cloying love and sentimentality. It is worth comparing these briefly with what fourteen-year-old working class girls were reading at the beginning of the 1940s.

The most popular papers then, apart from the film magazines (picturegoing was a very popular activity), were *Girls' Crystal*, *The Miracle*, *The Oracle*, *Family Star*, *Red Star Weekly*, *Red Letter*, *Silver Star* and *Glamour*.[5] Girls also read 'Pocket Novels' and romances like those contained in the *True Love* series, as well as the occasional *Woman's Weekly*. All these, except *Girls' Crystal*, brimmed over with tear-jerking tragedy or thrilling love fantasies. But at the same time girls of this age were avidly reading *Beano*, which carries on dauntless to this day. Apart from the 'Nazi schoolboys', it seems to have barely changed, and Lord Snooty and his pals still appear. Pearl Jephcott observed that heroines occupy rather inferior positions, and this, too, shows little alteration over time.

Girls' Crystal covered a similar range to comics like *Bunty*, *Judy* etc. 'Would Sallie Discover the Secret of the Idol' (1 March, 1941) shows little change in style today – see 'Jennie and the Green Goddess' (17 August, 1974). In the 1941 issue, there was a story exposing the evil-doings of a form mistress, and another of a crook; it included a detective thriller – 'Danger at the Haunted Crossroads', and a story called 'The Skating Impostor' which deals with the familiar female rival and wrongly accused brother; there was an adventure in foreign parts with Jean who is companion to Jasmin, daughter of the Emir of Marakand. *Girls' Crystal* seems to include more boy and adult male heroes than today's equivalent, and has more stories about mystery, secret passages and hidden rooms. *Bunty* and others of its type show much concern with pony riding and gymnastics and sorting out family problems and situations, and bow to changing fashions and technology by giving space to transistor radios, pop music and groups, but otherwise the style is very similar. We can compare *Girls' Crystal* with *Bunty* of 17 August 1974 which includes a statue that comes alive as a brilliant ballet dancer – 'Dorinda from the Deep'; 'Katy the Cabby', who uses her horse to pull a cab while her father is in hospital; 'Leave it to Lottie' – who is road manager to the 'Oggies' pop group, and who brings a member of the group and his mother together again; 'Josie the Gymnast', and 'Cindi's Search', a story about the Second World War in which the heroine and her little brother seek their mother.

Other papers in the 1940s contained short stories and serials in written form. They had titles like 'Her Way to Keep his Love', 'His Brother Stole his Girl', 'The First Man She Met', and 'The Night She Would Never Forget'. They can be compared with the 'true life' romances that are read in this form today, like *Loving*, and *True Love Stories*. *Red Letter*, read in 1941 and still published now, but to a much diminished readership, looks rather faded and fusty, but carries on regardless with titles such as 'Not the Man for Jenny', 'This Man means Trouble', and 'Fear not the Memory'. Pearl Jephcott describes *The Oracle*, for 27 September 1941 which

brings love to a shop girl, an ex-dancer in the Cafe Mena in Cairo, a munitions worker, a factory girl, and an innocent (though suspected guilty) young wife. This love comes however against a highly glamourized background, a world apart from the tenement house in Gas Street where the reader herself probably has to live. Unpleasant people and situations are the very stuff of the tales, which are weighted with sordidness and harshness. Love 'comes', but it comes in a sea of jealousy, scandal, revenge, lying, guilty secrets, murder, bigamy and seduction.[6]

Modern love comics are free of the more 'sordid' features of these stories in acknowledgement of a younger readership and rely on more superficiality and banality, but all these aspects may be found still in the true romance magazines, their impact reduced by the changing views on sexual morality.

The picture-strip love magazines of today did not exist thirty years ago, they were introduced for girls in their early teens and provide an easily digested sop to their appetite for discovering what 'love' is all about. The love-story magazines of 1941 were probably read by a much wider age group the younger of whom were considered old enough to take things like bigamy and seduction in their stride or were perhaps expected to be still reading *Girls' Crystal* and *Beano*. The equivalent magazines today are similarly worldly and oriented towards more adult tastes.

In the early 1940s the problem page was as important as it is now and added a touch of reality in the middle of the wild fantasy. Many of the letters raised the age-old problems associated with going out with boys. For example, one letter published in an issue of *Silver Star* in 1941 could just as easily have come from a current issue of *Jackie* or *Loving*. It read: 'I am only fifteen, but I have been going out with a boy who is eighteen. I love him dearly, but when he took another girl home, she said he told her that he only takes me out to please his pal. When I asked him about it he laughed and said not to listen to tales.'[7] In the same way the more 'adult' romance magazines dispense advice about contraception and marriage upsets. People's real life problems are very specific and personal, and those besetting the love-story couples are less ordinary and more glamorous and mysterious. But the solutions described for all of them share a common failing in not considering the more basic social problems that many are facing in terms of low wages, bad housing, and unemployment. Evil is always lurking within people rather than within a system. The world is represented as a glamorous place where love triumphs over all wickedness and the heroine beats her rivals and gets her man. Girls are not blind to the basic problems, but are probably quite pleased to step into a wish-fulfilling dreamland, where daily problems like money and meeting people don't arise and where life is made up of spontaneous romantic happenings. The influence of these papers is probably not immense, but neither is it completely insignificant. If girls read little else they are encouraged to see their lives as properly devoted to the search for fun, fashion, pop and boyfriends and their minds will become smothered and dulled by these trite literary offerings. This rather moral-sounding condemnation was strongly endorsed by Liz Waugh (quoted previously) who found that the girls she taught who only read these sorts of comics and magazines had little knowledge or opinions to give on anything else. 'The hairdressing apprentices I teach are obviously intelligent girls, but their mental diet of *Jackie* etc. together with the salon atmosphere creates an extraordinary vapidity. Their only answer is "I don't know." I'm not the only teacher who has noticed this.' This literature probably only acts as a reinforcement to the limited views and interests that have already developed, but it is important for what it omits from its content. Like much of the mass media, it endorses the *status quo* by leaving out any suggestions for the possibility or desirability of change.

GLOSSY GUIDELINES

Moving on from picture stories and pop stars, adolescent girls find the glossy magazines, like *Honey* and *19*, and the less expensive *Petticoat* – now retitled *Hi*. These depart from comic strips to more adult feature articles and stories, which may range in subject from the problems of black teenagers in England, to what it's like to be a *'Penthouse* Pet'. Music (pop or otherwise) is now approached in a more analytical way, with the emphasis on content rather than a singer's physical appearance. In a topical mood one article asks 'Why should men have all the fun? Are you satisfied to be a female in today's society or would you rather be a man?' and although good in some ways, the article not surprisingly fails to give any clues about how to change the situation. In it a psychiatrist warns potentially aggressive girls that men will see them as a threat and so they should 'be easy on them'. These magazines try to be more aware and sophisticated, choosing fashionable clothes and topical features. They are useful on beauty hints and bargains, but in avoiding any political perspective, their feature articles consequently vary from liberal concern with social problems to conservatism. Compared with these, *Spare Rib* magazine is specifically feminist and devotes its pages to issues of far greater relevance to the situations of ordinary girls and women. It provides invaluable and honest information on aspects of health and on issues like contraception and abortion; it examines the position of women at work and at home and reports women's struggles towards change; it reviews the arts from a feminist viewpoint, and demonstrates that glamour and reputation are of minimal importance. Sadly, girls who are attracted to the commercial appeal of the other women's papers and magazines may reject *Spare Rib* for not exploiting the things they see as closest to their hearts. The 'love' they want to buy is the sort done up with hearts, flowers and wedding bells. The really expensive glossies like *Vogue*, and *Harpers and Queen* can be left aside for the purpose of this book; they are published for the rich who can afford the ideas and fashions with which they deal and for those who either aspire to be rich or who enjoy the material fantasy world these magazines portray.

Today, the biggest selling women's papers are the stalwart weeklies *Woman* (circulation just under 2 million), *Woman's Weekly*, and *Woman's Own*. These are mainly geared towards housewives and mothers, but the young and single girl can learn a lot from them about her future role. Their immense circulation figures reflect the need women have to find new ideas for their homes and children. They also help isolated women to find reassurance and a sense of solidarity from reading about other women's experiences and problems, and give them something with which to fill their spare time. These familiar papers contain useful hints on coping with the role of home-maker. They are orientated towards the family and include enthusiastic philoso-phizing about its care and maintenance. This is woven around the cookery recipes, patterns to sew or knit, home-crafts, beauty advice, advice on medical problems, child-care, home-care, love fiction and personal columns. Readers writing letters to these magazines about their home and personal miseries are usually recommended to be patient, resigned and passive in order to solve their problems. Everything seems geared towards doing or making things for other people, and a gentle blanket of emotional blackmail adds an extra layer to the contents. 'Decorate a cake to show you care'. It is easy to see how to be a 'good' mum. Beauty tips show housewives how to look and feel years younger! The practical domestic information is very useful, but is obviously made the province of women. The effect is so inward and home-directed as to exclude the concept of real happiness in the world outside.

While girls progress from their young comics through the love story world, to more adult women's papers and glossy magazines, what are the boys reading? They go on reading comics like *Valiant* for longer than girls read *Bunty* etc., and they are also consumers of the younger pop papers, like *Popswap*, or *Look In* (the junior *TV Times*). At some point in their mid-teens, these will be outgrown, and their place is taken by football papers, the more adult music papers, like *Melody Maker*, or by specialized and technical magazines about cars, motorcycles, Hi Fi, and other things. But whatever is chosen it is clear that boys are not steeped in the same amount of romantic sentimentality as are girls. Nor are they likely to live up to any high levels of romantic fantasy when they confront teenage girls with their gauche reality. Girls have been smothered by love stories for so long that the 'natural' origins of their emotional fantasy world are cast very seriously in doubt.

ADVERTISING

[Advertising] is not merely an assembly of competing messages; it is a language in itself which is always being used to make the same general proposal. Within publicity, choices are offered between this cream and that cream, that car and this car, but publicity as a system only makes a single proposal: it proposes to each of us that we transform ourselves or our lives by buying something more.[8]

No one can avoid advertising in some form or other, whether in papers and magazines, on public hoardings, or on television and cinema screens. To some extent it can be ignored, but never totally, and this assumption is basic to the industry. In advertising, the ideals that girls and women are supposed to be striving for are taken away, polished up, and returned – at a price. Problems are recognized and stressed, and solutions offered for sale. Advertisers want to sell a particular product in the most effective way possible, and to do this they gather up all the beliefs about what people should be like, and offer to sell aid. They acknowledge day-to-day problems of living and offer de-sensitizers. They realize sex is a good sell and include it wherever possible. The irrelevant use of women's bodies to sell products totally unrelated to them can be seen everywhere. Pretty half-naked girls appear on advertisements for bricks, aluminium, cars, garage doors, drink, cigars, tobacco and other products. These 'attractive propositions' declare that 'every factory should have one', and are a blatant example of the way that women are defined and 'sold' in terms of their sexual attributes.

The world of advertising categorizes women in many of their other traditional roles, as girlfriends, wives and mothers. It suggests that if you buy the product luxury, beauty, grace, cleanliness and happiness will be yours. Married couples nestle blissfully together, babies chuckle, meals are sumptuous and sizzling, and kitchen gadgets look fun. This ideal of course does not exist except to exploit and perpetuate the problems of the real world. Although both men and women face this barrage of propaganda, it is girls and women who are most vulnerable. They, being more dependent on the approval of others, are sensitive to the images that are held up for self-comparison, like being an attractive girl, or a good wife and mother. For a working woman, pressures may be more emphatic, as she may be unable to employ the amount of time-consuming care and attention that happy advertisement families imply that she should.

Throughout comics and magazines there runs a continuous stream of advertising. Even the junior comics advertise things to tempt both boys and girls, but apparently neutral things like a junior typewriter will be illustrated differently for either sex. For boys it is represented as a tool for a career as a journalist or a writer, while for girls it is advertised as a machine on which to write love letters. As soon as girls become old enough to notice, the ads make them aware of their looks and the possible flaws in them. The boy-deflecting dangers of spots and pimples are described and teenage papers are full of antidotes for them. Girls' and women's magazines are sprinkled with ever-increasing aids to beauty. The message is not to be content with what nature gave you. 'Let him think nature gave you a flawless complexion.' 'When it comes to your hair, even nature needs a helping hand.' To get her man, a girl must strive to be beautiful, slim, and sexually alluring, and there is always room for improvement. So much is made dependent on looks. 'I so want this job – but I don't stand a chance with skin like mine.'

'Some are born beautiful and slim – most of us have to work at it,' comments one advertisement – and at great expense of time and money. Advertising works an endless confidence trick that makes it impossible to be natural – like being told 'How to do your hair so that it looks as though you don't.' Being natural also means being odourless, delicately scented like a summer breeze! Women fear giving offence through any 'natural' smells, and the rise of vaginal deodorants fed this fear, persuading girls to use chemicals which were harmful to sensitive areas in order to alleviate this artificially-created insecurity. There is a perpetual need to keep a woman clamouring for products, and no area or space in a woman's body or life is free from the prying, manipulating and exploiting presence of advertising.

Advertisement women play the roles that the product demands, and these are also geared to the popular images of women at any moment in time. Girls are seen being successful with men, feeding them and loving them satisfactorily and bringing up happy children. They are adorers and appendages of men. They are recognized as being inferior in many ways, although they may be patronized: 'Being a woman does not mean you can't appreciate good wines.'; and are given credit for being the 'power behind the throne', like 'cooking the meal that sealed the deal'. But when images are changing, the advertising copywriters are quick to follow, showing girls making the breakthrough to 'freedom' in their modern underwear and tampons. Even simple electricity can free girls from drudgery: '. . . you'll find a liberated kitchen through electric cooking can bring you much more time to be together.' Quick and easy cures are offered for today's problems. Depressed women are advised to buy something to cheer themselves up, tired and overworked housewives and mothers are sold multi-vitamin tablets and tranquillizers rather than being provided with improved housing and nursery facilities.

Advertising is capitalism's soft sell. An anonymous mass of people called consumers have each to be persuaded to need whatever a product can give them, to buy it and to keep on buying. Girls growing up, and women housewives worried about fulfilling and achieving their roles, are the foremost consumers. They see in advertising imagery reflections of society's attitudes and ideals often taken to extremes and caricatured. They may not be persuaded to buy the products, but they absorb the images. They do not learn their roles from this source, but it is a strong reinforcer. Advertising sets out to make people identify with characters in advertisements, with their situation and needs, to make them jealous of the person they would become if they bought the product. It captures girls' fluttering images of themselves and pins them up for sale.

MUSIC

At ever-earlier ages, as the comics illustrate, children are becoming aware of pop music and its idols. The extent to which they are exposed to this, and the amount that they enjoy and demand become intermeshed as the exploiters of the pop world turn on their supplies to fill the demand that they are partly responsible for creating. Other technological developments have helped this movement, in a way unknown to the original fans of young Frank Sinatra and Johnnie Ray. Television has enabled the stars to be shown to the people, and young children are quick to notice and take over the responses of their adolescent elders, who are so obviously getting a strong emotional injection out of the pop scene. They start to read *Popswap* and *Look In* alongside their *Bunty* or *Valiant*. Their parents are the generation who welcomed in Rock 'n' Roll, Rhythm 'n' Blues, Soul, Tamla Motown and the rest, and who are still playing and enjoying it. Their children therefore don't have to forge their own music culture, although they can shape the figures within it. They do not shock parents with the crude and 'unmusical' sounds that burst through in the 1950s. Their nappies were changed in time to the Beatles and the Rolling Stones, and this music is just part of the sound-scene of growing up.

As they approach and explore the music, they take in the familiar distribution of roles. Almost all the significant and successful stars, individuals and groups are male, as are their managers, promoters, publicity agents and critics. Girls are cast as the inevitable followers, the fans or groupies, who demonstrate acts of adulation for their idols. Pictures are collected, television shows are avidly watched, live shows are attended where girls scream and shout and cry, showing amounts of emotion completely misplaced in real life. Girls make up the bulk of the all-important market, the people buying the records. It is an unstable but extremely profitable business. Mistakes by a star, or fickleness by fans can lead to a swift crumbling of the pedestal. Girl fans therefore do have some power, but in a dubious way which represents no real change in the role structure. It is merely a transference from one man to another, not unlike the power of the 'little woman behind every big man', who may leave him undermined by taking up the same position with another. The pop music world is similar now to many other male-dominated occupations, in which entrance is barred to all but a few girls. It is complicated by the apparently whimsical nature of public demand (whose whims are cleverly manipulated by record promoters) which confirms men as those with popular talent, and women as those who support them, and maintain and sustain their success.

The reasons for this lie predominantly in three areas: girls' conceptualizations of themselves; their need and their role in relation to men; and the music and record industry, whose energies are focused on expanding markets and selling images to a largely female audience. To begin with the first of these, girls have never been encouraged, or had the chance to think of themselves as exciting and initiating figures. It is always boys rather than girls who buy guitars and drums to learn on, who get themselves together in a group to practise in back rooms and old church halls, and who eventually either drop out, or make their way to success through a circuit of gigs in pubs and dance-halls. Very few girls participate in this, apart from taking the role of sexy female singer, or just 'with the group'. They automatically assume the secondary parts. On the other hand there is no sign that they would succeed if they tried, as neither record companies nor papers, nor any other influential body give many encouraging hints.

The second area is based on a girl's 'need', as fed and fostered in love magazines, to have a man to love and to idolize. The position of men as artists and performers with girls as their fans corresponds to the same relationship in love stories in the comics and papers. It is no accident that all the heroes look like film or pop stars, and have the heroines falling head over heels for them in no time. Girls are fitted into a sexual framework which demonstrates and sustains the idea of their dependence on acquiring a man. Now that the 'weenyboppers' are being brought into the scene, and the record companies are finding more and younger pre-pubertal boy singers for them to rave about, girls are being primed for their roles even earlier. The same little girl who doesn't really like the little boy next door says she just cannot live without Little Jimmie Osmond.

The record and music industry is only interested in female performers to the extent that they are saleable, popular and will make money. The industry makes and creates music to male standards, and sells it to a predominantly female audience. There is of course a male audience, but they have a less sexually oriented relationship with the artists whose records they buy. They, like girls, buy music mainly by male performers, whom they judge to be good and worth listening or dancing to. They don't idolize these figures, but nor do they many, if any, female singers whom they may acknowledge as good-looking and sexy but may also reject for making unexciting or unprofessional sounds. Both male and female performers have to exploit their own sexuality, helped by their promoters, in the competition to gain attention, popularity and therefore sales.

Folk music is the one area of popular music which has a place for women. But even here their role is defined: they are the singers of love songs. They usually stand passively, or sit perched on a stool, pouring out heartfelt emotions. Nothing too gutsy is allowed because that is unfeminine. But since femininity in this form is unexciting, and unexciting music has a small following, nothing greater than moderate success can every be hoped for.* There have been a few pounding female rock singers, like Brenda Lee in the 1950s, and Lulu, and Suzie Quatro today. Janis Joplin invested and ultimately lost all of herself in giving a tremendously live and exciting performance. Women like The Supremes succeeded with Tamla Motown, but it seems that the sound was selling rather than the girl singers, who rose and fell with their style of music, although Diana Ross managed to break out into

---

* The success of singers like Joni Mitchell and Joan Baez is an exception to this.

individual success. Success as a pop group is the hardest area for women to break into. This traditionally male stomping ground is defended by fans and critics alike, who scrutinize female groups as if they were freaks and deride them in a male chauvinistic way if the music they make is not twice as good as the best.

In the same way as the structure of the pop music industry reflects and reinforces the inferior social and political position of women in real life, so also the song lyrics faithfully record and exaggerate it. As the old song says, 'girls were made to love and kiss', and this is a much-repeated theme – initially expressed in the 'Crying Talking Sleeping Walking Livin' Doll', and continuing to filter through most lyrics ever since.

But although girls are obsessed with young pop heroes they do not identify with them specifically but with the fantasy of having a relationship with them and all the accompanying glamour. For instance, when the Ealing girls were asked what famous person in the world they would most like to be their choices mainly fell within the glamorous world of music, television and film. The preference was predominantly female, they most frequently chose to be Elizabeth Taylor, Olivia Newton-John, Diana Ross, Raquel Welch and Twiggy. Some wanted to be closer to their idols by choosing to be, for instance, Marc Bolan's wife, or Mrs David Cassidy. Most did not actually wish to be their favourite male star, but wished to be married to him, or to be a female performer with a glamorous status. Girls are less interested in keenly following female singers, and although they like them it is the male individuals and groups like Donny Osmond and Gary Glitter, Slade and the Jackson Five that really turn them on. Their preferences are geared by sexual attraction and by the way they are learning to relate to boys and men. Therefore female performers count with them for less, and they may adopt the same critical attitudes towards these performers that men have. Only the appearance of more girl singers with more varied music, together with a reduction of the popular brainwashing that young girls go through, will change this situation.

To succeed for themselves and to stop being typecast solely as sweet faces singing sweet songs, women have to gird themselves with all the self-confidence that is usually lost to them, and blaze out their own music trail. And beginnings are becoming apparent: embryonic here and more developed in America, women are making and demanding their own sounds. The enthusiastic audiences for bands like for instance the Chicago Women's Rock Band in the States, and singers like Joan Armatrading and Jo Ann Kelly in this country, together with the increased production and popularity of women's folk and country rock music all testifies to this. There are many good things emerging which must not be co-opted and exploited away by sales and gimmick-conscious promoters. To a girl confronting the harsh world of commercial pop music, the only way may seem to be the humiliating and self-destroying male route through non-stop package tours centred around publicity and promotion. This process can annihilate talent and leave only commercial glitter behind. Performers become mere products to be exposed and sold to an audience, and this audience is predominantly female and prefers sexy male singers and musicians.

Women are right to be reluctant to expose themselves to this process, even if it seems to be the only way into the music world. While the record companies use women on record sleeves to sell male products, justifying this abuse by claiming that women performers don't sell, it is little wonder that women merely hover tentatively in the wings of the great noise emporium.

OTHER MEDIA

Newspapers, television, radio and films all portray women and make assumptions about them. I will only consider these briefly because each of them really needs an in-depth analysis inappropriate to this book. Besides, much of what I want to say about them simply repeats what I have already said about other things in this chapter. Newspapers, for example, have many ways of showing and judging women, from the sexy pin-up and their coverage of rape cases which often show more of the uncoverage of the victim, to their frequent identification of women as wives of their husbands instead of self-contained individuals.

The television set has become an integral part of most homes.

It can deliver hour upon hour of unbroken excitement and glamour entertainment, punctuated at intervals by news broadcasts and documentaries – a constant intermingling of fantasy and reality. Throughout the development of the various mass media, radio, cinema and television particularly, the potential influence and effects of each has caused waves of anxious concern. This was expressed by assuming a simple relationship between what is portrayed and susceptible young people who may imitate it or change their social behaviour as a result of seeing it. For instance, the greatest cause for concern in recent years has been the possible effects of television violence on delinquency. Results so far indicate that this is probably just one part of an interactive process in which television plays a contributory role.[9] All individuals are different and effects will depend on what a person brings to the media and how he or she uses it at any particular time. It is certainly not a one-way process in which everything on the screen is mentally mopped up by the viewer. The completeness of these conclusions is however hampered by the lack of evidence on effects on pre-school children, especially those whose lives have included television programmes from the moment they could focus their eyes. In so far as they may use television for gaining information about the world, it could well have a more important effect at an early stage, than later in life.

In transmitting information about the nature and role of the sexes, it will have a reinforcing effect on top of the role divisions that children already see around them, thus broadening the validity of these divisions and increasing the immutability of masculine and feminine. Children take in and learn from observing people on television and retain the content relevant to situations they may one day face themselves. Boys are more likely to identify with and recall actions of male figures, and girls are more likely to identify with and recall those of female figures. They learn more when the scene portrayed seems real to them.

As well as gaining insights into customs, attitudes, socially acceptable behaviour and moral aspects endorsing 'right' against 'wrong', they will perceive that it is essentially a man's world. Most of the exciting action series have male heroes. Westerns have indestructible sauntering cowboys; detectives uncover crimes, follow clues and disentangle knotty plots for the re-establishment of law and order; marathon domestic serials trivialize or stereotype most of their lady characters; and humour is doled out by male comedians who use women for many of the butt ends of their jokes. On the serious side, men run almost all the documentaries and chat shows, they read the news (with a few exceptions), and last thing at night they look to our salvation. Women feature as girlfriends, wives and mothers, singers and dancers, and as helpers on children's shows. It is a predictable reflection of the way things seem to be and confirms them. Occasionally women can step out of place and into a fantasy series, like Emma Peel of the 'Avengers'. In terms of intelligence, physical attack and defence she was allowed to be as good, sometimes better than her companion Steed, and certainly more attractive. But more frequently she was rescued by him and ulti-mately seen developing an affection for him. Because the events involved were often fantastic, she took on a cloak of fantasy and so could be excused her 'eccentric' talents and behaviour.

On the radio the forces are weaker than those on television, and as if as a result, there are a greater number of women announcers and interviewers. But the major parts still go to men who pre-dominate in the news, documentaries, profiles, humour, etc., although on some of the newer commercial stations women seem to have more scope. On the continuous music stations, the disc jockeys are invariably male, apart from the occasional woman, such as Anne Nightingale, who herself admits that she is the token female disc jockey for the B.B.C. and that this is no expanding trend.[10] On children's programmes and those for schools, the attitudes towards women show little variation from tradition.

In the cinema the roles that women play again follow a stereo-typed pattern. While this medium is perhaps more specifically defined as one of fantasy, it has also a more intense impact on the viewers who are in a social situation where they have to sit quietly and watch the film. The effect of the images portrayed, like television, will not teach or radically change people's views on men and women, but will add to the direction already taken. Very few popular films show characters, particularly female ones, who are honestly attempting to come to terms with the changing roles of the sexes and the way this affects their lives. Jane Fonda in *Klute* is perhaps an exception. It seems as if (male) producers and directors cannot cope with the alteration of women's role and the potential of their new sexuality.

Throughout the media, girls are presented in ways which are consistent with aspects of their stereotyped images, and which are as equally unrealistic and unsatisfactory. The contrast between male and female, expressed both in character and opportunity, emanates from every source. The chance is seldom given to girls (or boys) to see girls and women doing things which require strength of character and initiative. Finding a man and looking after him, helping others and solving personal problems are the only activities women are allowed to undertake. By the time a girl reaches adolescence, her mind has usually been subjected to an endless stream of ideas and images incorporating sexist values. She has struggled through reading primers and children's books, watched endless hours of television, has absorbed thousands of comics, keeps *Jackie* in her school desk or borrows it from a friend; she browses through her mother's *Woman*, listens to the radio, and enthusiastically follows her current music idols. She identifies with the love stories she reads to find out all she can about love and sex. In real life, most of her time is filled with school and homework, which seems of little relevance and plays a limited part in the world reflected by the media. Here school may appear as a setting for comedy, but makes no apparent contribution towards a girl's success in finding a man and falling in love. Unless a person is 'brainy' or dedicated to study, – self-definitions from which many girls, especially working class girls, exclude themselves – no connection between their lives at school and their growing sense of womanhood is ever portrayed.

Notes

Chapter 3

1. Quoted in the article 'Goodbye Dolly', in *Shrew*, Autumn 1973, which devotes the whole issue to examining the sexist content of reading primers and children's books.
2. Madeline Francis, 'Girls Only', *New Society*, 28 September, 1972.
3. Mary James, 'Honest Consumers, a Review of Children's Books', *New Society*, 13 December, 1973.
4. Corinna Adam, 'Locking up Your Daughters', *New Statesman*, 2 August, 1974.
5. Pearl Jephcott, *Girls Growing Up*, Faber & Faber, 1942.
6. ibid.
7. ibid.
8. John Berger, *Ways of Seeing*, Penguin, 1972.
9. For more information on this subject, see J. D. Halloran, R. L. Brown and D. C. Chaney, 'Television and Delinquency', *Television Research Committee Working Paper* no. 3, Humanities Press, 1970; and W. Schramm and D. F. Roberts, *The Process and Effects of Mass Communication*, University of Illinois Press, 1971.
10. Interview with Anne Nightingale in *Spare Rib*, no. 18.

CHAPTER IV

Contradictions in Female Education

Domestic science is another popular lesson. The girls regard it as a serious business and are prepared to work hard at it. This attitude appears to be fairly general. An older girl who said that she did as little work as possible when she was at school . . . still thinks of 'cooking and laundry' as lessons which did not turn out to be a waste of time. Senior girls, who perhaps spend one whole day a week, for six months, in the school kitchen, set about their work in a business-like manner, are not afraid to handle ovens, and have a confidence in their own abilities that is in marked contrast to their hesitating approach to such subjects as letter-writing or history . . . A good many girls indicate that they do not really think school work has any bearing on their future . . . 'When I was in the senior school . . . I didn't really bother. They don't teach you no more than last year and I was bored stiff. I used to give out the tea and the milk. I wish they taught you something a bit useful.'

Girls Growing Up, 1942[1]

The domestic crafts start with an inbuilt advantage. They are recognizably part of adult living. Girls know that, whether they marry early or not, they are likely to find themselves making and running a home; moreover some quite young schoolgirls, with mothers out at work, are already shouldering considerable responsibility, a fact which needs to be taken into account in school house-craft programmes. There may also be some girls who are far from enthusiastic, because they have had their fill of scrubbing and washing-up and getting meals for the family at home; and yet they may need all the more the education a good school can give in the wider aspects of homemaking and in the skills which will reduce the element of domestic drudgery.[2]

Newsom Report, 1963[2]

We did a load of cookery and needlework at school . . . I used to hate it. We did biology and chemistry, but all we had for equipment was a couple of old bunsen burners and you got five bad marks for turning them on. Only a couple of people did physics – I don't remember ever having the chance. You hardly ever found anyone doing it for O-level. We never had the chance of doing technical drawing or anything. We really hated needlework and cookery – we would've jumped at the chance to do anything different. I used to rip my needlework up every week so that I wouldn't have to finish it the following week.

> Jane – student at further education college,
> ex-East End Catholic convent school.

The advent of mass education in the last century broadened the educational opportunities of both girls and boys. But as we have seen there was widespread discrimination by sex and class. The separation of girls' future roles in life from those of boys greatly influenced the content and form of teaching and girls' own self-expectations. Today these are still with us, although many are concealed beneath an umbrella of professed equality. Women are taking and assuming an increasing role as workers while their responsibilities at home have remained almost intact. This has many implications, as schoolgirls try to balance out the academic demands of school and the changing image of working women on the one hand, and the traditional role of wife and mother on the other.

Girls' attitudes to school are affected by their social back-grounds, personality and ability, and the sheer implications of being female. These influence their views on the value of education, the best time to give it up, and the sorts of jobs they want to enter. It is well known that many children obtain little satisfaction or enjoyment out of school. Working class children in particular, whose social position has always influenced the kind of schooling they received, see education as of relatively low value or relevance to the opportunities that are open to them. Their position in schools has traditionally been at the lower levels, where they are categorized as 'less able'.

For girls, there is no relationship between academic and tech-nical schooling and being a good wife and mother. This point has been consistently emphasized throughout their history and has only changed with the development of a need for certain sorts of workers and with the demands made by an increasing number of educated women. But the contradiction still exists for many girls, for whom school represents a compulsory and boring prelude to the time when they are allowed more independence and freedom and given adult status. Their most popular job choices are those demanding minimal qualifications and make it meaningless to extend schooldays longer than necessary. Earlier physical maturity and sexual awareness emphasize the discrepancy between adolescent girls as developing women, and the child status and prolonged lack of responsibility accorded them by the school. The attitudes of schoolgirls who become pregnant, and their immediate removal from the school, for instance, demonstrates that child-bearing has no place in the curriculum.

The Ealing girls were vociferous about the boredom and dissatisfaction of school:

I do like school but I find it's a bit routine, everything's the same, week in, week out. They ought to make it more varied, the subjects. Sit in classrooms too much doing writing – don't go out enough. They also expect you to do too much home-work. I know you have to do a certain amount to get anywhere, but I think they expect you to do too much.

I think school is getting too over-crowded and it does affect people at school. This one is far too over-crowded. It affects the teachers because they have to cope with it. It's not fair to the teachers, more like clerk work to do with the register. I've spent all my life at school so far – it seems a waste of time. Most of the things I learn at school I don't use, and you get qualifications on what you know at school and I just think it's wrong that they should take you on what you know.

Don't like school – too boring. They don't let you choose your own subjects or anything in the first year. You have to wait right until the fourth year and then the subjects are not very good.

Most looked forward to leaving, whether or not they were discontented with school life. A third of them wanted to leave at the first opportunity, at fifteen, a third at sixteen, and the rest at seventeen or eighteen. They felt 'shut in and bored', and wanted to 'work independently to a certain extent without staff etc. breathing down my neck'. Some wanted to 'get a good job and get married', wanted to 'earn my own money and not have to depend on my parents to give me pocket money'. Others felt they were wasting their time because 'I don't really have a set ambition', or thought 'you can get good jobs whether you leave school later or not'.

> I would stay on but I want to be a receptionist, so if I stay on when I do not need qualifications for the job I want to do, it will be a whole year wasted.

> Might as well leave really, 'cause I'm not really doing anything. It's all right up until the third year, but once you get into the fourth year you don't do hardly anything. The teachers don't bother. Sometimes the teachers bother, some care and some don't. I'm not really getting anywhere. I was gonna leave next year but I might leave at Christmas. We don't do nothing. All we do is geography etc. and we get so bored with it. We don't learn anything. We might as well be doing something useful, something worthwhile.

Doing something worthwhile seems to have little connection with being at school every day, being treated like children, and being taught many things that apparently bear no useful relation to their situations in the present or the future. Yet this girl would probably disagree with the one in 1942 who saw things like cooking and laundry as useful school subjects. She is aware that there is more to life than household skills, although exactly how this relates to the rest of the school curriculum may not be clear.

For some girls the boredom and irrelevance of school has led to continual truanting until such time as they could legally leave. It is interesting that girls truant as frequently if not more so than boys, but whereas boys often move into delinquency, girls' truancy is not particularly associated with delinquent behaviour. Their rejection of the monotony of school and its imposed rules and constraints is not re-channelled into anything very anti-social.

I talked to two girls who truanted regularly. One, whose task it was to do the housework while her mother was at work, spent her time doing this, going out, or staying at home playing her records. But she also got bored at home:

> Sometimes you can have a laugh in school, and some of the lessons are really good, and you get a load of friends in school that you can rely

on for company. If I get bored at home in the morning I can come in the afternoon for a laugh. I like English 'cause I'm good at English, but half the time, when we don't have English we have maths and I can't stand that.

The other girl had a supporter in her mother who used to make excuses for her with the school board inspector. Her father had left home, and since then her mother had had a nervous breakdown and liked her daughter to be around with her. The daughter 'hated school', found it boring and didn't like the rules. But she had her life approximately worked out: the first year after leaving she would stay at home with her mother, and after that go into floristry or hairdressing since she had relatives who owned their own shops.

There were, however, certain days when the frequent truants I spoke to did like to attend school. These were the occasions of community activities, like Task Force and organizing playgroups. One girl told me: 'I don't like school itself. I haven't been here for ages. I come on Monday because in the afternoon we go to a children's playgroup, a community service, and on Wednesday morning. I don't come the rest of the week.' The situation is not helped by the crowded classrooms in which teachers struggle to keep order and where children have little chance of individual attention. At a special school set up for truants in Hackney, the teacher-pupil ratio was very good and the children benefited greatly. The intention of this 'school' was to persuade the children to go back to their proper schools, but this did not work as they were well aware of the advantages of their 'special' school.

School is a very artificial world and assumes the predominantly middle class belief in education for its own sake. The ambitions of many, especially working class girls, are more immediate and practical. They almost certainly hope to be wives and mothers at quite a young age, and look forward to working predominantly in offices, shops and factories, and some in teaching, nursing and similar work. The paradox of trying to make school seem less irrelevant is that this seems to involve doing things that relate more obviously to their lives, like perhaps cookery, needlework and baby-care, as advocated by so many official reports since education began. Yet it is this aspect of their futures that needs to change. The association of girls' education with their domestic roles has been consistently voiced in official reports, while it is simultaneously being modified by the accompanying decrease in household skills brought about by the development of time-saving products and cheaper mass-produced clothing. In a similar way, the teaching of typing and shorthand in school led several girls to express their opinion on the usefulness of these classes, but it also meant that they were already conceptually confined within the four walls of an office.

In schools today, domestic science has lost much of its intrinsic appeal for girls while academic studies still appear too abstract and arduous. Doing community work and helping with children and playgroups through school is enjoyable and rewarding, but still confirms girls in the traditional servicing and maternal roles. The growing level of social and community studies teaching could help to widen horizons by giving girls the concepts and context in which to examine their own position, but implies no necessary critique. The teaching of 'women's studies' has much potential, but is not yet available in many schools. This specific-ally involves looking (critically) at women's position and could have great consciousness-raising value, although even then it is often too late: girls have already got their ideas sorted out, and questioning these or altering them does not appeal.

Many girls consciously object to the way that school treats them like children until perhaps the magic status of the sixth form, if they stay that long. They are often very mature by the age of fifteen or sixteen and may be already taking responsibility for certain jobs inside and outside home. They are allowed to wear adult clothes, many are physically able to bear children, yet the discipline demanded by the school institution allows no exceptions to its rules. Adolescence is a very 'marginal' time, when girls and boys can gain adult status through going to work, while others of the same age suffer the non-status of schoolchildren. One girl expressed this specifically as her reason for wanting to leave school:

It's the general responsibility. You're treated more as a grown-up really. If you say you're at school they expect you to come in short ankle socks still, pleated skirt down to the knee, school blazer, satchel and everything else. I go around to a job after school, in a sweet shop. The woman who owns it, she is very good to me you know, she treats me like a friend.

But not everyone was keen to leave school. Some wanted to stay on for several years to obtain qualifications and emphasized 'the importance of a good education'. Others were nervous and frightened of leaving the familiarity and protection of school life. Those who wanted more education did not necessarily enjoy school, but those who doubted their ability to cope with independence emphasized the enjoyment of school and the importance of their friends.

I feel that I'm not ready to leave and rely on myself for all my needs.

All my friends are at school. I am shy and don't make friends easily.

I enjoy school. School sort of protects me. I don't like being out there in the world, trying to find your own way.

NO LOOKING BACK

The ideologies that girls take on and hold during the formative and uncertain years of adolescence have a crucial effect on how and where they direct their energies and enthusiasm, and help to determine the roles they will find most appropriate. Although such ideas, attitudes and values should not be isolated from the surrounding economic and social structures, and it should not be assumed that change in these has radical effects on either girls' behaviour or the structures themselves, they should not be neglected or dismissed as incidental and unimportant.

The alternatives faced by girls at school may seem fairly straightforward at first, and based on their measured performance there. If they do well they stay on for the qualifications that will provide a better job or entrance to college or university. If they don't do well, they begin thinking about leaving, getting a job, earning money and developing socially. If on the other hand they are not very good but they and their parents have high aspirations, they will struggle on to get through the necessary examinations.

The implications of this stretch much wider, however, and the way that girls see themselves and their abilities determines their range of job opportunities and also combines to temper many of their views on for instance the substance and value of working and having careers, getting married and setting up a home. Their future intentions build on these sorts of foundations, interacting with what they have learnt and feel about 'femininity' and female role. Today all kinds of ideas about women's position are presented and school cannot be accused of putting forward a totally biased picture. Successful women are in evidence and equality is becoming a commonplace word. But it takes more than passive demonstration of this to counter the strength of traditional beliefs which are more acceptably reinforced. Adoption of self-appropriate ideology rests on deeper sources, and unless girls belong to the minority (mainly middle class) that move upwards into higher education, they tend to fall back on the familiar expectations of feminine roles.

Every girl (or boy) has a unique view of the world and life, and usually shares common goals and values with friends. This is formed out of their 'informal' education: for instance through their own experiences, family, friends, the media, and the teachings of the law and church; and the 'formal' education of school. (Analogous to the 'formal' and 'informal' ideologies discussed in chapter 2.) As Chanan and Gilchrist put it:

> From these elements each individual fashions the store of behaviour models, moral and aesthetic touchstones, criteria of action and reference points of meaning that he carries round in his head. These are not passively ingested, and are not fixed once and for all, but are creatively synthesized, and the synthesis is either recharged or revised at each encounter with new works of art or entertainment, other people's values, public customs, laws and institutions.[3]

Most girls retain a strong hold on many of the traditional ideas about womanhood and this is not surprising. It reflects a depth of internalization of 'femininity', lack of confidence about change, uncritical acceptance of the ways things are, and a lack of viable alternatives, rather than simply the effects of social conditioning.

Even where girls recognize and understand their position and its limitations and discriminations, it is hard to conceive of realistic ways to change this. Girls have seldom been allowed much experience outside home and school, and have read relatively little that deals comprehensively with aspects of their own lives. They see many of their relatives and friends doing jobs from which they seem to gain minimal enjoyment. It therefore makes sense to make their priorities love, marriage, husbands, children, jobs and careers, more or less in that order.

Their feelings and views affect areas of decision in their lives already circumscribed by factors like sex and class. They consider and arrange opinions subjectively and objectively, in ways which do not necessarily coincide. These are weighed up with personal needs, self-image and actual school performance to set in motion the motivations that can have irreversible consequences. Girls are aware of the value of academic achievement but see this still as more to do with boys and men, whose relative non-conformity and irresponsibility does not seem to prevent them from gaining the higher positions. It becomes easy for girls to acknowledge the objective worth of scholarship while excusing themselves for not being 'that sort of person'.

Many girls' lives follow a similar pattern – boredom with school, early leaving into a local job that has marginal interest, finding a steady boyfriend, saving up to marry, settling down and having a family. Marriage and home-making appear as a meaningful distraction or welcome release for those with boring jobs or those who have no intention of making work a central part of their lives, Girls' needs and feelings about this form part of an evolving self-identity. This is still malleable and open to change, but the consequences of choices made at this stage are often irreversible. Once technical or academic courses have been rejected it is very hard to pick them up again. Women who have left education a long way behind them while pursuing family roles often realize the vacuum when their children have grown, but their lack of qualifications and training makes only mundane work available. The paucity and narrowness of re-training schemes for women still leaves most with the typical range of lower level employment.

School does not give equal opportunities to girls and boys whatever (formal) egalitarian ideology it may seem to represent. The way forward is far more clear-cut for boys who still face a life of continuous working. Whatever level of job they are steered towards, they look unambivalently towards a working future. Girls, however, are still schooled with the marriage market in mind, although this may not be acknowledged consciously. This inevitability in their lives provides as much excuse within the school, as for girls themselves, for their ultimate under-achievement. The belief that a girl finds her deepest and truest satisfaction in a husband and children is very prevalent (and many of the Ealing girls endorsed this), despite discussions about sexual equality and women's increasing presence in the work-force. It shows the power of and the market for the romanticism portrayed in magazines, but also shows an investment in the care and needs of people that is perfectly understandable in the light of women's working history and their alternatives.

In the present circumstances, in which housework and child-care are not social activities, it is practically impossible for women simultaneously to care for children and participate fully at work or be politically active. This difficulty is evident to those within the Women's Movement itself, and is even more insurmountable for most women outside the Movement, who may not have yet conceived of even the possibility of alternatives. It is not necessary that any direct or conscious conflict should be felt by girls between the idea of marriage and its accompaniments, and that of achieving a qualified position or career. It is more reasonable to suppose that the expectations of marriage serve to cast an intrusive shadow over the continuity of their views of the future and make long-term planning a more difficult commitment to make.

Energy spent in scholarly pursuits generally means some deferment of social activities, while an active social life precludes time spent in studying. Possibly an effective compromise by some girls is to see social goals as forms of achievement. It is easier and safer – the competition for getting a husband does not involve much real work although it may present its own share of worries and fears. Being a housewife and mother does not demand the passing of examinations. This is not failure but success in the terms of our old-style 'femininity', and bringing up children involves skills in its own right. There is no need to risk a venture into higher or more unusual aspirations unless you are obviously bright at school or you and your parents are intent on your reaching a certain career or level of education.

If there seems to be an over-emphasis here on the needs and problems of educational progress, it is because many of the advantages that school has to offer have been largely denied to working class girls. Social and domestic roles have consequently overshadowed the possibility of other interests and occupations and have increasingly narrowed their lives. Although educational reforms alone cannot be effective in changing the inequalities on which the economic system still depends, changes in upbringing and the nature of girls' education could widen their interests and the perceived scope of their lives. They could learn to understand and criticize society and gain the skills, knowledge and self-confidence that raises consciousness. The demands being made by higher educated women inside and outside the Women's Movement today are making it harder to discriminate openly against women, but real change can only begin if links are made between women struggling at every level.

'CAREER GIRLS'

Marrying and having children and leading a working life are no longer assumed to be incompatible, although in practical terms the facilities for combining these have shown little change. Girls no longer choose one or the other, but many have decided to add a career to their domestic role in life. Where marriage is accepted very much as the primary aim, girls still have to work for the money necessary to support themselves; and where a career is confidently chosen, marriage is usually also a definite part of the future although it may seem vague and further away. The experiences of those for whom marriage has always loomed like a large heart on the horizon, and especially those who have not progressed at school, need not include any clash of interests. The way forward is self-apparent, and the prospect of investing time and effort in a specific vocation can be implicitly dismissed.

Since everyone has to get a job when they leave school, many girls now see it as something more than a time-filler before marriage. They recognize the need to work after getting married, and when their children are old enough to be left, and not necessarily just for the money. Most stop short however, at wanting to do anything carrying the deep commitment they see as characterizing a 'full-time career'. For this requires a special type of woman, with attributes that they see lacking in themselves. They erect a barrier between the capabilities of this imaginary person and themselves, despite the relatively interchangeable use of the terms 'job' and 'career' in schools today. Girls acknowledge the dichotomy between marriage, home-making and a 'full-time career' which has its roots buried in prejudiced attitudes and the very real lack of facilities for women to work successfully outside the home. Many effect a solution in which they express their intention to take their chosen job more seriously.

Some of the Ealing girls had definite ideas on girls who committed themselves to a career:

A person who does do full-time and doesn't have any breaks at all I don't think should have any children anyway as it would interfere with her career. I think people who do go in for full-time like that don't stop for anybody. The whole of their life is round their job.

Well, if they are career-minded, or they don't want to get married for a couple of years, they're welcome to have a career. It's a bit hard to combine a career and marriage – for some it may be all right, but for others it would be hard work. Depends what sort of career – if it's one where you travel around it's a bit hard.

[Career girls are] . . . girls who don't want to get married – well they do, but they want to get married at a later age – about thirty – after they've done their job and that, got set up in it – not like me.

I think men should [have careers]. If they [girls] want to they can, but I think it suits men really. Once men start out on something, I suppose they go ahead, but women they always change their minds, and never do good in full-time careers really.

But not all girls accept this kind of thinking so easily –

Well, [women's] brains are just as good as a fella's. They're just as intelligent and that. Just because they're supposed to be weaker than men doesn't mean that they are. Not every girl will get married, and even if she does get married, she'll have something to fall back on, and if she takes a career for a few years she can do it after she's had her children. When she's about thirty-five to forty she's got nothing. She can always take a refresher course and go back to work . . .

Girls and women have been forced and accustomed to embrace a fundamentally ambivalent position. Many have drawn a lot of satisfaction and enjoyment out of activities specific to their 'domestic' role as women, while these are generally assumed by society to be inferior to the activities of men. They are attracted to a role that stands in second place. It is a double-bind situation: if girls go after what society deems most important, succeeding financially and academically in a career, then they may lose in 'femininity'; while if they concentrate on their 'proper' role, it is inherently of lower economic and ideological status. However fervently women's role in motherhood may be extolled, especially at times when the 'quality' and future of the nation has seemed to be threatened, this has never been reflected in women's treatment and position in society.

Marriage is something that most girls include somewhere in their future regardless of their opinions about jobs and careers. Motherhood is assumed to go with marriage and adds to the reluctance that many have felt towards the commitment they see involved in pursuing a career. Most of the Ealing girls hoped to marry, many before they were twenty years of age, and almost all by the age of twenty-five. They probably do not differ significantly in these hopes from an equivalent group of girls drawn from more middle class backgrounds, but as they grow older and their opportunities grow narrower, early marriage and having children appears increasingly more meaningful than further study or work.

At school, some girls are already experiencing a clash between studying and having a good time and do not want to regulate their social lives according to homework. Boys, love and romance have been part of their thoughts and conversations, if not their activities, for several years already. Meeting and keeping boy-friends is an important and time-consuming business, and it takes a strong commitment to studying, or very strict parents, to keep a socially active girl's mind on work. One fourteen-year-old who was hoping to leave school in the near future felt this very strong-ly.

> Now they leave [taking O-levels] too late. They leave it till the fifth year and by then most girls want to leave, and the boys. A few of my friends, not all, want to leave. Most of them go out with boys and I think it's too much if you have all the homework to do for school and be socially-minded at the same time. I don't do my homework – just go out.

SCHOOL PERFORMANCE

In spite of so many girls' enthusiasm to get out of school, there is plenty of evidence to show that in fact they are more successful than boys at primary school and through much of secondary school.[4] At pre-primary ages, tests of general intelligence show girls scoring higher than boys; and in reading, writing, English and spelling at primary school, the average 11-year-old girl beats the equivalent boy.[5] She excels in the whole area of verbal ability, speaking and reading earlier, and with greater articulation. Although she does retain some measure of superiority over boys in these skills at secondary school, she does tend to fall behind in other subjects. For instance, in areas needing arithmetical or numerical reasoning boys have already moved ahead, and have usually attained a better level of analytical ability. They have a greater interest and capacity for areas needing an objective approach, such as maths, geography and science. But in con-sidering these differences in ability, it should be remembered that there is always a considerable overlap between boys and girls and the range of differences within a sex can easily be as great as the differences between them.[6]

Girls achieve better results and do better in examinations than boys throughout much of their school life. However, there is an inconsistent relationship between their actual intellectual abilities and performance before leaving school, and their subsequent employment. This means that while girls of poorer intelligence go on to achieve accordingly, this is not necessarily the case for girls of higher intelligence. Whatever their abilities, girls are found in general office-work, shop-work and other occupations with few prospects, as well as being full-time housewives and mothers. Therefore, at some point during their adolescence, girls begin to *under-achieve* in relation to their real capacities. This is often around the onset of puberty, and coincides with the time when both boys and girls are becoming increasingly aware of their sexuality and their future adult roles. For boys, this includes an emphasis on intellectual and practical achievements, and on various strengths of physique and character. For girls, conformity is more appropriate, and achievement may be translated into the context of appearance, social life and popularity. School pressures become ineffective when set against social pressures.

Fear of Failure: Fear of Success

Girls are in an ambivalent and contradictory position. On one level, there is pressure to succeed academically, which is rewarded by school, parents, and the self-satisfaction of doing this. At this level, boys and girls alike may be hindered by the fear of failing, which involves a lack of self-confidence and a reluctance even to try for success. In all the vast literature that has accumulated about 'achievement motivation' in our competitive society, it is the effects of 'fear of failure' that have frequently been emphasized.

For girls the situation is more complex, and girls are often omitted from achievement motivation studies because they do not yield consistent and meaningful results and therefore 'mess up the model'! The increased awareness of feminine role stereotypes particularly those promoted by the media fosters the belief that it is not desirable that girls should be as clever as boys. This implies that 'over-achievement' involves losing an important ingredient of 'femininity'. The majority of the Ealing girls agreed that boys do not like girls to do better than them in school-work.

The implication is therefore – if you want to attract boys, don't start by showing how clever you are.

This is not to suggest that a girl's role demands that she be stupid, but she must modify her success in relation to that of the boys (and sometimes girls) with whom she wishes to be popular. She should ideally confine her 'success' to acceptable 'feminine' pursuits which don't involve male competition. In American society, Margaret Mead noted that: '. . . throughout her education and her development of vocational expectance, the girl is faced with the dilemma that she must display enough of her abilities to be considered successful, but not too successful . . .'[7] Girls may therefore experience a 'fear of success' which hinders their performance, and interacts with the reinforcing belief that academic success is unimportant for a girl anyway.

Competition is the important underlying factor. Few men like to compete with, or be beaten by a woman. Since her status is inferior, it reflects badly on the men beneath her. There are areas in which girls and women can succeed, indeed excel, but these are the ones in which few men even bother to compete – or if they do it is for the top positions. These are of course subjects related to cookery, needlework and child-care, in which female success will be ultimately put to male advantage at home. Competition is a disguised form of aggression, and society disapproves of aggressive women. A girl who both competes and succeeds in a male-dominated area, is often not regarded as a 'normal' woman. Both girls and boys hold their own stereotypes of the successful 'career woman', who frequently appears as a domineering and sexually unattractive battle-axe, especially if she commands a directing position over men. Even at a lower level of achievement, a working class girl who does well academically may find it hard to draw her male friends from the boys that she intellectually left behind.

In real life there is less antagonism between men and women at work than is actually feared, but this is often because the competition is made less direct by some means, or because, like the girl apprentice featured in the B.B.C.'s *Women and Work* programme, she loses her female identity in the eyes of her male companions and becomes 'one of the lads'. But the fear still persists, especially among those girls and women who have succeeded against men and are concerned not to appear 'un-feminine'. It is significant that men denigrate the sexuality of women who are above them; if they can seduce them, this is one way of stripping their power, and finding that they are 'only women after all'.

Interesting research has been carried out into women's 'fear of success' in America. One study[8] involved first-year male and female college students in writing a story about a mythical student who came top of a medical school class. For the girls, the principal figure was a woman, and for the male students it was a man. The results showed that almost all the men (90 per cent) completely accepted their hero's success, but most of the girls' stories (65 per cent) tried to explain away their heroine's achievement. They either described her fear of being socially rejected and possibly losing friends of both sexes, or they expressed her anxiety and doubts about her femininity and normality; or they tried to deny the validity of the situation by finding some excuse for her being at the top. This is an example of one story.

Anne is an acne-faced bookworm. She runs to the bulletin board and finds she's at the top. As usual she smarts off. A chorus of groans is the rest of the class's reply . . . She studies twelve hours a day, and lives at home to save money. 'Well, it certainly paid off. All the Friday and Saturday nights without dates, fun – I'll be the best woman doctor alive.' And yet a twinge of sadness comes thru – she wonders what she really has . . .

Since girls are brought up to be less competitive, their attitudes towards success are more likely to be mixed with doubts and lack of confidence. Studies have indicated that girls are indeed pessimistic about intellectual success. For instance six- to nine-year-old girls in one study showed little self-confidence, and expected to fail in situations where boys expected to succeed. They also took the blame for failures while boys tended to project blame on to something else.[9] Another study found that girls preferred to return and repeat a task that they had already done successfully, while boys preferred to move on to a new one.[10] In my own research, girls were very willing to accept responsibility for intellectual failure, while success was seen to depend more on chance or the whims of others.

School success can therefore be more easily and consistently pursued by those girls who are less concerned about testing and maintaining all aspects of the feminine stereotype. It is also an advantage to be supported and encouraged by family and friends. Working class girls are therefore more likely to feel the pressures towards 'feminine role' earlier because they and their families are usually less orientated towards achieving high academic goals. Their 'under-achievement' is consistent too with the nature of the most popular and available jobs which frequently require minimal qualifications and make it appear unnecessary to linger on at school. Girls' lower level of schooling, segregated education and sex-role learning interact with this to place them in the ranks of the less skilled workers. Middle-class girls who continue their education do not escape these pressures, but they may be postponed until they reach the apparent equality of the lower levels of middle-class occupations. Moving out of these positions may then prove more difficult.

Upbringing, Personality and Ability

It is necessary to look at the relationship between upbringing and personality in order to discover more about the origins of 'under-achievement' in girls. It has already been noted that the traditional feminine personality presents characteristics ill-suited to making progress in a world where competitiveness, assertiveness and independence are the axioms of success. The early experiences of the majority of girls denies the development of such qualities and adds a psychological block to the existing obstacles. The upbringing of boys and girls reflects the different goals that are assumed for them. A son is brought up to make some impact on his environment, while a daughter is protected from her environment. He is being taught to control and direct, while she becomes malleable and dependent.

I must once more emphasize that my argument should not be interpreted as advocating that girls develop the more destructive and inhibiting aspects of masculinity, or that their aim should be to emulate and compete with men, but as declaring that they should be encouraged to develop the autonomy, confidence, independence and assertiveness that would increase understanding and facilitate conditions in which they might change their own position.

A lot of differentiation by sex has already occurred within the family long before children begin to demonstrate their different abilities at school. Boys for instance are already more independent and adventurous, while girls are restricted, protected and given little chance to 'stand on their own feet'. A mother's behaviour is very important here – whether or not she closely supervises her daughter, what expectations she expresses for her, and how much she criticizes or praises her successes and failures. A girl is seldom given the opportunity to develop, test and assess her abilities for herself, and consequently she often under-estimates herself and is unconfident of doing things alone. She obtains her sense of identity through relationships rather than actions and becomes dependent on the approval of other people for her self-esteem. If she has been mainly disciplined by withdrawal of love as girls often are, she may become even more dependent on gaining affection, an attitude of mind which promotes passivity and conformity.

This treatment of girls is very important since a relationship is thought to exist between intellectual ability and independence. A key part of this ability concerns analytic thinking: the capacity to perceive problems in more global terms, to apply general principles to them, and to use analysis and reasoning to solve them. This is particularly relevant in science and related fields. Several psychologists have suggested that early independence and mastery-training is the most important characteristic in the development of this ability: which refers to whether and when children are encouraged to use initiative, take responsibility and solve problems for themselves instead of relying on others. Witkin[11] for instance found that mothers of 'analytic children' had encouraged them in initiative while those of 'non-analytic children' had encouraged dependence and discouraged self-assertion. The upbringing of many girls obviously militates against this, and since independence and mastery training also seem to have some influence on children's orientation towards achievement, girls are once again at a disadvantage.[12]

The effects of parental support and encouragement also play their part. Boys do better when their father encourages them, and their mother gives them emotional support (although this need not be the only model). Girls too, need some pressure, encouragement and support. It has been shown that primary school children's attitudes to school-work and their performance improved when parents showed a high degree of interest and encouragement. Working class children were more positively affected by encouragement, while parents' 'interest in school-work' benefited children of all social classes and especially girls.[13] Therefore girls may be held back by the affectionate protection of their parents if it is given in the absence of any serious inspiration to do things for themselves.

According to most of the Ealing girls, their parents had adopted a passive supporting attitude in which they wanted for their daughters whatever the girls wanted for themselves. In several cases where parents gave more explicit encouragement, girls did have significantly higher job aspirations. For example, one girl had parents who were both teachers and who wanted her to go to university, and she herself wanted eventually to do some kind of historical research. Another who wanted to become a doctor or a radiologist said that her parents 'wanted for me what they never had'. Interest and encouragement clearly not only varies by sex, but also by class, and the greater value and investment placed in education by the middle class is especially beneficial in the ways that it is transformed into help and interest.

Other factors prejudice girls' ultimate success from the start. One of these is the implicit conflict between the demands of schooling and those of the adult feminine role. For girls, the pursuit of 'femininity' leads to a multitude of distractions, such as attending to physical appearance, fashion, boyfriends, and the sentimentalization of love-stories and romance.* This leads to

* In an American national survey of adolescents in 1966, it was found that 65 per cent of boys compared to 21 per cent of girls worried most about achievement, 16 per cent of boys and 44 per cent of girls worried most about acceptance by others, and 19 per cent of boys and 62 per per cent of girls worried most about personal characteristics.[14]

apathy and lack of interest in anything to do with studying and school and influences the subsequent nature of their life and work. One girl reflected on this just before she left school to be an office junior – 'Well, I've never been interested in school and therefore I've never bothered. Well, I have, but even when I do I don't seem to get anywhere. I used to say that I wasn't interested, and it made me feel that I wasn't. I probably could have been interested in more things if I'd tried.'

SCHOOL AND THE 'HIDDEN CURRICULUM'

School reinforces what children have learnt about sex roles in the family, through the media, and in everyday experiences outside the home. Children find for instance that boys and girls are treated differently, boys' activities have higher status than girls', and that boisterous aggressive behaviour is less tolerated for girls. Inside school these sorts of sex inequalities and differences are perpetuated, together with those of class and race. Like a self-fulfilling prophesy, the various 'labels' that children fall under, like female, working class and black, the particular schools they attend, and the streams to which they are allocated all channel them in certain directions, often downwards towards low-level jobs.

The main function of school is ostensibly to educate and pass on knowledge, but it has other important social functions which include the suppression of unacceptable social behaviour, and an emphasis on the social importance of control and subordination – the acceptance of discipline. The exaggeration of this aspect of school can extinguish autonomy, confidence and curiosity in its pupils, many of whom become skilled at negotiating or flouting the authority structures.* Other pupils may react by tolerating

---

*In certain areas of London and other big cities, such as Liverpool, schools struggle to control boys and girls who fight, swear and taunt and reject everything associated with the school structure. Here, the girls concerned may be less physically aggressive than the boys, but are equally non-conforming. Often their social and family situations have alienated them to such an extent that they are unaffected by any threats or sanctions at school.

discipline as a necessary evil or accepting it as correct and desirable.

Schools are fairly effective in 'domesticating' and pacifying the 'masses', but the further assumption often made that the dominant values of society are passed on through teachers is an over-simplification. It would be hard to find consistency in values either between individuals or contained in how and what they teach. The need for acceptance of authority, discipline and subordination is certainly demonstrated if not learnt, but adoption of social values is not a straightforward process. It comes through family and individual experience, and values may coincide with and be influenced by those emerging from particular teachers and the content of their subjects. But as I emphasized earlier, there is often a gap between public acceptance of attitudes and values, such as the importance of education, and the consequences in terms of behaviour, which in this case would mean staying at school to get the maximum education.

There is an implicit contradiction between institutional conformity and the idea of 'free' intellectual creativity. The 'right' answer and good behaviour become the important criteria for success. Form rather than content becomes the primary consideration. Illich[15] has emphasized this in his theory of the 'hidden curriculum' and has shown how the structure of schools can have as much influence as the knowledge taught in them.

The early social experiences and training of girls predisposes them to accept the school's demands for conformity. Their increasing awareness that feminine status is lower may add to this process. Kohlberg[16] says the girls reach a 'good girl' stage earlier in their development than boys reach the equivalent, and stay there longer. He suggests they have to distinguish between 'prestige of goodness' and 'prestige of power' in sex role learning, and since little power is allocated to women, the only alternative is to be a 'good girl'. This would also link up with the studies of aggression which found girls performing more 'pro-social' acts.[17] Therefore the 'domestication' that schools try to impose on their pupils is more effective on girls and more important in its implications for their later roles.

Class Consequences at School

There are many ways in which it is easier for middle class girls to concentrate on studying and achievements at school (although similar conflicts between work and 'femininity' may be faced later if they move on into the predominantly 'male' arena of further and higher education). Social and educational aspirations are very much part of middle class life. The continuing inequalities of the education system mean that although all parents want 'the best' for their daughters, some 'bests' will be better and more accessible than others, and it is more likely to be the middle class who can provide most for their children. They have often benefited from education themselves, and give helpful interest and support, as well as better and quieter facilities for studying.

Working class parents seldom have the time or the energy to involve themselves deeply in their daughter's work and progress, and usually have less faith in the usefulness of a long academic training. They often adopt the verbally supportive but passive attitude of 'it's up to you what you do, as long as you end up in something respectable'. Also they may combine a relatively limited knowledge of available jobs and careers with a narrow view of what is more suitable. It is notable that the class system of our society allocates more worth to those with academic qualifications, whatever socially 'useless' work they do, and implicitly under-values and downgrades less 'brainy' manual work.

Level of school performance is very important, since success will contribute towards interest and enthusiasm in subjects, as well as increasing expectations that affect performance and attitudes towards studying. If in the early years of school a girl does not do well, and is placed in the lower forms, she defines and labels herself as not being intelligent, and absorbs and reflects her teachers' limited expectations of her. Working class girls (and boys) and immigrant children are often placed in this position, and become well aware of their status in the school. The apathy and lack of interest characterizing many third and fourth form girls shows that they have understood only too well that academic interests are not for them and often directly clash with social pursuits, forcing them to do work for which they can see little relevance.

Looking around her, a working class girl will see a tradition of early marriage and early child-bearing. Men will be involved mainly in some type of skilled work, while women work in offices, shops and factories, or full-time at home. It is very easy to fall in with this tradition. The schools themselves help to perpetuate the pattern. They increase the alienation felt by their pupils by upholding middle class values and couching ideas in middle class language. Few teachers can be identified with as working class, and many subjects, like history and English, tell a predominantly middle class story. There are few explicit models to show working class children, and especially girls, that there is any point in going after individual or intellectual achievements.

The gulf between middle class and working class children at school is linked to the difference between education inside and outside school, i.e. 'formal' or 'informal' education. School institutionalism tends to ignore the autonomous thinking and tastes of its pupils, suppressing their interests and current images of the world and attempting to impose another approved model. Connections are rarely made between the formal areas of culture that have to be learnt and the informal knowledge about life that is built up and reassimilated every day.[18] Language emphasizes this separation, and the work done by Bernstein, which is important in its exploration of this area, has also served to reinforce stereotyped ideas about working class intellectual inferiority. Middle class language and culture is still regarded as superior and the working class social background is seen as culturally deprived – as needing compensation and change. This attitude rejects working class language and expression merely because it does not meet the stringent requirements of neatness, grammatical correctness and clarity with which most teachers, examiners and other judges of ability are obsessed. It is in fact questionable whether middle class modes of expression are superior.[19]

Schools only respond to certain acceptable attitudes and to pupils who are thought to be suitable for formal education. They are seldom concerned to establish common reference points with pupils and therefore a large number of children fail to relate their own everyday preoccupations to the relevant areas of formal knowledge. School then seems to have nothing to offer them and although the capacity for interest and the ability are often present, the incentive to use any part of this education is missing.

Girls, and more especially those from working class backgrounds, are seen and see themselves primarily as aspiring girlfriends, wives and mothers, and then as aspiring typists, secretaries, nurses, teachers and so on.

One girl was aware of the perpetuation of attitudes and ideas: 'It's the mother and father's position in life that helps what the child thinks, the way they act at home – and if they're quite well-off, they have different views than what the poorer people have. It all depends how children are brought up – most children get the same sort of views as their parents.'

The 'Femininity' of Primary School

Due to their close associations with caring for children most primary school teachers are women. Their job usually involves controlling and teaching a large number of children because of over-crowding and under-staffing. Inevitably they demand obedience, silence, passivity and conformity from their pupils – all features of traditional female behaviour. For boys and girls alike, their primary school thus confronts them with an almost totally 'feminine' environment – not only through the teachers, but also through the type of behaviour that is being enforced. Differentiation within the family contributes to the different reactions of boys and girls to this situation. Girls find that the school's demands coincide with the way they are expected to behave at home, while boys experience a conflict between the two environments. In fact, the primary school values directly contradict the independent assertiveness that parents usually try to encourage in their sons. Although teachers may obtain some obedience and conformity from boys, it is likely that they see primary school as being a more appropriate environment for girls.* As a result boys

*One study suggested that both boys and girls label objects in the classroom like blackboard, book, desk etc. 'feminine', rather than 'masculine' or 'neuter'.[20]

have less incentive to work hard, and become more difficult to control. This may partly explain why girls do better at primary school than boys.

There is a lot of evidence to suggest that primary school teachers tend to expect boys to be more difficult and unresponsive than girls. They see them as less hard-working, less able to concentrate and less amenable to discipline.[21] Boys often rebel against the enforced 'passivity' of school but this need not put them at a disadvantage, on the contrary, it has been suggested that teachers spend more time interacting with troublesome boys, giving them both disapproval and encouragement.[22] It is claimed that this helps boys in their approach to learning, but if this were true, a lot more working class boys in lower forms would succeed than do at present. It is more likely that the advantages of such pupil–teacher interaction work in conjunction with other forces, such as class.

J. W. B. Douglas has suggested that the situation could be changed if there were more men teachers in primary schools, but this still would not alter the 'feminine' characteristics that are deemed necessary to maintain school discipline. Nor would it necessarily make boys behave better in the classroom. It is true that men are identified as figures of authority, much like fathers in the home, and this image is often endorsed by the figure of the headmaster who rules over a primary school largely staffed by women. But there are many other models that have already shown children their appropriate roles and behaviour. At home, for instance, the noisy aggression and naughtiness of boys is more often overlooked as part of their 'nature'. This is reinforced by literature such as children's reading primers and stories in which the same sort of behaviour in girls is absent or discouraged. The sex-differentiating process begins early and most children will already have started conforming to its tenets before they enter primary school, and are therefore unlikely to be helped significantly by a different male–female teacher situation.

For girls, there is less conflict. The characteristics which have led to reward at home gain even more implicit approval in the classroom. In fact the quietness, obedience and passivity of girls is often held up as a mark of their greater maturity and responsibility. It is ironic that these same attributes are later used to demonstrate inferiority! Nor are these characteristics likely to encourage the independence associated with intellectual curiosity or analytical problem-solving. Girls and boys alike also absorb the idea of a hierarchy that places men in the top positions from which they issue directives and make important decisions. Girls get on well at primary school. They rate high according to its 'feminine' values and rules, and achieve well. But they are already beginning to realize more about their present and future roles through its teaching.

A Secondary Education

The span of years at secondary school covers a time of important events and crucial decisions. The advent of puberty and increasing maturity begin to emphasize the distracting presence of sexuality. The adult world holds out a wealth of temptations but reproves those who respond to them too quickly. As 'adolescents' schoolchildren are in a situation characterized by an uncertain and ambivalent status. Friends and interests are quickly made and lost. Some school subjects are selected and others dropped, and the choice of alternatives becomes narrower. Decisions are made about further education and jobs, and working futures come into clearer focus. Social activities start to proliferate and every boy-friend is a potential husband. Attitudes, beliefs and values settle into an appropriate pattern, out of which emerge the contours of a life-style.

The secondary school plays a part in instilling values during this process of person-formation. Through the knowledge they are taught, and the value-judgements which accompany it, and through implicit expectations of class and sex, children's choices are nudged in pre-determined directions. This is illustrated by the range of subjects open to boys and girls. There has already been some divergence at primary school where girls do needlework and boys do drawing or woodwork if there are facilities, and games are clearly segregated. At secondary school the differences become wider and deeper. Subjects can be broadly classified into 'girls' subjects' and 'boys' subjects'. 'Girls' subjects' include the 'arts', and, more exclusively, cookery, needlework, typing and commerce. 'Boys' subjects' are scientific and technical, involving mathematical problem-solving and analysis, as well as the practical skills of woodwork and metalwork. Both boys and girls tend to avoid those subjects which are the more exclusive domain of the other sex, but while girls often reject maths and science because they see them as being too difficult and technical for them to understand,* boys reject domestic subjects as simply irrelevant for them. However, boys do take and succeed in arts subjects, which implies that they are capable of working at anything, while girls are viewed as being relatively incapable of succeeding in 'boys' subjects', especially the exclusive ones like metalwork and engineering. Their success at science, although increasing from year to year, according to the figures of passes at O-level and A-level, impinges little on either the sexual division of scientific labour or the conventional stereotype.

It is not surprising that many girls have relatively little interest in or understanding of scientific or technical subjects. Their lack of experience of these at home, the absence in their characters of the independence associated with analytical abilities, and the apparent non-scientific nature of women's adult role contributes to this. Technical toys have always been reserved for boys, and when something is constructed or repaired at home, it is boys who are taken aside to be taught, rather than girls. This exclusive knowledge has made women dependent on men inside as well as outside the home. Most of the gadgets that women use in everyday domestic life are put together and break down on fairly elementary scientific principles. Yet few women know what these are, or how to use them to repair or improve things. Science remains an abstract mystery, full of apparatus and experiments peculiar to a school laboratory, and apparently meaningless to girls' future lives at work or at home.

The problem lies in neutralizing the 'masculine' or 'feminine' labels. It is no use, for instance, trying to make girls interested in science merely by showing its relevance to housework. This only

---

* The influence of culture on this attitude is indicated by the variation which exists between different nations in the extent to which girls participate in science and mathematics courses.

reinforces the old stereotypes and keeps girls firmly embedded in the domestic sphere. Similarly useless is the suggestion made to increase girls' interest in chemistry by showing them how to make cosmetics. Although it might work to a certain extent, it could have the additional effect of causing the subject to be divided into girls' science and boys' science.* It is necessary to encourage girls and boys to do all subjects right from the early years, when assumptions about sex and role are already forming.

It is also necessary to change the present sex-discriminating occupational structure. Making it possible for girls and boys to study all subjects is of no use unless the jobs that the subjects relate to are seen to be accessible, suitable and acceptable for either sex. If this condition is not fulfilled the exclusion and inequalities will continue but with curriculum restrictions removed, and the reasons for boys' and girls' continuing rejection of the other sex's more exclusive subjects will provide even more justification for the assumption of 'natural' aptitudes and abilities.

The school curriculum often deprives girls and boys of their freedom of choice by assuming that they will not want to study certain subjects, and by arranging the timetable on the basis of those assumptions.†

Our timetable was worked so that if you did art, you couldn't do technical drawing, or woodwork or anything. No girls done woodwork. I wanted to do art, so I couldn't do technical drawing – I couldn't do both.

We did a lot of cookery and needlework at school. No technical drawing, no science subjects except biology. You never had a chance to do chemistry or anything until the fifth year – but everyone left in the fourth year anyway.

> Reflections by two further education students.

The situation has improved slightly and there are now more

* It has been shown that when maths problems are re-worded to include home-making terms, girls' scores improve, even though the abstract reasoning required for the solution remains the same.[23]

† One survey of 587 mixed schools discovered that 50 per cent had some subjects only open for boys, and 49 per cent had subjects exclusive to girls.[24]

opportunities for girls to take technical subjects. But care has still to be taken to ensure that they are given the same opportunity as boys to develop skills. For example, in subjects demanding manual dexterity boys tend to be given access to the more complex tools and are consequently enabled to produce more advanced pieces of work than girls in the same class. A double-standard is then created whereby girls are praised for the obviously less sophisticated objects they manage to produce.

It is therefore necessary to change the attitudes of teachers and pupils to 'exclusive' subjects, and to provide opportunities for both girls and boys to use common skills in the occupational world. Segregation of education has channelled girls into courses leading to devalued and under-paid jobs. False beliefs in ability differences based on sex have blocked many avenues for girls, and in so doing have justified and perpetuated the subsequent economic discrimination. In opening up new areas, however, care must be taken that women are not once again used to fill up the lowest levels.

Other areas of the school curriculum leave much to be desired in terms of their content. History, for example, is basically that of men, written by men. Women's history is barely considered, and although there are now several books available to fill this gap,[25] it will doubtless take some time before these penetrate the schoolroom. English literature may cover the better-known women writers, but often omits discussion of the position of women at the time, and also ignores many lesser-known female authors. Furthermore, in a lot of fictional works, women are portrayed as being passive and ineffectual, and taking action only for personal or destructive reasons. In social science, or social studies, which are increasingly entering the school curriculum, there is more room for discussion of the position and role of women. This may be included within a study of 'The Family', but a conscious effort must be made to prevent such a study from merely describing the current conventions of society. Psychology too has based much of its research and conclusions on basic 'biological' differences between the sexes, and has made the common error of equating 'human' with 'male'.[26]

One ability that is rarely taught in schools is how to be critical.

The rule and word of the teacher is too often accepted wholesale or rejected on principle. It is only the few who move on to higher education who suddenly find that they are expected to have critical opinions of their own about their subject. Many women are now trying to set up courses of 'Women's Studies' in schools and colleges to provide the incentive for girls to make up for some of these gaps in their education, and increase their self-awareness. It would be a great step forward to provide such an arena in which girls could assess their own position, but it should not be seen as an end in itself, isolated as another 'special' subject. It should be seen as a necessary but temporary measure until the general curriculum is revised and the existing segregation and bias are removed.

Teaching the Differences

Every teacher is a former pupil. Every teacher has already been through the process of learning the roles for each sex. Therefore each reflects consciously and unconsciously their own attitudes and expectations in their treatment of their pupils. This has implications for both sex and class. Teachers ultimately expect less from girls than from boys, and less from working class than from middle class children. These expectations are picked up by pupils with devastating effects.

An experiment carried out on elementary school children in America showed that teacher expectations could have a crucial effect on pupil performance.[27] In this experiment a number of teachers were told at the beginning of a school session that certain of their pupils were going to show marked intellectual improvement in the coming year. Unknown to the teachers, these pupils were randomly selected rather than chosen on the basis of their ability. At the end of the year it was found that the children for whom intellectual growth had been predicted had indeed made dramatic gains against their measured I.Q., as compared with a control group of children. Therefore the teachers had successfully passed on their expectations to these children and had probably given them more attention and encouragement. Although such research methods are always open to criticism, the implications of the 'self-fulfilling prophesy' shown here cannot be denied, and the expectations of teachers at any level of education will doubtless have equivalent effects on those being taught.

A survey conducted by the National Institute of Industrial Psychiatrists on the attitudes of female teachers found that in general they considered men to be better in roles of authority, more patient and fair, and capable of generating more respect.[28] These attitudes will doubtless be transmitted in subtle ways in the classroom. This finding is also supported by an exploratory American study in which a short form of the Broverman Sex-Role Stereotype questionnaire[29] was used to assess the sex role ideals of teachers by asking them to use it to describe what an adolescent girl or boy should be like. Over three-quarters of them produced the stereotype for boys and girls, wanting girls for instance to be submissive, dependent, unassertive, emotional and concerned with their appearance. And as in other studies, almost all the items associated with male ideals coincided with those of greatest social desirability.

Some of the Ealing girls talked of ways that they had noticed that their treatment differed from that of boys. Teachers seemed to be more sarcastic to boys, and more respectful to girls. (Boys can 'take it' better.) Girls are expected to be more tidy in their ways and in their work, neater in handwriting and the presentation of material. Boys however could get away with messy books and untidy behaviour. This is a subtle form of restriction of expression, and may develop into an obsession with form rather than content.[30] The Ealing schoolgirls also thought that boys got blamed for things more than girls, as a result of the sex labels that they had been given.

It is around adolescence that girls are struggling to find out what sort of people they are, and what they want to become. They are very tuned in to the things that will bring social approval, and quickly pick up cues from inside and outside school. Whether they accept or reject (as many do) the advice, treatment and curriculum of their teachers they still absorb the form and the sex-differentiated assumptions that these contain.

For girls and boys the secondary school represents a slightly less 'feminine' environment than the primary school, since unless it is single-sex, it usually contains more male teachers. Individual achievements begin to be stressed, and this implicitly contradicts the conformity of behaviour that is still demanded. Such achievement is still largely equated with masculinity however, and girls ride an ambivalent course through an education that could lead them to a dead-end or a high-flown career.

SEGREGATED EDUCATION

The majority of schools today are co-educational and employ men and women teachers, but the issue of mixed versus single-sex schools remains unresolved. Both types have their advantages and their disadvantages and the evidence supporting either is inconsistent. In single-sex girls' schools, for instance, it has been said that girls find it easier to concentrate, without the distraction that boys present. Science is taught by women and is not so blatantly a 'boy's' subject' as it is in co-educational schools where men usually teach the scientific and technical subjects. Women also hold all the positions of authority in contrast to the staff structure found in mixed schools which puts men in the top departmental posts and invariably makes them heads of school, and leaves women in the lower ranks.

However, there are many disadvantages: for instance, all-girls schools are often very insular and protected places, in which girls learn to perform well in their school-work, but are left inadequately equipped to deal with the mixed social world outside. Many girls recognize the artificiality of this environment and want to get out. Also, in spite of the increasing provision of science subjects for girls who wish to study them, the absence of boys leads school heads to assume that it would be irrelevant to provide the facilities for normally male-exclusive technical subjects like woodwork, metalwork and technical drawing. Therefore the opportunity for doing these does not even arise in all-girls schools.

On the other hand it is possible that co-education draws attention to and thereby reinforces the boundaries between the sexes. The continual presence of the opposite sex and of assumptions about the differences between the sexes implied by 'exclusive' subjects, at a time of self-consciousness and need for identity, may contribute towards maintaining the separation of the sexes. Also, the false incompatibility between female sexual attractiveness and intelligence may be emphasized in mixed schools. It has been suggested[31] that co-educational schools are more like boys' schools than a mid-way compromise between girls' and boys' schools. The debate around this issue still carries on, however, and it is not clear whether mixed or single-sex schools are of greater value in releasing girls from sex-stereotyping.

In conclusion, many working class girls find school life boring and irrelevant. They look forward to leaving as soon as they can obtain a job that will provide money, some interest, and the freedom for which they yearn. The education and class systems have always discriminated against them for being female and working class. They absorb a self-image that is academically low and their own performance may confirm this. The likelihood of school achievement is reduced as existing incentives are eroded, and as careers based on qualifications fade into impossibility.

They have grown up with feminine role models that show love and marriage and a husband and children as more important and immediate goals for a girl. They have little reason to invest in school, with its constant interference with their social preoccupations. School provides no connection between their activities, interests and experiences outside school and the knowledge and qualifications that are offered through education. It upholds a predominantly middle class image of the world and bases its judgement on this. Instead of aiming for the goals and achievement upheld by school, working class girls turn their energies towards maintaining relationships, in which success is more real and satisfying. People come first on their list of priorities, and this attitude affects their choice of jobs.

In the absence of incentives or pressures to study, school-work and the accompanying rules and regulations are largely seen as a waste of time. Even girls who start by doing well may finally be discouraged by counter-pressures and 'fear of success'. Middle class girls face a similar situation but the advantages of their home backgrounds together with the aspirations and expectations expressed for them by parents and teachers, help them to achieve relatively easier success and to experience greater long term commitment. It is mainly in the pursuit of higher education that the conflicts and contradictions in their situation are revealed.

From the beginning girls are seldom allowed to develop the autonomy and independence that is associated with analytic thinking and ability, and the confidence and initiative that combine to facilitate academic success. For many working class girls this is complicated by their alienation from and lack of interest in the formal expectations of education. Although they are sometimes under relatively less strict parental control or supervision than many middle class girls, and take on responsibility for themselves and their homes, they have little incentive to apply their confidence and independence to intellectual activities. Girls who are more protected by their parents become dependent on their image in the eyes of others; learning how to please and be pleasing, how to avoid being openly argumentative, and how not to hold too many opinions. Other people's approval becomes essential to a sense of identity and a feeling of well-being.

School differentiates and points children in directions that exaggerate pre-existing inequalities. Boys may experience early discomfort with the 'feminine' primary school but are soon aware that the official discouragement given to their 'masculine' over-activities is undermined by the status and success that these command. The more consistent conformity that many girls slip into does not necessarily bring them corresponding school success, and any relationship between the 'formal' subjects at school and their contemporary experiences is too often lacking.

A lot of girls like school for the friends they meet there, and for some of the lessons, like English, but see no point in most of the other subjects. What for instance is the use of knowing Australia's imports and exports, or the chemical reaction to make hydrogen, unless you are committed to a career that involves these, or you unquestioningly accept knowledge for its own sake. Domestic science teaching is no alternative, whatever Crowther or Newsom have suggested. Where, for example, community studies have been taught girls have usually found them interesting and meaningful, and local projects have made them aware of the relative situation of themselves and their families. But for a girl, community studies does not lead to very much except low level work for social services unless a proper training or degree course is taken. The sexual-segregating process of school and the division of labour in the work force outside interact and reinforce each other in a circular process.

Notes

Chapter 4

1. Pearl Jephcott, *Girls Growing Up*, Faber & Faber, 1942.
2. Newsom Report, *Half Our Future*, 1963.
3. G. Chanan and L. Gilchrist, *What School is For*, Methuen, 1974, p. 27.
4. For a further discussion of this evidence, see Ann Oakley, *Sex, Gender and Society*, Temple Smith, 1972, chapter 3; and Eleanor Maccoby, 'Sex Differences in Intellectual Functioning', in Eleanor Maccoby (Ed.), *The Development of Sex Differences*, Tavistock, 1967.
5. J. W. B. Douglas, *The Home and the School*, Panther, 1967.
6. H. A. Witkin, *Psychological Differentiation*, John Wiley, 1962.
7. M. Mead, *Male and Female*, Penguin, 1950.
8. Matina Horner, 'Woman's Will to Fail', *Psychology Today*, 3, no. 6, 1969.
9. V. Crandall, W. Katkovsky and A. Preston, 'Motivational and Ability Determinants of Young Children's Intellectual Achievement Behaviours', *Child Development*, vol. 33, 1962.
10. V. Crandall and A. Rabson, 'Children's Repetition Choices in an Intellectual Achievement Situation Following Success and Failure', *Journal of Genetic Psychology*, vol. 97, 1960.
11. Witkin, op. cit.
12. See also Eleanor Maccoby, 'Sex Differences in Intellectual Functioning', op. cit.
13. J. W. B. Douglas, *The Home and the School*, Panther, 1967.
14. Quoted in N. Frazier and M. Sadker, *Sexism in School and Society*, Harper & Row, 1973.
15. Ivan Illich, 'After De-Schooling — What?' *Social Policy*, September to October, 1971, reprinted as a pamphlet by the Writers & Readers Publishing Cooperative, 1974.
16. L. Kohlberg, 'A Cognitive-Developmental Analysis of Children's Sex-Role Concepts and Attitudes', in Eleanor Maccoby (Ed.), *The Development of Sex Differences*, Tavistock, 1967.
17. R. Sears, 'Development of Gender Role', in F. Beach (Ed.), *Sex and Behavior*, John Wiley, 1965.

18.   See G. Chanan and L. Gilchrist, op. cit., in which this problem is discussed in greater detail.

19.   See H. Rosen, *Language and Class: A Critical Look at the Theories of Basil Bernstein*, Falling Wall Press, 1972, for discussion of this and other questions.

20.   J. Kagan, 'The Child's Sex Role Classification of School Objects', *Child Development*, 35, no. 4, 1964.

21.   J. W. B. Douglas, *The Home and the School*, Panther, 1967.

22.   N. Frazier and M. Sadker, op. cit.

23.   D. Bem and S. Bem, 'We're All Non-conscious Sexists', *Psychology Today*, 4, no. 6, November 1970.

24.   C. Benn and B. Simon, *Half way There: Report on the British Comprehensive School Reform*, London, 1970.

25.   For example, Sheila Rowbotham, *Hidden from History*, Pluto Press, 1973; and *Women, Resistance and Revolution*, Penguin, 1974.

26.   See N. Weisstein, '*Kinder, Kuche, Kirche* as Scientific Law: Psychology Constructs the Female', in R. Morgan, (Ed.), *Sisterhood is Powerful*, Random House, New York, 1970.

27.   R. Rosenthal and L. Jacobson, 'Pygmalion in the Classroom: An Excerpt', in M. Silberman, (Ed.), *The Experience of Schooling*, Holt Rinehart & Winston, New York, 1971.

28.   Quoted in an article by Maria Loftus, 'Learning, Sexism and Femininity', in *Red Rag*, no. 7, June 1974.

29.   I. K. Broverman *et al.*, 'Sex Role Stereotypes and Clinical Judgements of Mental Health', *Journal of Consultative and Clinical Psychology*, 34, 1970.

30.   See H. Rosen, op. cit., who criticizes this emphasis in middle class education.

31.   J. Shaw, 'Some Implications of Sex-segregated Education', unpublished paper, given at the British Sociological Association Conference, 1974.

CHAPTER V

A Nice Job for a Girl

I think some girls don't want jobs what boys do, because you do not see women or girls driving buses nor trains, girls do not do anything mechanical. And you do not see women being butchers, nor being porters etc., because women and girls are not strong enough to do men's jobs.

Jean

We had careers advice altogether in a class. Someone would say, 'I wanna be such and such,' and she'd tell you about that job. But all the girls in the class just made up their minds that they were going to work in offices and banks.

Carol – ex-further education student
working as receptionist.

I wanted to do something useful but I don't know – might need qualifications. I wanted to do cosmetics – you know, putting make-up on people, but you need art and I'm not doing art this year, I picked the wrong subject. I decided this a bit late. I'd like to do something useful, but most jobs in art and music, only boys can have, like recording and producing – are mainly men that do this more than girls.

Anne

... my exam results weren't all that good this year. I went to the [careers] adviser and they said, 'Well, what do you want to do?' – the *big* question. So I said, well I wanted to be a doctor. 'Oh,' he said, and we'd talked about it before, and I don't think I've got – I think I'd have to be really brainy to get in, because I'm a girl. My teacher suggested radiologist.

Margaret

I was willing to stay on [at school] – but I wanted to get out and earn money, but the main reason that I wanted to leave was because every night I go home and do me mum's housework and I hate doing that, so the only way I can get out of doing that is to go to work. Me little sister does it too. My mum goes out to work to earn more money for clothes and things like that for us, and she's always gone out to work, and she went on condition that I took charge of the house, and got meals for the evening and things like that, so I took over the housework when she went out to work . . . I've got a job already . . . I'm supposed to be an office junior, but it don't sound much like it. I take a few calls on the telephone . . . then I can make tea or coffee, whatever I fancy . . . I would have liked to have been an actress. I've always wanted to be an actress. I always wanted to go to drama school, but my mum and dad just couldn't afford it and I knew that, and really all the people I spoke to about acting as a career, they said really the best bet would be to get a place in drama school, but I couldn't get the money to do that, my mum and dad couldn't get the money to do that, so I just thought, oh blimey, if the only hope is a drama school, then it isn't worth it.

Michelle

The approach of school-leaving age finds every girl and boy looking around for a job or career. The grown-up world of work that lies outside the sheltering security of the home and school threatens some and entices others with the promise of money and independence. Girls now accept that they have to become employed when their education is over. Even those who still see work as a time-filling activity before marriage are drawn through an automatic process of careers advice and job selection. Many girls who intend to work both after marriage and after having children, are trying to align this with the traditional priorities of domesticity and motherhood. They survey the apparent job market with enthusiasm, anxiety or indifference, and their choice of work illustrates the way in which the range of careers open to girls depends upon their treatment and experiences within school, and the assumptions they have made about the nature of their role.

EXPECTATIONS

The girls from the Ealing schools had already gathered some firm ideas about future careers, and why they thought they would like them. They covered a range of over thirty different jobs, although this is reduced if for instance the hospital jobs are considered as one. It is further reduced by the fact that just over four girls in every ten chose some sort of office-work. The variations within this included personal secretary, ordinary secretary, shorthand typist, copy typist, clerk typist and junior office-worker, but most girls specified shorthand typing and general office-work. Office-work is obviously the favourite work for girls especially in a dense urban area like London where opportunities are plentiful.* The frequency of this choice is a reflection of the enormous growth in demand for office-workers during this century. The popularity of office-work points to its respectability and to the way it can accommodate a wide range of girls varying in their intelligence and qualifications.

The next most popular jobs were as teachers, nurses, shop assistants and bank clerks – which altogether accounted for about a quarter of the job choices. Following these were girls who wished to become receptionists, telephonists, air-hostesses, hairdressers and children's nurses or nannies. The narrow range of careers so far selected took up over three-quarters of all the choices. The remaining preferences, although quite numerous, were made by only a few individuals, and included employment in the womens' services, or as a ground hostess, kennel maid, laboratory researcher, fashion designer, computer operator, social worker, radiologist, physiotherapist, continuity girl, beautician, actress and model. Professional choices such as doctor or lawyer were rare, and more often chosen by Indian girls who were in the higher forms and had fathers in professional jobs. All the chosen careers were safely in the realms of 'women's work' (with the exception of the choices of doctor and barrister). There was little venturing into male or even neutral occupational territory. It was interesting that the choices bore no relation to the national distribution of women's work which places most girls and women (and especially those from working class backgrounds) in factory work, clerical work, shop work and service work (catering etc.).†

* See Appendix for more information on careers for girls in different areas of Britain.

† In 1970 women formed 71 per cent of service workers, 48 per cent of sales-workers, 67 per cent of clerical workers, 38 per cent of technical and professional workers, 20 per cent of production workers and 7·5 per cent of executive and managerial workers.[1]

I wanted to find out more about the reasons for their job preferences, and what it was about them that the girls thought they would enjoy. On the face of it, the great popularity of secretarial and general office-work is based on its considered suitability for girls, and the relative ease of entry. It has many obvious attractions. It is a clean respectable job. It has some glamorous appeal because it involves dressing up for town and the possibility of meeting and working with men. It does not need Saturday work, and is relatively well-paid, especially for girls proficient in typing and shorthand. It needs few qualifications and there is a demand for people prepared to do this sort of work. All things considered, it *seems* a nice job for a girl.

The Ealing girls were attracted by this work because they hoped to do interesting things, meet people, travel and earn good money. Some also mentioned their current enjoyment of typing. Here are a few of the ways that potential secretaries, shorthand typists, copy typists and office juniors perceived their future work and the particular things about it that attracted them:

If I can work my way to a really good secretary I hope to be able to travel about (if the boss I work for travels).

Money. Working under a handsome boss.

Meeting different people and having an interesting and varied job.

The standard of work and dressing up as a new experience.

I like this job because you can get good wages and lots of promotion.

Working at an office is a comfortable place.

You are able to help different people and this is what I like doing.

I like typing and prefer to work in an office to a factory.

In reality, these hopes may prove something of a disappointment. For example a girl may not meet many men if she is working in the typing pool. If she works in the office, it may well be that the number of new people passing through is very small, and the ones already there are not exciting. Secretaries and shorthand typists hoping to travel with their bosses will find themselves left behind, or merely transported to another part of town. It is clear however, that this sort of work is very easy to slip into, for many valid reasons. One of these is expressed in some other girls' answers to the question of why they wished to do this work: 'I don't know, but as I am doing shorthand and typing at school I think this job will be all right.' And, 'It is what I am learning mostly now. And it is really the only thing I could do.'

Many schools are today well-equipped with departments where girls learn typing and shorthand, and do courses in commerce. While the boys are being taught technical skills and expertise in woodwork, metalwork, technical drawing etc., the only practical skills that girls can learn, apart from cookery and needlework, are shorthand and typing. Therefore, at whatever age a girl decides to leave school, if she has taken these courses, she has these skills to sell. She has little need of other qualifications, except perhaps English, and she has already acquired an idea of whether she would like and could cope with a secretarial job. When a lot of these girls claim that they like typing and shorthand they are basing this on their own experience, and they avoid the trouble or risk of exploring new skills and occupations. The schools have made similar assumptions, and office-work is almost totally a 'girls' subject'.

The expansion of business and administration particularly since the war has produced a constant demand for office-workers. Demand usually leads to higher wages but in this case the parallel enthusiasm of girls for this work has meant that in the main female office-workers have remained as under-paid and exploited as they would be in any other women's job. Office-work is, however different from other women's occupations in that it contains so many variations in status and pay. For instance, secretaries can command very high rates of pay depending on where and for whom they work. In London young secretaries can start with a salary as high as that of a qualified nurse, while in provincial and rural areas and in some small firms and businesses in London the pay is much lower. Secretarial work also has the attractive and deceptive appearance of a career structure which rises from pool typists to executive secretaries and yet seems to demand relatively little in the way of lengthy training or qualifications. This overlooks the fact that there is no guaranteed progress from one level to the next.

Thirty years ago, young working class girls would seek employment in the local factory, and move regularly from job to job within it, often covering as many as twenty jobs before they were this number of years old.[2] They did not consider office-work as this usually demanded a secondary school education. Today girls have moved away from factory work as a result of the availability and desirability of office employment (although opportunities differ a lot by region). I spoke to a careers officer with reference to this phenomenon and was told that: 'Girls who really should be working in factories making handbags and clothing are in offices.' But neither girls nor their parents would agree. Factory work can be dirty, and is usually given much less status than a clean comfortable office job. Even if a girl's father or mother work in a factory themselves, they express hopes that their daughters will find something better. Only two of the Ealing schoolgirls expected to work in a factory. One explained 'It has good money. It is not too far away from my home and I know a lot of people who work there.' The work had little interest for her, only convenience and familiarity. The other girl was more concise. She anticipated liking 'nothing' about her future work.

Working with People

Part of the legacy of women's role is that they should be involved less with themselves than with caring and looking after others, and the upbringing of girls makes them dependent for identity and self-esteem on their relationships with other people. This was illustrated by the comments from the Ealing girls on the jobs they expected to get. The jobs they chose reflected, of course, the jobs that were normally open to them; these, in turn, were usually extensions of their 'feminine' role and exploited some supposedly feminine characteristic.

Many of those Ealing girls who wanted to go into some kind of secretarial or office-work spoke enthusiastically about the different people they hoped to meet, and for others the possible 'people involvement' acted as the determining factor in their choices. Here are some of the reasons the girls gave for other choices. They show great consistency over the various types of work. (The expected job is given in brackets.)

I mostly like having to help people. I like to know what is wrong with them and would like to help in any way.

(Doctor)

It's very interesting and you're meeting different people every day.

(Nurse)

I enjoy having children around and I'd like to meet people and have their company.

(Children's Nurse)

I come into contact with people and the work differs from day to day.

(Radiologist)

Helping people, meeting people, and sorting out their problems.

(Social Worker)

The thought of working with children appeals to me. I like helping children or people and children are more willing to be helped than adults.

(Teacher)

Meeting different people every day.

(Bank Clerk)

It seems interesting. You are meeting different people and helping them. The receptionists always look smart and kind. Also it is good money.

(Receptionist)

I think being a telephone operator you come to know about many places and people and I like meeting people.

(Telephone Operator)

I like the idea of meeting people and of travelling and learning about the things in everyday life in other countries.

(Journalist)

The travelling, meeting people from different backgrounds, being independent, money.

(Air Hostess)

You get the chance to meet a lot of people and a chance to travel.

(Interpreter)

Meeting different people, seeing all types of people, helping people (an office job would bore me).

(Shop Assistant)

It is a friendly sort of job and you meet a lot of people.

(Hairdresser)

This job is very interesting, – you meet a lot of different people and you get to know what people are really like.

(Policewoman)

Being concerned with people is a very positive aspect of 'femininity' and it is wrong that this concern is so unevenly distributed between men and women. The stereotyped view of women sees them as naturally more adept than men at working with or for people, and taking care of them. Nurture is supposedly based in the maternal caring role, and serving is contained in their falsely assumed inferiority. The great investment in other people demonstrated by girls' commitment to being wives and mothers influences the vocational directions of their minds. Men on the other hand, are supposed to be more concerned with proving their own individual success by individual strivings. They are seen as better with 'things' than people, and can cope with scientific and abstract problems.

I can remember finding conflict between the personal and the abstract in my own life. When I left school, I rejected any idea of continuing at university the pure sciences I had studied at A-level. The thought of concentrating on such intensive abstract science frightened me and I was convinced that I was not good enough. I went to work as a technician in a medical research laboratory, and I specifically chose this sort of research because it had some ultimate connection with helping people and entailed working with other people. This gave it some tangibility and meaning. If however I had stayed there, I would never have acquired more than a limited autonomy, and would always have been carrying out someone else's experiments. Almost all the careers for women that involve intensive care and service of others contain the implicit contradiction that the very aspect of the job that makes it worthwhile can also wear away or suffocate women's sense of individuality. Continual attendance on the needs of other people at work, as at home, leaves little time or energy for self-expression. People are very demanding. Self sacrifice brings its own rewards but it is unjust that only half the population should accept this as part of their basic personality and role. Men also should become more 'people-involved', instead of themselves making up a large proportion of the people that girls and women are concerned with nursing, teaching, typing for, cooking for, serving and waiting on.

Most girls seemed fairly content with the sort of work that they expected, and when they were asked to name any job that they would like to do given all the opportunity in the world, quite a lot repeated their original expectations. However the number of those who had previously selected some kind of secretarial or office job was cut to a quarter, and this coincided to a large extent with the underlying fantasy of exchanging this work for something more glamorous. Future clerks and typists aspired to be air-hostesses, actresses, models and film stars. A few moved more towards the less glamorous but highly qualified levels of barrister, doctor, vet, scientist and journalist. The attractions of these were divided between the glamorous aspects of the work, the travelling, and again meeting people.

To the extent that these can be taken seriously, they highlight another contradiction which has also emerged from the attractions of and expectations about work. This lies in the girls enthusiasm for travelling as well as meeting people. The enjoyment and hope of travel is particularly expressed in their choice of an ideal job, but one girl in ten also mentioned travel in her reasons for liking the job she actually expected to take up. These desires, however, conflict with the traditional role of women, which assigns to them the relative isolation and stationary nature of housework and child-care. One characteristic that the glamorous careers like air-hostess and actress have in common is their incompatibility with the stable and grounded demands of marriage and motherhood. At the moment, the Ealing girls' hopes and dreams fly freely, in optimistic co-existence with their acceptance of the feminine role. But not for long. They will soon be imprisoned by the responsibilities and limitations of a relatively low-paid or dead-end job, of marriage and of caring for a family of their own.

For some, the assumption that they will marry had already put boundaries around their perspective of the future. For instance, when asked the question 'What would you do if you didn't marry?', two girls gave the following replies: 'If I didn't get married I'd travel a bit I suppose and see a bit of life.' 'I'd start living my own life, doing things for myself.'

Almost by definition hopes and dreams are often far removed from real life. The constraints placed on girls by the mere fact of being female and the further implications of being working class or black mean a narrow scope of actual opportunities. Girls' dreams are increasingly invaded by love, romance and sexuality, which are modelled on the glamorous actresses and film stars that they might dream of becoming themselves. Ironically these popular women have themselves little chance of successfully combining their public lives with the femininity and married family life that they frequently portray in plays and films as the most satisfying destiny for girls.

'Careers for Girls'

I've wanted to do this [research for history] for quite a long time but I don't know enough about the sorts of jobs you have to do for these sorts of things – you just get to know about things like air-hostesses and teachers. They don't tell you enough about more unusual things. Careers officers come round now and again and ask what you want to know about but they tend not to know about that sort of job – just teachers and nurses and that sort of thing.

Jenny

When it is time to think about choosing careers, the sources that girls have to draw on are the images found in books and magazines, on television and through observing and discussing with the people immediately around them. These invite them to become nurses, teachers, telephonists, secretaries, bank clerks, and the rest of the familiar jobs for girls. Among the girls from the Ealing schools, we saw that this range, plus shop assistant, receptionist, hairdresser and air-hostess accounted for over 80 per cent of job preferences.

In careers books, however, such as 'Careers for Girls' by Ruth Miller,[3] there appears to be an abundance of opportunities for girls. Over a hundred areas of work are defined, some of which involve several sub-categories of job. For some careers, further educational qualifications are necessary, but not for others. There is therefore an enormous discrepancy between what is supposed to be available and what is actually taken up. How many girls who do not have high educational qualifications are thinking of becoming, for example, an architectural technican or a chartered surveyor, a dental ancillary, a cartographical draughts-woman, an interior decorating assistant, a dispensing optician, quantity surveyor, pharmacy technician, landscape architect, meteorological technician, or anything in horticulture or agri-culture? Why, if there is indeed such a wide range of possible choice, do girls stalwartly continue to pursue the same old sets of jobs?

Many girls who have plodded fairly aimlessly through their school curriculum and have ended up amongst the 'girls' sub-jects', meet the suggestion that they should try one of these unfamiliar jobs with reluctance or horror. 'What? What's that? Oh, I don't think I could do anything like that, I think I'd be happier in an office.' A girl needs a lot of nerve to enter 'un-feminine' kinds of work, especially if they do not appear very openly available. It is not easy to strike out on your own when school has consistently encouraged conformity to convention and regulation. A few will be able to do this and encouragement would help others, but most have already held set ideas about 'girls' jobs' for many years.

If for instance a job is labelled as a type of 'technician', this may be construed to imply some scientific connection; an assump-tion not necessarily justified, but enough to frighten off a girl who has defined herself as nonscientific. These are also seen as potentially 'masculine' jobs, which is also a reason for dog-matically avoiding them. The necessity of further training also scares away many prospective girl candidates, who see it as an extension of school, and therefore likely to be similarly authoritarian in form and irrelevant in content. Many are ignorant of the real conditions of further education, and on-the-job training. They do not realize that they can learn in an atmosphere which is much freer than school, and about subjects which can be more interesting or have more direct application to their jobs. It is too easy to drift into a factory or shop, or go into clerical or secretarial work in which training is unnecessary, or merely involves an evening class in shorthand. The propularity of short (three to six month) secretarial courses, often quite intensive, shows an irrational exclusion of this from the general rejection of other sorts of further training.*

If a girl is not content to settle for a slot in the more popular careers she can further explore the facilities offered by the local careers office, as well as those provided in her own school. The minimum provision is that every school-leaver should have at least one personal interview and one talk or discussion with a careers officer. It is a difficult task to present a range of jobs to a girl when the officer has little personal knowledge of her and only some notes about her academic background. It may be possible to broaden her horizons but more often in a horizontal way that just extends the same areas: such as suggesting physiotherapy to a would-be nurse, rather than encouraging something unstereotyped and different. These possibilities are also likely to be caught in a double trap of tradition. If a girl asks about a job she is interested in, it will more often than not be in one of the familiar occupations and she will be given the appropriate information. If she has a blank mind about what she wants, then it is likely that the advice will again recommend these sorts of jobs, on the reasoning that if a girl does seem not to be interested in anything, then she will certainly not be enthusiastic about 'unusual' sorts of jobs.

Careers officers keep reports and records according to sex, and may recommend jobs in direct relation to current vacancies for girls in local offices, shops, factories etc. Their job is not an easy one as they cannot make job vacancies for girls in areas of work

---

*This is not totally irrational however, because the present lack of further education opportunities for girls means that this sort of course is the one most easily available.

where none exist. Careers officers differ, some are more modern and enlightened about girls' careers, and some are still entrenched in the old attitudes. I spoke to one of the latter about the possibilities of girls doing work normally prescribed for boys. He saw no reason at all for girls to want to do boys' jobs. Why should they wish to get dirty or messy? He thought that one girl who had expressed a desire to assist in some sort of engineering was having a fantasy and just wanted to get dirty! Fortunately not all careers officers take this view.

Today an increasing amount of attention is being paid to providing careers information in schools. Although it is left largely to the discretion of the school, most have made one or more teachers responsible for this in addition to their specially reduced timetable of other subjects, and some schools have taken on full-time careers teachers. Hence it is possible to widen the scope of career knowledge for girls, and hopefully for boys as well, by introducing a whole spectrum of possibilities at an age before sex and job separations have completely hardened. Careers and the nature of work should be a subject frequently discussed and explored. It should involve projects which cover an understanding of all sorts of work, and which examine the attitudes and values that are held about different jobs, and which, for example, downgrade many women's jobs.

The Ealing schoolgirls themselves wanted earlier careers teaching at school, and the provision of more activities like visits to places of employment.

We don't get [careers] literature. We get the careers officer coming round about twice, and Mrs — talks to us sometimes. And we have films, but they tend to be about the same sort of things and not all on careers. I think we need more visits – I think the fifth formers do go on visits to factories and police stations and so on but I think we should have them younger because if you give them in the fifth form and that's when you want to leave, it doesn't give you much time to decide. They should give you a lot of this sort of thing, especially for boys because a lot of your life depends on what you do, so you should have a lot of time to decide what you want to do.

If we did things like the fourth form leavers do – they go round looking at different jobs and things, and work in children's nurseries and things like that. If we could do that I think more people would stay on and they'd enjoy it.

Careers officers and teachers are not the only active influences in a girl's choice of job. Mothers are very important, as well as fathers, and female friends and relatives who are already doing certain sorts of work. A relative minority have been absolutely swayed by one person, and it is reasonable to assume that most base their choice on their assessment and perception of themselves, their picture of what the world offers to girls, and their immediate opportunities. This invariably leads to a conventional career.

Many mothers go to work today for all kinds of reasons and the acceptability of this might be expected to influence their daughters' attitudes to working. I did find a tendency, although not very significant, for girls with working mothers* to reject the home-based assumptions and satisfactions of women's role more than those with non-working mothers. Their job choices do not bear any relation to this however because few of their choices approached the over-all low-level nature of their mothers' work. A few wanted to join their mothers who were working as typists, secretaries and nurses, but the majority had mothers who were involved in canteens, cleaning jobs, shop or factory work.

Most parents, whether mothers were working or not, did not pressurize their children about jobs although some definitely wanted their daughters to stay on at school. As noted earlier parental attitudes were usually either expressed through giving blanket support: 'It's entirely up to you, it's your life,' and 'Whatever you will be happy doing'; or in similar vein but specifying certain exceptions: 'You can do what you like, *except* work in a factory, shop, or anything not quite respectable.' Anything not quite respectable, at present, usually includes the less traditionally feminine, less 'appropriate' jobs for girls, and even if the girls were to think about such jobs they would face parental opposition.

At present girls are largely excluded from certain male enclaves, from, for example, apprenticeships in crafts like printing. But

---

* Over two-thirds of the girls had mothers doing full-time or part-time jobs.

apart from straightforward exclusion they usually lack the self-confidence to undertake jobs they have never heard of or which seem to be predominantly male preserves. In addition girls often lack the opportunities for day or block release from their jobs for further education, they are given little encouragement to try for unusual jobs and information is often inadequate or given too late.

'Girls Don't Do This Job'

The irrationality of sex-stereotypes was illustrated when the Ealing girls were asked to name a job they might have chosen had they been boys. Most selected the skilled male jobs that were frequently the hoped-for careers of their boyfriends and the boys in their forms, like mechanic and engineer. When they were subsequently asked why, if the job was different from their own expectations, did they not choose it as a girl, they were not at a loss to provide answers. However these were mainly expressed in a succinct and dogmatic tautology describing the present situation. Here are some of their answers, followed by the job that each refers to.

You don't often find women working in garages under the cars doing dirty work.

(Mechanic)

It is a man's job, I'd look silly in a pair of dirty overalls under a car.

(Mechanic)

Girls are not interested in engineering.

(Engineer)

You do not hear of any female executives.

(Executive)

Girls don't do pilot work.

(Pilot)

Girls don't do technical drawing.

(Draughtsman)

It is not right for a girl to be the same as a boy.

(Engineer)

They had simply accepted that if a job was categorized as man's work, it was therefore not right, or suitable, or interesting, or appropriate for a girl.

There were other sorts of reaction, and for instance some girls realistically recognized that 'male' jobs are often blocked to girls, either by entry requirements, or through the implicit preference given to boys. They showed awareness of the social restrictions but accepted them. For example:

They never want a girl to be a mechanic.

(Mechanic)

This job is wanted by men mostly and they have more chance of getting it because a lot of people like men driving instructors better than women.

(Driving Instructor)

People would say it's not done for a girl to do this. But if I had guts I would.

(Electrician)

Boys are much more approved of than girls, because girls are said to be liable to run off and get married thus wasting the ratepayers' money for their training.

(Doctor)

Nobody would trust a girl as a pilot and I would never be given the time to prove myself worthy.

(Pilot)

Other girls mentioned stereotyped female characteristics that are said to make them incapable of coping with certain sorts of work. The belief that women are weak, faint-hearted, and less intelligent was brought out like a white flag surrendering to male superiority.

A man is tougher, and girl journalists might have to see and report something that really upset them whereas a man wouldn't be so soft.

(Journalist)

You don't have girl lorry drivers because usually the stuff inside the lorry is too heavy for a girl to lift.

(Lorry Driver)

It's unladylike.

(Bricklayer)

I don't think I could face it as a girl but a boy is less squeamish.

(Vet)

Boys should be able to put up with things a girl can't.

(Doctor)

I think this job would be too complicated for a girl.

(Computer Science)

These old beliefs are repeated in spite of the everyday instances of women doing heavy or distasteful jobs. For example nurses have to lift heavy patients, and witness many gruesome sights.

Another justification for girls keeping away from male-dominated territory was found in the acceptance and deference given to a boy's greater need for a good job because of his future necessity to support a wife and family.

Girls do not have to earn quite as much as a boy as he will soon support a family.

(Banking)

There is more money in printing and boys need a steady bank balance if they're to get married.

(Printer)

I have not described these reactions in order to provoke either surprise or pessimism but to show how much the divisions need to be questioned and discussed as well as making changes in the real job structure. The reasons behind the avoidance of male-labelled jobs are often simplistic and irrational and therefore rest on apparently flimsy ground. However they are tied up with much deeper feelings of feminine identity and role and merely logically to deny girls' dogmatism or reasoning, and increase opportunity, would not produce an automatic movement into these and other areas of work. The same difficulties would be encountered in any attempt to persuade boys to enter 'women's work', but this would be complicated by their attitude towards such work which they would see as inferior as well as unsuitable.

It takes self-confidence and courage for girls to break through the prejudice that surrounds entry into male-dominated careers. Throughout school life, they have experienced the separation of sexes and subjects, and have moved towards the safer 'feminine' areas of interest. They learn that much of the work men do is associated with 'male' characteristics such as aggression, strength, stamina, competitiveness, ambition, and a technical or analytical mind, which are qualities that conflict with the myth of 'femininity'. Therefore bricklaying, as one girl said, is obviously 'unladylike'. If girls are not well-equipped with these qualities, it is at least partly related to the nature of their upbringing, and if they are, they are reluctant to use them to advantage and prefer to see themselves as inadequate. It is less anxiety-provoking to opt for work in which girls are welcomed and it is not appealing to forge a path into areas that may be hostile and competitive. Although girls see working with people as an important factor, it is often as important that these people should be friendly.

Industry has tried to attract girls with less than moderate success, and one study[4] reveals in detail the attitudes of girls to science in general and to engineering as a career in particular. A bias against industry due to the following reasons was discovered: belief in prejudice against girls; ignorance about the range of work involved; acceptance of the common view that engineering means having dirty and disagreeable working conditions; a wish to avoid stiff male competition; and a preference for work to which they could easily return later in life. Although the research was done in the early sixties, the comments that girls made about engineering still ring true today. Here are two examples from girls who were at that time taking A-level science subjects.

I was interested in engineering but was advised against it because of the competition from boys. Girls can't get into sandwich courses.

I would like to know about openings in industry. Engineering interests me, but I think it's a man's job. It's dirty.

Girls are not usually frustrated mechanics, engineers, lorry drivers, electricians, pilots, journalists and doctors. Most of them have an inbuilt cataloguing system in which the reasons and dogmas, like those expressed above, come under the section concerning common sense and the way of the world. They not only reject these more traditionally male jobs, but also the subsidiary careers connected with them, and other less well-known jobs which are overlooked or avoided through ignorance of their existence or nature. They lack the confidence, the opportunities and the desire to challenge the strict divisions of work. Attitudes, popular ideology and the economic and occupational structure all contribute to girls' inhibitions. Their real opportunities are manipulated by employers (invariably male) who hold the power, wealth and means of production, and have highly reactionary ideas about women and their role; while male employees who are themselves exploited hold grimly on to the exclusiveness of their skills, backed up by the operation of protective legislation and job evaluation.

WORKING CLASS GIRLS AND FURTHER EDUCATION

The girls in the Ealing schools were predominantly from working class backgrounds, and despite professed equality of educational opportunity, it is obvious that working class children of both sexes still receive a lower level of education. This happens for many reasons already discussed. There are also real economic problems for some families and in addition girls are well aware if their parents find it hard to support them, even without having to pay the extra that would be required to send them to college.

A great many working class girls who would benefit greatly from further education neither know of its existence nor feel encouraged to find out about it. They are very anxious to leave school and do not realize how different further education can be.

I saw a careers officer when I left school. It was so boring you know, I can hardly remember. They said I could be a clerk. Ever since I was a kid I always wanted to teach, always. But I never knew anything about further education. All I knew when I was fifteen was that I wanted to get out of there. I found out about further education by chance, from my teacher at night school. Further education changed my life coming here, I'll tell you that. So different from school. But I still think they ought to offer more courses. I mean, I wouldn't want to do engineering or anything, but that's only because of the way I've been taught.

Jane, further education student.

The provision of further education, day release and block release is inadequate for both girls and boys, but particularly for girls. In 1973, 10·4 per cent of employed girls were taking day release compared with 39·7 per cent of boys. Provision for apprenticeships was similar, 7 per cent of girls were apprenticed compared with 42 per cent of boys, and of these girls, over three-quarters were in hairdressing. Since the Industrial Training Act of 1964, Industrial Training Boards (I.T.B.s) were set up to remedy the post-war shortage of skilled labour and to combat the arbitrary quality of training given by many employers. There are now twenty-seven such boards, to cover fifteen million workers, but if one examines the existing figures they seem to have made little impact on further education opportunities for girls. The I.T.B.s have an equally divided membership of trade unionists and employers. In 1969, the T.U.C. made several suggestions: that special grants be allocated to firms who trained women for jobs outside their traditional range; that re-training opportunities for older women should be given; and that grants be given on condition of equal provision for girls. These have not been carried out.

If we examine the meagre day-release that is provided, it is found that public administration gives the highest amount – to 70 per cent of its girl employees, but public administration provides less than 10 per cent of all jobs for girls under eighteen. The next highest are given in transport and communications, gas, electricity, water and chemicals, which provide day-release for clerical workers, but not for manual workers. (These give further education to approximately 23 per cent of their girl employees and 88 per cent of boys.) The scientific branches of the Civil Service and the Medical Research Council give day-release to their technical staff of both sexes, but they are fairly unusual in this. In 1970, there were 110 female apprentices in engineering and related industries compared to 112,000 boys. (In the same year there were 15,801 girl apprentices altogether, 11,336 being in hairdressing and manicure.) It was noted by the T.U.C. that, ironically, it was those industries employing the largest number of women who gave the lowest amount of day-release. For instance, in the distributive trades (shop-work) only 2 per cent of girls were 'released', in textiles 2·4 per cent, and in clothing and footwear also only 2·4 per cent.* Altogether these make up a pitifully small amount.

Opportunities for further education are seldom offered from clerical and other office-work apart from large institutions like the Civil Service and nationalized industries. Girls either make the best of the learning and skills they have gained at school, or they embark on a training course at their own expense. Figures show that girls and women make up the majority of the members of evening classes and part-time courses, many of the former however are non-vocational. If girls have high ambitions in the secretarial and clerical field, they need the determination to heave themselves up by their own shoe-strings. There is little help from employers who want consistent service from them rather than aspirations. The attitudes of employers and girls too often coincide and hinder any solid demand for more opportunities. Employers are content to see girls as short-term investments, on whom it is not worth spending money since sooner or later they are bound to leave for another job or for marriage. They also assume that girls themselves do not wish for further education and this may often be the case since many girls are so pleased to have left school that they perceive further education as a step backwards in freedom and maturity. They have had no chance to realize that further education colleges can be much less restrictive than school, and need not interfere with their financial independence. Employers should be compelled to make these oppor-

* Most of this information on further education for girls was collected by Arsenal Women's Liberation Group.

tunities available to all girls and boys.* Also a wider variety of subjects should be offered to each instead of the rigid sex-defined courses that are offered at present. Apart from the usual O-level and A-level subjects, the main courses that girls are found in at further education college are business and commerce, which includes a disproportionate amount of shorthand and typing, and hairdressing. A whole range of technical subjects is available to boys, and they also take business and commerce but their courses are oriented towards management and they don't learn the 'feminine' skills of typing and shorthand.

The lack of these facilities for girls is paralleled by a similar lack of places for wives and mothers who want to return to work. Many women who abandoned education or work for marriage and motherhood find that they want to do some kind of job, but only have access to low level and unskilled jobs. Four years ago (1972) there were only 11,000 places at government training centres for women returning to work; there were 10,000 names on the waiting lists and 2,000 applicants every week. The range of womens' work that re-training offers is limited and this is reflected in books that give advice on careers for older and 'late-start' women. These consist of the familiar jobs for women in social work and the hospital services, teaching and clerical work. But even the opportunities that are available involve time, expense and training – and thus are totally out of reach for women whose previous experience of education has been unenthusiastic and scanty, who may have very little money, and who may still not be completely free from family responsibilities. The class bias of educational and occupational opportunity acts at each stage of life and presses women back into their rationalized position at home.

Both boys and girls are capable of undertaking a much wider spectrum of skills and occupations, but sex has become an organizing principle of capitalism and working men and women at home and at work have to accommodate themselves to their ascribed slots within the system. It would be a misinterpretation

* Compulsory day-release for sixteen- to nineteen-year-olds has been one of the demands made by the Association of Teachers in Technical Institutions (A.T.T.I.) for the past six years.

however to think that a female invasion of male work or vice versa is more than part of the challenging and dissolving of gender roles. The breakdown of these needed to provide greater choice for both sexes has to involve fundamental social and economic changes as well as changes in ideas, beliefs, attitudes and values.

Notes

Chapter 5

1. M. Galenson, *Women and Work*, figures from the International Labour Office.
2. Pearl Jephcott, *Rising Twenty*, Faber & Faber, 1948.
3. Ruth Miller, *Careers for Girls*, Penguin, 1966.
4. N. Seear, V. Roberts and J. Brock, *A Career for Women in Industry?*, Oliver & Boyd Ltd, 1964.

CHAPTER VI

Sophisticated Myths

The sexual division of labour is a monumental fact of life. It has history on its side and is accepted as an essential condition for the survival of society. But does it stand up to closer scrutiny? It appears to rest on a number of very doubtful assumptions.

Many of the differences assumed to exist between men and women have been generated from the biological fact of women's capacity for reproduction. Their subsequent preoccupation with pregnancy, childbirth and child-rearing has been seen as excluding them from many other sorts of activity. This view has been the dominant ideology for many centuries and is still widely held today, an anachronism in the midst of modern scientific and technological progress. The old belief for instance that 'proper' women (i.e. middle class women) are incapable of, or unsuited to, heavy or physically demanding work has been expanded to keep them from doing many other things outside the home. Their nineteenth century status as the property of men, the sign of male affluence, and the producer of future heirs, has contributed to their devaluation and to paternalism. That a woman's place is at home looking after husband and children is a myth which helps to validate the continued cheap reproduction of workers and, therefore, the maintenance of capitalist business and industry.

The belief that the condition of women in capitalist society springs from something universally true of women is contradicted by the existence of cultures which do not contain the same division of labour. Much anthropological evidence illustrates this.[1] If, however, anthropological evidence seems rather remote and one is tempted to dismiss such societies as 'obviously not like us', there are closer examples to be drawn from women's situation in our own society both past and present. For instance, the idea that housework and child-care are light jobs suggests that women as housewives and mothers have a soft option. But this is far from true. Admittedly housework has become easier over the years, but it used to be very hard work, and remains so for those who today cannot afford household aids. In the earlier part of this century, and long before that, domestic servants worked an endless round of drudgery, doing things which the most physically fit person would find tiring. Child-care can be even more exhausting, needing virtually endless amounts of energy. Children are physically and mentally demanding at all times, even when they are asleep, for mothers learn always to stay alert for the sound of crying. It is no light task to carry round a two- or three-year-old child. In the area of London near my home, the terraced houses have six or eight steep steps leading up to the front door. Every day mothers strain to pull heavy prams up these steps, as well as shopping baskets on wheels crammed with the family shopping. It is hard to see all this as light work.

Many other jobs also provide ample evidence of women's physical strength and stamina. The hospital services are one good example, where not only do nurses have working hours and shifts that are in themselves exhausting, but they are also required to do a lot of heavy lifting. Physiotherapists are continuously involved in physical activities, doing exercises, massages and supporting people. In another area of work, women cleaners working in offices and industry have to move large machines around from floor to floor, and room to room.

The emergency substitution of women in men's work in the past provides further proof that women have a vast reservoir of abilities. The two World Wars showed this very clearly, when women were drawn away from their homes and children to fill the gaps in industry created by men joining the armed forces. Heavy work was often carried out, requiring the same strength needed for tasks at home:

At many jobs that they had rarely or never done before, women proved to be quicker and defter than men, with their small fingers used to knitting and sewing. Women were easily trained for welding, which gained much ground in British engineering during the war. But even the jobs that required sheer physical strength were not always beyond middle-aged housewives who had been used to struggling with shopping baskets and small children up several flights of tenement steps. No woman went down the coal-mines, but in most jobs beneath that level of sheer strength and stamina, a few could always find a place.[2]

No one cried out then that a woman's place was only in the home, but when the war was over, it was conveniently packaged and labelled as a temporary crisis. Women were applauded for their special efforts, but were encouraged to return home, or were automatically made redundant.

Myths about women's role and abilities persist in spite of past and present illustrations to the contrary. The reasons for this were discussed earlier, and linked the economic and social structure with ideology and women's psychological sense of identity. It is economically necessary that women provide their free services in the home, maintain a family and pass on their own example to future generations. Although in reality nearly 40 per cent of the work force are women, and 64 per cent of married women are working, this can be overlooked in the belief that a woman's work role is secondary to her domestic role which both men and women have grown to accept with unfortunate consequences for women. 'Everyone knows that if something is called women's work it means it will be low paid, probably very essential, often uninteresting, and unpleasant, and men don't want to do it.'[3] At one time it was considered that women mainly worked for pin-money but this idea has now largely been discredited. The accompanying moral disapproval takes longer to dissipate, but it is perhaps a generational judgement that younger people no longer make. Although many women have always worked out of the sheer need to make ends meet, there are other equally valid reasons. For instance, the need to find social companionship, to break the isolation of the home, and to gain economic independence are all very important.

The division of home and work activities into primary and secondary has saddled women with two jobs. Even if they are out at work all day, the household tasks and child-care are still made their responsibility and women's guilt is easily aroused by accusations of possible neglect. The inaccurate and often horrific accounts of 'latchkey' children have made many women either stop work or feel torn with anxiety.

> I get up in the morning round about 5.30 and I pop downstairs and put the kettle on because I do like a cuppa tea; and then I usually cook my husband's breakfast and my boy's breakfast because I feel guilty coming out to work, to be honest I do feel guilty. It's only because I feel guilty that I like to know that they've had a good breakfast.

From an interview for the B.B.C. programme
Women at Work.

MOTHERHOOD

Two perspectives on the demands of motherhood have reinforced each other to preserve this role for women. The first is concerned with real conditions, and the second with ideology. In this country every mother with young children is faced with a widespread lack of nursery facilities. If she wants to work she often has only the choice of putting her children in the care of any available and willing relatives, or leaving them with a paid baby-minder who may lack adequate facilities for the care of more than a few children. Day nurseries are relatively few, and most have permanent waiting lists. A young mother needing work who is without access to any of these has no choice but to stay at home, or be exploited as an outworker.

There were plenty of nursery facilities during the Second World War, when state-sponsored nurseries were crucial to facilitate women's employment, but there are no signs of any increase in nurseries to cope with today's expanding female labour force,* and because of the absence of nursery provision, it becomes necessary for mothers to stop working for long periods of time. This contributes to the discontinuity that characterizes women's working life. It frustrates those who really need to work or who enjoy it, and reinforces employers' dogmatic pre-

---

* In 1974 London boroughs provided day nursery places for only 1·5 per cent of children under five years of age.

judices that women are only a temporary, frivolous or surplus labour force, worth less than men and treated accordingly.

The ideology supporting this is contained in the myth surrounding the importance of motherhood. Girls are brought up to believe that the most fulfilling thing in life is to have children, and to be good mothers. Women who cannot bear children are pitied, those who do not want to are considered peculiar and unnatural and mothers who are indifferent or unenthusiastic about their own children are condemned. A child needs its mother, and the mother needs to have her child. These two assumptions are seen as inextricably bound up together, and in many modern societies this is thought to be 'natural'.

This can again be questioned by another look at other cultures. It is true that women have to undergo the biological process of reproduction, but it is not only them who can care and provide for children. This is shown by the Australian aborigines for instance, and the Arapesh who involve both sexes equally in child-care. The Matebele in Rhodesia have a system in which a child has a 'Big Mother' and a number of 'Little Mothers'. These are all called 'Mama' by the child, and: 'It is thought unnatural for the biological mother to show more interest in 'her' child than in those of her sisters and cousins.'[4] This frees many Matabele mothers for work in the fields and in the towns and enables them also to have their children looked after independently. Another example can be drawn from Victorian England, when upper class families usually provided nurses for their children from birth. This left the mothers free to carry out their social duties, and to visit the nursery as often or as seldom as they liked.

What is it that has produced this relatively recent emphasis on the importance of exclusive mothering? Is it perhaps part of the advanced scientific knowledge of a civilized system? It is certainly true that the development and extension of state education has meant that children now remain dependent for longer than before, and the expansion of psychology and Freudian theory has laid the responsibility for a child's personality and behaviour firmly at the door of the family home. However, a less civilized, and more backward result has been to tie women more and more to the home, making their whole lives an investment in and a sacrifice to their children, and making them feel guilty if they cannot adapt to such a life easily or willingly.

But many other props have been brought in to support the idea of a special mother-child relationship. The belief in a maternal instinct is one, and although this instinct is present in many animals and is necessary for their species-survival, it has no proven physiological basis in human beings. A mother's love and protectiveness for her child need be no more intense than that of its father, or in fact any other person who becomes very involved with it. Another belief is that women innately possess the 'right' characteristics for motherhood. This grows out of sex stereotyping and social conditioning but is given substance by the typical feminine personality which develops as a result of the differentiated nature of girls' upbringing. Girls become dependent for identity on other people and relationships and this leads naturally into an apparently 'natural' predisposition for motherhood. Girls have many rehearsals with dolls and through observing their mothers, and may often be made responsible for the care of smaller brothers and sisters. The present organization of work makes it economically valid for women to be primarily concerned with home and family, leaving men free to sell their labour outside. Since women have always lacked an officially acknowledged place in the external world of production, they have had little alternative other than to sink their identity into their ascribed role, into caring for those closest to them. Motherhood has become an integral part of this. But today changes have made it impossible to deny the importance of women's work outside the home. However the economic need to use them more efficiently by tampering with the mothering role is an issue which has been carefully avoided both by a ruling class and a popular ideology that associates any alteration of family structure with social chaos.

The growth of psychology in the 'twenties and 'thirties and the subsequent recognition of the importance of a child's early experiences resulted in much theorizing and research. The consequences for a child of early separation from the exclusive and continuous care of its mother were scrutinized. The doom-laden concept of 'maternal deprivation' was formulated, predicting delinquency and personality defects. This condemned mothers who were separated from their young children through work or for any other reason. One of the earliest proponents of this view was John Bowlby, who in 1947 declared: 'It appears that there is a very strong case indeed for believing that prolonged separation of a child from his mother (or mother-substitute) during the first five years of life stands foremost among the causes of delinquent character development and persistent misbehaviour.'[5] He later modified this, but the essence remained: that there was an 'autonomous propensity' by both mother and infant to develop a deep attachment towards each other.[6] Many of his followers carried this further by extending and misinterpreting his and their own findings. Bowlby's early research has been much criticized, since it was based on children in residential nurseries who thereby provided an example of the effects of institutionalization rather than maternal deprivation. The central theories of exclusive attachment and mothering have also been attacked.[7] Numerous studies trying to test these have only produced inconclusive or contradictory results, and indicate the complexity of the concept. But the belief in a special mother–child bond is still very strong and its spell has yet to be broken.

Soon after Bowlby and similar researchers had made their theories public, these began to be used against mothers who worked. For instance, 'It has been claimed that proper mothering is only possible if the mother does not go out to work [Baers 1954] and that the use of day nurseries and crèches has a particularly serious and permanent deleterious effect.'[8] In spite of inconclusive evidence, working mothers over the past thirty years have inevitably become linked with child neglect and have been made very responsible for the future development of their children.

It is undeniable that a child needs to make close bonds with at least one person that she or he can trust, love and depend on. What is incorrect however is the claim that there is one exclusive and primary relationship between mother (or a specific mother-substitute) and child which must remain virtually unbroken during the child's first five years of life. The consequent reluctance to remove children from mothers has even kept some children in very unhappy family situations in preference to going to a 'good' foster or children's home. A child that is badly treated, or who grows up with a background of instability, insecurity or rejection does have a greater probability of developing problems. But this is just as likely to happen in the idealized family home with a full-time mother who cannot cope or who may not be suited to devoting herself to domesticity and child-care.

By comparison, the importance of the father's role has been very under-researched, but the indications are that a father is equally able to have as intense a relationship with a child as its mother. But for men to participate fully implies entering the 'less valued' world of women. Research on men who look after motherless families found that:

Those fathers who continued to work had to regard their work in a new light. No longer could they look at it from the point of view of its economic rewards, the satisfactions, if any, which it brought and the other criteria by which most people assess their job. For many, a new and over-riding criterion asserted itself – the compatibility of work with the care of children.[9]

Men who had to give up work found this particularly disturbing: 'Most fathers drawing supplementary benefit didn't like doing so . . . Fathers felt they ought to be at work. Without a job they were less than men.'[10] The research also found little support for the claims of maternal deprivation in these circumstances. But even if male reaction to increased 'fathering' was favourable, the present division of labour by sex, with its emphasis on efficiency, would not permit working men to include this in their role. Men usually work all day and often late on shift-work or overtime and have little opportunity to spend much time with children.

The myth of maternal deprivation and neglect remains rooted within a deceptively simple concept of motherhood. It would perhaps be better to abolish the terms 'motherhood' and 'father-hood' as they serve to isolate responsibility for children. Although a substantial amount has been written about it, attempts to produce general theories about it have not proven very meaningful.

I think that an individual approach would be far more appropriate to the present situation. For instance it has been shown that the satisfaction felt by a woman towards her position, whether it be a working one or not, has a more positive effect on her children than her blanket acceptance of the need for all mothers either to stay home, or to work.[11] Dissatisfied mothers can produce the same 'harmful' effects as negligent ones. Too often the happiness and satisfaction of a mother is neglected in the theories and research lavished on the needs of her children. Concentration on the possible bad effects on children resulting from their mother's working has ignored the possible benefits to both mother and child. For instance, one working mother commented: 'I don't think it does the child any harm at all by the mother going out to work, in fact I think they benefit. The child who's gone to a nursery and has been surrounded and has been taught to share things will mix far more easily in a school than a child that's been with its mother.'

Unfortunately it takes more than counter-evidence to permeate and erode such a monument to women's subjugation, and one that is so much a part of social structure and beliefs. The scarcity of nurseries, the unequal pay that makes man's work outside the home more important than a woman's, and the deep investment of feminine identity in the happiness of family life, form a combination of levels that must be broken down before women can freely share the mothering role with men as well as other women.

Probably neither children nor their families have heard of Bowlby or other similar researchers, but they have learnt through the way that families are organized and from books, magazines and the television, that a mother and her children have a 'special' attachment. Girls and boys see fathers going out to work as the stable economic provider, while mothers are either full-time housewives or do work in addition to their household tasks. Many mothers who work because of economic necessity have to take manual or semi-skilled jobs and may justifiably complain about the amount of work they have to do. Their daughters gain little idea from them that mothers could work because they want to, and not because they have to.

Several of the Ealing girls who had full-time working mothers said that when they had a home and family of their own they would make sure that they were waiting at home when their children came back from school. They did not expect father to be there, or other friends or relatives. The present structure does not encourage them to question it or seek alternatives, but only to compromise and adapt to it. It is reassuring to come home *to* somebody, after school or work, but there is no rational reason why it has to be mother. But once again it is difficult to break the pattern since it is with their mother that many children have already had to form their closest attachments through the isolating circumstances of the nuclear family. Their dependence on her makes her presence hard to find a substitute for and reinforces the belief in this as the crucial relationship. If care and responsibility for children was consistently (but not confusingly) shared amongst more people, and other attachments were made and nurtured, there would be less pressure on mothers, and children would be able to benefit from a number of different relationships with adults of varying personality and role. But it is hard to construct a different and shared way of child-rearing in the midst of the old ongoing system that emphasizes privacy, property and possession of people as well as things. Experiments in raising children in communes and similar environments have consequently encountered problems as well as advantages.[12]

FEMININE OCCUPATIONS

Curiously, as a housewife and mother, a woman is regarded as someone who 'doesn't work', whose activities, although necessary, are not 'real' work. This attitude is extended to any work she does outside, and consequently 'women's work' has been under-valued, under-paid, and very exploited. '. . . women do work which is both dirty and physically tiring when it appears as an extension of housework. Indeed, the more closely work resembles housework, the less it has the status of 'real' work. Cleaning is a clear example of this.[13] Also secretarial work often involves little more than being a 'substitute wife'[14] to bosses, carrying out all the low-level menial tasks and drudgery. In a recent survey, two out of three secretaries said that running personal errands was part of a secretary's job. They are treated as sexual decoration for the office and the male ego. The crucial part they play in their bosses' success goes unrecognized.

A vicious circle is set up in which women's work, like the status of women themselves, reinforces their own devaluation:

In our money economy, women have relatively little money in their own right. They sell their labour in the bargain basement, at cut prices, and so they are given a cut-price valuation in all spheres of activity. When you sell your labour power you are also selling your time, your life-time, the stuff of life itself, and if it fetches low prices you are yourself valued low.'[15]

There are many reasons for the persistence of this circularity, and for the continued separation of jobs according to sex. Employers for instance have little wish to change the situation, because they benefit from women as a cheap labour force. They, and most other men and women, accept many assumptions about women's suitability for particular jobs. In male-dominated areas of work, there is strong opposition to women's entry from the men who are fearful of dilution, lowered wages, and unemployment. Opportunities also vary by region, and outside the highly-urbanized centres, women wanting to work have to choose from the limited jobs available. Many women have to take on the boring repetitive jobs that they are supposed to be so well suited for, because there is nothing else, or because with their double work load inside and outside the home, they cannot cope with jobs needing concentration and responsibility. But to declare that women do not find this work boring, or that they even enjoy it, is wrong. In the words of one woman worker:

It's very tiring work in the way that – it's boring you know. You put the same bits in, and if you can't think of anything else you just think of the bits you put in. I switch off, myself. I don't know what the other girls do but I can't think of work all the time otherwise I'd get real depressed. The sort of people who usually work on printed circuit are young people, the reason being that it's very monotonous work and a younger person can usually stick, whereas an older person would crack up, something like that. With my job, the boards come up, and

there's a lot of bits out some days and it gets on top of me and I feel
like picking 'em up and chucking 'em on the floors.
                    Woman factory worker interviewed on *Women at Work*.

One characteristic of many popular jobs for girls is that they are
one-level occupations. They contain little opportunity for moving
into anything different or higher. Most women's work remains
'stationary' apart from the professions, in which women still
form a small minority, and such jobs as teaching and hospital
work. In these a rise is possible, but less likely for a woman than
a man. Movement is horizontal from job to job, with little progression to anywhere except marriage or old age. (Where
women's position and pay in the form of allowances and pen-
sions is still lower than men's!)

For instance, although office-work does represent a good respectable job for a girl, it has got a very low ceiling in terms of
prospects. This is especially so for working class girls who often
go into it with lower qualifications, or merely lack some of the
refinements of accent or manner acquired by middle and upper
class girls. Office-work has built up it own hierarchies, from the
'pool proletariat' to the executive secretary, and discriminates
accordingly.

Within this vast cross-section of the female population, there are
many distinct gradations of social class, which are translated into distinctions at work. It is often assumed that an office girl slowly progresses
from the typing pool to the carpeted office of the 'executive secretary'.
But in fact few girls seem to make much progress once they enter the
office. It reflects enduring social distinctions as faithfully as does the
school system ... The selection goes back as far as birth and is reinforced by the prestige gradations of secretarial schools.[16]

Therefore a secretary or shorthand typist usually progresses
only to a position where she is working for a more important
boss. She is unlikely to become anything other than a secretary
herself. In work such as television production[17] and publishing
secretarial work is used as a side-door for women into positions
that men would apply for directly, and there is no guaranteed
promotion. Similarly, receptionists, telephone operators and shop
assistants do little more than swap jobs. A female bank clerk is

viewed differently from a male bank clerk, every one of whom is 'a potential bank manager'. Women as 'rank and file', and in servicing roles to men's occupational superiority are taken for granted in a view that places men at the top of a hierarchy of power and women at the bottom and disregards the real usefulness of their work.

The situation will not be solved however by getting women into management and top jobs, for this does nothing to remove the inequalities everywhere else. In fact, as Audrey Wise has said, 'what we want to do is abolish top jobs'. It is more important for instance to give all girls the opportunities to learn various sorts and levels of skills and to give them self-confidence in their abilities, instead of exploiting them through myths of femininity that imprison them in the 'bargain basement'.

We have seen that since feminine characteristics are not ones that are highly valued in this society, women's work is treated as inferior. Women are seen, and see themselves as not having the appropriate qualities to cope with men's work. But this does not necessarily constitute a criticism of women. On the contrary, men can be seen as sacrificing themselves to the acquisition of more money, either through desire to make profit, or in desperation to make enough to feed and clothe a family. The overwhelming concern that the Ealing girls showed about people and about interest in a job reflected their emphasis on 'human' aspects rather than money. Men surrender to a de-humanizing rat-race, agreeing to productivity deals which make work more unpleasant in return for promises of increased wages, which soon get swallowed up in inflation while conditions remain the same. Women have traditionally been excluded from this at home and those who have had to work have been more exploited than men, but in the increased female militancy of recent times, women sensibly do not want to follow men's example in their demands.

Indeed, sometimes women have shown apathy or antagonism on the question of equal pay itself, precisely because they fear that more wages will mean worse conditions, forced nightwork etc. The woman who says: 'I don't want equal pay.' sounds very backward. She is often really saying: 'I don't want to worsen my working conditions even for more money', and this is *not* backward.[18]

Women in jobs such as teaching and nursing, have begun to be militant, and many are realizing that they must demand better conditions as well as pay. Men may accept working under almost any conditions for more money, and these contrast greatly with the easy conditions and service they expect from their private sanctuary at home. But women are more sensitive and resistant to such compromises. Their actual or ideological exclusion from total involvement in work has preserved in them a sense of being apart from the system. They are less easily conned into exchanging conditions for cash.

YOUNG HOPES: OLD PREJUDICES

If we consider the potential working life of girls today the grounds for prejudice and sexism fall away. Firstly, families have become smaller over the years and nowadays the average family only contains two or three children. The technological progress and publicity connected with contraception has meant that more and more women can control their own bodies, their families can be planned and their lives are freed from the unpredictability and tyranny of pregnancy. Secondly, women have longer lives than men (about seven years on average), although presumably due to being the 'weaker' sex, they retire five years earlier than men. Thirdly, there is no substantiated reason why it should be considered harmful for a woman to work if she wishes to during most of her pregnancy and fairly soon afterwards. Therefore assuming free and easy access to nursery facilities a woman with two children need only spend about three years of her life preoccupied with pregnancy and lactation. This represents a tiny proportion of her life-span. If she wants to be a full-time mother until her children are well into school, this still leaves between thirty and forty years of her life when she is able to work. Of course not every woman wants to work, but the important thing is to have the choice, and not just the choice of low level and boring jobs. Many women would like to do some work if the right opportunities existed, and they should be able to do so without being rejected on the basis of outdated and unfair reasoning.

There is for instance little difference between a girl leaving a trade or industry, and a man moving from job to job. If some areas of work seem to have a high turnover of girls, it is more often because the job is so boring, or offers such little prospect, that the only sensible thing to do is to move on for a change. Many male apprentices leave on completion of their apprenticeships, using these as vehicles to greater things. What is the difference between a boy doing this, and a girl leaving to have a baby? There are some indications that since the late 1950s girls of fourteen to fifteen years of age have indeed begun entertaining ideas and hopes of working after getting married, and to some extent after having children. One study[19] (carried out in 1956) showed that 'an unexpectedly large proportion of girls were hoping to continue in paid work after marriage'. 61 per cent said they would continue to work after marriage, (18 per cent full-time and 43 per cent part-time); and 50 per cent said they would take up work again when their children were old enough to be left (9 per cent full-time and 41 per cent part-time). The trend indicated by this result can be seen in the hopes expressed by the girls whose attitudes to science were being explored in a study[20] around the same time. 85 per cent said they would work until the birth of their children (55 per cent full-time and 30 per cent part-time), and 52 per cent intended to work after their children were fifteen years old (17 per cent full-time and 35 per cent part-time). The researchers at this time concluded that girls saw their home-making role as their primary role, while the work that they planned to continue with was a secondary interest. In a more recent survey,[21] 97 per cent of the girls between the ages of fifteen and eighteen years who were asked about their working plans said that they would work after marriage, (43 per cent part-time and 54 per cent full-time); and although 91 per cent said that they would not work before their children went to school, 93 per cent said that they would work while they were at school, (82 per cent part-time and 11 per cent full-time), and 93 per cent also said they would work after the children had left school, (36 per cent part-time and 57 per cent full-time). Therefore although part-time work is still emphasized, there has been an increased tendency towards full-time work, especially after the children are self-sufficient. It seems odd however that so many of these girls still thought that marriage necessitated relinquishing full-time work for part-time work, and that such a high proportion would not work at all before their children went to school. It points to the variation in and changeability of ideas and attitudes through time and between regions – which should be kept in mind when generalizations are made. For instance, it is likely that living in London gives girls a broader perspective on the idea of working mothers than they would be likely to get in a small town.

The girls who are today contemplating the world of work view it with fragile and incomplete images of their future lives, but with hope, and with some awareness of the changing ideas about women and their role. The girls from Ealing schools provided some illustrations of how they intended to cope with future homes and work.

I think [working after marriage] is important because I think you tend to vegetate a bit if left at home doing housework all the time.

I think it's important for a girl to work as well as being married– unless she's got small children. Apart from the extra money, if any thing went wrong with the marriage she would have to support herself, fall back on her job. If you're too dependent on one person, the husband, it's very tempting for the husband to make the wife more the slave.

Over 80 per cent of these girls said they would definitely carry on working after they married, and one was very emphatic that a girl should go for a 'proper' career:

Oh yes! Because if you get a job like this and you get married, you can always go in for some job that isn't so demanding after you're married. But I think it's stupid to leave school and go into some silly office job, because you're wasting your life and you only live once.

Most expected to stop work when they had a family, and stay at home while their children were very young, but many also expressed strong views that women should go back to part-time or full-time work as soon as they could put their children into nursery school.

... when you have a baby you don't say, right, now I'll pack up working and be a housewife. I don't agree with that at all. When they're small, O.K., but once you can get them into a nursery, then, when they're about three, go back to work again.

If you're indoors all the time, you can get bored and fed-up with it. I don't think they should leave their children when they're ever so young, but when they're about four they should be back at work.

It would be rash to make wide generalizations about these findings. Some girls have definite ideas about the necessity of long and full-time motherhood, and others, declaring their working intentions now, may find them hard to fulfil when the time arrives. In areas outside London traditional values retain their strong though dusty footholds, opportunities are fewer, and changing ideas make less sense and take longer to permeate. The nature of the available work is important and may turn out to be less attractive than working at home. In the absence of economic necessity, staying at home is then chosen with relief. Caution is also necessary when trying to infer action from stated attitudes and intentions, especially for girls at this age whose real futures may be hazier than the impression given by their answers. However, to the extent that their ideas reflect their own absorption of a general and changing opinion about women and work, they can certainly be taken optimistically and seriously.

The number of women working has increased greatly over the last ten to twenty years, largely as a result of married women continuing to work or returning to it later. Ideology is changing and people are beginning to recognize that being permanently at home is often both boring and unnecessary and that taking a job is a 'good thing' for those women who can and want to. Although complete acceptance of this view is still some way off, in many quarters it is becoming another model for behaviour. Some full-time mothers and housewives are finding that their commitment is called into question by this model which is increasingly being held up as the only 'right' course. But conditions are not keeping pace with ideology and those who advocate such a new model blandly assume that children will be taken care of elsewhere and thus betray the middle class nature of their thinking. I have met several young full-time mothers living in the suburbs of London who felt that they should be working although they did not want to; they held Women's Liberation to blame for the pressure that they felt rather than the changing social and economic climate.

The acceptance of married women working is related to their own changing attitude to jobs, and increased education for girls has led to a heightening of their expectations from work. As the long term possibilities of work are assumed, 'interest' (which includes meeting people) is accentuated as a characteristic which is as important as or more important than other factors like convenience or money. This varies by region and according to opportunity: for instance if all local jobs are equally boring and uninteresting and marriage takes on a high value then money will clearly be the most important criterion.

'Interest' was very important to the Ealing girls, whose contemporaries thirty years ago would hardly have considered this as a possibility as they moved from job to job, usually working in factories and workshops. Shop-work was perhaps the nearest thing to being interesting and unmonotonous. At this time, girls at school might have vaguely hoped that the jobs they went into would be quite interesting, but it was far more important to earn money to help the family than to seek job satisfaction.

It was significant that for the Ealing girls money was not considered to be the most important thing, in fact this was specifically denied in several instances. Although this may be a specifically London phenomenon, for them at least the emphasis had moved more towards the content of work – its interest and satisfactions, and the possibility of a girl 'making a career for herself'. Considering the mundane, boring and non-promotional jobs that are the lot of many girls there is bound to be some disillusionment. But whether or not girls would now be content to transfer their expectations back to a home and family remains to be seen.

Women and girls growing up today are trying to combine marriage, children and work for all kinds of reasons and with varying success and satisfaction, and most constantly battle with real obstacles that make this very difficult. Girls thinking about their futures are beginning to realize these contradictions in their role. A few are thinking deeply about it, and one expressed it in this way:

If a lady is to be anybody she's not to be at home all the time. I mean – she is a person after all. She's not a person you put away in the cupboard that cleans up the house and has children, and the husband does everything else. No, it's not fair – after all, she's living. She should go to work, not even for the money, but to be someone and do something. If she's got young children to begin with, she'll wait a couple of years maybe three, and say she's decided to put it in a nursery, that's good for the child because it makes them more stable when they're about five, and if she gets it so that she can fix it in with nursery hours, she'll be all right. My Mum did that with my brother in a nursery and she worked out all right. As long as there's not too many children and they're not too untidy, they should get on all right.

Christine

Notes

Chapter 6

1. See for instance Ann Oakley, *Sex, Gender and Society*, Temple Smith, 1972; Ann Oakley, *Housewife*, Allen Lane, 1974, chapter 7; M. Mead, *Male and Female*, Penguin, 1950.

2. Angus Calder, *The People's War*, Panther, 1971. (The Second World War.)

3. Audrey Wise, 'Women and the Struggle for Workers' Control', *Spokesman Pamphlet*, no. 33, 1973.

4. Edgar Moyo, 'Big Mother and Little Mother in Matabeleland', *History Workshop Pamphlet*, no. 12.

5. John Bowlby, *Child Care and the Growth of Love*, Penguin, 1947.

6. John Bowlby, *Attachment and Loss; Vol 1: Attachment*, Penguin, 1969.

7. See for instance Lee Comer, 'Myth of Motherhood' *Spokesman Pamphlet* no. 21, and her book *Wedlocked Women*, Feminist Books, 1974; Michael Rutter, *Maternal Deprivation Reassessed*, Penguin, 1972; Ann Oakley, *Housewife*, Allen Lane, 1974, chapter 8; and R. P. Wortis, 'The Acceptance of the Concept of Maternal Role by Behavioral Scientists: Its Effects on Women', *American Journal of Orthopsychiatry*, 41(5), October, 1971.

8. W.H.O. Expert Committee on Mental Health, 1951, quoted in Michael Rutter, op. cit.

9. Paul Wilding, 'Motherless Families', *New Society*, 24 August, 1972.

10. Paul Wilding, op. cit.

11. M. R. Yarrow, 'Maternal Employment and Childrearing', *Children*, 8, 1961.

12. See for instance C. Bookhagen, E. Hemmer, J. Raspe and E. Schultz, 'Kommune 2: Childrearing in the Commune'; and G. Zicklin, 'Communal Childrearing', both in H. P. Dreitzel, 'Childhood and Socialisation', *Recent Sociology*, no. 5, 1973; also *Children's Community Centre — Our Experiences of Collective Child Care* published by a group of people involved in this in Dartmouth Park Hill, London, July 1974.

13. Sheila Rowbotham, *Woman's Consciousness, Man's World*, Penguin, 1973.

14. M. Benet, *Secretary*, Panther, 1972.

15. Audrey Wise, op. cit.

16. M. Benet, op. cit.

17. Liz Kustow, 'Television and Women', in M. Wandor (Ed.), *The Body Politic, Stage 1*, 1972.

18. Audrey Wise, op. cit.

19. J. Joseph, 'A Research Note on Attitudes to Work and Marriage of Six Hundred Adolescent Girls', *British Journal of Sociology*, vol. 12, 1961.

20. N. Seear, V. Roberts and J. Brock, *A Career for Women in Industry?*, Oliver & Boyd Ltd, 1964.

21. Unpublished survey carried out by Anna Coote and Laura King, 1973.

The Chosen Sex

Is it Better to be a Girl?

I like being a girl and being feminine. I also like boys. I think being able to have a child is wonderful, whereas boys can only help.

I think it is better to lead a girl's life because girls don't get hit because they are feminine. Also they don't get told off as much as boys do. Girls can wear sexy clothes.

Boys can't wear pretty things and be emotional over a film or book etc. and if you're a girl you like boys and little children and if you were a boy you wouldn't be able to do this.

It's easier and nicer to be a girl – boys have so much responsibility.

Or a Boy?

I'd prefer to be a boy, because they have a much larger choice of jobs than we do, also they seem to have far more fun.

Boys can get out of doing things round the house, and it is natural for a boy to get into trouble, not a girl.

[Boys] don't have to wear skirts, and parents let boys do more things than girls.

[What I dislike about being a girl is] having to have children, why can't men have them. Having a period, we have to go through pain where the men don't. Girls do the housework and cook when she comes home from work, where the men have everything waiting for them when they come home, and then they laze about.

Boys' and girls' satisfactions with being male or female are one part of a constant self-evaluating process, and the mirror into which they look for self-appraisal is framed with the comparative values and standards set up by society. It is hard to question a biological fact of birth but not impossible to assess and criticize the consequences that follow from it.

Their perception that femininity and the feminine role are often considered less important or meaningful than equivalent areas of masculinity lies uneasily alongside women's enjoyment of them. The ambivalence that this can produce questions the happiness derived from female activities. This same unequal value system has explained the acceptance of tomboys and the rejection of 'sissie' boys. Girls may be envious of boys' abilities and facilities but the reverse is rare.

When boys and girls are young they differ in the amount of preference they have for activities associated with the opposite sex. Girls have as great an enthusiasm for boys' roles, toys and activities as they do for 'feminine' things whereas boys firmly adhere to their appropriate 'masculine' role and activities and often contemplate those of girls with derision. Some work done in America has illustrated the nature of sex-role preferences in young children.[1] For example, girls aged between three and a half and five and a half years of age divided almost equally into those preferring feminine things and those preferring masculine ones, while 70 to 80 per cent of the boys in this age-group favoured masculine roles. The differences widened with increasing age and six- to nine-year-old boys became more enthusiastic about masculine expressions of their role, while girls too showed a greater preference for masculine choices than for feminine ones.

This is the time when it is quite permissible for girls to be 'tomboys'. But as they move towards and into adolescence, they feel and respond to pressures that point them in a more feminine direction. They internalize much of their role without even being aware of it and there are many models readily available. Increasing age and experience has given them an idea of how life is organized and they begin to structure their present and future perceptions accordingly. The tomboy preference for masculine activities gives way to an emphasis on appearance and the recognition of a future status that depends on becoming girlfriend, wife and mother. The switch from masculine preferences to feminine ones can be rationalized through shared involvement in the social trappings of femininity and through acknowledging the more enjoyable aspects of being female.

This has already started happening for many children before they reach their teens, aided by earlier puberty and easy access to information about sexuality and womanhood. In one study of twelve-year-olds,[2] both girls and boys were asked what sex they would have chosen to be if they could have chosen for themselves. 93 per cent of the boys and 81 per cent of the girls chose their same sex again rather than preferring to be the opposite sex. The reasons given by the boys for their choice were mainly connected with physical superiority and the claim to have a 'better life', whereas the girls most frequently mentioned appearance and clothing as the attraction of being female.

The Ealing girls were also asked this kind of question and a similar proportion (75 per cent) of them replied that they would have chosen to be born as girls. The rest would have preferred to be born as boys. Their reasons were various and those who favoured being girls were mainly concerned with the traditional activities of the feminine role. They had progressed beyond the earlier twelve-year-olds' emphasis on clothes and appearance, and although these were still important aspects they were superseded by the anticipated joys and satisfactions of becoming wives and mothers and caring for homes and children.

Girls at secondary school are already very aware of their feminine role especially where it concerns reproduction and motherhood, and this necessarily affects their future hopes and ambitions in other areas of life. As we saw earlier, the under-valuation of femininity has skirted deceptively around motherhood in terms of ideology, while the real conditions for instance for working or unsupported mothers are discriminatory and oppressive. Glorification of motherhood has always concealed the amount of sacrifice and the struggle that this involves for women. Nevertheless motherhood remains one of the most positive aspects of the feminine role for many girls.

I love having children around me and when you have your own children I suppose you look after them more than your husband would be able to.

I'd rather be a girl because I love young children and I think a mother is closer than fathers to young children.

Girls have more happiness in life, bring up a family, wearing nice clothes, and not having to go out to work when they're married.

I like being a girl and would like to be a housewife and have children.

A girl may have her own home and cooks and cleans for her husband if she gets married and she may not have to work all her life.

There appeared to be no conflict in their minds between their futures as housewives and mothers and the generally low social value associated with this role. Their love of children makes motherhood a very attractive and worthwhile goal. The sexual division of labour has placed women primarily at home, produced the discontinuity in their potential working lives and reinforced their assumed 'inferiority' as workers, but it is this very factor that enhances the feminine role because it seems to imply greater choice. For instance, 'Girls can do more things, they get married, have children. They can stay at home or go to work. Men cannot.' It is an attractive proposition not to have to work all your life, as men have to do, and they were pleased that being girls excused them from this, as well as from other sorts of responsibilities.*

I enjoy being a girl and I hope to get married and have a family of my own. I don't want to be a boy because they have horrible jobs to do for fifty years.

I like feminine things, and boys; and boys, when they grow older, have to support a wife and child.

It is part of the traditional male role to assume responsibility and to take the initiative, at work, at home and in developing personal relationships. This has equivalent drawbacks and advantages and there is no reason apart from custom for boys to do this rather than girls. Girls sometimes mention the fact that boys have

---

*In a study of five- to eleven-year-olds in America, Hartley found that with increasing age girls disliked the thought of working outside the home and preferred the idea of a domestic life with children.[3]

to ask girls out as being something they do not envy while others complain that waiting to be asked is just as bad. For the Ealing girls, these and other feminine activities, such as wearing fashionable clothes and make-up, being sensitive and emotional, and being treated more gently and respectfully, all enhanced a picture of frivolous irresponsibility against a background of future maternal responsibility.

I would prefer to be a girl because most boys are rough, don't have a very good reputation at school. If you were a good-mannered boy, you are normally laughed at. I also like being feminine, I don't want to be rough.

Girls have better clothes and bright colours suit them.

I think it is better to lead a girl's life, because girls don't get hit because they are feminine. Also they don't get told off as much as boys do.

Girls can wear much prettier clothes, can have children, can be emotional over books and films, have a gentleman to pay for you and go out with.

I think a girl can have a bigger choice of fashion, and when they're upset a girl can cry and let it out but a boy keeps it inside him and makes it worse.

It is easy to identify with the way they feel and understand how attractive women's role appears compared to that of men. Women's lives are not as directly tied down to earning money. They have a husband to pay for their upkeep and although in real life it has become far less possible to keep a family on a single wage, this is the assumption made by the state in all its rules and dealings with married women. And although women may seem separated from production through being at home, this is deceptive as we saw earlier, and women have a crucial part to play in organizing their own domestic labour so that their house-keeping money can be stretched in every possible way to make ends meet. Working class girls in particular are well aware of the struggle that maintaining a home and family can involve, and are also conscious of working class women's traditional need to work. Many of their mothers exemplify this and work in badly paid and unsatisfying jobs. When we consider girls' reactions to questions about being girls, it helps to take into account their context of socio-economic conditions and ideology. Work is then not seen as attractive but as an unfortunate necessity of life and therefore the apparent opportunity to avoid it seems one of the advantages of being a woman.

In addition to this there are other inducements. For instance children are more worth spending time and energy on than many boring and alienating jobs, since they actually respond and grow. The apparent choice of whether to work or not after marriage and after children, and the ability to organize life in the home without supervision gives an illusion of freedom and greater choice of action. If girls accept that their life will be fulfilling by having a husband and bearing his children, then this does provide a defined and tangible goal, one that can be reached without too many qualifications or too much competition or training. Inasfar as their role is concretely defined as being at home and with children and still only vaguely defined in terms of work, it provides girls with a necessary framework in structuring and organizing their lives. Girls' lives have traditionally been set out for them, the major question often being *who* they will marry rather than what they may become. This can be interpreted as 'easier' to the extent that they do not have to bear (in theory) the major economic responsibility for family survival. In practice this is not so.*

There are many other errors and deceptions in this picture. What seems like 'freedom' and 'choice' has its own confining limitations. The value of being able to choose whether or not to work is diminished when it is realized that the only available jobs, for someone without qualifications and training, may be uninteresting, unprogressive and under-paid. Part-time work, which many women want, is often hard to find and may be almost full-time work for a half-time wage. Housework may seem to offer freedom to be your own boss and organize your own day, but it produces its own monotony. Although it has become less time-consuming with modern aids, housework offers little permanent satisfaction and the aids have removed most of its skills or

---

* Figures from the 1971 census revealed that one in five women were the chief economic supporters of the household.

made them redundant. Freedom becomes isolation and autonomy condenses into a choice of radio programme.

Many of the forty housewives interviewed in 1971 by Ann Oakley claimed that 'the "best thing" about being a housewife is that you're your own boss, you don't have to go to work and you have free time.'[4] However this 'freedom' becomes compromised by always having to be enjoyed in the place where work is to be done, and as Oakley comments:

The housewife is 'free from' rather than 'free to'; the absence of external supervision is not balanced by the liberty to use time for one's own ends. The taking of leisure is self-defeating ... Housewives experience more monotony, fragmentation and social isolation in their work than do workers in the factory. Somewhat predictably perhaps they have more in common with assembly-line workers than with those whose jobs involve less repetition and more skill.

Motherhood offers a more meaningful role but ironically this is also one which is in perpetual conflict with that of the housewife. Children bring dirt and untidiness and constantly create housework. Caring for them has many rewards but it can also become overwhelming and intermittently depressing, as their constant demands leave women no time to themselves, no time to think, no time to give expression to their own individuality. When at last they do have time, their early youthful enthusiasm and capacity for self expression may have drained away. But whether the satisfactions which come from looking after a home, husband and family are great or small, they do not have to fill a life-time. When children have grown up and are self-sufficient, their mother's 'primary' role is apparently over and time may stretch into the future filled with nothing but housework. The thought of working again is often frightening after so many years at home, and without skills the choice of work may now be rather limited.

We have seen that the way a girl sees herself and her aims and values is critically important to the way she pursues the various threads of her life. Although each of the Ealing girls had her own attitudes, hopes and expectations to guide her future, they also expressed some consistent values and goals as a group. They thought for instance that it was important for them to have lots of fun and friends, to be independent and earn lots of money; they wanted to be successful with boys, to get married and have a home of their own, to have children and to feel needed. The relative importance of more studious aspects, like being good at school-work, and having a full-time career, although not insignificant, faded in the light of social aims and ambitions. It is part of the confusion of old and new images of feminine role that women's job intentions and expectations continually bump up against the forces of marriage and family life.

The Ealing girls showed little feminist consciousness, if by this is meant criticism or rejection of any of the traditional features and expectations of the feminine role. However their endorsement of traditional features of femininity does have positive and optimistic aspects that should not be overlooked. They are responding in a realistic and rational way to a social structure over which they have little individual control. Most recognize only a distortion of Women's Liberation ideas at the moment and if they were to reject their role as women there appears to them to be nothing to replace it. Women's oppression has always been characterized by isolation at home – producing a lack of solidarity which has hindered the development of any women's movement. The pleasure and confidence that girls express in being female is a stronger basis on which to build solidarity than is a preference to be male and a rejection of women as inferior or unimportant. From this basis the good aspects of the feminine role can be emphasized and the onerous and oppressive ones can be challenged and changed. It would be wrong to assume as some socialists did in the past that the worse the state of people, the more discontented they become and therefore the more militant. It often happens that it is when people are growing strong and confident in themselves that they are able to examine their situation and demand change.

In examining the more positive features of the feminine role, the masculine role also comes under scrutiny and its disadvantages are taken into account. For instance, the girls' reluctance to have 'horrible jobs for fifty years' is very reasonable and is one of the many disadvantages of being male. The fact that fathers are often less close to their children than mothers, and are not generally found in many jobs that involve child-care is a major gap in their meaningful experience. Furthermore the development of 'manliness' demands the public suppression of all but the more destructive emotions.

Many girls are enthusiastic about the things they like about being female and feminine, and gloss over the realities and hardships. They are well aware of the pain and struggle that can be involved but accept this as the way things are and should be. At present they have little idea that change might be brought about by themselves rather than imposed from outside and so continually try to compromise and adjust.

I'm not really sure, I like a lot of things about being a girl, like clothes, but I think at the moment boys get a fairer deal in a way, so maybe I'd prefer to be a boy. At present, a lot get more money for what they do and get better positions in their jobs, and more politicians and things. I suppose it's partly because girls don't go in for things like that but they do tend to get on easier than girls. I think girls have to fight harder to get better jobs.

Penny

Some girls expressed a preference for girls' jobs and said that these were more interesting, or that girls had better opportunities. The correctness of their assumptions about opportunity and prospects is dubious, but it is true that the 'women's work' that involves personal interaction, in places like hospitals or offices, does seem more relevant than for instance producing parts for cars.

The girls who would have preferred to have been born as boys placed a different interpretation on the characteristics of the feminine role. The joys that were anticipated by other girls in housewifery and motherhood were retranslated into pain, inconvenience and lack of freedom. Their general contention was that 'boys have it easy' because they have better jobs and opportunity in life, no periods or pregnancy, less responsibility and more freedom.*

* In the study of twelve-year-old children's attitudes cited earlier each sex saw the opposite sex as having the 'easier life', but while this was the only reason given by the boys, the girls gave many other reasons why they envied men.[5]

A boy does not have the worry of staying home all day and looking after the children. He also has the chance of a better job. Boys have more chance of getting on in life than girls.

Boys do not have as many problems as girls have.

I have always wanted to be a boy and am always dressed in jeans etc. Boys always get on better, they can just go up to girls and talk to them. Girls have to wait until they are approached. Boys get all the pleasure and girls get all the pain.

Boys do not have to worry about leaving their jobs because they do not have children.

Boys seem to be a lot freer than girls, and parents don't worry about them as much as they do to girls.

Boys – the way I look at it, they get away with a load of things we don't get away with. My mum and dad don't worry about them the way they worry about girls, and they seem to trust them more.

Girls have a long history of restricted mobility. Middle class girls in particular have for several centuries been tied very closely and protectively to their homes. For working class girls this has happened more gradually since their home situations were often so cramped that it was a relief for parents to have them out of the house. But at the turn of the century their restriction was accelerated by the increasing awareness of 'respectability' amongst certain areas of the working class. 'Respectable' families did not let their daughters wander the streets.

There are also all the other ways in which freedom has been constrained. For instance there is little encouragement within women's role for exploration and adventure, and girls' upbringing does not allow them to develop much confidence in doing this. The conception of women as property and producers of 'heirs' has ensured their close supervision in the past and the 'weakness' of their sex has made them prey for the sexual desires and superior strength of men. Despite the so-called permissiveness of society today, girls are still kept under quite a strict family control which has consequences beyond the simple one of their protection.*

* Such as inhibiting the development of analytical ability.

Parents fear for the safety of their daughters if they are out at night. But rather than equipping them with knowledge and confidence about 'the facts of life', many of them prefer a method of strict control. However much they do trust their daughters it often seems to girls that parents have little trust in them and that ways have to be found to get around this. The Ealing girls were conscious of their relative lack of freedom, often made explicit by the comparative treatment of their brothers.

My brother, he can go out any time of the night he likes – come in any time of the morning he likes – and if I did that, there'd be hell to pay. It's just not fair. My mum still thinks my time is at half-past nine. I think that's ridiculous!

They are right to complain about their lack of freedom and opportunity and their future domestic responsibility just as other girls were right to contemplate their enjoyment of children and a freer expression of emotions. What they are doing is describing the unequal advantages and disadvantages experienced by both women and men. Each has a life that is circumscribed and justified by the organization of social beliefs and economic conditions. Each bears the consequences in different ways but women have borne these in not just one but every area of their lives.

BOYFRIENDS AND MARRIAGE

At the moment I'm going out with a fantastic guy and I'm really enjoying being a girl.

Boyfriends feature heavily in the thoughts and activities of teenage girls whether or not they have actually got one. They represent social success and status, a secure symbol of acceptable femininity, someone with whom to share experiences and tentatively explore love and sexuality, someone to take them out and give them a good time. Girls are surrounded by constant reminders of the importance of attracting boys. Two-thirds of the Ealing girls said that they had current boyfriends, most of whom were older than them and working, mainly as mechanics, electricians or in similar jobs. Both girls and boys develop ideas about the most desirable qualities to look for in the opposite sex. They survey the stereotyped possibilities that are hung up on the media line as prototypes for approval and imitation. Handsome and rakish men confront and conquer sexy women, who manage to retain the required amount of demure coyness. But how far do these mirror the real desires of girls and boys, and the criteria by which they judge what is attractive?

One study by Jacqui Sarsby[6] of these ideas in children of fourteen and a half to fifteen and a half years indicated that the emphasis is different for each sex. In order to get a range of social classes, boys and girls attending private, grammar and secondary modern schools were studied. In addition to the differences in ideas between the sexes, differences were also discovered between the schools which, of course, were broadly related to social class. The majority of boys set great store by looks and sexual characteristics, concentrating very much on the shapeliness of a girl's figure. This approach was rather different from the girls, who 'mentioned good looks in equal proportion to the boys, but the difference was that they often stipulated that they didn't *really* matter, or that they weren't the main thing'. The girls were less concerned about sexual attributes, and placed the accent on things like colour of hair and eyes, and height. What they were more concerned with however was a relationship based on something more supportive, – 'their answers emphasized a desire for someone to understand them, not to laugh at them, and to be kind to them if they were depressed. They stressed their need to be cared for and treated with sensitivity.' This attitude provided a great contrast to the boys' pin-up figures.

The girls' hopes of finding someone with a kind and understanding personality bore little similarity to the boys' physical ideals. Those boys who did mention personal qualities thought for instance that it was important for a girl to be respectful or obedient, and others spontaneously referred to the desirability of marrying a virgin. This double-standard, although in a gradual state of erosion, was still prominent for some boys, and also caused a comment from one of the Ealing girls:

It's funny really, 'cause when you go out with a bloke, they expect you to give them a bit, . . . but when they want to get married, they want a girl who's a virgin, and yet they've just taken some other girl's virginity – so she can't marry a bloke who wants her to be a virgin. It's daft, it really is!

Michelle

Sarsby found the greatest differences between the private school girls and the secondary modern girls. The former were relatively more concerned with the intellectual compatibility of their future husband and stressed equality, independence and understanding. They did not feel that their husband should dominate and make all the decisions. 'The secondary modern girl, on the other hand, was looking generally for an honest, reliable, moderately good-looking, sexually experienced male, who would be faithful, provide a regular income and sexual satisfaction, and be kind and understanding . . . His intelligence was only fairly important.' The secondary modern schoolgirls who were mostly from working class backgrounds put more emphasis on security and the practical sides of marriage, they showed anxiety about sexual faithfulness, and tended to wish to give their husbands the major load of responsibility. Their male counterparts however saw their ideals and needs in other terms: they wanted good looks and sexual satisfaction, and wished to be looked after by a competent housewife. Less stress was laid on faithfulness and some degree of independence was demanded.

Sarsby concludes that there is great variation in ideas of what marriage is, what needs each partner expects it to fulfil, and what they expect from one another. She suggests that if these indications are true then marriage across class lines may encounter special difficulties in the consequent clash of expectations.

I did not ask questions about prospective husbands, but a few girls spontaneously mentioned the unreasonable demands they had experienced from boys. For instance one girl complained that:

They don't like girls to swear, goodness knows why. *They* can swear of course. They like them to be feminine, like them to be sort of – not laugh a lot. Sometimes I'm like that, and sometimes I shout me mouth off. They don't like them to giggle. I do I'm afraid. I can't stop sometimes when I start. I think they like them to be more feminine than they are. They say you can do what you like, but if you go off – you say I'm going out, and then they examine you the next day. They ask you, what happened, and what time did you get home etc. They say Oh I'm not possessive but they really are.

These differences in expectations also reflect the perspectives with which boys and girls grow up to view their ftuure lives. The encouragement boys are given to seek independence and adventure conflicts with the eventual necessity of marriage and the responsibility of having a family. Most adolescent boys perceive marriage with a sense of uncertainty, as a time in years ahead when they will settle down in some sort of security with a 'decent girl' who will look after them.* But marriage makes a relatively small ripple on the surface of their continuing life outside home compared with its enormous impact on girls. The obsession with physical features and lack of concern of Sarsby's boys with the personality characteristics of their prospective girlfriends and wives is probably related to their age and level of maturity (which is usually lower than girls at any school-age). But it is true that men's initial perception, judgement and treatment of women as sex-objects continues throughout their lives.

The importance and inevitability of marriage turns every boyfriend into a possible marriage partner. Most (82 per cent) of the Ealing girls wanted to marry – a third of them hoped to be married by the time they were twenty, and three-quarters of them by the 'critical' age of twenty-five. At the age of fifteen, ten years hence seems almost another life-time away, and the occurrence of marriage during this time is almost taken for granted.

For some girls, the failure or miserable conditions of their parents' marriage makes them hesitant about the prospect of their own, but it is hard to reject it for this reason alone. Fictional romance and the rosy glow that surrounds young married couples help to foster the hope that it could all be different for them.

In ways I don't want to get married because me mum and dad's marriage ain't worked out all that good and I wouldn't want mine to

* In the earlier study of twelve-year-olds, 90 per cent of the girls expressed positive attitudes to marriage whereas the boys were split in their views: 57 per cent were positive, 34 per cent were negative and the rest were neutral.[7]

work out the same, but I expect I will get married. I'm going out with me boyfriend at the moment and I wouldn't mind him really. He's dropped a couple of hints but I pretended not to pick 'em up, you know, be a bit difficult.

I do think about marriage and I don't want to – I'd like to but not for a very long time. You'll see my mum at home, and children, her depressions and frustrations. I don't think I could put up with that. I think if I get a career I might not get married. Everyone says I shall but I'm not so sure.

Since my father left, I've had it sort of drummed into me that, well, never trust anyone, and things like this, so I don't think I will get married, not yet anyway. I got a couple of boyfriends but I don't go with anyone steady or anything. Just a different one every night or every time I go out.

By their attitudes, many girls implicitly accepted that a husband and family were the most satisfying things in a woman's life. They thought having children was still of great importance, but they found the old cliché that says that women's place is in the home to be far less acceptable. The ideological climate concerning women's equality exposes the implied put-down in this statement as male-defined and offensive; other aspects of women's role cannot be so easily rejected.

The importance of marriage in girls' lives has also been illustrated in a batch of essays written in 1968 by fourteen- and fifteen-year-old girls from a London grammar school. These were discussed by Eva Figes in her book 'Patriarchal Attitudes'.[8] The girls were told to write an essay in which they imagined looking back on their lives at the age of eighty. Eva Figes concluded that they had 'their thoughts firmly fixed on marriage and motherhood' and very little else, and that '. . . after the birth of the children the future often became little more than a dim fog, with grandmotherhood at the end of it'. These girls seemed to view work differently from the Ealing girls, and only spent a hypothetical ten or so years at work during their life-time. They became 'what they called "an ordinary housewife" at the age of about forty-five'. It is possible that changes in ideas and attitudes about the position of women at home and at work, which have certainly had a great shaking out and airing since 1968, have broadened the minds of girls at school.

An earlier study, carried out in the mid-1950s, looked at girls' attitudes to work and marriage and, in this too, girls wrote autobiographical essays in which they imagined looking back on their lives in old age. 90 per cent talked about their marriage, and more than half wrote of their work as well. Many of them were uneasy about combining work and marriage; much of this uneasiness has since gone, though real conditions have not changed significantly. Another aspect that emerged from the essays was that 'large numbers of girls (37 per cent) recorded the deaths of their husbands when their husbands had performed the limited function of providing them with children'. Perhaps this is related to the tragedy and pain that has been historically and romantically linked with women's destiny. On such tragic foundations are built the stories of noble and suffering women. '20 per cent recorded various forms of violent death, some for two husbands, in train, air or road crashes, by cancer or strokes, in war or in accidents at work.' Their wives however then got down to the business of living and bringing up their children which they seemed to do quite adequately without men, their lives fulfilled and their needs subsequently provided for by their children and grandchildren. It may be that male fears and insecurities about the protection of their power and indispensability are more well-founded than is generally thought!

FAMILY LIFE – PRESENT AND FUTURE

The close mother–daughter relationship that Young and Wilmott[9] wrote about in their East End families can be found in varying degrees in other families in different areas. Although the continuation of this relationship after marriage may be less usual outside close working class communities and less available in certain places through housing problems many young girls find their mother a greater source of empathy and understanding than their father. This is rooted at least partly in the close relationships that mothers have with children during their earliest years, and the mother–daughter identification that occurs as a result.* This empathy is strengthened by the accepted attitude towards women, which sees it as natural that they should talk freely about personal feelings and problems, but regards the same behaviour in a man as an admission of personal failure. Women's role in the home also makes them far more easily available to talk with than fathers, and mothers are the confidantes in many difficult situations. They act as a source of emotional reassurance while fathers are seen more as sources of information. The way parents are perceived and related to again reflects their different personalities and knowledge. Dad is often seen as distant and impersonal, factual and worldly-wise; mum is usually softer, more protective and more sympathetic to problems, although she too has to be tough in other ways.

I find it easier to talk to mum compared to my dad – most people get on better with their mums than their dads. Girls I think will find that their mum will understand more because they've had to go through it all.

Helen

If there's anything I wanna know and I know that he's got the answer, he'll tell me the answer. But I can talk about anything I like to me mum – she's not embarrassed to tell me the answer to any of the facts of life or anything like that and I'm not embarrassed to ask her because I know that she'll answer me and she won't say – that's best not talked about.

Michelle

I go through patches. On the whole I seem to get on with them fairly well. I get on better with my mother because my father's very Victorian. If he's talking about girls he'd say – Oh yes, she was pregnant by the way, a schoolgirl, whereas my mum would just say, silly girl and we would talk about it. My father wouldn't talk about that at all – very Victorian and his father was too. We all have a good old moan together in the family when we get together – all the men go out.

Margaret

Some of the girls were asked whether they would bring up a daughter of their own any differently from the way they had been

* See the theory of early socialization suggested by Nancy Chodorow and discussed in chapter 2.

brought up and several mentioned changes that they would make, for instance:

I'd try to bring her up to like school, because I really hate school, and I hate coming. Every time I have to get up I think ugh, school, I wouldn't like my daughter to be brought up like that.

Janice

I think I'd be fairly strict with her in some ways, for example schoolwork. I'd like her to do well at school, but I don't think I'd insist on her going to university or staying on for A-levels, although I suppose I'd like her to. I wouldn't be too strict about clothes, and I'd let her go out to work on Saturdays, but not in the evenings. But however much she may not want to do her homework, she ought to. But I don't think I'd be too strict.

Penny

I'd tell her things straight, not go round the houses when I'm trying to tell her something. When she is depressed I know personally there are some things that would do her good, like going out and seeing friends and doing something really interesting ... I'd also like my daughter to be popular because popular girls get on, they have a really good life – I think they do. Personally I don't think I'm all that popular at school.

Christine

The only thing I would not do is – I've 'ad a load of responsibilities laid on to me and I don't mind 'em, but they just annoy me sometimes because in the holidays I look after me little sister and it stops me going out where I would really want to go, 'cause I'd have to take her and I can't afford to pay for her, and half the time me mum and dad can't afford to pay for her. I don't suppose I'd give [my daughter] as much to do as I've had to do, but otherwise there's nothing wrong in the way my mum's brought me up.

Michelle

When asked whether they would like their own future home and family to be like their present one, nearly half the girls gave a negative reply. Over a third of their dissatisfactions lay in the nature of family relationships which they wished to make closer, more united and understanding.

I will talk more to my children about life and problems. I'd be a friend and mother.

I would like it to be nice and peaceful and I will trust my children.

I would make it feel more together and loving.

The others desired changes that revealed their frustration with old-fashioned ideas, and their intention to give children more freedom and independence. They also wanted better and more modern houses, instead of the old terraces and cramped flats in which many of them lived. Their hopes for the future spring out of their conditions in the present and their optimism about the possibility of change. But it is the wider social and economic conditions about which they complained, such as bad housing, that themselves affect and exacerbate the family tensions that many girls were determined to avoid.

Sharing the Housework

The double responsibility of working women has always officially gone unrecognized, but with the increasing demand for and supply of women workers, the turnover of ideas in the last decade, and the public attention given to women's changing status, it may be wondered how far this atmosphere of change has influenced ideas about the division of housework. If the Ealing girls are any indication equality has not got very far where housework is concerned. Although it is thought useful if a man is handy about the house, and fair for him to help with the washing-up, domestic work remains largely exclusive to women. As Oakley has observed, 'During childhood an identification with the mother or other female adult who cares for the housewife-to-be instils a sense of housework as a feminine responsibility. The mother is not only the female child's role-model for feminine behaviour but for housework behaviour also.' An orientation towards housework becomes bound up with the rest of the female personality. Twenty-eight of Ann Oakley's housewives named housework as one of the worst aspects of their role but all saw it ultimately as their responsibility. Similarly more than half of the Ealing girls disagreed with a suggestion that being a housewife would be very dull and boring, and implicitly accepted housework and child-care as being part of their rightful role.

If I get married, everything bar housework will be on a mutual setting, bank account and everything shared. Housework – I don't expect him to do it although I don't like it much. I'm hopeless at cooking. I hope I can find someone who can cook!

I think they ought to help. My dad helps my mum quite a lot you know, washing-up and things, but I think my mum works harder on the whole.

I expect him to wash up now and then, but I wouldn't lay everything on him. I wouldn't say – right, I'm going out to work, you get on with the washing-up.

I don't agree with the wife going out to work and the husband staying at home and looking after the kids. I'd rather stay at home all day if it was that way, really. I think there's a certain bargain in the home and for the woman that's her children and they need her more than the father.

So housework is still clearly women's work, despite some husbands being willing to help out with peripheral things, like washing-up and doing the vacuuming and occasionally going to the launderette. The emphasis is very much on 'help' rather than share.

Housework is low status and menial work and the separation of the sex roles at this point is very resistant to change. It is considered unmanly for men to take more than a token and circumscribed part in housework, and social judgement may even condemn a woman whose husband appears to be exceeding his share. Men's own avoidance of housework is often complemented by an equally strong reaction by women themselves to protect their role from male intrusion. Women whose identities are bound up with being indispensable wives and mothers do not always welcome the knowledge that their work can be diluted and shared.

Women may also be concerned with their social image and may be frightened of being judged as 'bad' wives if they fail to do certain things for their husbands. The sexual division of labour again makes some sense of this through men being at work all day and women being traditionally at home or in 'easier' or part-time work. Although both may be equally tired by evening it seems unreasonable to many women that they should now persuade their husbands to help with 'their' work. For women who are at home all day with children this is reinforced by the assumption that theirs is not 'proper' work.

Ann Oakley suggests[10] that middle class and working class women have differing orientations towards housework. More middle class than working class women tend to have a detached ('instrumental') attitude towards it which is influenced by the length of their education. More working class than middle class women have a 'traditional' orientation in which the housewife role is closely bound up with self-image. Their relative lack of opportunity for becoming involved in meaningful work and activities outside the home contributes to this.

Girls from working class and middle class backgrounds today are destined to have a longer working life than previous generations due to social and economic changes that include contraception and smaller families as well as their own increasing desire to have some element of a 'career'. The continuing acceptance of separate domestic roles for men and women, however, still leaves women with the double load. Ideas about sex discrimination and women's equality are publicly discussed but do not deeply enter the consciousness of many girls. However the idea that women do have rights which have been withheld from them is one with which the new generation is growing up.

Most girls have heard of Women's Liberation, even if they have only absorbed its misrepresentation in the media and think members of such a movement must be ridiculous or freaky. Some of the Ealing girls mentioned this subject spontaneously, at other times it came up as a natural extension of discussion. Their ideas and impressions were mixed – often unclear and fragmentary – a reflection of the way that they had been picked up. The aspects of Women's Liberation concerning equal pay and anti-discrimination were usually mentioned and approved of but the Ealing girls were rather doubtful and confused about altering roles or personal relationships.

I think girls have got an advantage over the boys. Apart from Womens Lib. which I think, it's not very strong, it'll die out in a little bit, although I think some people will persevere and keep the standards up, something like that. But I don't really believe in Women's Lib.

Equal pay part – that's all right, but when it comes to marriage I think most women like to be dominated to a certain extent, and the man probably needs to feel important to dominate. They always do it like that and I think it's the best way. Most women think – Oh, I'm equal to a man – but they aren't in many respects. But when it comes to marriage I think, I suppose, you have to have discussions between them – the important matters. Not 'I want you to do this'.

Anne

Another girl also expressed the idea that it was important for a woman to be dominated by a man. She was a person who had consistently brought up her own quite radical ideas and opinions about girls and women, and their equality and treatment, but she was still very much in the process of exploring these, and coming to terms with what she really felt:

Sometimes I like playing at Womens Lib. Go around pretending you're a fella, but that gets boring 'cause I know I can't be a fella. I have to be a girl no matter what. I was born a girl so I suppose I had better be a girl. I think it's fair that they should get equal pay and get the same amount of rights, but to actually – although they say they want to be equal, some women get on top of their husbands. Although they'd like to be equal, you can't really be that equal. There's got to be somebody on top, just a little bit, to say 'Right, we'll do this', because you can agree on some things, but not on all things. Got to have one or the other. But it might be different for different things. Not very much on top, I agree, most of the time, but I should imagine a husband has a bit more say, because if he didn't, he'd have no purpose. Women have the children and the housekeeping, and he's the worker. I know we can't do without men, but, he's – I was going to say, not useful, but he is. Maybe women shouldn't be in the house so much. I mean you get just as good male nurses as female nurses, so I don't see why you don't have female executives, paid the same money as male executives – because they've got just the same amount of brain as men. Just because their body's a bit different it doesn't matter.

Christine

Most of the others who talked of 'Women's Lib', were also prepared to sanction equal pay and opportunity but nothing more radical. Like many other people, they had taken in the media send-up about 'bra-burning' and rightly thought it was absurd. Unfortunately they associated Women's Liberation with this

image, which produced an artificial gap between the true ideas
of the Women's Movement and their own embryonic stirrings.

I agree with some of it but not all of it. Some of it's stupid – burn the
bra and all that. It's a waste of time because they're not getting anywhere. They should worry about getting equal pay and things like that.
If a girl wants to drive a lorry, she should be allowed to. There's a lot
of jobs that girls would like to do but just haven't got the chances.
Should be allowed to do it if they wants to. There's a lot of boy's jobs
that a girl could do better than a boy, but she's never had the chance to
do it.

I agree with some of it like equal pay and equal opportunity in jobs,
but I like men to be domineering and I don't like women always trying
to be better than men.

Boys and girls are more equal than they used to be now. It's not that
just the girls are taught how to cook and iron and all that, and the boys
taught woodwork now. I think that's a good thing – up Women's Lib! I
don't believe in girls not doing housework and going out to work. I
wouldn't go as far as that – or burning your bras.

And one West Indian girl was very much against women's liberation, but at the same time was determined not to accept her
traditional role of ultimate responsibility for children:

I think that Women's Lib. is the most stupid thing that occurred for
ages. Honestly, it really is mad. How can a woman be equal to a man? –
that's what I'd like to know. My mum, she believes in Women's Lib,
in a way – she thinks a woman should have the same wages as a man –
oh, it's stupid. Men should bring in more wages, shouldn't they?
'Cause men, – I can't say they're more strong, 'cause that's got nothing
to do with work, but, men's more – well, not more advanced, we have
the same brains, but *better* than women. I think it's stupid anyway.
Boys are more intelligent and everything – us girls always giggle . . .
But if my husband left me I'd chuck the kids at him. I'm not going to
be left with kids to bring up on my own. I wouldn't. I'd just leave or
have a nervous breakdown. I'd make sure he comes back.

Gloria

Some of them were visibly wrestling with their opinions, and
trying to line up and work out the logical reasons for the traditional ideas they were reluctant to part with, such as the impor-

tance of male dominance. They often found little more than spontaneous conservatism to back them up, which nevertheless has an apparent validity that should not be underestimated.

As I emphasized earlier, being a girl and a woman, and having a 'feminine' identity involves a deeper self-investment than merely taking on a superficial role. Any discussion simply concerning the disadvantages and inequalities of being female overlooks the way girls and women feel about themselves and what they think will make them happy. For instance, much of girls' concern with future happiness is bound up with personal relationships and family affairs, which is after all where their role and their responsibilities have traditionally rested. Changing the basic organization of these aspects of their lives is much harder than agreeing with and working towards improving women's position at work.

It is hard to make the necessary connections between women's role at home and their role at work, between their personal and sexual lives and the parts they play in production. While girls and women still see themselves as separated from the mainstream of productive work in society they will emphasize, as did many of the Ealing girls, that theirs is the 'easier' and more enviable position. And although they are right in some of their reasoning, this camouflages the way that the social and economic system separates and restricts the lives of both men and women.

Notes

Chapter 7

1. D. G. Brown, 'Sex-Role Preference in Young Children', *Psychological Monographs*, 70, 1956.
2. S. E. Clautour and T. W. Moore, 'Attitudes of 12-year-old Children to Present and Future Life Roles', *Human Development*, 12, 1969.
3. R. E. Hartley, 'Sex Roles from a Child's Viewpoint', paper read to the Annual Meeting of the Orthopsychiatric Association, 1966.
4. Ann Oakley, *Housewife*, Allen Lane, 1974.
5. S. E. Clautour and T. W. Moore, op. cit.
6. J. Sarsby, 'Love and Marriage', *New Society*, 28 September, 1972.
7. S. E. Clautour and T. W. Moore, op. cit.
8. Eva Figes, *Patriarchal Attitudes*, Panther, 1972.
9. M. Young and P. Wilmott, *Family and Kinship in East London*, Penguin, 1962.
10. Ann Oakley, op. cit.

Black Girls in Britain

In the urban and more industrialized parts of Britain, school classrooms contain children of many different races. White English girls and boys share streets and lessons with children whose familes have come from countries such as the West Indies, West and East Africa, China, Cyprus, India and Pakistan. Immigration from the West Indies and the Asian countries in particular has increased significantly since the last war, and those who came over mainly settled in London, the industrial Midlands and the North. Although initially they went to these places because they produced the highest demand for labour, as time went by this was combined with and reinforced by the need to join friends or a local community that was already established. They settled in working class areas where they could find work and accommodation, and so communities developed and grew. In Ealing the main immigrant communities are the Asians in Southall, who live in what is probably the largest Asian settlement in London, and the West Indian community who live mainly around Acton. They have found work in local light industry, in food and clothing factories, engineering, service industries (transport etc.) and at Heathrow Airport. The original focus of my work was to investigate English (white), West Indian and Asian girls at school, and their perceptions of the feminine role, and therefore I specifically chose schools in an area that contained a relatively high proportion of black children. It is the situation of black girls that I want to turn to next, and their responses to the same sort of questions that I put to the working class white girls.

The English girls came from varied backgrounds but most were working class in origin and had fathers who were in skilled and semi-skilled manual work or were in routine clerical jobs. A minority had supervisory or higher grade non-manual jobs and a few owned and managed their own business. Seventy per cent of their mothers worked (22 per cent full-time and 48 per cent part-time) and most came from families containing between one and four children. By comparison, almost all the West Indian girls in my research had fathers who worked in skilled, semi-skilled and unskilled manual work, which included working as train drivers, machine operators, mechanics, carpenters, panel beaters, porters and in general factory work. Several of them however either had no father or did not know his occupation. A higher proportion of West Indian mothers worked (78 per cent : 61 per cent full-time and 17 per cent part-time) and most had families containing three to six children, (27 per cent had over seven children) although not all the children were necessarily in this country.

The Ealing Asian girls mainly came from India (67 per cent) and East Africa (22 per cent) and only a few in this particular group came from Pakistan and none from Bangladesh. The Indian and East African Asian girls were distinguished by a sprinkling of fathers who were professionally qualified as lawyers, barristers, and teachers or who held non-manual jobs, but otherwise they too had fathers in various levels of manual work, mainly semi-skilled and unskilled manual work. Fewer of the mothers worked (for reasons discussed later), and all the families were large.

Although they live in a similar environment to white girls and face the same demands from school and from the social system and economic structure outside, the actual situation and prospects of black girls are different because of their colour. Furthermore, they have come from different backgrounds which have moulded the perceptions and expectations they have about their lives here. How they feel, their ideas, attitudes, aspirations etc., become clearer by being placed in an historical and social context. So far as I have been able I have used their own words in the context of some background material which will allow the reader to make sense of them. In addition to the black girls from Ealing, I also talked to some sixteen- to eighteen-year-olds who were attending a college of further education in East London.

WEST INDIAN GIRLS

The main period of immigration from the West Indies to Britain began in the 1950s and escalated during the 1960s, until the Immigration Act of 1968 placed restrictions on entry by means of the voucher system. The demand, in Britain, for unskilled labour after the Second World War was largely met by an immigrant labour force recruited from, among other places, the West Indies. Unemployment, exploitation and poverty in the British West Indies made many people turn to Britain, which they had been taught to regard as the mother country, as a solution to their problems.

In the West Indies there were English-speaking schools taught by teachers with English middle class values who used English textbooks. This kind of influence had been prevalent for so long that many had understandably grown to see themselves as an extension of Britain. Their passports said that they were British citizens, and they were unprepared for the hostility and discrimination that greeted their arrival. Here West Indians, together with other black immigrants, found themselves forced to live under the same social and economic conditions that have historically characterized the British working classes. Since they could only find low-level and low-paid work, and were discriminated against, they gravitated to bad and overcrowded housing in traditional working class areas and their children attended ill-equipped and overcrowded schools. But as immigrants their conditions were exacerbated and complicated by race and racism.

As their numbers grew, antagonism and prejudice against black people appeared in every area of life in schools, housing, employment and in everyday social interactions.* Their children were channelled into the lower grade schools and even into E.S.N. (Educationally Sub-Normal) schools; decent accommodation was difficult to find and discrimination operated in the system for obtaining jobs and progressing within them. In order to pull

* Exploding into the Race Riots in Nottingham and Notting Hill in 1958.

together a diversely scattered community and to gain a sense of identity over here, men and women organized social activities and set up their own organizations and clubs. Religion and the church are important in the West Indies and continued in this country as a way of seeing to the welfare of the community. Women often formed the regular basis of the congregation and were involved in setting up outings, meetings and other activities through the church. Some adhered to the Church of England and the Roman Catholic church while others belonged to the more exclusive and strict religion of the Pentecostal Church or the Seventh Day Adventists. These activities helped to provide an early social focus and to sustain a situation characterized by isolation and hardship.

One reaction in Britain to their immigration was a great concern with 'integration' and 'assimilation' into the English community. This was taken up in academic study and research and throughout the 1960s a 'Race Relations industry' gathered momentum. But although it has advanced academic disciplines and furthered the careers of researchers, most of this work has done relatively little to help the people being studied. Inequalities have remained untouched. White middle class assumptions and values were imposed on black communities and an emphasis was placed on the 'integration' of the immigrant into the 'host' society. This was a very one-sided approach, assuming little responsibility on the part of the so-called 'host' community and ignoring the source and effects of the social and material conditions of immigrant life.

It is possible to interpret the black immigrants' own response to living here by examining the legacy of slavery and colonial rule, and the 'culture' of the West Indies. This is relevant, but it does not explain certain features of their life in Britain. The fact that West Indian communities encounter a vast number of problems in 'adapting', and are well-represented on the files of social workers is not merely because of their 'culture' or history. It is as much a product of the conditions of their contemporary situation, which implies that aspects of the oppression that defined their past ways of life still exist in present-day Britain. Their situation here is closely related to the days of slavery, colonialism and life under imperial rule, and past and present combine to ensure continued exploitation in Britain.

Studies and reports about West Indian immigrants in Britain have therefore focused around 'problems'. For instance, apparent 'instabilities' of their family life compared to the Western ideal family have been studied in terms of their success or failure in 'adjusting' to a new and different culture. But the situation is more complex than this, and although it is essential to look historically at the family structure and the role of women in the West Indies, which I have tried to do in the brief outline that follows,[1] this cannot be separated from the conditions and demands of the contemporary situation of West Indian women and their family life in Britain.

In the West Indies, familes are extended to include aunts, cousins, grandparents and other relatives. There, women have taken the major responsibility for home and children in a way that is different from the contemporary English ideal of the small husband–wife–children unit. Their role developed out of the conditions imposed on them by slavery and colonial rule, which distorted their family life and structure when Africans were brought to the West Indies as slaves two or three centuries ago. Although at that time monogamous marriage was the official ideal of white people and the slave owners, it was denied and made meaningless to the slave. Slaves had no rights, and women were the property of the white master. Slave owners used women as labour, for breeding more slaves and for their own sexual gratification. Men, women and children could be separated at their master's whim, and therefore there was no chance to develop a slave family.

Under slavery, the slave owner took over many of the functions usually performed by a father in other societies, such as giving children their name and status, education, food and a home. The biological father had no rights or responsibilities towards his children. Illegitimacy, the taboo of respectable English people, was imposed on West Indian people as a feature of life. After slavery was abolished (Emancipation 1834) the situation became less defined and several sorts of family structure were possible. However, influenced by their ex-master's model and the dominant colonial ideology, the ideal of formal marriage and the stable patriarchal family system was taken over and accepted by most and became associated with property and status. According to this model, a prospective husband had to be able to provide regularly for his family so that his wife should not have to work, and he held nominal authority in the home. Thus many did not consider formal marriage as a possibility because of widespread poverty and unemployment. Most men and women cohabited in 'faithful concubinage' and common-law marriage, which were more egalitarian structures in which authority was shared and both men and women worked to support the family. These relationships rested on an understanding that they might eventually develop into marriage, or they might be broken at any time.*

Therefore in all situations apart from formal marriage, which was confined to the emerging middle class, the paternal role was inhibited as men and women were independent and could separate completely, or in the periods when the men had to go away to seek work. In cases where separation occurred, however, it was the women who were left with all the care and responsibility for the children. In the West Indies then and now, this responsibility has generally been shared through the extended family system, in which grandmothers, aunts and cousins are available to help and free the younger women for work. But in Britain there was no extended family to help and the women who emigrated found themselves struggling hard and often alone to accommodate home, work and children.

The maternal role was therefore stronger in the West Indies than the marital role, and the leftover Victorian doctrine of respect for marriage within an authoritarian father-dominated home co-existed with a situation in which it was often impossible or unlikely that men could fulfil such a role. And since mothers provided most security, stability and discipline for their children, relationships were usually much closer with them for children of both sexes. Therefore, although women worked whenever possible (unless they were middle class and richer), their role in life

* It seems ironic that in Britain today West Indian girls find it relatively easy to marry while young middle class white men and women have begun to reject 'bourgeois' marriage and live together instead.

was mainly defined as one of having children, working hard to raise their family and in old age being supported and looked after by their children and through the extended family.*

Fertility had a high value, as in the days of slavery, and it was consequently thought unnatural and pitiable for a woman not to bear children. As in many other societies, including our own, maternity was a normal and desirable state of womanhood, but this was so emphasized in the West Indies that a man could even desert his wife for childlessness. (The advanced knowledge of contraception today still comes up against the belief that the mark of womanhood is to bear a child, while the proof of man's virility and manhood lies in his ability to make a woman pregnant.) Therefore parenthood was the hallmark of adulthood for both sexes, but a man was not assumed to be responsible for the children he produced.

It is out of this kind of historical development that West Indian women came to Britain and have tried to build a better life for themselves and their children, only to be confronted with numerous obstacles. There is less difficulty here for those who wish legally to marry, and the marriage expectations of young black girls today are similar to other girls in Britain, but the struggles of men and women against poverty and unemployment continue. Any 'instabilities' in marriage and family life should therefore be seen as being related to the conditions under which they live and work rather than merely as inherent West Indian characteristics or 'maladjustment' to English life.

Family Life in Britain

My dad died when I was two. Mum came over here and we were back there – she left when I was one. They came here first and we were left behind with foster parents and relatives of hers. We came here in 1966. In some ways I never knew her, 'cause when you're a small girl, y'know you forget – all we had was a photograph of her. She never came back to visit. She used to promise that she'd come back, come and see us, but

*'The main reason for a matriarchal system evolving in the Caribbean [and black America] was the fact that the woman with her historical experience of being a productive slave in her own right, was not economically dependent on the man.'[2]

never came. When I came I wanted to go back. We didn't want to come, oh we were crying and we didn't want to come over. When we got here we were having breakfast and we were crying, and she started to cry as well y'know 'cause we said we wanted to go back, didn't want to stay. But after a while we settled down. There was nothing else we could do but stay – we got to know her.

> Sonia, seventeen years old. At further education college.

Many families were split up during emigration, and children were frequently left behind in the care of grandmothers or other relatives while their parents came to Britain, either separately or together. After a time, the children would be sent for, and would arrive in England to find a new father, and probably new brothers and sisters. They were not only transported from a familiar rural setting to a strange urban one but into a new family scene as well. If the members of a family do not get on well together, a dangerously fraught and tense situation can be produced. Conflicting relationships between children and their stepfathers have been a source of concern and unhappiness to many young West Indians. They may find themselves confronting a new father who resents their presence. Sometimes men object to supporting children that are not their own and this opens the way to clashes between them. Alternatively, if the step-children are female a man may find them as attractive as his wife and may for instance try to relate to them sexually or strictly control their social activities to keep them pure and protected for their own sake or for himself. A detached youth worker told me that many of the problems of black girls that he encountered seemed to stem from the strain of such relationships. Some of the Ealing girls lived with their mothers and stepfathers, and Gloria, for instance, talked of the antagonism between her stepfather and herself.

My big brother and my sister and me were all born out of wedlock, you know, illegitimately, and my sister and all this other lot after me were born when my mum got married. My brother's daughter is illegitimate, and my brother lives with his girlfriend, but we don't get on – well, I don't care what he does anyway. And my dad's got two others – his son and daughter back in Barbados – supposed to be my brother and sister but I never seen 'em before in me life. They're all scattered about, my family. That's why my dad and me don't get on 'cause he don't think I was his really – I don't care anyway, 'cause my big brother and my big sister aren't my dad's you know, and my dad didn't think I was, so that's why we don't get on together really. But I don't care what he thinks.

Gloria

Since being in Britain an increasing difference of attitude and expectation has developed between those who came over in the early years of immigration and their teenage children who came over at a younger age or were born here. Many parents cling to the hopes they once had of opportunities in Britain and are willing to accept their situation and work within it. Their children, however, often find their parents' attitudes too passive and constraining. They want independence and better jobs than those that are offered to them, and they are unwilling to accept low-level alternatives. To the parents it often seems as if their children are rejecting the chances that they have struggled to give them. Clashes may ensue, especially between mother and daughter. I spoke to another seventeen-year-old girl about the possible reactions to her leaving home.

It's hard to leave home because the parents, West Indian parents – when you get say to eighteen or so, then you leave home and want to live by yourself, the parents they start 'Look how long I've been working for this child, brought her up and everything and she don't pay me back in no way, as soon as she goes to work just take her things and go,' that's what you hear, you hear that a lot; 'she wants to leave home, we don't allow boys to come in here so she's gone about her business,' do what she wants and that and have a bit of freedom of her own. The white girls, their parents they say if you want to leave home and get a flat of your own it's O.K. but West Indian parents: 'You think you're a woman, you want to leave, after we've brought you up and we give you this and we give you that you don't turn round and help us in no way, you just go about your own way, I don't know what's wrong with you.' I wouldn't be like that to my child if she ever wanted to leave – talk to them yeah and help them out but run them down, no.

Floretta

These clashes become more understandable when we consider the real struggle that parents have been involved in for the sake of their children.

The Ealing West Indian girls at fourteen or fifteen, were a bit young to be thinking seriously of leaving home, but we did talk about their family situation. Many of their answers to questionnaires about the concern and interest of their parents implied that although parents were concerned with their progress at school, personal problems and worries were seldom discussed and even everyday experiences at school were frequently left untold. Fathers were often remote figures, and like the English girls, they almost always had a better relationship with their mothers. This is understandable when we consider the traditional role of he West Indian mother; but this mother–daughter relationship itself is affected by the gaps in experience and understanding between the two generations. Some girls thus found it hard to get on with either of their parents and had little knowledge of the closeness that is idealized in the myth of family life. But it is the social and economic conditions under which people live that largely contribute to distortion in personal relationships within the family. Fathers often do shift-work in unskilled and low-level jobs or are unemployed, and the cards that capitalism has dealt them make it hard for them to stake any serious long-term bets in life. This perpetuates their lack of close involvement with their children, who are therefore still very much the responsibility of women, and will remain so while work conditions outside determine and extend into the division of labour and relationships in the home.

West Indian women themselves spend much of their time in full-time or part-time jobs, or do outwork to help maintain their families. Consequently their children are given less time and attention than they may have had in the West Indies where at least there would always be a relative to look after them. Here in Britain, their young children are often cared for by child-minders, whose facilities for child-care are very variable. West Indian women have to work, but there is a pitiful amount of nursery provision for children of any colour. There is perhaps less awareness amongst black mothers of the theories about 'maternal deprivation' as they have been less exposed to the propaganda. But all children benefit from a stimulating environment and a number of close, stable relationships which may be lacking in the child-minding facilities that have to be used. The conditions that many West Indian families are forced to live under make the ideal happy family life even more complicated and difficult to achieve than it would be in favourable circumstances. The girls I spoke to were very aware of stress at home. Here is Gloria again:

I don't get on with my dad all that much ... he's a train driver, works at nights so he's out in the daytime, so we don't see each other all that much. Can get on with my mum, like a house on fire. Sometimes have off-moments but that's soon patched over 'cause you've got to talk to her all the time ... But I don't like talking to my mum and dad, they don't understand people. They think I talk in riddles so they don't listen to me. I don't care anyway. I keep everything to myself. Don't talk to nobody. I keep it to myself. I don't have to talk to anybody. I don't need to talk to anybody. I can solve my own problems. I only have problems sometimes, but I can solve them myself. I wouldn't tell 'em to my mum and dad for anything.

I've never spoken to my parents sat down and spoke to them and joked with them like some children joke with their parents about different things. We've spoken, me and my mum, as we're always in the house, we talk a lot ... but when my dad – he does shiftwork – we hardly ever sit down in a group and talk about life in the future or anything like that. But they make it rather difficult for me really, 'cause when my mum and I start talking about something, my mum starts saying, When I was young ... this and that – it gets on my nerves. They don't think forward, it's funny. Sometimes I try to put myself in their place and say, I see what they mean, but they don't seem to want to know what we mean or understand or anything like that. I just don't bother myself to go to them and talk to them or anything like that.

Audrey

There are seven of us: five kids and my mum and dad. My mum's rather loud, quick-tempered and all that. My dad's quiet. I don't like him – well, he isn't my father, see ... Don't talk to them at all. [I talk to] my sister, she's fourteen, I'm sixteen. My brother's nine. He tells me his problems, or he tells my mum. He's the favourite 'cause he's a boy. Mum says she wishes she had a boy first, and dad wishes he had all boys. [If I had a daughter of my own], one thing, I'd talk to her. My mum don't talk to me. I'd try to understand her when she grows up – tell her all about boys. I wouldn't tell her to keep away from them. Sort of mix, with the right sort.

Sharon

Boyfriends, Sex and Marriage

Relationships between many West Indian parents and their daughters are not helped by the strict rules imposed about boys and the constraints on girls' social freedom that are consequently enforced. This lays a basis of resentment in girls who find that going out is constantly monitored and controlled and that boyfriends may be banned completely until an approved age. Their parents draw a simple equation between boys, sex and pregnancy and adopt a preventative solution that tries to deny their daughters opportunities for social and physical contact, rather than explaining, discussing and working out other alternatives. Girls are brought up similarly in the West Indies, but the situation becomes more emphasized here where education and opportunity are at stake. Many girls object to this attitude and feel that it implies an absence of trust and understanding. This was prevalent in the lives of many of the Ealing girls.

Mum knows I do it [go out with boys] but I don't tell her I do it. She suspects. She don't know about the two boys I go out with now . . . She says boys are trouble. She thinks most boys nowadays just make you pregnant and then leave you. Parents don't trust girls, most of them. They think the boys are much better. Think girls leave home, run away from home. They won't get an education. All they think the girls think about is boys. Well, we do, but not all the time. My parents think that most girls want to get themselves pregnant, get trouble. They don't talk to their kids about this, don't try to understand more.

Sharon

That's one thing I disagree on, the fact of having boyfriends. They both think that when you have a boyfriend, the only thing you're going to do is have sex, which you're going to end up, you know, in a sticky position kind of thing. If they hear that one young girl about the age of fifteen, is pregnant, they say, well you're going to do the same and they don't seem to find out by letting me have a boy. They just jump to conclusions and that's that for them.

Audrey

One girl, who had a black father and a white mother, felt very constrained within her family. Her social life was controlled, and boyfriends were out of the question.

Now my brother, he's got a girlfriend, believe it or not – only thirteen – and yet I'm not allowed to have a boyfriend ... Now the summer holidays are coming up, I've been asked out several times but I'm like scared to say Yes in case something goes wrong or I have a row. I'd rather go without boyfriends than have a row with my parents. They used to tell me I was too young but they can't do that anymore because I keep arguing that one out. I think getting pregnant is the worst thing. They're frightened of it, just in case I do. I've got friends, boys, who I have round to the house. We generally sit about and talk and that's all right, but for me to actually go steady with a boy – they'd be frightened.

Nearly three-quarters of the Ealing West Indian girls said that their parents never or seldom allowed them out with boys. Nevertheless, over half of them claimed to have a boyfriend.

I also talked about this to the girls who were attending further education college; they were in a similar predicament.

You don't talk about boys in my family – you can talk to your mum, yeah, she's someone who understands, but with your father you can't. 'Cause y'see fathers they more protect their daughters, and boys can go out when they like and where they like and girls have more protection. According to my dad, my dad goes – the boys today in this world they're no good, all they think about is getting girls pregnant and gambling and going to parties and that, that's all they care about. They don't think there's not one boy in the world that's good. They think they're all bad, well my dad does. My parents, when I leave college, they don't really mind me having a boyfriend but I can't talk of boyfriends while I'm at college. They say I should be studying my work instead of boys, but they let us go out, that's the trouble, they let us go out but when you say you're going with a boy, that's something different!

Floretta

When boys touch you – they all go – 'What's the matter with you, why can't I touch you?' And I go 'Leave off, don't touch me.' That's how our parents brought us up in life – not to mix with boys at all. They used to laugh at us at first. I used to think to myself, when I get older things like this have to happen. I thought to myself it's all part of nature. My mum said, don't let boys touch you or nuffink, don't let boys kiss you or nuffink – and when I was about twelve years old a boy kissed me on my cheek. I ran home, into the bathroom and washed it off – scrubbed my face. My sister found me in the bathroom and said

'What's wrong? What's wrong?' 'Oh don't tell mummy don't tell her please, a boy kissed me on my cheek.' And my sister started to laugh – she go 'Poor you.'

Janet

Girls who come from religious families belonging to the Pentecostal or Seventh Day Adventist churches find that this can affect the strictness of their family and social life. Valerie, aged seventeen, whose mother belongs to the Pentecostal church, said that:

When we go out, she reckons be back before 10 o'clock – I don't understand it because when my mum was back in the West Indies she used to be out late, and she reckons how it's more safe over there, because over here, London's so big you know what I mean, and I just can't understand it. If she had freedom why can't she let me have freedom ... It's just their minds – probably what *they* did they think we will do, when we go out – know what I mean. It's just their minds, 'cause there's no part of the Bible say you can't go out. No, there isn't, and I always say that to my mum.

Another girl spoke of a friend who could only move between college, church and home, and was ignorant about sex:

Because this girl, how old is she now – seventeen, and the other day we was talking y'know and we were saying something and she asked us what was that y'know, and we expected her to know. So we said haven't your parents told you nothing and she said No. So we sat down in the Quiet Room and we told her all what we could. Them religious parents they don't expect their daughters to do things like that.

Daughters are brought up very strictly, both here and in the Caribbean and their parents try to impress on them the dangers of men. The fear and concern about daughters becoming pregnant is expressed so frequently and vigorously that it tends to exaggerate the extent of its actual occurrence. But exhortations to stay away from boys, unaccompanied by reasonable explanation or helpful sex education can result in girls experiencing a lonely and frustrating time and being very naive about sexuality. According to the view of one youth worker involved with helping black teenagers, a girl's first sexual experience may be with an older man and she may even be raped – too inexperienced, innocent and frightened to resist. If girls are not allowed any sexual knowledge or experimentation they can find themselves plunged easily and unsuspectingly into compromising situations.

Sex education is something which is only just beginning to be explored in any sympathetic and meaningful way, mainly through schools. Black and white girls alike suffer from the consequent vulnerability of sexual ignorance. Some girls are lucky and have mothers who explain and talk to them about it. Annette was one of these, and her mother also put her on the pill when she was sixteen and going seriously with her boyfriend.

I was saying, I don't wanna go on the pill, nothing's gonna happen y'know, and my mother said, just in case because you never know when. And with my mother in some ways I think she's more understanding because she's made a lot of mistakes and she knows, and therefore she doesn't want me to make the same mistakes and she's taking all the precautions that can be taken. But other black mothers, they don't talk to their kids so much, I found that out because of my cousin, my aunt never explained it to my cousin . . . and my cousin grow up resenting her mother for not sort of explaining things to her and thinking she was too childish to learn.

If a girl does 'get trouble' and becomes pregnant, she may be treated quite severely by her parents who may even turn her out of the house. For some girls this is a very real possibility, while for others it is more of a threat.*

She'd be mad at first, my mum would probably chuck me out, she would – she'd think of what my auntie and uncle would say and she'd think, no, she can't have me there, and chuck me out. She thinks of them first. But, well, let's face it I think all parents are like that at first – what would the neighbours say – and then afterwards they swallow their pride. But some of them chuck them out.

Amelda

*This may also exaggerate the relative occurrence of pregnancy in that if young white girls become pregnant this is kept as private as possible and they usually either have an abortion or get married. But to the extent that black girls are turned out of home (and I have no access to any facts or figures for this), this makes their situation more 'public' and therefore a 'social problem'.

If it was me, if it was only my mum that lived at home it would be all right. If I came home pregnant she'd tell me off yeah, but she wouldn't chuck me out, no. But my dad, if I came in pregnant now, he'd chuck me out, because he keeps on saying that he doesn't want it to happen again.

Floretta

Other reactions are not so severe, and a child may be born and adopted into the girl's own family. If the boy and girl concerned want to get married, this is of course much more acceptable. Abortion however has not been an approved solution, although one girl did say that she thought young pregnant girls were beginning to have abortions because their parents wanted them to carry on at school.

The attitude to daughters becoming pregnant is usually that they have let down and shamed the family. In the experience of one social worker, 'I was trying to persuade a West Indian family not to throw their daughter out, and finally pointed out to the mother that her daughter was illegitimate and was only doing what her mother had done. The mother replied that the girl had had more chances, more opportunities than she had ever had, and should know better.'[3]

Since illegitimacy was part of the enforced conditions of life throughout the history of the Caribbean, its continued occurrence in this country has sometimes been interpreted solely as a left-over 'cultural pattern' from a time and place where this did not bear social stigma. But this explanation is incomplete and further reasons can be found in the distorting nature of family life and sexual relationships under the combined pressures of race and class.

There would be less problem in the Caribbean since a pregnant girl, although often ritualistically turned out by her mother, is taken in by relatives and then reabsorbed into her family, who help to care for the child. An illegitimate birth may be publicly disapproved of for the sake of demonstrating adherence to middle class values, but it has been made part of life for the black working class. But in this country, if a pregnant girl is turned out of her home, she is often quite alone. She may seek help and be referred to social workers, but they cannot offer much since the social services are geared towards accommodating families, not unsupported and unmarried mothers and certainly not young black girls. It is very difficult to find alternative accommodation for black girls who have left home for any reason as they are seen as potential 'trouble'. There is a critical need for accommodation for them. Girls who do not seek help from the social services sometimes go and live with their boyfriends or other friends, or live in squats, as an increasing number of young homeless and jobless men and women have begun to do.

Under the pressures of inadequate living conditions and frustrations at home, it helps to believe that all might be different in the future. For instance, many of the Ealing West Indian girls firmly intended to make their own future home and family life very different from the one that they were experiencing. They wanted to have bigger and more modern housing to live in, much closer personal relationships, and they intended to give their children, especially daughters, the freedom and independence that was withheld from them.

Growing up in my family is hell, my parents just don't have any understanding at all and through their mistakes I'll make my family's life different

It will be better and I will want my kids to be more truthful and closer to me than I am with my parents.

There would be more peace and quiet and I would let my children go out more.

I would like to have a big house with a room for my girls and a room for my boys.

I tell you, if my daughter got pregnant I wouldn't chuck her out of the house I wouldn't. I'd more or less try to understand, I don't want to make mistakes like parents do today. I want to try and understand her. I don't want them to think that parents never understand them.

Amelda. A student at further education college

Valerie, at seventeen, connected her freedom with wider changes:

Girls are brought up in such a way, you know what I mean, I wonder if you can't break that kind of way. I mean, years and years of 'wash the dishes, cook the dinner, clear the place, make yourself look nice and just sit in the house and watch for this young man to come along, and get married and have kids, and I'll be the grandmother.' I can't stand that. I like to live a life of my own, you know what I mean? I don't like to work to rules. There ain't no rules saying that you must wash the dishes and clean. I said that I'm a girl, therefore I'll wash the dishes, I'll clear the place but when it comes to goin' out, don't stop me, you know what I mean.

The restraints imposed on West Indian girls through their parents' fear of sexual exploits causes many of them to yearn for more freedom and independence. Boys are certainly not subject to such restrictions, and recognition of this was reflected in the response to questions asking whether they would have chosen for themselves to be girls or boys. Half replied that they preferred to be female, while the rest preferred the idea of being male. Those who preferred a boy's life were often very conscious of the problems, burdens and 'pain' that were part of their feminine role. But instead of extolling positive virtues of masculinity, they were more concerned with describing the negative aspects they perceived about being female, the struggles involved, and the fact that boys did not have to go through these.

[If I was a boy] I'd be allowed to go out more like my brother who is younger than me. I wouldn't be able to have illegitimate babies and get into trouble with my parents.

A boy don't have to do so much housework, and they go out more often, and mothers don't nag about them all the time.

I choose to be a boy because if you are a girl, you have to go through a lot of trouble such as pain and all different things. Although boys have pain but not as girl.

I would have chosen to be a boy because they've got more freedom and we've always got to keep ourselves out of trouble and find ourselves hands around the house.

It's more likely a boy can leave school and get any odd job right away, then later on do training and have further education, whereas a girl would have to struggle maybe for a long time before she can make something of herself.

The other girls gave a mixture of reasons for preferring to be girls, and many just enjoyed the way they were. Clothes and fashion were often mentioned, particularly as an area in which girls were seen to have a much better range than boys. A few thought that girls had an easier life, but this reason, combined with the future joys of being a wife and mother which were so popular for the white English girls, was noticeably lacking. Marriage was not given much emphasis, and the importance given to having children was much less than that expressed by the white girls, and contrasted with the large familes from which they came.

As a girl there are more nicer clothes about, and I think that life is easier for girls.

Boys are stupid sometimes, and anyway, boys can't wear tights and high shoes and all girls' stuff anyway. I am glad I am a girl.

It's much more exciting being a girl. Boys are sort of dreary. Boys get in trouble more – although when they are in their teens they are let out more than girls. Boys always get into fights, getting cut up. I'd rather stay the way I am. Girls are superior to boys. They can always wrap them round their little finger. Girls stand out in crowds, boys don't. Although they want to have better education than girls and get better jobs. Girls can have better jobs as well if they want to.

Sharon

These ideas seemed to be couched far more in the present, than in promises of the future. There was so much that was potentially enjoyable in their lives, so much to be learnt or to struggle against that stereotyped visions of their future role concerned them less than they did the white girls. Dreams of boyfriends, love and marriage were nonetheless important, but marriage itself was approached with less immediacy and more reservations. For instance, only half of these girls were prepared to commit themselves to saying that they wanted to marry, a few (10 per cent) said that they did not wish to marry, and the rest were unsure. If they did marry, like the English girls they mostly thought this would happen in the unpredictable and broad span of the next ten years. They did however incline slightly more towards the latter ages, and this preference and the reasons for it was expressed in some of their own comments.

I wouldn't get married *now*. Not until I'm about thirty I suppose. I want to live a bit first. Supposing you marry someone, got to live with them first, find out if you want to stay with them.

Evadne

I wouldn't like to be very young – I wanna enjoy myself first. Well, you could, if you got a fun-loving husband like my sister, but you know I think you don't enjoy yourself all that much, and once you get children, no fear, you can't enjoy yourself anytime. So I'd like to get married when I'm around twenty-seven, somewhere like that.

Gloria

Some days I say I might get married and the next I say I might not get married, 'cause my parents go on a lot. They think it's good to get married in some ways but I just say, what's the use? Why can't we just live on our own and enjoy ourselves instead of getting married. But then I think it would be nice to have children, looking after them and setting up a home and everything, but I don't know. Once my cousin said that she wasn't getting married, and she's twenty-five now, and my parents said to her that she's stupid – what does she mean she's not getting married? It's not that I wouldn't want to get married but, I don't know. I think marriage is necessary if like you're going to have children. I don't see the use of it apart from that, because before you're married, if you're faithful to somebody, then you should be able to do it without getting married.

Audrey

Whenever anyone asks me if I want to get married, I say No, or Maybe, but never Yes. Don't want to get married, at least not yet. Want to be independent, I don't want to depend on somebody. Be free for a while I guess. That's what life is about, getting married and having children. I want to do something different. That's why I want to continue. You can have children and that's that. Looking at people gets you thinking sometimes.

Barbara

Janet at further education college thought that whether or not the girls wanted to get married, the boys certainly did not.

A lot of the West Indian people, no, some of them, they want to get married at this age, get married young, but the boys nowadays, you just can't talk about marriage to them. They don't wanna know. Married! Me? You must be joking! – and that's all you get. You have to find a nice one if you want to get married early. The young boys they're wild – they run from girl to girl, and they don't want to get married. Most of 'em want to get married at a later day in life. That's what our parents want though. They don't want us to get married at sixteen or seventeen. They want us to get married at a later day in life y'know. Like my mum says, when you get your good education you can go all over the place and see everything first before being tied down. Not like her – she got married early.

School and Education

When West Indian women came here, one of the hopes uppermost in their minds was to give their children the chance of getting something better for themselves. They have since impressed this wish on their children and see education as the primary way of achievement. Many of them had had relatively little education themselves, as it was expensive and scarce.

Schools are different there I think, but now, in the past nine years they seem to be developing much more, education is getting better. But the education here is free. Back there you have to pay, especially for your books, especially if you want to go on and do, like go to secondary school or college, you have to pay for that. Everyone has to pay and if you haven't got the money you can't. Unless you get a scholarship – that's if you're really brilliant.

Sonia

They [parents] all want to see us brought up the right way not the wrong. They want us to get as much education as we can because back in the West Indies y'know, some parents didn't really get a lot of education. So when they come over here, they want their children to get as much as they can. They go on 'Oh yes, my daughter is this, my daughter is that,' that's what my dad says. He's sort of pushing us to be something. What he says, he goes – 'I want *you* to be a lawyer, I want *you* to be doing medicine, I want *you* to be a professor.'

Floretta

The opportunities that were opened to their children however were limited by the social and material deprivations that also faced the indigenous white working class community – by poverty, by overcrowded homes and schools, and by the lack of the influence and knowledge that benefits middle class children at school. This was aggravated by prejudice and discrimination within schools, by the language problems, at first undetected, and by the culture-biased intelligence tests that put many black children in E.S.N. schools.*

Teaching is dominated by middle class values and language and the progress of schoolchildren is judged by the same standards. This militates against working class children of any colour. But black children suffered even more from the hierarchical rigidity of the streaming system and, as a result, from the bad behavioural problems inherent in the classes in the bottom streams taught by constantly changing teachers.

The teachers vary – the teacher we had for English, he's left because he was getting married and not able to get any home here and they were too expensive for him. And I find that if he was to take me I would really get on well, but then after he left my work just dropped lower, just went right down, like that. Every term nearly we have different teachers for different subjects and with one you get a high mark and with another you get a lower mark, and when I go home and tell my parents my problems they don't think the same as I do, they think there's something different the way I don't get the same marks or higher marks as I should. They come out with all sorts of ridiculous things. They say that I'm either thinking of my boyfriend or something like that. To me it's the teacher I have and the way it changes every minute. All the time things will be changing, a different teacher here, a different teacher there, and all have different ways of teaching the same thing. I think that's what it is but my parents don't think so.

Audrey

West Indian children have a reputation for boisterous and bad behaviour at school, and lack of concentration; these must be considered in the context of the comparative strictness of schools in the West Indies, and of the mode of behaviour often imposed by parents at home. The relatively easy atmosphere in the class-

* This is discussed in much more detail in Bernard Coard's pamphlet on *How the West Indian Child is made Educationally Sub-Normal in the British School System*, New Beacon Books Ltd., 1971.

room provides a catalyst for letting off steam or releasing repressed anger or frustration. But these characteristics are also rooted in the social patterns produced by slavery, the unsettled nature of West Indians' historical background and their consequent lack of identity. Knowing this, however, does not make it much easier for them or for the teachers to alter the situation.

Many black parents, particularly mothers, were very distressed to find that their children were being allocated to the worst schools and placed in the lowest forms. In most schools today, as in the Ealing schools, the distribution of black children is such that most are at the bottom and their numbers decrease up towards the higher forms. The assumption of lower ability compared with white children in the same forms has often been implicit in school organization. Militant activity by mothers alleviated this situation in some places, for instance by setting up supplementary schools in black communities in Birmingham, Nottingham, Leeds and London, and by campaigning against racist practices by education authorities (for instance against the 'banding' of black children into special schools in Haringey in 1968), and against particularly bad schools (for instance Cowper Street school in Leeds in 1973).[4]

One girl told me about the action her mother took a few years ago when she was dissatisfied with her daughter's treatment at school. She is rather unusual in that she was the only black girl in a girls' grammar school.

The teachers were against me an'all, and my mother went up and spoke to them and said that she was the only black girl in the school and you should try and make her feel as if she's accepted 'cause all she does is come home and chuck her books on the floor and say she wants out, she don't want it anymore. Then after that the teachers started on about my work wasn't up to standard, but up to that day it was O.K. So my mother took all my work to the headmaster of another school and the headmaster y'know said he can't see what the teachers are finding wrong – he said that some of the marks aren't fair because the work is up to standard, and this got my mum uptight and she went up to the school again and started on at them again – so after everything the teachers wouldn't bother. If I handed in my work they would look at it, tick it and that was it, and during the lessons if I put my hand up it was 'hang about a minute' – hang about two hours! So by the time exams came I was just fed up with it, all I wanted to do was leave, I didn't care about anything else.

Annette

The girls' own response to education is ambivalent. They feel the boredom and irrelevance of school as much as the white girls, but at the same time they place more emphasis on the importance of qualifications and of education itself. Their replies to questions concerning education and careers showed enthusiasm and ambitions, and while some may have given what they felt to be the 'correct' response to such questions, others were probably expressing genuine and serious aspirations. These reflect the assimilation of their parents' hopes for them, and the acknowledgement that Britain offers better education than they would get in the West Indies.

About an equal number of them wanted to leave school at sixteen, seventeen or eighteen years of age, and relatively few at fifteen years. They wished to stay at school longer than the English girls, most of whom wanted to leave at the age of fifteen or sixteen years.

If I stay on a little longer I would be able to know and understand the work better and to leave school well-educated hoping to get a good and well-paid job.

If I leave school at fifteen years old I might not be able to get a job that I really like because I might not have any qualifications for the type of job.

Nearly half the West Indian girls gave this kind of reply. An equivalent number however, keenly looked forward to leaving, whether sooner or later, seeing this as their opportunity for independence, freedom and money to spend as they liked. But whenever they expected to leave, there was an overall emphasis on the importance of doing well at school, gaining education and making a career.

The hopes impressed on them by their parents are often much higher than their actual performances in school, which is not altogether surprising when their position in the school hierarchy is taken into account. Many girls said that their parents often told them to do better at school and got cross if they did not.

Every time my report comes in all they expect to find is just one straight line of A's to say that I'm brilliant at this and that. I try to talk to them about that and say that this is not all that matters, but they sort of go – yeah, you wouldn't think things like that.

Audrey

At the moment, because I am still going to school, my parents wants me to only think of my lessons and nothing else which I find rather difficult at my age and when I leave school at least I won't be tied down with looking after younger brothers and sisters as they will be somewhat older.

Vera

Their home situation makes it even harder for them to study seriously, because, for instance, of the cramped space, absence of helpful books and materials and the domestic duties imposed on them. Although their parents are willing to work hard and sacrifice a lot for the sake of education, it is hard to translate this into meaningful help for their children. Like many working class white parents they do not have much time nor the means to stimulate and encourage their children's school-work. And the girls are given housework to do as well as having to look after their younger brothers and sisters, especially while their mothers are out at work.

In the lower forms, taking and passing exams is a longer process and if these girls stayed on as long as they wished to, their qualifications would still not be very high. Many were aiming at O-levels, but a substantial number did not know what sort of exams they might take and will probably end up with a few C.S.E.s. Much of the reluctance to leave at the earliest opportunity was also accompanied by apprehension about going out into the world and finding jobs, and the necessity for more education to prepare them better for this. But to achieve even limited goals will mean overcoming the factors that implicitly oppose their progress.

By investing in education they are trying to work within the system – but this is not the only response they might have made. Among black teenagers today, there is evidence of a growing alienation from and resistance to striving within the educational structure, and black experience has begun to change the will to perform.[5] They are recognizing that they are schooled for low-level employment and are rejecting what is offered to them. This has begun to happen, mainly in areas of high unemployment. It probably occurs more in male than female youth, since girls have been able to get 'better' work more easily, like clerical work (although this is limitedly available to them) and nursing. The situation can also be understood by taking into account the way that the male upbringing and role makes it easier and quicker to translate frustration into aggression whereas black girls and women have to confront the consequences of not only their colour but of femininity as well. The lack of applicants to take up the level of work offered in Brixton, London, which has possibly the largest population of black unemployed youth in the country, has shown this, and the situation is duplicated elsewhere in Britain.

The statistics don't tell the whole story, because a large number of black unemployed youth refuse to register with state agencies and support themselves by drawing sustenance and strength from the life of the community. They refuse the work that society allocates them . . . Their rejection of work is a rejection of the level to which schools have skilled them as labour power, and when the community feeds that rejection back into the school system, it becomes a rejection of the functions of schooling.[6]

Black Girls and Women at Work

The historical conditions that West Indian women lived under in the last two centuries made it economically essential for them to work, either on the land, in domestic service, in unskilled work or in skilled work like dressmaking. The prevailing ideal of white middle class marriage defined the wife as someone who did not work, but was supported by her husband. To attain this, as outlined earlier, West Indian men had to have enough regular income to keep their wives from working and therefore material conditions ensured that West Indian marriages were kept to a minority for a long time. But as a result of this, West Indian women have had a different experience of economic independence from English women, who have always been dependent on their husband's wages if they were middle class and on adding to his wage if they were working class. Therefore West Indian women have for a long time borne the most consistent responsibility towards providing both materially and emotionally for their families. Those women who came independently to Britain to work and improve life for their children were continuing this tradition and still do so today. White women are now in the process of emancipating themselves from the dependency of husband and home, by venturing out and being increasingly drawn into work, and by demanding equal pay and opportunity. West Indian women have had such 'independence' thrust upon them but in a way that has been far from emancipated.

Not surprisingly they do not want their children to go through the same struggles, and work in the same low-level and exploited jobs as they did. They want secure, well-paid and respectable employment for them, and their children should in theory be able to work their way up to this through the education system. Their aspirations extend to boys and girls alike, but in reality both face a similar job selection to that of the white working class; although their opportunities are reduced by the interwoven effects of race.[7]

The West Indian Ealing girls had job expectations that were very similar to the white girls, except that they covered a narrower range. Office-work and nursing, which are respectable jobs for girls in the Caribbean, were the choices of the majority, and over two-fifths of these went for secretarial and general office jobs. The rest of the girls hoped to be bank clerks, teachers, social workers, children's nurses, hairdressers and models.*

None of them expected to work in a factory. Again, this may be a characteristic of London, with its plethora of clerical and commercial work, but even taking this into consideration, the job choices (apart from nursing) are not those in which black women have yet been found in any great number. Black women have been concentrated in the worst jobs in terms of pay, conditions and status, and provide a pool of unskilled labour for industry.

*The wish to be a model became very popular when the choice of 'any job in the world' was given, and parallels much of the interest in fashion and clothing.

In the service sector, they have been given the kind of work that occurs behind the scenes where contact with the public is minimal. For instance in 1966 about 13 per cent of white women were salesworkers, compared with 7 per cent of Asian women and only 1 per cent of West Indian women.* It may have been significant that none of the Ealing West Indian girls wanted to be shop assistants, receptionists or air-hostesses – all quite popular choices with the English girls. The popularity of clerical work accompanies the large proportion of girls doing typing courses (like the white girls), but the actual incidence of black girls and women in this sort of employment is proportionally much lower.

The nursing profession is an area where a high percentage of immigrant labour is found, and is a popular job amongst young immigrant girls. The roots of this can also be traced back to the days of slavery and colonialism, where wet or dry nursing, and looking after other people's children was regular work for West Indian women. Up to 30 per cent of nurses are foreign-born, and in 1966 nursing accounted for 22 per cent of black female immigrants.† Long hours and low pay accelerated the decline in the numbers of British girls taking up this career, and nurses from overseas have come to provide an integral part of Britain's health service. At first immigrant student nurses were supposed to return home after completing their courses but this rule was later relaxed to help our critical need for nursing staff. In 1970, about 19,000 student nurses came into Britain from Ireland and the West Indies, and increasing numbers came from Malaysia, Mauritius and Hong Kong. 'What used to be a vocation for women of the middle class is now a job for women of the working class, and particularly for black and other immigrant women.'[8] Many are admitted to Britain as students, but find themselves excluded from the best training. They are often directed to take

* This is changing in some urban areas like London where black girls are employed in fashion shops and boutiques, but the situation is always bleaker in the provinces.

† As compared to 10 per cent of the British female labour force. In the West Midlands in 1966 four times as many West Indian girls were nurses as were in other white-collar occupations.

the S.E.N. (State Enrolled Nurse) course – a two-year lower-level course, instead of the higher S.R.N. (State Registered Nurse) three-year course, which can be used outside Britain and is a professional qualification with the potential for promotion. As S.E.Ns, they can be used for the unpleasant routine jobs and generally exploited as a trained work-force relegated to low pay.

I asked the Ealing West Indian girls whether their mothers worked and what sort of jobs they did. 61 per cent of them had full-time jobs, 17 per cent had part-time jobs and only seven out of fifty did not work. This is a higher proportion than the figures found by the 1971 Census which showed that 68·4 per cent of women from the West Indies engaged in some kind of economic activity. The girls' mothers were mainly employed in factory work or nursing, with a smaller proportion working as cleaners and home helps, or on London Transport. Clerical jobs were minimal and there were no higher-level jobs represented. Their position was very different from that reflected in their daughters' aspirations. Of those who wanted to be nurses (nearly 20 per cent) some were following their mother's example, while others made this choice against their mother's advice. Some of them spoke specifically about their views and those of their parents on a career in nursing.

First I thought of going into the W.R.A.C. 'cause it sounded interesting, but my mum wants me to be a secretary. But that's the worst thing. I wanna be a nurse and be with a lot of children 'cause I love children. I'd rather be a nurse than anything else. I'll probably end up working in a factory somewhere. I've got a feeling I would anyway. That's the only job that's going.

Gloria

Mother, when I told her I wanted to be a nurse she said, 'A nurse?' – 'cause she's a nurse herself. She said, 'You don't want to be a nurse. I won't let you be a nurse. You can be anyone else but not a nurse, and you're not working in any factory or shop assistant.' So I said O.K. . . . mum says that as long as you do some worthwhile job it's all right with her. She's not going to tell me what to do, it's up to me as long as I don't work in any low-down thing.

Barbara

It is this generation of black school-leavers that are feeling the greatest effects of being working class and black, as their hopes and expectations and those of their parents are frustrated and crushed. With comparatively low qualifications they have to make do with the work that is available and with the high level of unemployment there may not be any. For boys, this is resulting in the rejection of such low-level work,[9] while for girls the effects are diluted through the availability of a few unskilled office jobs, which offer work but few prospects. A minority do get higher qualifications, and form a black élite who may be used as a model to deny the existence of discrimination, but most will emerge from school a product of material and social conditions and bearing the consequent bias of class, race and sex. The Ealing West Indian girls, at fourteen and fifteen, showed enthusiasm and faith in the education system. The jobs they hoped to do are not impossible to obtain, but the likelihood is made remote because of discrimination or the demand for qualifications that they may not have. Later, if they are stuck in the 'bargain basement' of jobs, the struggle to survive becomes critical if they have children to support and perhaps a husband who cannot find work. It is hard for women to be militant when the household depends on their labour.

Nevertheless, West Indian women have become involved in militant struggles in Britain since the late 1960s and with the general growth of women's industrial activities. They have played a part in fights for equal pay and union recognition. Within unions black women have also come up against forces of neglect and discrimination that pertain specifically to their sex and colour. In 1972, they took part in the auxiliary hospital workers' strike, and in 1974 in the nurses' strikes. And throughout the duration of the night-cleaners' campaign which culminated in the 1971 strikes, black women took an active role.

There are also many individual struggles that go unreported and unnoticed. As well as older women, girls growing up in the last ten years have entered work here and encountered elements of hostility and discrimination. Some will have tried to confront these, and a further education student that I talked to described one of her own battles.

Then I got a job in Sainsbury's. Any time you want to get wound up just work behind the cash desk, 'cause, y'know the customers used to come in and they wanted us to ring their stuff and pack their bags at the same time, and one time I was doing this woman's bag and she turned round and she called me a black bastard, or something like that. So I turned round and I dumped the things down and pushed her things and ignored her – 'cause if someone's as ignorant enough to go on like that I'm not going to argue with them to go down to their standards, so I just left her, an, she's screamin' and shoutin' at me at the back, an, I'm getting really wound up on this thing and banging on it. So she went to the manager and told the manager that that black girl won't wrap her bags for her, so the manager got someone else to relieve me off the till and took me upstairs. And when he asked me why, I said well, for one, if I had done what my mum told me to do she wouldn't have been able to come up to you, I said because I don't like sitting down and being shouted at for little or nothing. So when he heard what she'd done he said well, if you'd have packed her bags you'd have got rid of her quicker. I said to him I don't stand for things like that y'know. So he said to me that you're too hot-tempered and if anyone does that again just ring your bell and call for me and we'll sort it out. And that was that. And then – I always seem to get places where black people are treated wrongly, and I hated it because they used to have black kids mopping up. All right, you've got part-time kids – you've got part-time black, you've got part-time white – the white would do the stacking on the shelves and you'd have the blacks on their knees scrubbin' here and scrubbin' there. I don't like that sort of thing. If they'd treated them equally, I mean if whites were doing it as well it wouldn't bother me. The whites would get treated completely differently you know, like the whites are too clean to be on the floor but the niggers can do it, know what I mean? – and that got me, so I had an argument with one of the managers about it and they took no notice, so one time me an' a girl called Gill got all the blacks to say we were going to walk out. They were all big until the time come and then none of them moved, and I was really annoyed y'know, 'cause, Thursday and Friday it's majority black working there, so that time if we'd have walked out we'd have had to get what we wanted, or the shop would have to shut. When it come to the time, those black kids were going, no, where they going to get another job and this nonsense and just before that I'd been offered promotion to work in the office, and I told them this and I says I've got more to lose than you but it don't bother me because they might treat me nicely because I stand up for myself but they're black people as well and if they can treat me that way why can't they treat the others, but those kids wouldn't move, so I left that as well. I told them where they could stick their promotion and everything else.

Annette

Racial prejudice is an integral part of black experience in Britain and is perpetuated through a divisive social structure. In schools it is concealed to some extent by a supposedly neutral atmosphere which theatens punishment for any very explicit demonstration of hostility. However, in any multi-racial school there will be racial undercurrents, if not explosions, and many children are constantly aware of this potential. Experiences of prejudice can only be meaningfully described and understood by those concerned, and I purposely did not make it a focus of my inquiry. For all black girls and boys, however, it will have crucial effects on the way they see themselves and their lives. It did crop up spontaneously in talking to some girls, such as Barbara. She lived with her mother, who was a nurse, and her stepfather. She had been boarded out since she was four years old because of her mother's work in the hospital. She was in the top form of her year.

I don't know what sort of career I want yet. I don't want any old job, I want something that people will look up to you and respect you for. School sort of protects me. I don't like being out there in the world, trying to find your own way. I like it here, don't know how to explain. I don't think I'd like to start going out to work yet . . . [There would be] great differences between work and school. I'll get a lot of enemies, I know that much. I won't get what I want straight away – because of my colour. They say it's not this, but I know it is. And another thing, I don't like people pushing me about too much. There isn't colour prejudice at this school, but in other schools I went to when I was younger, you find children would be against you because I was coloured. But here everybody's all right – there are more coloured children here anyway. You can make your own friends so its all right. But I found when I was younger I had to fight my way to make people understand. I wouldn't let people push me about because I was a coloured person. Went to a boarding school for a while and it was mixed, and the boys used to enjoy pushing me about, so I had to fight to let them know that just because I was coloured I can do something for myself. So my reports were quite bad then, and I went on to a girls' school and my work improved after that. They reckoned I'd get to a grammar school but I didn't get through because their syllabus is different. I went to a boarding school when I was ten, left at eleven and then went to a girls' school for three years, and then I came here. All in England – I was born in England . . . Getting the money's the best thing about working. Finding the job, trying to get the job may be the worst – don't know yet. If I got qualifications it shouldn't be difficult to get a job, but these people, they're just prejudiced I'm sure. Even your own colour turn you down – just like that. . . . I want to do all sorts of things. I doubt if I'd get there but I could easily try. A woman Foreign Minister – would have to do the job much better. A woman really is just as intelligent and knows what it's all about. I suppose a woman could use her face and her body and all that, but a man, he'd do the talking. I like to talk. I don't want – Oh, she's got a pretty face, I'll do this just for this, and all that. I like to do the talking.

In Britain, young West Indian girls (and boys) face many conflicts. These occur between black and white, and within generations as the young are encouraged to integrate into a society that inherently discriminates against them. Being born here, as an increasing number are, does little more than sharpen the contrast between what they are entitled to and what they receive. What really happens to the Ealing girls in the future may bear little similarity to their ideas and hopes expressed here. And in the light of inflation and growing unemployment, cutbacks in jobs will be made and they will find that being black, female and working class makes them very vulnerable. They will have to confront the situation with the determination of their mothers, but perhaps with the added benefits of education, more awareness and self-confidence, and fewer illusions.

ASIAN GIRLS

I am seventeen years old, lucky to have received some education in England – hopeful to become a nurse. I am British Asian, my parents come from India, a village, the customs of that village are law in my home. I have three sisters, the youngest fourteen, the eldest nineteen. My father is contemplating finding four husbands in the village, they would come here and would get permission to stay because we are British. I am sure there must be hundreds of girls in our position. What can we do? What chance have we got to have even limited freedom? You talk of discrimination, few of you know what it is like to belong to a background such as ours. I myself may be luckier, because I have good friends who help, but when I see my sisters I worry. I read your maga-zine in the newsagent's, I wouldn't dare buy it.

Letter in *Spare Rib*, No. 29.

There are three main Asian communities living in Britain: Indians from the Punjab and Gujarat areas of India, Pakistanis from West and East Pakistan (now Bangladesh), and East African Asians (mostly from Kenya, Tanzania and Uganda), the majority of whom emigrated from their home countries within the last twenty years. For those from India and Pakistan coming to Britain originally meant settling temporarily to work and earn money, sending it to the family at home and finally returning. It was for this reason that many Sikh and Pakistani men came over alone in the early years of emigration, but rumours of impending restrictions and controls on entry which were implemented in the Acts of 1962 and 1968 panicked them into suddenly sending for wives and families and forced many to settle here who would otherwise have eventually returned home.

The various countries from which they have come reflect their relative economic status and position here. For example, the high level of poverty in Pakistan and Bangladesh brought many people here, and they generally make up the poorer section of the Asian population in Britain. Most originally came from rural back-grounds and had minimal education. There was little money to invest in education so schools were poorly provided and there was no compulsion to go. Teachers were neither well-qualified nor well-paid and parents could ill-afford to buy school materials for their children. Relatively few went further than primary school.

The Sikhs, who originated as a reform movement within Hinduism in the fifteenth century, make up the largest proportion of Indians in Britain. They come mainly from the Punjab, a small and densely populated part of Northern India. The largest pro-portion of Sikhs who have emigrated to Britain are *Jats*, a caste of land-owning peasant farmers, as well as other castes, such as *Ramgarhias*, traditionally a caste of craftsmen who emigrated to

Britain and to East Africa. Their background contains more in terms of education and opportunity than that of those from Pakistan. Primary education is free and supposedly compulsory in the Punjab although it is the present generation who have benefited most from universal education. School may include some teaching of the English language, but many of the Indians who initially emigrated here were neither literate nor spoke English and were at first very dependent on those in the communities who had a good command of the language.

The number of Hindus that came to Britain has been comparatively small, and they have mainly come from Gujarat in the western area of India. They have been shown generally to be a more urban and educated community, but at the same time often stricter in their observance of things like caste distinctions in marriage. The Indian community benefits from having a very strong sense of identity and being traditionally more tightly and efficiently organized, and has, for instance, set up organizations like the Indian Workers' Association to look after its interests.

A significant number of the East African Asians have come from the urban areas of post-colonial Africa and have a rather more cosmopolitan background. They speak more and better English and are usually quite middle class and sophisticated in their original work-skills and experience. As a result many of them are comparatively accustomed to European ways of living. Those with qualifications and skills or resources of their own can sometimes make some progress, but the greater proportion are unlucky. For instance, most of the Ugandan Asians came here quickly and traumatically after their expulsion and lost much in the way of money and goods. Since they came involuntarily they came from urban and rural areas alike and from the working class and the middle class. Once here, their concentrated numbers and their language difficulties forced them to take any work that was available, and so in spite of their skills many found themselves in unskilled jobs and in areas of work far removed from what they were accustomed to in Uganda.

The reasons that each person has for living in Britain will affect their perception of themselves here and the extent to which they wish to integrate and take on a British way of life. They too feel the effects of a one-sided concept of 'integration', but unlike the West Indian people they wish to preserve their separateness and strong cultural identity. Britain makes great demands on all immigrant people in terms of ideology and behaviour and in terms of the social and economic structures we insist that they work in and the critical and inflexible way we perceive and treat their adherence to cultural customs. We think we are doing them a favour and that they must respond by showing their conformity to a dominant culture. Asian people have a deep sense of their own culture and community. If they see their future lives as lying in Britain then there is perhaps more reason for an aspiring family to loosen their close observation of traditional ways of living, but where life here is temporary, or they feel alienated and threatened by aspects of it, then they will continue strictly to preserve their own cultural hegemony for self-protection and communal help. For those whose future is confused and hazy and who are struggling to survive here, drawing on their own community offers more security. Many are continually sending money home to relatives and some send it back as capital investment in some enterprise they are building up, and such capital commitments at home will add another dimension to their perception of their lives in Britain.

Asian groups are community-oriented and socially cohesive and family loyalties are very strong. This has been of great help in alleviating the conditions under which many Asian families live in Britain. For instance, the hardship caused by the unemployment of the Ugandan Asians was eased less by the British Government than by the financial support of their relatives and community here. Horror stories of large families packed into one or two rooms shocked the country ten years ago but are no longer news, although they remain a continuing part of the lives of Asians here and the social services never have sufficient facilities to accommodate them. Work is not easily obtained, as most immigrant groups have found, although those with some education and a good command of English can now get a few positions in banks and offices. Some have followed a tradition of shopkeeping and have opened small local stores. Others have set up workshops or factories, often in dressmaking or textiles in which they employ other Asian men and women. This has particularly formed an outlet for those women who would not be allowed to work in places where there were many men or other 'unsuitable' company.

Asian men and women mainly work in factories and local industries in which they are exploited like their white working class neighbours. However, like the West Indian people they suffer further from prejudice and discrimination, and they too usually find employment limited to menial and low-paid work in semi-skilled or unskilled jobs. They undertake the night-work, the awkward shifts and many of the hard and dirty jobs. Even if they have professional qualifications they are usually placed in the junior grades. Occupational figures show them as having a high representation as clerical workers but these have been slightly exaggerated by the inclusion of white people born in India. Men generally work in engineering, transport, metals and the car industry, and in the clothing and foot-wear industries (particularly Pakistanis). In West Yorkshire many of the mills are dependent on their labour: for instance the introduction of new machinery necessitated special night-shifts that were intolerable to local women workers and employers now recruit men direct from Pakistan.[10] Asian women who work have jobs as machinists in the clothing industry, in laundries and local factories, canteens, cleaning and outwork, all of which are extremely exploited. There are also a small number of both men and women who are well-educated and professionally qualified, and who work as doctors, teachers, nurses, barristers, civil servants etc., and some men whose entrepreneurial skills have built up successful businesses.

Religion plays an important part in all Asian communities and guides the principles around which they live. As a result of living in Britain, if not before, these principles have been inevitably confronted by those of a more advanced capitalist society and by the adaptive pressures that this exerts on the way people work and view their lives. Religions vary according to the country of origin and the regions within it. Those who come from India for instance are usually Sikh or Hindu, and those from Pakistan and Bangladesh are predominantly Moslem. These beliefs and principles determine their moral ethics, and form the social climate under which they live into one centred around many stern requisites of behaviour. Such requisites include moral conformity, loyalty and cooperation; self-discipline – which involves strict obedience to the social order; recognition of the dominant authority of the father and other elders; respect for marriage; and the advocation of modesty and restraint.

In some ways the ideal personality implied in this is one that contrasts with today's ideals of individualism, initiative and competition. For instance, the Sikh community puts great emphasis on *dharam*, meaning duty to the family and community, and *sewa*, meaning religious duty and service done without desire for reward. However in other ways the emphasis on such aspects as preservation of order, self-discipline, conformity, and respect for marriage are easily in keeping with conserving a system based around accumulating capital.

Modesty and restraint are stressed for both sexes, but particularly for girls and women, and this is manifest in their upbringing. Asian children usually make up the quieter and better-behaved elements inside school classrooms in Britain. The comparative level of freedom and permissiveness allowed to young people here greatly outrages religious and moral principles and is looked on with disapproval by Asian parents who fear that their own children will pick up some of these ideas. Thus they try to protect them as much as possible from contact with any 'harmful' influences.

Women

Asian women traditionally occupy a subordinate position in the community. This is not always explicitly inferior, although in Moslem society in particular this has a historical and religious basis which has resulted in rigidly enforced seclusion and subordination of Moslem girls and women. More often women are esteemed in their 'proper' place which is at home bringing up children. Theirs is a private life of meekness and modesty within the joint patriarchal family. Men are very much at the head of their families, acting as public spokesmen and negotiating with the outside world. The 'purity' demanded from women requires them to be confined and protected from external influences.

Moslem women in particular are traditionally kept in strict *purdah* away from men who are not relatives, and command little authority even at home. The Sikhs, however, 'pride themselves on their relatively progressive attitude to the position of women in society. The teachings of the gurus on this subject amount to a rejection of the negative aspects of Hindu and Moslem traditions, in particular the ideas that women are "unclean", prone to sinfulness, inherently weak-minded, and created mainly as a temptation by the Almighty.'[11] One guru described women as 'the conscience of man', an attitude which regards the immoral or irresponsible behaviour of a woman as being far more serious than such behaviour in a man. Any compliment that this implies is deceptive since its consequence has been to lay an unfair and heavy burden of moral responsibility on women, and severely restrict their freedom. They are revered as mothers, for passing on and maintaining tradition, but at the same time they are often not even permitted to go shopping alone.

In many communities, Asian women are still seen primarily as producers of sons and maintainers of the home and are dependent in every way on their husbands, who have to be 'respected' regardless of the nature of their characters. Families who have lived in Britain for some time may change their ways of thinking and behaving, but it is often these moral traditions that are strongly adhered to when people feel confused or threatened by the influence of a more 'permissive' way of life.

Women's traditional position in India, Pakistan and Bangledesh or East Africa is quite easily preserved in the extensive rural areas although education and communication has increased the likelihood of Western influence. In Britain however, this is much harder to preserve since interaction with British society is bound to provoke at least a slight change or widening of ideas. Few escape all external influences, but this has happened to some of the women living in very large Asian communities, such as in Southall, who speak little or no English and only use Asian shops and other Asian facilities. One consequence of this, however, is to cause a gap between them and their children who attend schools where they learn the English language and other features of English life. Some children have found themselves in the role of interpreter for their own parents.

Although the proper role of women is at home, some women have broken out of this through going to work. According to the 1971 Census figures, 40·8 per cent of women from India were engaged in economic activity here compared with 20·7 per cent of women from Pakistan. Figures for East African Asian women are more complex because they are mixed up with African figures and with those for India and Pakistan, depending on place of birth. This situation has also changed since 1971 with the expulsion of the Ugandan Asians in 1972.

Educated women with professional qualifications such as teachers and doctors have sometimes managed to continue working in Britain, but with difficulty, and have often found themselves confined to the lower grades in their professions. Other women have had to go out to work here because of basic financial needs. In India or Pakistan whether a woman works or not depends on whether her family is high or low caste, rich or poor, and whether it is based in a town or village. Large numbers of Asian women came to Britain as dependents with little or no experience of working outside the home. Many have not worked after arriving here, but economic pressures have driven others out into mainly semi-skilled or unskilled work. Like other women, they have found it impossible to keep a family on the single and often low wage of their husbands. Often their work-place will be limited to a predominantly female environment in factories and small workshops (sweatshops), laundries etc., where they may be overworked and exploited. Asian families themselves may own workshops which use female relatives as cheap labour. This arrangement makes conditions harder to check and also makes it harder for the women to improve their pay and conditions. This has happened in Southall for instance, which was the home of most of the Asian girls that I spoke to, where local clothing manufacturers have taken advantage of the traditional Asian skill of dressmaking. Outwork is also readily available at incredibly low rates for those who have to work at home. Amongst the Ealing Asian girls, 43 per cent had mothers who worked, of whom 62 per cent were from India, none from Pakistan (there were only a few girls represented from Pakistan), and 38 per cent from East Africa. Many of them had found work in the canteens and kitchens of Heathrow Airport, and others were employed in sewing, ironing, laundry work and in local factories making sweets, rubber and chemicals.

Many women felt the loss of the joint family system on coming here and their isolation at home often led to intense loneliness. But at the same time some Asian women, like English women in the past, have found an enjoyment in working and a relief from being confined in the home. Rajinder, an eighteen-year-old Indian, who was born in Tanzania and spent one year in India before coming to Britain six years ago, talked about the experience of her mother.

Dad works at Fords, and my mum works in a sweet factory, full-time. My mum, if she stays home there is no one to talk to her and she gets bored with it, but when we came from India she stayed home for a month and nobody used to talk to her and she really got bored so she said you know I want to do some job and now she's working in the factory and there are so many Indian ladies working down there too and they're ever so friendly and get along well and she likes it up there better than home. She says 'Oh it's nice peaceful and quiet down there and I've got some ladies friends', and I said, 'What's wrong with us!' In India she didn't work she used to look after me and my brother, she wouldn't have worked because my dad was in Africa and she was the only one to look after us and we used to live in a flat down there.

It is only the richer, more highly educated professional élite who have modified or rejected the exclusion of women from public affairs. However, young Asian girls who have attended school in Britain are increasingly being allowed to work, if only until their marriage. This has brought its crop of concern and worry to families about the possible consequences of this for girls' marriage prospects. The girls themselves feel the pull of both cultures and straddle a chasm between them while trying to accommodate the ideas and demands of both.

Marriage

In Asian families, the birth of a son is far more cause for celebration than the birth of a daughter, and this stems largely from the economics of the marriage system. Marriage is highly respected and its sanctity is unquestioned. Divorce is deeply frowned upon, and although for example in 1955 the Hindu law was revised to allow for it, the actual instances of divorce are negligible. Although divorce is similarly permitted by the Moslem religion, this is qualified by the statement: 'The most hateful of all lawful things in the eyes of God is divorce.' If a marriage does recognizably break down and divorce is carried through, women are at a disadvantage compared to men. The option of remarriage which is open to men, is a course disapproved of for women. Widows face similar discrimination, in contrast to marriageable widowers.

Marriage is a form of social contract. It is not based initially or primarily on love – a marriage is arranged first and the time for falling in love comes later. The parents of a boy and a girl are responsible for the arrangement, and the most suitable choice is made by investigating backgrounds and family histories. Stars and horoscopes may also be important as signs for a good marriage and Hindu-arranged marriages often begin with an exchange of horoscopes so that temperaments may be matched. In a Sikh family the chosen boy or girl is usually someone of the same caste but from a different *goth*, meaning clan or sub-caste, and in India they are generally sought from a different village from that to which the family belongs, since many of those in the same village may be from the same hereditary *goth*. The betrothed couple should not have known each other before their marriage.

Parents are very afraid of anything that will 'taint' their daughters and thereby lessen their chances of making a good match. This mainly explains girls' lack of freedom, since they are forced to remain separate and tucked away at home to avoid any opportunity for temptation. The main fear is contact with boys and men, and therefore Asian girls are not supposed to have any associations with them. This is more rigidly enforced for Moslem girls and makes life almost intolerable for some girls at school, who have to mix and do lessons with boys, while at the same time any rumour that they have been seen talking to boys may result in their being removed from school. The prevalent fear of gossip can pervade a girl's life both before and after she is married. Rajinder, quoted above, spoke about this, although she was fortunate in having parents who were not as strict as many others.

My dad, he was very strict before, but he doesn't like me going out with boys, but if they are as brothers as my brother's friends then they're all right and they come round to my place and spend time and chat away and walk about. He doesn't mind, it's just that in Indian families if somebody sees you with a boy they start gossiping and they say she was with this boy and that and he [my dad] doesn't like that, but he doesn't mind. There are some parents who are very strict. They wouldn't even let their daughters go out and if she does then they go with her . . . I wouldn't get married at this age but after five years I don't mind, but not at this age, I want to enjoy myself. Because actually in Indian religion if you get married and you go out too much they start, you know people will start talking about you that she is married and she doesn't even bother to stay home. They will start to break our marriage, by gossiping telling the other people that she's not like this or that. And people start talking you see inside families, the people, relatives, they start talking and everything goes out, out of the family and other people knows about this too and they start gossiping . . . Not many people have divorces, they live separate but they don't have divorce. You see if you get divorced then nobody would marry the girl the second time. The boy can get married, but is problem for the girl. But it's up to the girl, if she wants to get a divorce she can get a divorce but it's hard to find a second husband for her. For boy is all right.

Such rumours are also feared for the possibility that they may be relayed back to India where the response to Western 'vulgarization' is severe and may affect a girl's chances of having a husband brought to England. The demand for moral purity is also extended to young adult women, and therefore they and girls alike may be denied the company of men apart from members of their own family.

For Asians living in Britain, some of the anonymity of the

marriage arrangement has been removed.[12] For instance photos may be exchanged and meetings are usually organized between boys and girls as prospective marriage partners. The biggest consideration in many cases, however, is still the financial one – the dowry.* Amongst Sikhs in 1974, dowries ran at about £150 and upwards, and some go up to thousands of pounds.[13] A boy or girl transported over from India to become husband or wife is considered a far better prospect than one living over here because he or she has not been 'vulgarized'.

Before 1969, it was possible to bring prospective husbands or wives over to Britain, but in January 1969 the Home Secretary ruled that Commonwealth citizens engaged to women living in Great Britain could not enter to marry and settle. This made it virtually impossible to bring over husbands for girls in Britain, while boys could still send home for their brides. It further made it difficult for any British women with foreign husbands to live here, and as such was a blatant piece of discriminatory legislation. By 1974, a situation was developing in which there were many marriageable girls in Britain who could only choose a husband from the boys already here, while the boys could bring over wives who were less influenced by Western life, and therefore would make 'better' wives.

Now Asian boys in Southall prefer to send back to India for wives, since they can expect them to be more dutiful and obedient. Several Sikh boys I spoke to said they did not like the girls brought up in England because they wore their hair loose, showed their legs [traditional Sikh women wear trousers] and spoke too much with boys. The girls complain that the boys chat them up and try to get them to go out with them, but consider them corrupt and unworthy of marriage if they respond.[14]

This had the result of increasing the cost to parents of marrying a daughter, especially since marriage in Britain involved three ceremonies – engagement, a civil and a religious ceremony – compared with one in India. Some girls found for instance that pressure was exerted on them to return to India to marry, since parents, like the boys described above, suspected that girls brought up here would be rebellious and discontented wives and

* Although now, amongst several other national aims, India professes to be trying to get rid of the dowry system.

less willing to share in family duties – therefore they were less likely to pick them as wives for their sons. Girls from Pakistan who are more strictly guarded than Indian girls are also more often sent back to Pakistan after their education, where they are married.

After a prolonged campaign in the press and in Parliament however, the ban on husbands was finally lifted by Roy Jenkins in June 1974. Now, provided the girl is a British citizen, she and her husband can settle here. This has thereby helped to resolve the predicament of British wives with foreign husbands, and the problems of parents who arrange marriages, but has also produced cries such as those from the girl writing to *Spare Rib** who have been to school here and do not wish for imported husbands. Another answer to the dowry problem of course is not to have an arranged marriage, and Rajinder's parents took this view:

My dad gives me good advice about what to do and what not to do. But he wouldn't talk about sex or anything, not even marriage to me. He doesn't like that, giving a dowry, and his friend said, when Rajinder gets married you have to give a dowry, and he goes, I'm not going to give a dowry because Rajinder's going to find her own fella and I won't mind that. They think I'm too young, they say I've got five more years to go. They don't want me to get married at a small age because I wouldn't have anything to enjoy or do anything. I'd have to stay home and do the cooking and that but after five years its all right. But they're not planning anything yet. If the girl stays here and nobody marries her then she goes to India and gets married down there. Their parents think that Indian boys are very good, better than London ones, because when they come from India they change down here and they're not what they used to be, you know, quiet and shy, but go out and parties and everything and they don't behave like the other boys, that's what they think.

Relationships between the sexes are strictly controlled throughout life. Girls' activities before marriage are rigidly circumscribed, and after marriage, when bride and groom leave the ceremony together, this may even be the first time that the girl has been totally alone with a boy and not within the security of home or accompanied by close friends or relatives. Most parents

* Excerpt from *Spare Rib* magazine, no. 29, quoted on page 261–2.

do their best, and often succeed in ensuring a happy marriage for their children, but there are bound to be some unhappy ones which may be covered up by the strong feelings against divorce. Since the partnership is not initially fired and bound by love, expectations from marriage are different in this respect.

It is interesting to find that in both Punjabi legends, and in many films shown in Britain at the Hindi cinemas, love is portrayed between Indian boys and girls and the subsequent conflict between this and the arranged marriage system forms the basis of many plots. The romanticism is even taken further to imply that the arranged marriage system is rather like a necessary evil, an unfortunate destiny that has greater power than love. In real life, although arranged marriage has become somewhat liberalized and boys and girls usually can make the final decision, love-marriages are still frowned upon and are relatively unusual. They may occasionally happen between more westernized or educated people like college graduates. But it is not approved of to marry outside your caste, and mixed marriages are another rare occurence. Rajinder's parents took a less strict view about boyfriends and marriage, but they did make qualifications about the boys concerned.

I've got a boyfriend, I've been going out with him for one year. My parents say that as long as he is my caste they don't mind but they wouldn't like me going out with white boys or Pakistani boys. In India they have religion, different kinds, and they don't like Pakistani boys – you see if you marry a Pakistani boy then you're out of your religion because you go in Pakistan side and you're not anymore Patel, not Gujerati, so they wouldn't like that and they wouldn't like me marrying a white fella. They would stop me, if I said I got on well with him and that, they'd say it's your life you're dealing with and if you get hurt and that then don't come to us. So really they're trying to protect me from you know, if I'm doing anything wrong.

If for example a Sikh boy marries a white girl, this will be accepted especially if she adopts aspects of Indian custom and dress. However, it is most unusual for a Sikh girl to marry a white boy, because this would have necessarily involved courtship, which would have been cut off in its early stages. Such a relationship is considered undesirable because of the consequences if their courtship did not lead to marriage. The girl's reputation would be spoilt as a result of her association, and her subsequent marriage opportunities would be severely impaired. Therefore, although Asian girls are very well aware of the existence and enormously high status of the adolescent love-affair, since it is read about, talked about, seen on films and television, and actually happening to other girls at school, for them it is out of reach.

In comparison to Moslem girls, Sikh girls have a little more freedom before marriage. The rules are less strict about speaking to boys and men, although they would certainly not be allowed to go out with them. They are also permitted to speak in front of their elders. A young married woman is in much the same situation, and is required to be quiet and retiring, leaving most organization and interaction outside the family in the hands of her husband. Middle-aged and older women however enjoy more status with age. They can be less reserved, and are treated with great respect by the younger people. But for all Sikh girls and women, fulfilment lies in having and looking after children, and their place is very much at home. The consequences of this in Britain may be loneliness and isolation, as they are so far away from the close family network of the Punjab.

Education

In British classrooms, Asian boys and girls try to understand and accommodate to the demands of school life. For many of them, language is a major obstacle, and yet seemingly the key to success. It is a more subtle part of the same discrimination that places black children in lower forms and makes prejudiced assumptions about their intelligence and ability without sufficient consideration of factors like language and culture. People who discriminate thus implicitly regard English as having higher status than Asian languages like Gujerati and Punjabi. These languages are important and form an integral part of Asian identity and home and community life. Some children have little difficulty with English, if, for instance, they have learnt it before coming here, or have spent most or all of their school lives here, but those who come at a later age find themselves trying to learn in a semi-comprehensible world. They may be put in special classes, and sometimes these have unfortunately been combined with general remedial classes, thus adding another handicap to their progress. In some areas where there is a high concentration of immigrants, such as Southall, the practice of 'bussing' primary school children is carried out, which means transporting them to schools outside their immediate area to preserve the required percentage (30 per cent) of immigrant children in local schools. This has a disruptive effect on the children, greatly reduces their involvement in school and makes it harder for their parents to visit their schools. Although Ealing is supposed to be phasing this out, with the present provision of schools and cutbacks in educational spending, this will probably take some time.

Asian parents have a great concern and enthusiasm for education in Britain. It is often seen as a way of acquiring social standing and breaking through the confines of the caste system. Sikh parents for instance are as concerned for their daughters' education as they are for their sons'. This interest is not new in India, as there were schools for girls in the Punjab in the early nineteenth century. But for girls particularly, education can also provide a route round the dowry system, and a way of bypassing the caste system. This is a response partly produced by the material circumstances forced on them in Britain. With the difficulties and cost of marriage, if girls' education helps towards getting them a better match it is a material investment.

But the ambitions of parents and daughters can create problems. On one hand the parents' demands often put great responsibility and strain on their children who are expected to stay in night after night to study. For girls in particular, for the reasons outlined earlier, going out is rarely allowed in any case. On the other hand, the girls' own ambitions begin to take off on their own. They start to view the traditional early betrothal with reluctance, and many want to delay this, preferably until they have qualifications and an established job. It is ironic, however, that the more time girls spend at school or college, and thus the more education they receive, the more opportunity they have for meeting boys.

And consequently in some ways they are becoming less eligible for a 'good' marriage.

If continuation of education is in conflict with the time for marriage, girls may be given more say in their marriage arrangements. They may be able to postpone marriage by choosing to carry on with their studies and it is also now common for them to have the power of veto if they have any doubts about their prospective spouse. Their lives are continually changing and education is always a dynamic and influential process. Although for some girls the initial aim of their education is to make them more marriageable, at the same time it is also constantly teaching them about other ways of life, and may lead them to question the organization of their own lives. Schools may be criticized for not always encouraging or meeting the interests of their pupils, but for Asian and other immigrant pupils this deficiency is even further accentuated through ignorance or neglect of their culture, although some schools have now introduced 'black studies' courses.

Some families have changed on coming to London, perhaps more than they might have done in the provinces, and have tempered their expectations from their children and loosened some of their restrictions. But this also depends on many other factors such as their country of origin, social and economic backgrounds and the strength of the ideas and attitudes they held before coming. It also depends on the extent to which they are living as part of a large Asian community.

Rajinder talked of her father's attitude to change:

My father says you got to live you know, if you're in London you live London-style and if you live in India then you live Indian-style, so instead of this he likes to live in London style but if you're in India then you live like Indians ... When I came from India I was so quiet and that, I wouldn't even go out, because the way, well, when I was in India I was like that. I didn't like going out and didn't have much friends, but when I came down here I had many friends and we you know used to get on fine and that and I started going out and everything and I sort of started changing you know, not really more Indian but mostly living in London.

But in areas where there are large numbers of Asians, young people are expected to conform, often without question, to the norms of traditional Asian social behaviour. Because they are frequently unable to relate these customs to their experience of the Western world, they often find themselves in a situation of conflict. Their position in Britain is at once marginal and ambivalent: they are safe and secure inside a stable and supportive family structure and a cohesive community system and yet are attracted by the activities and interests of the English girls around them. They find it neither simple nor satisfactory to juxtapose all the new and conflicting ideas and images with their own traditional ones. Their ventures into English classrooms have opened up worlds unprotected by parents or custom and have presented exciting new possibilities. The protection and seclusion of girls has been partially sacrificed to the demands for compulsory schooling and the importance and usefulness of education. The lives of many young Asian girls have long since branched off in directions away from those taken by their own mothers.

It is in this context that Asian girls go to school in this country. At primary but especially at secondary school level, the curtain is lifted on a completely new world which aptly fulfils parental fears. It is comparatively free and permissive when contrasted with their upbringing within the family or any other school experience they may have had prior to coming to Britain. Girls and boys are noisy and boisterous. They shout at each other and even at teachers, implying a lack of respect for authority. There are no limitations on girls and boys talking to one another, (apart from normal school demands for silence) and many girls go around with boys inside school, and go out to parties, dances and films. In direct contrast Asian girls find their lives confined to coming directly home from school, helping with the housework, doing their homework and then reading a book or watching television, and sometimes there are strict ideas about what television programmes are suitable for children to watch.

After observing such contrasting life-styles, they might be expected to feel some dissatisfaction with the restrictive boundaries that surround their own lives, and this was so for many of the Asian girls in the Ealing schools, who expressed their simmering discontentment. For instance, if they had been given the choice, few of them would have preferred to have been born as girls. (20 per cent – as compared to 80 per cent who would have preferred to be boys.) Even in the closeness of their own community, the relative freedom of boys showed up only too clearly. And throughout the reasons they gave for preferring boys' lives there ran a longing for greater freedom; in this their responses resembled those of the West Indian girls except that they were even more pronounced.

A boy has more feeling happy than a girl because the boys can do everything but girls cannot do it. A boy gets better jobs than girls.

A boy has a freedom of doing anything he wants but the girl has just to be tied in the house.

Life is easier for boys than girls, they can come in as late as they wish and have more fun than we do.

A boy don't get pregnant and the girls do. And anyway our Indian people don't let the girls to be free same as with boys.

I would be a boy. At least you can go to places and all that. They can go anywhere that we can't go to . . . you can't go alone anywhere. I mean, when I get home and I want to stand in the road for a minute, she tells me to come in, sit down, don't answer the door. If someone comes, she says don't answer it. At least boys can go out and enjoy themselves. I don't mind about boyfriends so much but I do want to enjoy myself.

It is true that the Asian continents have their token women in politics and in professions like medicine, but there are few of these and they are an unrepresentative élite. Educated women are usually from high caste families, who have grown less traditional through education and Western influence. Such families have thrown off some of the cultural restraints for girls and women as part of a process of becoming self-sufficient and independent from the Asian community. Some of the African Asians for instance are in this position through living and working in the urban centres of East Africa. I spoke to one Kenyan Asian girl, Manjit, who was very well-spoken and confident. She had been in England for four years and her father worked as a surveyor. She did not live with her parents:

> They work in Bedford. I wanted to study in this school so I stayed here when they moved to Bedford. They wanted me to go to Bedford but I didn't. My sister is here too. I live with my uncle and grandmother and sister who is younger. I see my parents every weekend and in the holidays . . . I like arguing, I do it quite a lot because my uncle, grandmother and me disagree on quite a lot of things, like parties and boys . . . we also argue about clothes. I have one brother and two sisters, all younger. I'm the eldest so I'm supposed to be a goodie-goodie and set them an example because what I do they'll do. This is difficult sometimes because when I express my views my grandmother doesn't like me arguing with her and so she says 'Don't argue with me – your sister will do that', so I can't really put forward my views . . . I prefer to be a girl because there is nothing special about being a boy. I would like to show boys that I can do what they can do because a lot of them are big-headed. My cousins – they tease me and say that the place for a girl is in the home, and sitting there, and you can't do anything, and the boys should go out to work and all that. I argue with them and it's usually left halfway – no one wins. They want me to stay at home and learn to cook so that I can look after my man, I have arguments about that. I don't care what people think I'm like. I don't want to be like everybody else. I think differently from my family already.

However, her going out was still strictly monitored, and she could not go out with boys until after she had finished her studies. She said that if she were to bring a boy home 'they'd pack me back to India I suppose, I suppose I'd be taken to Bedford to stay with my parents and they'd act as probation officers or something.'

Controls within the Family

Parental power commands great respect among Asians and is linked with that of the community as a whole to constrain members into cooperative conformity. The family also forms a focal point for any conflicts and contradictions that are being encountered by sons and daughters whose daily entry into school confuses their past and present values and ideals. The availability of self-comparison with life outside the family makes them more conscious of their restricted freedoms.

Asian girls like those quoted earlier thus find themselves looking at an alien teenage world. Understanding this new experience is aided through talking with parents, and this is usually possible on many levels since families live closely together. But there are certain topics that are less easily discussed, such as freedom, sex, and relationships with other girls and boys. Girls usually find it easier to talk about personal things with their mothers who are often more approachable and sympathetic. There is a tradition of close mother–child relationships in Asian families, but it may be hard to discuss such taboo subjects with someone who has never experienced similar conflicts, who is likely to uphold restraint, and who may herself speak little English and rarely mix with English people. For instance, it would be difficult to talk rationally about the problems of relating or not relating to boys at school when parents have made the implicit assumption that girls must mix with boys as little as possible. Girlfriends who share similar experiences may become confidants for problems like this, as one girl found – she had come from Tanzania a year and a half previously.

I can't talk to my dad or my mum. If I have some troubles I usually talk to my friends, I find it difficult to talk to my sisters. We're not so very close – in different worlds, so I talk to my friends or the teachers. I like to talk to them and I find it easy. I can't talk to my parents, no, I think they wouldn't understand. They just think that what they say is right and I've got to do it and not argue or anything and do as they say without saying anything at all.

Gita

It would be a gross misinterpretation however to suggest that they do not get on with their parents and most endorsed the loyalty and enjoyment of family life.

The frustrations expressed by the Asian girls that I talked to lay mainly in not being allowed to go out when and where they wanted and often not being allowed out at all; also in not being allowed to associate with boys; and in not having much control over their future lives. Of these, the most salient dissatisfaction at school was the taboo on boys. This could threaten girls' future school-lives since if they were suspected or discovered to be having any sort of relationship with a boy, however innocent, this could jeopardize their future educational prospects, as parents would take them away from school.* Almost all the girls I spoke to had some opinions, problems or complaints about the severity with which their protection from boys was enforced.

We're not allowed to go out with boys at all. It is an Indian custom. When a girl gets married her parents choose the boy, and they don't want me to go out with boys. My father doesn't like me to go to discotheques and things because he thinks I will get in contact with boys and they'll bother me and interfere. They have got the impression that all boys are bad – maybe because outside school sometimes there are Indian girls hanging around with boys, maybe he thinks I'll do that. It doesn't bother me that other girls can go out because most of my friends are not allowed to do that. I don't have many English friends I have Nigerian and Chinese friends and they have the same restrictions as me.

Manjit

They never allow me to go out with boys. [My father] doesn't let me go out. I'm too young. He thinks boys are just out to get what they want, or they're addicts, and they just leave you when they've had it or something. It's all right if my brothers go out with girls, but not girls going out with boys – not *me* going out with boys. My sisters used to go out with boys, but they wouldn't tell him you see. They'd just say they were going out with friends and then go out with blokes. But I feel different. Even though I don't like my father, I wouldn't deceive him. I have got a boyfriend and I'd really like to go out with him, and I'm so worried, if only he would let me. But I'm so scared – if he says No then I can't even talk to the boy after that and I feel really guilty. I want to go out but I can't do it to him ... sometimes I get so tired I think I'll just get married to some boy, the first bloke, whether I loved him or not, just to get away from him. [The boy] understands because he comes from my country too and he knows what parents are like, so even though he wants to go out, he really does, but we can't do anything about it.

Gita

* One of the Ealing Asian girls was subsequently taken away from school for associating with boys, and put to work in a laundry: an all-female environment.

They say, 'Don't talk to boys and be nice.' They don't mind me going to parties with boys and girls because we don't talk to them. I did talk in the school though. I don't talk much like my friends do. Their parents think the same as mine though. A boy asked me to go out, but I don't want to because if my parents found out I would be in trouble. They'd be angry. It's in the religion, which says that when the girls go off the parents must know the boy, and the girls must not talk to boys.

Naseem (who came from Pakistan five years ago)

Sometimes my mum says 'I hope you're not going out with boys.' Some girls go to school and go out with boys and talk to them. She says 'I hope you're not like that or I'll stop your school straight away.' She didn't go to school. In India there wasn't any school for girls – only boys went to school. If I go to work probably I'll have to go to work with my aunt or someone, I can't go to work on my own. They won't let me travel alone. They take me in a car and make someone go with me, an elder aunt or somebody. But if I come to school I come alone. They think you will talk to boys on the road. You must not talk to boys until you get married. Don't know what they'd do with us if we did. I've got [a boyfriend]. He comes to school and we talk together. Some of my friends have got boyfriends and their parents don't know. Some go away with them and their parents can't do anything – they go to another country. I think it will change. We don't want to be like this when we get older, it'll change.

Surinder

Only a small fraction of the Asian girls in the Ealing schools said that their parents ever allowed them to go out with boys, but twice that number declared that they had a boyfriend. And from their various remarks it would seem that in spite of the severe consequences of discovery, many girls inevitably talked to boys and some occasionally went out with them, although most would not admit it to their parents. Sometimes similar restrictions may be applied to boys going out with girls, although in general they have far more social freedom outside the home than girls. Marjit commented that:

They [boys] can go out – they can stay out all night if they want to, they don't worry much about boys. But a boy is not allowed to go out with a girl, as maybe when he gets married, if the girl's parents know he's been out with other girls, they may not let their daughter marry him because he's a bad guy or something.

Marriage by Arrangement

As we have seen, marriage is a matter much too vital to be left to boys and girls alone and is arranged by the family. This may be modified even further in the future with the increasing influence from English culture, but at present many Asian girls can still exert little power over either the time of their marriage or the choice of husband. They may continue their education in an effort to postpone marriage, or reject their prospective husband. But since parents go to a lot of trouble to select a suitable boy, it may be difficult to justify complaint or rejection, especially if the only impression is gained through a photograph. Many girls are well aware of their narrow alternatives but feel they have to accept the situation as a fact of life. They have a foot in two cultures, the new Western one and the traditional Eastern one, and from such a position they ambivalently absorb and question both sides. For instance, two girls who resented their lack of freedom, and disliked the idea of being presented with a husband, were simultaneously reluctant completely to discard their traditional marriage system. They pointed out that it had been used with apparent success for hundreds of years, their parents represented examples of such arrangements that had worked, and presumably the well-publicized breakdowns of so many English-style marriages do not make a good advertisement for security and happiness. They also trust and respect the decisions of their parents who are very interested and concerned for their futures. But in 'love-marriages' at least there is more choice and an increasing number of Asian girls are responding resentfully to their total lack of autonomy. One Indian girl who was aware of this expressed her own almost contradictory opinions and also spoke of the difficulty at that time of Indian girls finding suitable husbands at all in Britain.

My parents are going to get me married and then they'll go back to India. Boys aren't allowed to come to this country anymore – it's stopped now. About ten years ago they used to get the girls married to boys who came over from India. Not to boys already over here because they don't want their girls to be married to a boy that's like that. Now they have to find a boy here for you. Nobody likes that idea really. It's because the Indian boys here go out with girls and all that. They feel that an Indian boy isn't such a good boy if he's been out with other girls, so they try and find a nice boy for you. My parents will just choose one and send me him. They don't care if I like him or not. Some parents do ask girls, mine wouldn't. I don't like it. I think you should get married to whoever you like and you can see if it is the right one or not. At least you can like them or not! When I get married I'm not going to see him. When my mum got married, she didn't. My dad was about fifteen years older than my mum, and she was only about fifteen or thirteen years old when she married him – so small she was. But now we can see photos and all that, and sometimes he comes to your house. My parents made a very good marriage. Every marriage works out really – I suppose you get married and have children – it looks like they chose each other when they got married, get on quite well. Indian marriages don't break, they don't have to. All families are happy and when girls get married in India they are still happy. But now these girls got boyfriends and they won't get married.

Surinder

I will be eighteen when I go back to Pakistan and get married. My parents will stay here. I will have time to get to know him before I get married. I have met him. He's good, he's O.K., two or three years older. If I didn't like him, just don't get married to him I suppose. But your parents don't just give you away to another person, he is very carefully chosen. You can't choose someone of your own. My friends will do the same . . . If I stayed here, I don't want to get married – but my parents says I can't do [that]. That's what my cousins say – they don't want to get married, all of them – if they earn their own living they won't have to ask their parents for it and its O.K., but if you stay with your parents . . . After we get married we can do what we like, our parents cannot tell us. But as long as you live with your parents, they will tell you.

Naseem

I suppose I will get married. I don't know if I'll get married to an Indian, it all depends on the person. I would have to take some notice of my parents but they have said that I can choose my own man. My best friend's parents would choose her man because they think that they can choose the best person for her. They ask about how much land you have got, how many O-levels and all that. I don't like that idea. Some girls go back after schooling to their own country, not to work at all, because they think that if you get married in India or Pakistan, all the boys are innocent.

Marjit

Whatever the traditional advantages of an arranged marriage, the general unpopularity of marriage at this point in their lives, whether because of its imminence or the method of arrangement, was reflected in other parts of the research where both getting married and having children were dismissed or considered unimportant by the Asian girls. For example, when girls were asked if they wanted to get married, only a quarter committed themselves to saying Yes, just over half were unsure, and the rest said No. They consistently regarded school and a career as more important than marriage, and were less than enthusiastic about being housewives or having a lot of children. Yet family life is understandably of great importance in their lives and it is unsurprising that many simultaneously acknowledged future satisfactions in having a husband and family of their own. Their response contrasted with that of the English girls, whose current enthusiasm for social life, boys, marriage and children tended to overshadow more studious pursuits. While other girls are keenly increasing their experience of boys and love in their run-up to voluntary marriage, Asian girls are kept in frozen childlike innocence, and either contentedly, resignedly or resentfully accept the inevitability of approaching marriage.

School

The Asian girls, like the West Indian girls, wanted to stay on longer at school but they also expressed more enjoyment and enthusiasm for school than did either the English or West Indian girls. They did not find it boring and irrelevant, and most wanted to stay on into the sixth form, to the age of eighteen. There was a greater proportion of Asian girls in the higher forms compared with the West Indian girls, but many of them still clustered in the lowest forms and in special classes for those with language difficulties. Those who had come to Britain most recently had a slow and incomplete articulation and understanding of English. They all laid great emphasis on doing well, and systematically confirmed the importance of education. This can be seen partly as a product of the high value placed on education by their parents and their community in general, and partly as a result of its being linked to the prospect of a better marriage. But most girls also expressed the wish actually to use their future qualifications to make something of their own lives, commenting for instance – 'I like to study hard and become something really great,' and 'I want to get more education and live a better life.' Almost all had some idea of the job they might take up. But enthusiasm will serve little practical purpose for those girls who will be married soon after leaving school and may not work at all, or who will work until marriage and then have to stay at home. Others, especially girls from Pakistan, may be sent back there, where they may do some work but probably nothing very interesting or important. Almost all the girls expressed career hopes but these may turn out to be wishful thoughts. Those who come from middle class backgrounds and have parents in good jobs, especially professions like law and teaching, are more likely to make these hopes a reality. They are also more frequently in the higher forms and their home and family life has accommodated many British values and customs and provides more help and support for studying.

Education in Britain offers better school facilities and a much wider range of opportunity for girls than that existing in their own countries of origin, and some girls like Marjit were aware of this:

I've been over here nearly four years – came from Kenya. I went to school over there before. This school is much larger. Didn't have laboratories or advanced equipment – but not much difference. If I was still there I would probably have ended up as a typist because I've never come into contact with any girls who want to become barristers and I think that would have remained a dream.

But others were more concerned with the immediate problems of language and the clash of expectations between the social restrictions around their lives and the demands made at school. One girl who had been here four years was very miserable and desperately wanted to return to India, but her parents would not let her go. One of her basic problems was keeping up with the language – she was very keen to be a teacher, but every lesson brought the same difficulties.

School is all right if you're good at it. I'm not very good at it – is good if you're in your own country and you study. It's much easier and you learn more about your own country. Don't like it over here very much – the English language we study. In my language I know every word – but not in English. I don't *hate* school – it's all right, but it's not the way I want to be. If I was to go back to my own country, I would study and be a teacher. My course, I think I should change it – I choose it myself and now I find it difficult and I think the best way is not to do this course. Is German and I don't read German, not going to Germany. Also chemistry and geography – geography is all right but I don't like it. [I want to] be an art teacher. I could do art and be good at it. I don't know why they won't send me to India. My parents, when I'm eighteen, they want me leave school to go to work and get married but I don't want that.

Saranjit

Surinder on the other hand quite liked school because it was the only place she was allowed to travel to unchaperoned, although she too could not always understand what the teacher said.

Others had found that although they could to some extent revel in their freedom within school, there were some school activities that dangerously flaunted the constraints with which they had to conform. Talking with boys is one example already mentioned, but simply exploring and searching for project materials can cause problems.*

I like to go around finding out what's happening around you, like English girls do. We can't do that. Our teacher, she tells us, why don't Indian girls go around and find some things that are happening around you – and you can't, and if you tell, she won't understand. We can't go around because Indian parents don't want their girls to go around the streets walking . . . My friend used to go out with this boy last year, and this man saw her once talking to this boy, and he told her parents everything about it, and her mum she came to school and saw the

* Some of these girls may see and envy English girls wearing short hair and make-up, neither of which they are normally allowed, but I only found one reference to this.

headmaster and he said, I don't know anything about her going out with boys. And they stopped her from school and now she's home and she goes to work now, and now she's getting married. She's only about fifteen years old. She's got engaged, she told me two weeks ago, and she's going to get married before the summer. She doesn't want to get married because she's got a boyfriend and she was crying you know – 'I don't want to get married.'

Kamlesh

Wives or Workers

For at least four of these girls their continuing studies into the fifth and sixth forms were viewed with the certain knowledge that they would not be allowed to take up a job. Pakistani parents in particular are very cautious about letting their daughters work in this country, and will often either keep them at home after they have left school, or will send them back to Pakistan to be married. The girl quoted earlier, who was to return there for her marriage, did however intend to take up work over there.

When I get married I can go on working if I like, and I will. I will work at dressmaking because ladies can do this sort of work. Women can do teaching or dressmaking, and they have to go for a six-month course if they want to be a dressmaker. There are lady doctors. Can't do factory work because there are men and women together. In teaching and in hospitals, have to work together, but not in dressmaking, don't get any men dressmakers.

Naseem

There are various reactions to Asian women taking jobs, and this is often dependent on the kind of work involved. Girls are encouraged to qualify for certain professions that are considered respectable and carry high status such as teaching and medicine. Jobs in which the relationships between the sexes are clearly defined are preferred, and when possible these courses are studied at all-girl day colleges. Office-work is regarded with some suspicion as it involves social contact with men although bank-work is an exception to the rule. Some technical and scientific work is also acceptable. Older women are often found working in the textile industry, which is an all-female work-place where they work long and hard for little remuneration in company with many others.

As well as the preference for a female environment there may also be restrictions by caste. More conservative Sikhs for instance would consider it wrong for a *Jat* woman (one from a caste of peasant farmers) to work for someone who is not a *Jat*. Families in which wives or daughters are working often try to keep this knowledge hidden from relatives at home in India, where it would be considered as a loss of status. Thus:

> There are, in fact, two classes of Sikh working women: girls who have been to school in Britain and are waiting to marry (in the Punjab, such girls would generally have to stay at home), and older married women whose children are at school or grown up. Newly married brides or wives with infant children are expected to stay at home, often under the wing of mother-in-law. However, if they have professional training, they are more likely to continue working. It seems that young wives whose husbands' families have shops are allowed to work in these.[15]

In the same way as their desire to stay on at school can postpone marriage arrangements, so also working and earning your own living seems to some Asian girls to offer the chance of becoming slightly more independent of their parents. Surinder, the Indian girl who enjoyed school for the autonomy it gave her, was also very keen to go to work after she left school, since if she were to stay at home her parents would arrange for an earlier marriage. She would still have to be accompanied to work however.

> I want to be secretary job if I pass my shorthand and typing, but I don't want to work in a factory, I really don't. I want to pass my exams . . . they want me to get married – straight away if possible. If I go to work then I don't have to but if I stay at home then I have to get married in two years . . . Some husbands do let ladies go to work. My dad won't let my mum go to work. About five years ago no Indian women used to work, but now they've started working. I think it's nice. It's a good idea, instead of staying home all the time. Once you're married you can't talk to another man. My dad says you can't. My mum can't.

Despite the relatively narrow range of jobs that are approved for Asian girls in general, these girls gave job expectations that largely followed the choices made by their (white) English class-mates. A third, like Surinder, said that they wanted to do some sort of office-work, although this work is usually less favoured for Asian girls, but this is not an unreasonable choice since they do the same typing and commerce courses as their class-mates. Where they did differ as a group was in their greater choice of professional careers, such as doctor, lawyer and barrister, teacher and pharmacist. For instance, Gita from Tanzania commented: 'I'd like to be a doctor, and I'd like to go back when I've finished it and help the people in my country because the country's very poor and there aren't many doctors or really educated people and there's lots of diseases and I'd like to help them.' Gurdip, an Indian girl, demonstrated the other end of the scale of accommodating to professional and Western influences. Her parents were both trained as teachers and her father still taught although her mother had been unable to find a teaching job here. They had been in England for five and a half years, and she had plans to become a doctor: 'I want to be a doctor, or a nurse if I cannot be a doctor. My grandfather [first gave me the idea] when I was little. Some of our family are teachers, and some psychiatrist [her sister], and he wants someone to be a doctor.' She had all the advantages of a professional Indian family and was also less restricted in her social life than many of the other girls. She had even acquired a cockney accent.

Asian families have inevitably had to modify some of their behaviour and attitudes about women working in order to survive in an uncompromising environment, and these and other aspects of life have been influenced by factors which include the length of time lived in Britain, their country and region of origin, the size and cohesion of the Asian community they live in, their financial situation, education, and their command of the English language. Some, usually the richer and better educated, may be more ideologically adaptable, but not necessarily, since principles of behaviour may be even more rigidly enforced over here in order to help preserve the community and resolve ambiguity about different ways of living. It is ironic that Pakistani and Bangladesh families, who often have the strictest ideas about the role of women, are also often the poorest and would benefit from more income. Some women have had to break out of family seclusion to work in the factories, but in general figures show about twice as many Indian as Pakistani women work.

Thus a serious attitude to education combined with a personality in which modesty, meekness and respect for authority are integral elements, has meant that teachers are usually faced with a set of quietly-motivated pupils. For Asian girls at least, their relative shyness and timidity contrasts with the boldness of English and West Indian girls in the same classrooms. Mischievous eyes and giggling whispers substitute for the noisy boisterousness of the others and their relative studiousness benefits from a more secure sense of identity. But while their motivation and the ideology within the school are in accord, the appropriate application of this in the future is uncertain.

The picture drawn of Asian girls and women becomes rather stereotyped into one of timidity and shyness which does not permit much public self-demonstration. This however disguises the determination and spirit which can be seen in their own ambitions, and in clashes within the family, and also has been especially apparent in the recent strikes involving Asian women workers. The Imperial Typewriters strike at Leicester for instance started in May 1974 and lasted three months.

But however deep their discontent, it is hard for young Asian girls to conceive of rebelling, rejecting, or running away from any destiny planned by the family. Rebellion loses itself in a strongly instilled sense of respect and conformity, as well as in fear of the consequences, for it implies the sacrifice of security at home, however constraining, to the potential insecurity and vulnerability that lies in the hostile and unfamiliar world outside. Parents are concerned for their daughters' success in marriage, and girls will tend to go along with their wishes. Concern for their happiness is an important consideration that most parents have not forgotten, and this further complicates the logic of girls' resentments. Protests can be made and will be received, for the family, although rather authoritarian, depends on cooperation but this may do little more than postpone marriage for a year or so.

But perhaps if change is going to come, it must come from the girls themselves. Men are after all notoriously backward in implementing change in situations that alter their status and power over women. As the present generation of girls grow up, those who are frustrated by the extent of their own lack of freedom and control over their lives and futures may be fired with the determination to free their children from these constraints. Several of the girls tentatively expressed such intentions:

I will help my kids with all their problems and let them go out with friends more often.

I will give my children a little more freedom. They will be allowed to put their views about things forward.

I'd let [my daughter] do what she likes – what we can't do. Wear fancy clothes wear make-up. Wouldn't like her to go out with boys. I would like her to choose her own husband.

I'd let her go out with boys definitely. I'd like her to tell me what she's doing and not like I do to my parents – say I'm going round to a friend's house when I'm not.

They are still rather cautious, but appear nevertheless to want to make these kinds of change. But it is very confusing to try to balance out changing beliefs and expectations of the past, present and future. They are not simply swapped around, but tend awkwardly to co-exist together. Like the English girls, only much more so, they are confronting a situation in which the nature of feminine role is no longer so clearly defined for them.

Under the present restrictions of parental rule, it may often seem more tempting to exchange this situation for the only approved alternative of marriage. But then the authority of the husband takes over which may be equally limiting. However some girls hope for instance to be able to continue with their career after marriage. Gita, from Tanzania, who was not going to have an arranged marriage, said:

I'd try to talk to him and make him understand that it would be better if I did work. I think boys have changed their ideas. They don't really mind girls going out to work after they're married and after they've got a family – so I hope I'm a lucky wife . . . If I got married early I'd like him to keep on with my training because I really want to be a doctor and I'd like to go on with it, so if he understands and he wanted me to get married quite early, well I would but as long as he let me do my training. [My mum] doesn't work. You don't have these sort of things in our families. They wouldn't let mothers go to work. The girls do now but mothers usually stay at home. I think this is a bit stupid – ladies, girls, can work if they have a family – not when the kids are very young but when they are about two or three and they start going to school. I think a mother should work because the father can't support the whole family. *I'll* work, yeah I'll keep on working. Once I'm married [my family] wouldn't really mind what I do – I could do what I can do and what my husband says I can do.

The cockney Indian girl quoted earlier also had 'modern' views on work and marriage for girls and sounded determined not to be stuck in a traditional role. The realization of her wish also to be a doctor would make this a more likely prospect.

Definitely all for it [women working]. When you've got your kids into a nursery and that, go back to work. That's what I'll do. I don't want to stay at home doing nothing. I'll talk to him [my husband], get him to see that I don't want to stay home and do nothing. I don't want to stay at home waiting till he gets back. That's old-fashioned. Girls can get married and just come back to their work – nothing stopping you.

To many others however, the obstacles preventing this may seem insurmountable.

Talking of change is unavoidable when a minority culture is trying to co-exist within a larger society with different customs and values and both must live under the regulations made by the dominant society. However 'integration' is not a simple process and as I emphasized earlier, our concept of integration is very one-sided and our judgement of immigrant groups is too often based on how 'English' they have become. We forget how meaningful it is for them to retain their own cultural identity. One Indian girl was sensing this when she said:

Friends play together when they're young and do all things together, but when you get older you don't do things together so much with [English] friends. They don't try to understand your ways. Some English girls don't want to change their set ways – eat Indian food etc. Indian food is very good, especially for vegetarians. Especially for my mum who is a vegetarian. Don't know what she'd do if she had to eat

English food. About clothes – it's the same as food – they're not interested. The reason why English people accept West Indian people more than Indian people is that they dress English, they're taught English. But we – as I get older, I want to wear my dress because I'm proud of it. Saris – they're beautiful they are. And my English friends say – why don't you change your dress? Why don't you wear English dress? They wouldn't take off their dress and wear Indian dress!

The position of women in Asian societies is not a simple one. From an immediate feminist standpoint it is obvious that Asian women have long been denied any equality of opportunity or individual freedom, and their control by men is one that has always been handed on from father to husband through the pre-arrangement of marriage. But although our experience of sex-discrimination is a shadow of theirs, the adoption of women's more emancipated role in Western society is not a complete answer. The position and exploitation of women under Western capitalism is no blue-print for liberation, although it certainly does admit to some of the ideas of sexual equality and a certain individual freedom of expression. And while I am certainly not advocating the arranged marriage system it cannot be naïvely dismissed as an unreasonable or male chauvinist custom. It is far more complex and meaningful than this. For instance, from this viewpoint it is worth speculating just how much time and mental energy is devoted by other 'freer' girls in the contemplation of their future 'love-marriages'. At present surely nothing provides as much willing distraction to developing more individual freedom of expression and interest than this.

For most other girls the romance of love and marriage leaves them spellbound and ensures their voluntary capture. It is taken for granted as a positive and integral part of the feminine role for which there is elaborate preparation and competition. They can gain a wealth of experience through having boyfriends and practising with different sorts of relationships. Love can be dabbled in and tested. Every boyfriend is assessed as a possible husband. Marriage and setting up a home appear as a natural extension of this and there is no reason to postpone them if both parties are prepared to work and save some money.

Thus they have many of the freedoms that are denied to and

yearned after by Asian girls like those I talked to. They can go out at night alone, with boyfriends, to films, dances and parties. Parents still apply rules more strictly to them than to their brothers but compared to Asian girls these are minimal. But for many girls, this precious freedom is not often extensively used to explore new areas of interest and individual possibility. It is mainly invested in a preoccupation with boys, love and dreams of wedded bliss, which seem like the most meaningful pursuits. Their 'freedom' has re-snared them into the marriage trap. For Asian girls whose marriage is predetermined, becoming a wife is a relatively involuntary process. (Although neither they nor Asian boys are normally forced to marry people to whom they object.) An article defending Hindu arranged marriages said that:

> The Indian mind is conditioned to the idea that 'you can always love the person you marry' as opposed to the Western idea of marrying the person you love . . . Romance need not culminate or end in a marriage. It can also begin with a marriage . . . If they (Indian youth) are caught by the arrows of Cupid (in India we call him Manmata, the God of Love and he has floral arrows), they will face up to that situation and follow it through. But they will not go out of their way looking for the right partner on their own. They will leave it dutifully to their parents and look forward to the marriage and the delight of discovering and knowing their partners. The percentage of love-marriages in India has certainly increased in recent years. But still it is a small minority.*

Thus Asian people view the prospect of marriage rather differently. Its inevitability removes for them much of the other girls' emphases on boys and romance, although in Britain some Asians may begin to be obsessed with what they are prevented from doing. Other Asian girls who resent their lack of control over the future may even develop a (probably temporary) rejection of marriage. Since an arranged marriage does not initially depend on love, it lacks the magical qualities that have overtaken other girls. Dreams of love at first sight and romantic encounters are less built into their views of the future as defined by custom,

---

*By Shakuntala Balu, defending arranged marriages, although the adjustments and compromises that she says women don't mind making make her own conclusions questionable, and her assumption of girls' acquiescence is doubtful if applied to those living in Britain.[16]

although they will certainly have scented and picked up the excitement which surrounds sexuality and love in our society.

This contributes to the emphasis laid by the Ealing Asian girls on education, qualifications and careers as opposed to love, marriage and children. Ironically the potential of the mental space and time that may be gained through a lack of social life and boyfriends is often restricted as part of their general control within the family, or they may get involved in a job, a special interest, or some career training, only to find that this pursuit has to be cut down or terminated on marriage. Much of their other feelings about themselves seemed bound up with present rather than future hopes and problems, embodied in their lack of autonomy and other restrictions. Their dissatisfaction with their lives as girls is reflected by so many preferring to be born as boys; and, like the West Indian girls, those few who did prefer to be girls gave reasons that were more concerned with clothes and job opportunities than with the joys of being wives and mothers. At present, opportunities at school and at work offer tempting freedom for Asian girls, but if their lives were changed and they were given all the freedom they wanted – to go out socially with boys, to choose their own husband and so on – would they also fall neatly into the accompanying fantasies which occupy so many thoughts and hours, and absorb all the elements of freedom that previously seemed so intangible? Already Asian girls have picked up much in this respect from the chatter and obsessions of their contemporaries, and there are plenty of other sources, such as books, films and television, from which it is hard for anxious parents to protect them.

Got a television. Father comes and switches it off, doesn't let me or my sisters watch films – I watch it when he's not home. He doesn't watch it, just my brothers and sisters and me. They have nice programmes on besides films, I watch the news and all that. I like the films best and that's what I can't watch. I watch them when he isn't there, but he comes in at ten to six and he never goes out . . . I just read my books, that's all I do, schoolwork and library books. I read all the stupid books you know, lovely books. I read this book, a love book, from the library, and my mum found it and saw the cover and said don't read this book again. I read them anyway. I took it out again and I

took the cover off and when I've read it I put it on again and take it
back. [Her mother could not read English.] She doesn't know though.
She wouldn't let me read them. She thinks if you read these sort of
books you start doing things like those yourself.

Surinder

Asian girls and women who have come to Britain have done
so as dependents – dependent on present or future husbands or
on fathers. But here their lives have brought them into contact
with the demands of an advanced capitalist economy and the
necessity for wage labour. Coming out of lives often exclusively
centred on the home they are experiencing a new and changing
relationship to production which affects their role at home, and
although exploited as immigrant labour they will find the potential power that lies in their own degree of financial independence.
Girls who have been to school in Britain and have adopted some
of our beliefs and values are beginning to resist their traditional
Asian role and are seeking more freedoms: such as freedom to
determine aspects of their own lives like marriage, and freedom
to sell their labour in jobs of their own choosing. Asian girls in
Britain are looking forward to the possibility of greater autonomy
and choice than they have had before or would have at home.
But the process of change, and the intricacies of female liberation
involve complexities that can perhaps be helped by a better
understanding of both their predicament and our own.

Notes

Chapter 8

1. The main sources of my information on this are secondary, and for more detail see for instance Edith Clark, *My Mother who Fathered Me*, Allen & Unwin, 1957; and Judith Blake, *Family Structure in Jamaica*, The Free Press of Glencoe Inc., 1957.

2. Dilip Hiro, *Black British, White British*, Eyre & Spottiswoode, 1971.

3. 'Unmarried Black Mothers: Problems and Prospects', *Race Today*, July 1973.

4. 'Caribbean Women and the Black Community', *Race Today*, May 1975.

5. Farrukh Dondy, 'The Black Explosion in Schools', *Race Today*, February 1974.

6. Farrukh Dondy, op. cit.

7. See Hermione Harris, 'The Location of Black Women in the Labour Force', reprinted in M. Wandor (Ed.), *The Body Politic Stage 1*, 1972.

8. 'Black Women and Nursing: A Job Like Any Other', *Race Today*, August 1974.

9. See 'The Black Explosion in Schools', op. cit, also reported in the *Guardian*, 21 June 1974.

10. Robert Moore, *Racism and Black Resistance in Britain*, Pluto Press, 1975.

11. A. James, *Sikh Children in Britain*, I.R.R., (Institute of Race Relations), Oxford, 1974.

12. See a pamphlet by Crishna Seetha, *Girls of Asian Origin in Britain*, Y.W.C.A., 1975, in which this and other aspects are discussed.

13. P. Harrison, 'The Patience of Southall', *New Society*, 4 April, 1974.

14. P. Harrison, op. cit.

15. A. James, op. cit.

16. Shakuntala Balu, 'Mine is an Arranged Marriage', the *Sunday Times*, 21 October, 1973.

CHAPTER IX

Prospects

One good thing in my house – my mother's never said that washin' up dishes is for girls and hammering is for boys. We take turns with the washing-up which is good. Most people they bring their kids up to be able to fix a window the boys, and the girls wash up and cook and that's it, that's all women are supposed to do. In my house, if my window breaks I fix it, if the carpet's comin' up I put it down. My brother can't tell you what wire goes in a plug. I do that. Therefore everything's mixed sort of thing. I think it's much better than bringing 'em up for a girl to think that all she's gotta do is get babies, cook dinners and wash dishes. A lot of black girls do grow up like that because parents have their boys going out because boys can't get into trouble you know, and they're always goin' out, comin' in, and the girls gotta cook, starch, iron, and I don't think that's right – but my family is different.

> Annette from the West Indies, aged seventeen,
> who hopes to become a draughtswoman

The English, West Indian and Asian girls that I have described share a similar situation, for although there are various differences as a result of ethnic origins and class, they are each in their own way trying to grasp a changing sense of the feminine role. For the English girls, this is mainly concerned with accommodating ideas of work as a more meaningful part of their future lives in addition to being wives and mothers. For the West Indian girls it involves striving for more freedom and understanding and demanding something more out of life than the continuous struggle faced by their mothers and grandmothers. The Asian girls are in the most complicated situation and move between two parallel ways of life which embody different and conflicting expectations. They want to attain greater freedom and control over their own lives than they have been allowed in the past. The financial demands of living in Britain have already changed their working lives. Although they often work in the most exploited occupations, they and other women have begun to experience economic independence and to realize the value of their own labour outside the home. This itself must alter their perception of their roles as women and their relationships with men. Their daughters too, who go to school here, are changing their expectations of the future.

It is one of the aims of education to relate the acquisition of skills and knowledge to adult life. Girls' education in Britain has developed and widened since the days when it revolved around either becoming thrifty housewives and domestic servants, or decorative, accomplished and eligible ladies. But the role of housewife has been devalued, helped by the expansion of higher education for girls, the emphasis on the value of work outside the home and the availability of household aids. Although recommendations about educating 'less able' girls for domesticity appeared in the Crowther and Newsom Reports of 1959 and 1963, schools officially aim to educate girls and boys towards academic and technical achievements. Few today would admit the aspiration of housewife and mother as totally sufficient or admirable for their female pupils, although this assumption may appear blatantly in the comparative treatment of girls and boys and in the organization of the curriculum.

Girls' ideas, however, remain mixed on this point, but the direction in which they consequently move through their own ability and motivation can define the way they spend the rest of their lives. Their opportunities have already been circumscribed by a number of inter-relating social and psychological factors. For instance, the separation of masculine and feminine interests and aptitudes in childhood leaves girls less familiar with scientific and technical things, and parental restrictions on independence and exploration can have far-reaching effects on self-confidence, assertiveness and the development of analytic ability. Learning within the family and identification with mothers and other women reproduce 'feminine' characteristics in personality and behaviour. These are reinforced by the further division of knowledge and skills in school, although the classification of 'girls' subjects' and 'boys' subjects' is just beginning to be broken down.

Working class education has always remained at a lower level than that of the middle class, and the combined consequences of sex and class place working class girls in the most stereotyped positions. For instance, they usually make less investment in school life and education in general and see this as having little direct relevance to their immediate lives and interests. Their parents often leave them to make all their own decisions about school and careers and they are inevitably drawn into traditional feminine occupations. They leave school early with few qualifications and go into lower level jobs where the pay is unequal and the nature of work sex-defined. They get more enjoyment and meaning out of social pursuits: boyfriends, fashion, music etc., which bear no relation to the goals and preoccupations of school. The separation of sex roles is implicit in these social interests, and for instance, in love magazines. The idea of finding true love with Mr Right is always the primary goal and the key to everlasting happiness. Middle class girls are not necessarily less involved with these things, but at the same time they are usually under other pressures through the family to invest more in education and careers. Their parents often expect more definite achievements from them and can be influential and effective in helping them through school and to a vocation. For them, the love story images are also attractive and persuasive but can accompany rather than dominate their lives.

Since the last war the working lives of all women have become increasingly characterized by a period of giving birth to, and caring for, children sandwiched between two periods of employment, and most girls are prepared to acknowledge this pattern. Before this time, marriage was associated with the termination of work, forever if possible, and Jephcott remarked about the working class girls that she studied in 1942, that 'They see marriage as a full-time career and literally want to make a job of it.'[1] But this has not radically changed in all parts of Britain, and a great many girls see marriage as an over-riding consideration, which can verge on an obsession. So it was for some of the English girls in my research, but at the same time they acknowledged the need and desire to work in a way that was more than just filling time before marriage. Sixty per cent of them thought that they would return to a job sometime after having children, 20 per cent thought they would not, and the rest were not sure. (This compared to 70 per cent of the West Indian girls and 60 per cent of the Asian girls who also thought they would return to work.)

When they left school they all wanted to take up 'feminine' occupations: mostly in some sort of clerical work as secretaries and typists, while others wanted to be receptionists, bank clerks, telephonists, hairdressers, shop assistants, teachers and nurses. Only two expected to do any kind of factory work and they were less than enthusiastic about it. In these jobs they optimistically hoped to meet people and have an interesting time. They dogmatically refused to entertain the idea of doing more traditionally male jobs since 'girls don't do these things'. These views and aspirations are also shaped by the labour market, and in this respect the narrow range of jobs for girls living in the provinces will understandably affect their preference for full-time marriage. The boring and under-paid work that is open to them turns marriage into a meaningful quest into which they can pour their emotions, enthusiasm and dreams of happiness. Finding a husband is a personal and an economic necessity.

Oakley suggests that the sense of identification with the housewife role is reduced for those women who have had more education and it is a commitment to education or work that conflicts most with marriage and domestic demands.[2] This was reflected in principle in the way that many of the English girls in my research were concerned with their social and marriage prospects to the detriment of their other prospects. In comparison most of the West Indian and almost all of the Asian girls expressed relatively high educational aspirations while they were less openly enthusiastic about married life or motherhood.

The English girls were also aware of the advantages that they saw in their role as women, and were glad that they were destined to be wives and mothers instead of being committed to the social evil of doing a job for the rest of their lives. They were enthusiastic about marrying quite early and having children. They were conscious of the existence of Women's Liberation and generally approved of legal reforms like equal pay. However, the idea of change in personal areas that might upset the male–female relationship of superior–inferior, and dominant–submissive was one that was less easy for them to accept. There are understandably a lot of contradictory areas in girls' lives today, for instance, many of them want more economic independence and opportunity and plan to return to work after they have had children. But at the same time they cannot simply reject their 'feminine' training and their expectations of traditional womanhood demand to be satisfied. The disillusionment of uninteresting work will also hasten many towards the sanctuary of marriage and any idea they may have entertained about a 'career' will quickly evaporate. The West Indian and Asian girls on the other hand were more concerned with the present restrictions on their freedom than with prospects of married life, and were more enthusiastic about education. But they too were tentative about the idea of Women's Liberation.

All girls will find that there are many other gaps between attitudes and real life through which ideas and hopes can fall. Unless you are very talented or very rich there are usually many compromises to be made. The overwhelming influence of immediate situations can change or destroy original intentions. For instance, we must not forget the influence of future boyfriends and husbands – and this emphasizes the need not only to change women's consciousness but men's as well. In my questionnaire there were several stories which required the girls to identify with the situation of the heroine and decide which of two possible outcomes they would choose. In one of these, almost half the English girls were prepared to give up a university place to stay with the boy they loved, and two-thirds of them would reject a training course away from home that would promote them in their job if their (hypothetical) husband was reluctant for them to go. This illustrates their low commitment to higher education and careers and also the dominant influence of love and men. University education does not represent to them the pinnacle of achievement that it does for the middle class. In contrast, over 80 per cent of both the West Indian and Asian girls would have taken the university place. Their response to taking the training course however was mixed. Just over half the West Indian girls, but only a third of the Asian girls would have taken it. This choice for Asian girls is of course affected by the customary protection of young wives by their communities.

IDEOLOGY, SEX ROLES AND CHANGE

The steady increase of women in the work-force has helped to expand the boundaries of the feminine role. Current ideas about sexual equality and opportunity have complicated what was previously a straightforward route to ideal womanhood through marriage and motherhood. Women themselves are now challenging their roles at home and at work and are active in trade unions and the Women's Movement. The contours of their place in our society have become blurred as their contribution to outside production becomes accepted. Many girls, although mainly middle class, have already developed individual ambitions in which marriage and children figure as desirable but also intrusive events and ones to which they would reluctantly commit the whole of their lives.

But although the role of women is now more varied, this change has occurred more as a result of an expansion of existing possibilities than from crossing sex-role boundaries, and men's roles have remained relatively unchanged. Married women are now finding that the adoption of a full-time life at home can be criticized as much as a life at work used to be. There is pressure on women to question their satisfaction with what would previously have been taken for granted. Contentment with being 'only a housewife' is now held in doubt. But success in a career is not sufficient by itself, because it denies the 'proper' family life which is nationally emphasized. It is somehow assumed that the ideal 'superwoman' has a happy home, husband and children on the one hand and an interesting occupation on the other. Unfortunately neither of these is easy to attain and the combination of both is usually limited to those who can afford it.

A confusion of ideas about women's role and femininity can tolerably if uncomfortably continue so long as it is unnecessary to act upon it. Demands for equality and role-sharing can be agreed on in principle but are difficult to act on if they conflict with real conditions. We are in the process of trying to create alternatives and a diversity of opportunities for girls and women, but at the same time we are also creating ambiguity in what used to be a more defined and structured area. In trying to resolve such ambiguity girls may be tempted to fall back on the familiar and approved versions of their role that have appeared constant through their formative childhood years.

These rest on the belief that sex-role differences are fundamental, and a small set of biological distinctions has produced a tidal wave of implications in every sphere of life. Although there is little evidence to show that girls and boys necessarily differ much in their abilities and characteristics the socialization of girls into 'femininity' and boys into 'masculinity' produces differences and perpetuates many myths about men and women. Women's role in reproduction and family life has separated them from outside production and has devalued them in the economic terms of capitalism. This is implicit in female status inside and outside the home and is contained within general ideas about the nature of the world. As described in the first few chapters, popular ideology about sex-roles is passed on through the family, school and the economic organization of home and work, and through the media and organizations like the church, and is set against a backcloth of history and tradition. It conforms to the economic division of labour and provides a reinforcing basis for the sexism that characterizes our social organization.

In trying to alter the conditions of sex discrimination, the Women's Liberation Movement has had to battle initially against the depth and forcefulness of ideology. This has become an integral part of women's political struggle alongside the need to change economic conditions. Socialists have often made the mistake of viewing ideology as something simply tied to economic changes and have thus assumed that changing the economic basis of society will also change people's beliefs and attitudes. But separation and discrimination by sex pre-dates capitalism and can therefore continue beyond it, and has to be changed consciously. Economic changes can leave vast areas of personal and sexual relationships untouched. Since so much of feminine self-identity is internalized in childhood, it will be modified neither easily nor quickly. In order to modify it, it is very important for women to understand and make sense of both old and new ideas about femininity, to share understanding with other women and to want to change their situation and their relationships. This is what is involved in the 'consciousness-raising' that has become an integral part of the Women's Liberation Movement.

In the past, ideology about women has changed as a result of a combination of social and economic conditions interacting with women's real needs and desires. These facilitate each other and if for instance the economy needs women to work, this is not only related to their personal and economic situation but is successful to the extent that women themselves want to work. This is also illustrated in the relationship between the drop in the population of Britain in the 1940s and the development of more efficient contraception. The lowered birthrate which caused so much concern about the future of the nation was due less to this development than to women's own desires for smaller and more manageable families and their consequent willingness to plan and to limit the numbers of their children. In the light of the increase in unemployment, the economy would perhaps benefit from keeping women at home and away from the job market. But this would be difficult unless women were willing to stay at home, and could afford to do so. The work and career expectations that have been encouraged in girls over the past years will not easily be reversed and they are likely to produce more resistance to the employment situation than there has been in previous generations.

In the last century the middle and upper classes passed down the idea that women's ideal place was at home dependent on their husbands. But this arrangement was economically impossible for ordinary working people and working class women have always had to work to supplement the family income. Throughout the twentieth century however, social and economic factors have contributed to the shift in and expansion of women's role. Women have at last become recognized as part of the labour force in many areas of work outside the factory, domestic service and the sweated jobs in which they originally found employment.

But this change has inevitably originated from above, through ruling class control of dominant ideology and its adoption by the aspiring middle class. The continuous labour of working class women in the past never affected the way women were seen in relation to production. But when middle class women wanted to work and it became economically necessary and desirable for them to do so, ideas about women changed more rapidly. All girls are now encouraged to choose careers at school and to aspire to jobs requiring education and training, although, inevitably, it is still children from middle class backgrounds that benefit most.

Middle class children not only have the advantages of better education, but also have the opportunities of getting the less sex-defined jobs. These jobs are, of course, generally the most creative and the people who get them work as 'thinkers'. They are the minority who both manufacture and enjoy the capitalist illusion of greater and greater opportunity. On the other hand the working class is employed, as a rule, in manual jobs, often demanding great ingenuity and inventiveness but not having much to do with the manufacture of ideology. The working class contribution to prevailing ideas has normally been in opposition to the job structure, in the trade unions and in political movements, rather than being supportive of that structure. So it is that so far as work is concerned the working class have always been on the receiving end of the ideas produced by the dominant classes. Hence it is not surprising that middle-class children at school are more open to far-reaching possibilities, to alternatives and to change. This openness reflects the way that they are encouraged to see themselves and demonstrates the advantages that they enjoy at home.

The increasing intervention of the state in people's lives in the last hundred years has contributed even more to the definition of sex roles within the family. This began with the establishment of state education and has expanded through the provisions of the welfare state which was originally set up to improve the family life and health of the nation. Women's central position in the family connects them closely with the workings of the state and their dependence on welfare constantly reminds them of the 'correct' and moral assumptions made about their role as women, wives and mothers.

It is easy to see examples of the way these are enforced through women's everyday needs and interactions. For instance the lack of free state nurseries is based on the assumption that mothers should not have to work. Many of those that do exist are open either in the mornings or in the afternoons, or finish at a time like three o'clock, all of which are useless for women with full-time jobs. Social security investigates women's personal lives, and the cohabitation rule assumes that if a woman sleeps with a man for more than two nights he is keeping her. This financial relationship is also implicit in the lower scales of unemployment benefit received by married women. In state schools sex divisions are part of the organization and girls move on into appropriate jobs.

In the area of contraception and abortion, the idea of sex without reproduction has only relatively recently gained acceptability. In the past the ruling class has been concerned about it from the point of view of controlling morality as well as reproduction. In Britain today contraception is easily available and mainly free, and its approval coincides with the needs of a planned society, the need for women in the work-force, and fears about overpopulation. In fact the Ross Panel which reported in 1973 about the need for a population programme in Britain actually suggested that in the event of a policy for population stabilization, the incorporation of women into wider aspects of society would discourage them from having children and help to reduce the birthrate. And as for abortion, the past and present debates have preserved the control of its availability in the hands of the state.

In all these areas women and children are directly dependent on the state and each encounter reinforces the implications of female status and role. It is also working class women who are most affected because of their greater dependence on welfare. It is therefore not surprising that it is in areas like these that the

Women's Movement has concentrated, setting up nursery campaigns, making demands for equal educational opportunities, free contraception and easily available abortion etc., and working in the community and the family as well as in campaigns for equal pay, anti-discrimination, and trade union representation.

There are other and more intimate ways in which femininity and masculinity can be changed. From looking at the ways that children learn about sex-roles in the family we have seen how deeply the sense of psychosexual identity is internalized. Feminine characteristics are passed down from mother to daughter as part of this developing identity, and the 'double identification' of girls and their mothers links them closely with home-based activities and relationships. But if for instance men were to be equally responsible for child-care then boys and girls could start building relationships and identifying with both sexes from the beginning instead of mainly with women. But for this to be meaningful, women's status will also have to change since under the present conditions children would still grow up viewing men as superior and more powerful and women as inferior and irrelevant to other areas of life outside the home and family. This however would involve a fundamental change in man's relationship to production and reproduction which is hard to envisage under capitalism.

It is also necessary to alter the relationships of men with women, men with men and women with women. The individualism and competitiveness that is useful for a capitalist system works against cooperation between people and tends to distort personal relationships. Thus although it would benefit women to develop a more independent sense of individuality in order to pursue new areas and interests, this is not to advocate the same sort of single-mindedness that characterizes the pursuit of capital gain.

The protected upbringing of girls and the limitation on their freedom perpetuates their vulnerability and inhibits self-confidence. But giving girls a greater sense of independence and confidence also entails equipping them with some defence against that from which they are protected, which is usually connected with their susceptibility to physical or sexual assault. Providing them with some skills with which to handle such situations would be an improvement on stifling restrictions and warnings, and the fears that these can produce.

At school, too, girls hold many of the traditional concepts but these can be meaningfully questioned. It is very worthwhile to go into schools to talk about their ideas on jobs, marriage and children, and to set up Women's Studies within the curriculum. Girls' own experiences can be examined and critically reassessed, and although it is unrealistic to expect many of them radically to change their attitudes or life-styles, they will have been made aware of alternative ideas and behaviour which later may help them to understand and resolve real-life situations.

Although it is popularly assumed that women are making continuous progress towards greater emancipation, we should be cautious about accepting this too easily. In Britain today, popular ('formal') ideology as transmitted through such media as newspapers, radio and television has incorporated the modern and humanitarian ideas of sexual equality. But people rarely practice these in real life. They pay lip-service while following sex-stereotyped modes of behaviour. Employers also do this less discreetly to conserve male-dominated areas of work and keep women as a cheap and transient work-force. Many professed male sympathizers to Women's Liberation still expect their homes to be spotless and their dinner to be on the table. This is their 'informal' ideology and exposes the gap between general attitudes and particular situations. The danger in this distinction ('formal' and 'informal') lies in the possibility of the 'formal' ideas camouflaging the majority practice of the informal ones. The evidence of a minority of middle class women entering higher occupations with equal pay can disguise the extent of job division and discrimination at lower levels.

Official acceptance of women's equality through legislation like the Equal Pay and Anti-Discrimination Acts can produce a false sense of accomplishment and victory, and therefore apathy. In this respect the trade unions certainly slowed up their concern with equal pay after Barbara Castle's announcement of the Equal Pay Act in 1970, and today this is still not achieved. Furthermore, if the Anti-Discrimination Bill persuades people that equal opportunity thereby exists, the absence of large numbers of women moving immediately into new areas of work and ability will be seen either as showing their lack of interest and motivation or as justification for the belief that female biology and psychology makes women unsuitable for particular roles and jobs. Thus the separation of the sexes may be even more fully preserved by this kind of interpretation without allowing for the necessary time to erode and replace ingrained beliefs and dogmas.

TRENDS

The growing movement of women out to work has been accelerated since the last war by the increasing number of married women working. This happened through a combination of factors such as acute shortage of labour; increase in part-time work opportunities and shorter hours in general; expansion in the service industries; earlier marriage and small families; domestic gadgetry and convenience foods; and the depletion of the male labour force through National Service (until the early 1960s) and the raising of the school-leaving age. This process is not easily halted because the economy has become increasingly dependent on women's work. This has been accommodated in the everyday life of women and their families, and it has fundamentally altered their attitudes and expectations.

In education, figures for the late 1960s and early 1970s showed that the disparity in the number of girls and boys entering and passing G.C.E. exams in 'girls' subjects' and 'boys' subjects' respectively was diminishing.[3] Many more girls than ever before had taken 'masculine' subjects like maths, chemistry and physics, although there were still only about half as many girls as boys doing these. The increase in the number of exam passes at O-Level and A-Level was also proportionally greater for girls, and this occurred over all subjects. 140 per cent increase for girls compared with 63 per cent for boys. A similar trend occurred in C.S.E. exams. Girls also tended to have a higher pass rate and be more prominent in the higher grades. But while those with A-Levels have the chance to go to universities and training colleges, the others have very limited opportunities of further education. More recent indications (1975) however are now complaining of the drop in standards in performance in G.C.E. and C.S.E. examinations, but the reasons for this are not clear. Nor is it clear whether this applies to both sexes alike. Another very recent trend is the dearth of school-leavers applying to universities and other colleges of further and higher education. This will be partly related to the drop in the birthrate following the post-war 'bulge', but must also represent a disillusionment in economic terms with the worth of degrees and other qualifications.

In the area of employment, women made up 36·5 per cent of the work-force in 1972, which was an increase from 36·3 per cent in 1971 and 31·8 per cent in 1951. However, when this is examined more closely by occupational category, it is shown not to be an overall increase. There has been a decline in the proportion of women working in skilled technical, supervisory and managerial jobs and the higher professions, while they have been increasingly employed as clerical workers, saleswomen and shop assistants, and unskilled and semi-skilled manual workers. In a research study made on forty less-skilled occupations from 1961–6, a considerable rise in the employment of women was found.[4] The employment of women in all occupations had risen by 13·9 per cent over this period but the increase in semi-skilled workers was 23·1 per cent. The increase in women working therefore seems to have been taken up in less skilled work. The fact that so many women work on semi-skilled work is probably as much related to their being women as to the degree of skill involved. This trend is to some extent inconsistent with the previous evidence of girls' increasing educational achievements, but is probably complicated by the popularity of clerical work which absorbs girls of all levels of qualification. School-leavers with various levels of qualifications can find work in offices, as juniors, typists, secretaries and clerks. This has represented a rise in 'respectable' opportunity for working class girls who thirty-five years ago would have needed the rare chance of a secondary education to work in an office at all. But in other areas of work the semi-skilled and unskilled levels are still filled by working class girls and women and the higher and professional jobs are still reserved mainly for the middle class.

At the present time, we are looking towards a period of economic instability and depression in Britain. Work is becoming scarce and insecure, and wages constantly fall behind the cost of living. In the last decade, unemployment has probably affected women less than men because it occurred mainly in the industrial sector, while women had been largely recruited into the service sector. In places where women were employed in manufacturing however they were hit by unemployment more than men. In 1966–70 male employment declined at the same time as female employment was increasing but conflict did not arise because the areas of work did not coincide and men and women were not competing for jobs.

In a contracting economy there will be a financial need for women to earn money, but the worthwhile and interesting jobs desired by girls may turn into fantasies. The service industries that have expanded so much will also be those that are cut, especially in the part-time work that women have found so convenient. In clerical work secretarial agencies are already finding girls harder to place in jobs, and are saying that the heyday of the 'temp' is over. This will hit girls like those from Ealing, many of whom were hoping to enter secretarial and office-work and other areas of the service sector like teaching and nursing. The contraction of the economy is being felt in all parts of the occupational scale and white-collar and professional jobs are becoming as vulnerable as those in other industries.

A constantly growing need for women's work combined with an expanding economy might have eventually led to the socialization of some aspects of housework. This would have facilitated women working by providing nurseries and other community services and thus also increased markets by giving the family more income to spend on commodities. But in today's situation such 'luxuries' are out of the question as the government is trying to hold down wages and workers' consumption as a whole and encourage investment and export by giving profit incentives to business.

Therefore in the present perspective of continuing inflation and unemployment in Britain, the immediate outlook for improving the position of women is not good. Although economic pressures on the family will increase the necessity for women to work, the economic cutbacks will make it much harder for them to make any real headway within the system. Equal pay is already receding into the distance in spite of the Equal Pay Act, and as employment prospects get bleaker the opportunities for diversifying 'women's work' will diminish as these are guarded by and for men. Without the implementation of equal pay and greater opportunities it is hard for women to conceive of more economically viable alternatives to marriage and financial dependence on men. It is speculative whether the economic instability will mean that more pressure is put on personal stability via the family, since the family is always emphasized at times of national crisis. This would again endorse women's function at home, and they will have to recreate traditional wifely skills to expand the inflation-gripped housekeeping money, and make food and clothes more cheaply from raw materials.

Girls growing up and leaving school are already being hit by the present cutbacks in education and employment. In some parts of the North of England school-leavers have been unable to find any work, let alone the sort that they might have chosen for themselves. Recently the government announced the closure of twelve teacher training colleges and there are relatively few jobs for newly-qualified teachers now. This presents a great contrast with the situation in the 1950s and 1960s when the Robbins Report publicized the need for teachers. At this time girls were given strong encouragement to go into teaching and women were asked to return to it if they had left to bring up a family. Against this background the valid criticism of teaching as a 'feminine' job that extends women's maternal role outside the home has less impact as the opportunity for women to take it up declines.

But as I stressed earlier, the changes that have already taken place in girls' attitudes towards their lives will not be easy to reverse. Although the change in ideas and expectations has happened more to girls from middle class backgrounds and from areas in the South East of England, others too are starting to see themselves with needs outside those of housewife and mother, and are concerned with other ways of occupying themselves. I have only given examples of girls in London, whose experiences and opportunities will be somewhat different and wider than those who live in more rural and provincial areas of the country. The changes concerning women's role that can be accommodated in London are not typical of all parts of Britain, and it is much harder for girls to break away from social and economic pressures in those areas without becoming isolated.

It is however many of the women working in industrial areas who have been very involved with the recent upsurge in militant activities, and who have taken action on issues like union recognition, equal pay and better conditions. The period since the 1960s has seen a great increase in the incidence of industrial conflict and militancy. The combination of increasing inflation and unemployment has contributed to job insecurity. Control over workers has been tightened by the intervention of employers and the state into union affairs and by wage restraints. Rank and file militancy has occurred in industries which either have been inactive for a long time, or have no previous history of militant activity. Within these women have begun to realize the power of their labour, and the need to fight for their right to work. Unfortunately clerical work, the most popular choice for girls, is an area that is particularly difficult to organize. Secretaries, typists and other general office workers are diversely scattered all over the country in businesses of varying size, and union recruitment is rare and often meaningless in very small firms where girls can easily be replaced.

Most of the action involving women has been over redundancies, equal pay and wage agreements, and often even the basic right to union recognition. In many factories in Britain women have gone on strike alone or together with men, or have occupied their work-place as the Fakenham women did.[5] They have experienced a mixture of success and disillusionment in their encounters with employers and trade unions, but have also discovered their own strength and their enthusiasm for action. In the public sector, nurses, radiographers and other ancilliary hospital staff have acted in a way that the weight of social responsibility has prevented in the past. Faced with a similar situation, teachers and social workers have also taken strike action. Many of them have rejected the aloof professionalism of their jobs and have begun to question some of the aspects of their work, such as servicing private patients in hospitals. In all areas and across different races women have become more involved, and much of their power and energy is as yet untapped. They have set a precedent for women and girls to follow and are laying historical foundations for women's participation in life outside as well as inside the family. Girls can gain knowledge from their experiences, and self-confidence from their success in struggle, for their own is still to come.

Notes

Chapter 9

1. Pearl Jephcott, *Rising Twenty*, Faber & Faber, 1945.
2. Ann Oakley, *Housewife*, Allen Lane, 1974.
3. *The Education, Training and Employment of Women and Girls*, A.T.T.I. pamphlet, 1973.
4. ibid.
5. For details of women's strikes and industrial activities see 'Striking Progress 1972–3' in *Red Rag*, no. 2; and M. Edney, D. Phillips, 'Striking Progress 1973–4' in *Red Rag*, no. 8, reprinted in *Conditions of Illusion*, Feminist Books, 1975.

Appendix

A Brief Survey of the Regional Opportunities for Girls in Britain*

There is clearly a much greater range of careers in London than there is in most other parts of the country. This is mainly due to the extensive operations of the service industries: distribution, hotel and catering, transport, hairdressing and other personal services, insurance and banking, national and local government, and professional services such as education. These provide many of the most popular opportunities for girls. In London, 60 per cent of employment (of both sexes) is within these industries.

Service industry offers work all over the country, although the extent of this varies between regions. In *Scotland*, where the primary industries, agriculture, forestry, fishing, mining etc., exclude women, about 68 per cent of female employment is in the service sector, and other sectors follow a pattern that is familiar as traditional women's work: 20 per cent of women work in textile and clothing (e.g. knitwear and tweeds), and 30 per cent in distribution. Other work includes light assembly work (semi-skilled in the engineering industry), process work in food factories, and clerical work. In 1971, 25 per cent of girls going into clerical work took jobs in manufacturing companies; and 70 per cent of girls entering apprenticeships did so in hairdressing.

Moving south, into the *Industrial North*, which comprises Northumberland, Durham and the North Riding of Yorkshire, there is an increasingly high level of unemployment (in 1972 2,512 girls were unemployed in this area). The unqualified leaver may therefore have some difficulties finding work. (This region also has a lower school-leaving age than the national average.)

*This concentrates on employment involving relatively few qualifications and little training.

For girls, there are opportunities in clerical work in the ship-building and engineering industries, and in the chemical manufacturing industry, where there is also process work. There are some jobs in light industry, but very few technical opportunities in the engineering industries for girls. Civil Service and local government offer employment, and 'opportunities for girls have increased enormously in the past few years by the influx of clothing and textile firms'.[1]

There is also a great concentration of industry in the *North-west*, – Cheshire and Lancashire, which consists mainly of engineering, textiles, food, drink, tobacco, and vehicles. The textile industry, which has historically employed many women, has contracted over the last forty years, but this has been compensated for by the increase in service industries, especially the distributive trades. Some girls get laboratory work in the chemicals industry. Clerical work is available, but there is a relative scarcity of this in some areas, like the old textile towns of Burnley, Rochdale and Wigan. Recently there has been a growth in the mail-order industry, in Oldham for example, which has provided many jobs for girls and women.

In *Yorkshire*, the basic industries are agriculture, coal-mining and woollen textile manufacture (and steel production in Sheffield). Girls find work in the textile and clothing industries but for most other sorts of employment, apart from shops and other local jobs, girls would have to travel to the larger cities. There has been some expansion of the service sector especially in tourism, which has supplied an increase in opportunities in this region of otherwise low employment.

The service industries are booming in *Wales*, and absorb over two-thirds of both boy and girl school-leavers. About a third of all girls go into clerical or commercial jobs. In commerce, girls can work as machine operators, shorthand and audio typists and counter clerks, but it is boys who are set on the rungs of the managerial ladder. Girls also go into the prominent distributive trades, as well as post office jobs, teaching, medical services, local authorities, hotels and catering. There is far less industry in Wales and most of it is concentrated in the south-east, in the coalfields, and in associated iron, steel and tin-plate industries. Other manufacturing industries have grown up round these traditional ones, and offer jobs to girls as unskilled or semi-skilled operatives, process workers and machinists. Technician apprenticeships are theoretically available (as they are in other places), but it is doubtful if many girls apply or would be accepted if they did so. The Central Youth Employment in Cardiff makes this comment – 'Indisputably the most popular job in the eyes of many Welsh girls is hairdressing, with associated careers as manicurist or beauty specialist.'[2]

The *Midlands* has many manufacturing industries, and women have traditionally worked in the potteries, also in the hosiery and knitwear factories. It is 'the ideal place to seek an apprenticeship' for boys, but has little on this level to offer to girls. There are of course the usual commercial, clerical and business opportunities, and a third or more of girl school-leavers usually enter some form of office-work. Secretarial openings tend to be limited, but there is a steady demand for girls doing general clerical duties – the familiar dogsbody jobs and various forms of office machine work. There is also the rest of the service industries, especially retail distribution, and the nursing training is good in certain areas.

East Anglia shares with Cumberland and Westmorland the characteristics of being very rural and sparsely populated. In order to do a particular job, it is often necessary to travel long distances to towns, a necessity probably approached reluctantly by a lot of girls, and very inconvenient for wives and mothers wishing to work. Agriculture is dominant in East Anglia, but there are few lady farmers, only farmers' wives! There are operative jobs for girls in the towns; in shoe factories, electronics firms and food-canning factories. There are some laboratory technician posts, business and commerce offer secretarial and clerical jobs, and there is work to be found in hotels and catering along the coast.

Tourism is the ever-increasing concern in the *South-west*. In its background of agriculture this is emerging as a major industry, offering work to many girls, most of whom find themselves in over-worked waitress jobs. There are jobs for women in manufacturing, mainly food, drink and tobacco, and some office-work within the fields of public administration, insurance, banking etc.

In *London and the South-east*, which contains a third of the population of England and Wales, we find the commercial and financial centre of England. There are fewer people in manual and unskilled occupations here than in any other part of the country. There are a lot of manufacturing industries which give employment to about 30 per cent of the labour force in the *South*, as well as basing their head offices here. The radio and electronics industry is expanding rapidly in this area and provides jobs for women in light assembly work. Paper printing and publishing is also concentrated in London and the South but girls have few chances in printing. A lot of research (medical, Civil Service etc.) goes on close to London, and there are many girls employed in such establishments. The transport system offers technical, commercial and personnel opportunities, and there are also jobs in communications, the Civil Service, public service and the law.

Girls come enthusiastically to London to seek their fortunes, to find a job and a social life that their provincial or country origins cannot provide for them. Many start or end in office-work. If they have secretarial skills, there is no shortage of jobs, but it is very hard for them to extricate themselves from this sort of work and find something better. The slave, runabout, and 'substitute wife' of the office is in an unenviable situation, but for many girls it is probably a respectable and exciting job compared with what they see offered by a country village, or an industrial or provincial town.

Notes

Appendix
1. *Cornmarket Careers for School Leavers* 1973, Cornmarket Press.
2. ibid.

Index

References to notes are given in italic numerals